SHIP BOTTOM BLUES

A Novel

SHIP BOTTOM BLUES

A Novel

Daniel J. Waters

This is a work of fiction. Names, characters, places, organizations, events and incidents are either products of the author's imagination or are used fictitiously.

Actual historical or public figures are used in a fictional context with what the author hopes the reader will recognize as respect and genuine affection.

Text © 2019 Daniel J. Waters

All Rights Reserved

No part of this publication may be reproduced, stored in a retrieval system or transmitted in any form or by any means, electronic, mechanical, recording or otherwise without the prior written permission of the author.

Cover Design by James Zach / *ZGraphix* / *Mason City, Iowa*
Author Photo © Jean Poland Photography

THE BALLAD OF THUNDER ROAD
Words and Music by Robert Mitchum and Don Raye
©1958 (Renewed)UNIVERSAL MUSIC CORP.
All Rights Reserved Including Used by Permission
Reprinted by Permission of Hal Leonard LLC

LONG BEACH ISLAND MAP
Courtesy of Ryan Martz & Doug McCarthy / Fire & Pine
Bluffton, South Carolina
www.fireandpine.com
Used by Permission

*For Pam, Jessica, Michael & John-
The best Chapters of my Life*

*"The law they swore they'd get him
But the devil got him first."*

The Ballad of Thunder Road
Robert Mitchum (1957)

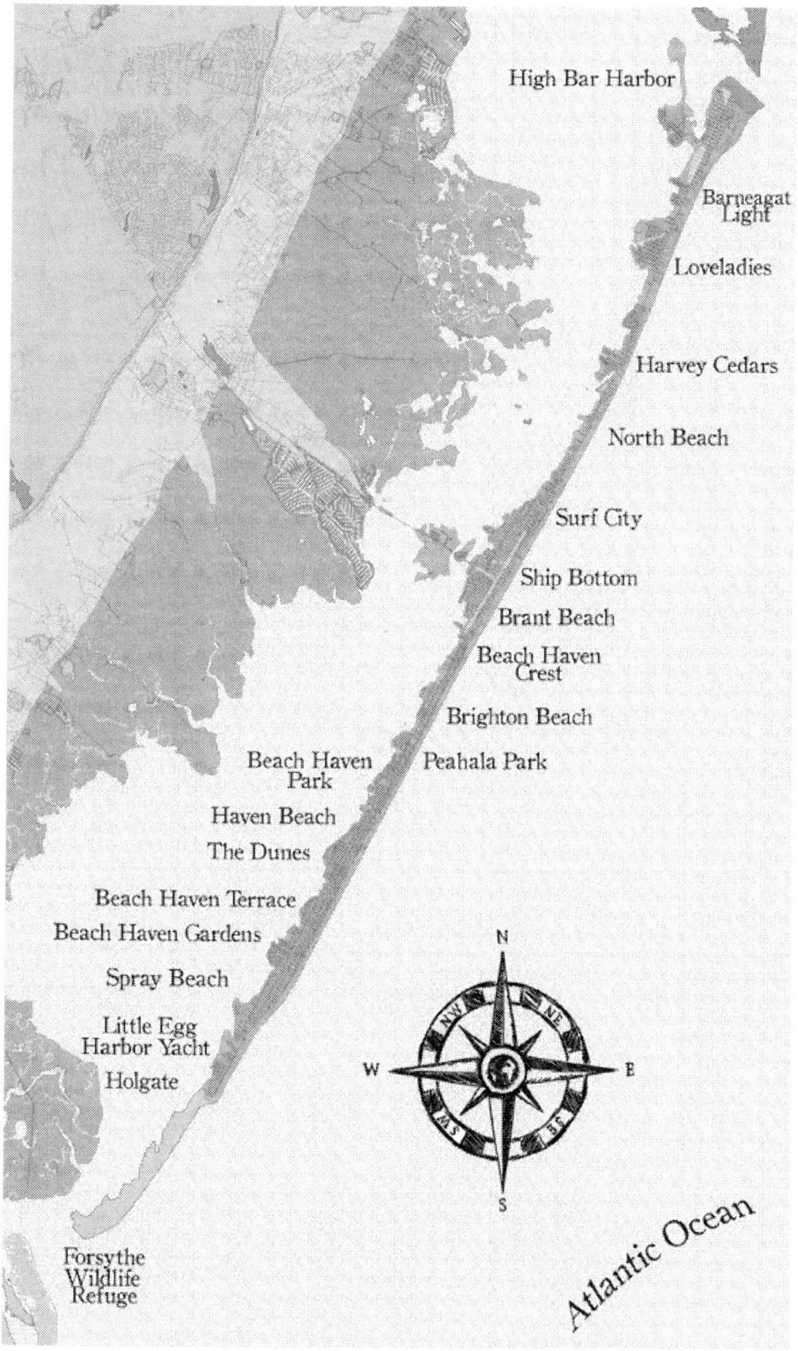
High Bar Harbor
Barneagat Light
Loveladies
Harvey Cedars
North Beach
Surf City
Ship Bottom
Brant Beach
Beach Haven Crest
Brighton Beach
Peahala Park
Beach Haven Park
Haven Beach
The Dunes
Beach Haven Terrace
Beach Haven Gardens
Spray Beach
Little Egg Harbor Yacht
Holgate
Forsythe Wildlife Refuge
N
NW
NE
W
E
SW
SE
S
Atlantic Ocean

AUGUST 1969

One

Long Beach Island, NJ
Ship Bottom Township

Years of stalking the small deer and the wild turkeys of the Pine Barrens had rendered BoDean Bowker immune to long periods of immobility. The position of the sun told him he'd been there for three hours, maybe three and a half. The truck windows were down but without a breeze he was soaked in a foul sweat.

The old man hadn't moved much. Must have a four-quart bladder, BoDean figured, given the empty bottles of Ortleib's next to his sagging lawn chair. He'd never seen anyone tap salt from a shaker into a beer before, so he thought he'd give it a try when he got back to the cabin after dark. BoDean was an Iron City man himself - big, round quarts, each in its own brown paper bag.

He ran calloused fingers over the object in his right pants pocket, careful not to touch the sharpened edge he'd created with flint and fire and a ball-peen hammer. A tiny smile creased his lips. There would be some justice in it, this weapon he'd created.

BoDean's thumb stroked the convex surface, seeing clearly in his mind the tiny details he'd observed while preparing it. The intense heat of the fire had burned off all the enamel but the raised outlines had survived. He'd handled it enough times that he could read the lettering with his fingertips.

The "S" and the "C" were the most prominent. Toward the center were the smaller letters. How many times had he looked at them as he sharpened and polished? The cutting edge ran from the pointed bottom to just even with where he touched it now. When embedded in a neck or a chest or a belly, the words would say everything he wanted. He knew it would work. He'd already used it to field dress small game, finally working his way up to a young whitetail. People's hides weren't anywhere near as tough as animals. It would slice skin like butter.

BoDean tried to picture the old man in a younger day. Sharp blue uniform, leather holster and sidearm, nightstick tapping an iron fence as he walked his beat with that swagger cops think only they have a right to. He didn't look so healthy now, Bo Dean reckoned. The pasty legs above the high black socks and leather sandals were a road atlas of purple veins; a big belly hung over a ridiculous pair of tropical-print swim trunks. BoDean figured would be doing him a favor, really.

But not today.

Maybe soon, but not today.

The old man was asleep, that much he could see. As BoDean shifted his weight the honed edge sliced deeply into his thumb. He bit down hard to stifle any sound. Blood was oozing now. He smeared some of it over the embossed lettering and was reminded of a time when he and his brother Billy were murdering an overly-efficient Bank Examiner as a favor to one of the New York crime families. The guy was older and scrawny and the job should have taken five minutes. But Billy always liked to experiment. He wanted to see how far he could get into dismemberment while still keeping him alive. After the hands, feet, one arm and part of a shin had come off the schmuck started screaming "Blood libel!" over and over until Billy finally got frustrated and sliced his windpipe with a skinning knife. BoDean didn't know what blood libel meant and never bothered to find out but he had liked the sound of it. With the help of several fence-wire tourniquets they were, he recalled, down to part of just one leg at the hip still remaining when the guy finally croaked.

Blood libel.

Billy would have approved. BoDean had strung the tiny wrist bones he'd pried out of the scorched soil by Billy's shack on a leather loop around his neck. With his free hand he touched them lightly.

Blood libel.

He settled on the thought and with the cooling and congealing drops of blood he traced out the lower set of raised letters in his mind: C...H...I...E...F

Two

Surf City, NJ

Michaela E. Cleary, Chief
Surf City Police Department
Long Beach Blvd
Surf City, NJ   17   , 1969

Dear Chief Cleary,

    Greetings and salutations from the Great State of Georgia. It's   er than hell here. I'm sure you're busy preparing for the upcoming   Weekend.

    I am being treated very well although I don't really have a great deal to do. Technically, I am considered a re-enlistee and I am certainly happy and proud to carry that designation. My ETS has not yet been determined and I am told it is apparently dependent on matters currently ongoing here at Ft.   I would have phoned but there is apparently a problem with the long-distance lines somewhere up .

If you see my parents, please apologize for my sparse communication and reassure them that I am healthy and in good spirits. My father will be pleased to know that my hair is cut once a week by a talented NCO barber/stylist and that my bunk and footlocker are completely squared away. Tell my mother not to worry and that I am sorry I had to leave on Day.

I hope you are doing well. Say hello to your Dad. Give my regards to Mr. W. Kelly and tell him he was most certainly correct in his assumptions. Please excuse the formality of a typed letter but current circumstances apparently require it. I'm sorry I am missing the chance to meet your lovely Sisters. And remember, there are no such things as ghosts.

River deep, mountain high.

Sincerely,

Pvt. Ronald F. Dunn, USA

Mickey Cleary refolded the letter, placed it back in its official envelope then tucked it into the pocket of the uniform blouse which hung behind her on an aluminum sand chair that had seen better days. She'd try to decode it later. A sea breeze kicked up and she tipped her chin to let it wash over her.
"I ever tell ya I had a boyfriend?"
Mickey smiled, amused by both the comment and the incongruous image of the woman sitting across from her on the beach.
"No," Mickey replied, "You never told me you had a boyfriend. I was in third grade, remember? Saint Rose of Lima. We never even knew you had a real name."
Sister Innocentia took a long drag on her Virginia Slim. "Christ, that was such a friggin' long time ago," she said, blowing out a contrail of blue smoke that momentarily encircled her headpiece. "For sixteen years I was Agnes Madonna Catanzariti and I was

the complete package, as they say. The wellspring of thousands of very, very impure thoughts, I can tell you that." She reached beneath her robe and made several grunting adjustments which rattled the large crucifix resting just below the circular arc of the white wimple.

"What are you doing?" Mickey asked with a laugh.

"Freeing the two prisoners."

"The what?"

The former Agnes Madonna Catanzariti clamped the long cigarette in her lips. "Lettin' my bazooms breathe a little, if you must know. God, you Irish are such a nosy bunch."

Mickey reached into the Styrofoam cooler and produced another can of Schaefer.

"Are they lookin'?" Innocentia asked.

Mickey peered over her shoulder at the four nuns and the seven girls splashing in the green Atlantic surf. It was hard to tell which group was having more fun. The nuns were in full habits which were now soaked with salt water. The girls ranged in age, Mickey figured, from about nine to maybe fifteen or sixteen. "That's all that's left?" Mickey asked.

Innocentia popped the tab on the beer and took a long swallow. "Yep. The Magnificent Seven. Be down to the Dirty Half-Dozen here in a few weeks when young Miss Donahue turns sixteen. I don't know how much longer the Diocese will keep us up and running – it's not like we make license plates or anything."

"And where will Miss Donahue go?"

"Got her lined up with a foster family over in Jersey. Ritzy suburb, private school, all girls no less. Says she wants to be a teacher. Trouble is she's got a boyfriend. *Frankie*. But I think he's a runner for the Ragone's already so..."

Mickey blinked at the mention of the name. "Frankie, huh? Got a spare chastity belt?" she asked and then reached for a beer of her own.

"Better," Innocentia answered. "I got her on the Pill. Might as well face facts, right? I tell her it's a vitamin. She's a good kid, though. Maybe a little on the dramatic side, but if anyone can make it out it's her. She's got a good heart."

Mickey sipped at the sweating can.

"Too bad about Ragone's kid," Innocentia said, fixing Mickey with a gaze.

"Yeah," Mickey replied. "Too bad for everyone."

"The old *goombah* made a very large donation to our cause not that long after the boy's funeral. Wonder who it was told him to do that?" Innocentia arched an eyebrow and dabbed sweat from her nose with her sleeve.

"Probably the Holy Ghost," Mickey said. "I understand he's a very religious man."

"It's the Holy Spirit now, Cleary, remember? No such things as ghosts."

An image flickered in Mickey's mind. The breeze had dropped but she suddenly felt cold. A small shiver passed right through the center of her.

"You alright here for a little while?" she asked Innocentia.

"Depends. How many are left in the cooler?"

Mickey stood up. "Enough," she said brushing sand from her thighs. "I have to check on my dad."

Innocentia stretched out her legs and pulled her habit up far enough to reveal a pair of flower-print bloomers.

"Second Vatican Council standard issue, I presume?" Mickey asked.

Innocentia drained the last drops from her can. "Well, all I can say is what Pope Paul the Sixth don't know won't hurt him," she replied. "Pretty sure him and them other Cardinals got together and had that sweet little John the Twenty-Third whacked. So in God I trust but everyone else remains a suspect. Patsy live here in Surf City?"

"No," Mickey replied. "I found him a nice one bedroom walk-out over in Ship Bottom. It makes him feel like he's independent, living in another town, although I could probably spit there from here."

"Bring him back with you if you want. An old nun and a retired cop. Be interesting to see who has scarier stories."

"My money's on the old nun," Mickey said as she pulled on her uniform blouse and trudged off.

Three

U.S. Army Fort Benning
Georgia

Ronnie Dunn sat hard and straight against the wooden chairback. The lawyer from the Army Judge Advocate General's office was young but with a clean shaven head and thick black GI glasses. He pushed the 8x10 picture prints in front of Ronnie.

"Know where these were taken?" the JAG lawyer asked. His engraved name badge identified him as "Huilinga." His brass hardware identified him as a Captain.

"No, Captain, I do not," Ronnie replied. "In country I'd say – but could have been anywhere and anytime."

"Do you recognize any of the soldiers?" Huilinga persisted.

"No, sir, I do not."

"How about this one?" Huilinga pushed one of the prints closer and pointed to a figure with the tip of a mechanical pencil. "Ever seen him before?"

"I don't believe so," Ronnie replied.

"Really," Huilinga said in a half-question. "Look closer. We believe this is someone you may have met, perhaps at some time prior to his deployment."

Ronnie leaned in, feigning intense concentration.

"He appears to be a platoon leader," Ronnie answered. "But I don't believe he is someone I am acquainted with."

Huilinga tapped the pencil on the photo. "I didn't say you were acquainted with him, Corporal. I said you may have met him."

Ronnie kept his palms on his thighs, letting his fatigues soak up the gathering sweat.

"Look hard. Think, oh, I don't know, four years ago. Fort Bliss. Anything?" The question came from the JAG lawyer seated to Huilinga's left. His name badge said Dugoni and he wore a smug impression and the same hardware.

"I met a number of soldiers during my short recall to Fort Bliss," Ronnie said. "I was there to evaluate a new sniper rifle and scope comb-"

"We know why you were there," Dugoni interrupted. "Do you really want to tell us you don't recognize the soldier Captain Huilinga is pointing to?"

Ronnie steadied himself. "Captains, with all due respect, the soldier in the picture is wearing a combat helmet and camo face paint and has what appears to be several days growth of facial hair. It would be very difficult to-"

"Quit fucking with us, Dunn," Huilinga said, snapping the extruded lead on the pencil for effect. "You know goddamn well who this is. You damn near broke his skull at an off-base bar, August nineteen, Nineteen-Sixty-Five."

Ronnie's mouth was filled with the cotton that topped off pill bottles. "I'm sorry, Captains, but I could not say with certainty that the soldier in the picture is the individual you are referring to. No sirs, not with certainty."

Huilinga and Dugoni looked at each other. Ronnie recognized that it was a practiced move. No good cop, bad cop here – just two bad cops, he realized. Neither was on his side.

Huilinga leaned in closer. "What if I told you that this piece of shit ordered his platoon to murder several hundred Vietnamese villagers, including women, children and old people? Would that help your memory, Corporal? Maybe tickle your sense of human decency to help us out here?"

"I am here to help in any way I can, Captains," Ronnie replied. "But I cannot say with certainty that the soldier in the picture is the recruit with whom I had an altercation at Fort Bliss on the date specified. That soldier had a fresh Army haircut and was clean-shaven at the time."

Dugoni reached into a leather satchel that was on the table and pulled out a folder. From it he slipped out several sheets of paper. "Maybe this will help," he said in a placating tone. "This is your statement to the MP's upon intake." He held the papers with both hands and read slowly:

"He was with a bunch of other FNG's and they must have been drinking for some time prior to my arrival at the off-base establishment. I was at a table nearby and this particular FNG was getting really loud. Saying he couldn't wait to get in-country. Said he had dreams about killing gooks with his bare hands. About fucking the young girls, first with his cock and then with his K-Bar. He continued with other fairly vile comments, even for a soldier. I told him to tone it down at which time he called me a chickenshit motherfucker. Said I looked like someone who'd obviously never seen combat. I had just returned from a Brown River Navy deployment on the Mekong River and so I understandably took offense to his comments. I drew my sidearm and struck him several times about the head until he slumped on the table and knocked over his beer. I asked the other FNG's present if they had anything to add. Shortly after that I found myself in the custody of the Military Police."

Dugoni took off his identical GI glasses. "Sound about right?"

"I believe that is the statement I gave," Ronnie answered.

Dugoni took on a conciliatory tone. "Look, Ronnie, we're going to try this eight-ball for murder and dereliction of duty and put his ass in a black hole in Leavenworth for the next hundred years. We want to establish that his behavior was not from the stress of combat or mortal fear, but rather a pre-existent disposition to extreme violence against civilians. Do you see where I'm going?"

"You wish to exonerate the U.S. Army's training and culture from having anything to do with this particular atrocity," Ronnie answered.

There was an icy silence.

"What do you mean, 'this particular atrocity'?" Huilinga asked. "Are you aware of other similar actions against defenseless non-combatants? Did you participate in any such actions? If so, now is the time to tell us. You may be called as a witness for the United States Government, so we consider you to be on our side. We don't want any surprises."

Ronnie waited until he could work up enough saliva to speak.

"I did not participate in nor am I aware of any actions similar to the one you have just described to me. May I have some water, please?"

"As soon as we're finished," Dugoni snapped.

Ronnie ran his tongue over dry lips. "If the soldier you have identified in this picture is the same one involved in the altercation with me at Fort Bliss then I will take your word for it. It very well could be. But as far as making a positive identification from memory and this photograph, I'm afraid I cannot do that with absolute certainty. However, I will not dispute that they could well be the same individual."

"They *are* the same fucking individual," Huilinga hissed. "And you fucking know it. We just need you to say it." He shuffled the pictures and replaced all but one in the satchel. "Take this back to quarters with you and study it. Intensely. You may notice some fine details that escape you at the moment." Huilinga turned to the MP at the door. "Sergeant, get the Corporal some water. Tall glass with ice, please. And a bottle of Coke to take with him."

"Thank you," Ronnie said. He slid the photo closer.

"Oh, and what exactly does 'River deep, mountain high' refer to, Corporal Dunn?" Dugoni asked.

"It's just a line from a song. Also the title, I believe." The MP set down the glass and the sweating green bottle of Coca-Cola. Ronnie drained the ice water in one long gulp. "Ike and Tina Turner," he continued. "1966."

"You really like that jungle bunny music?" Dugoni asked. His chair scraped the floor as he pushed back from the table.

"They just sang it," Ronnie said, standing slowly. "It was written by three white people if that makes you feel any better. Sir."

"Thanks for that little bit of intel," Huilinga said. "And by the way – if you've somehow gotten it into your head that *we're* the enemy, you are going to be here for a very, very long time."

Four

Ship Bottom, NJ

"Dad. Dad, are you asleep?"

The sagging form in the chair didn't move. Mickey looked at the beer bottles.

"Move so you're standing right in front of me, Michaela."

The voice came from beneath a salt-splattered fishing hat emblazoned with the words *"Life's a Beach on LBI"* in aquamarine stitching. Mickey shuffled two steps to her right and crossed her arms.

"You OK, Dad?" she asked.

Patsy Cleary didn't move a muscle. "Some guy's been staking me out for a few hours now. Pickup. Jersey plates. Chevy, probably a Sixty-One or a Sixty-Two. Lotta rust. Mud on the tires and in the wheel wells, not sand. But a funny kind of mud. Lighter. Thought maybe I heard him pull away but I didn't want to look up. Act like you're picking up the bottles and scope it out."

Mickey leaned over and followed instructions noting that most of the bottles were warm and still half-full. She carried them to Patsy's little porch and surveyed the surroundings on the short walk back to his chair. No Chevy pickup.

"If he was here, he's gone," she said.

Patsy raised his head and tipped back his hat. "Whaddya mean 'if'?"

Mickey laughed. "OK, Sergeant Cleary. Have it your way." She had brought back the one beer that was still reasonably cold and handed it to her father. "Why on God's earth would a guy be staking *you* out?"

Patsy took a drink. "What? Like I ain't important enough? You know, I seen what happened in that old station house of yours. I was there, remember? And to this day they ain't never found a single trace of that rat bastard Artie Petroni. I know everybody likes to pretend that all that stuff with you down here never happened but those ginzos, they never forget. *Never.*" He burped as if for emphasis.

"You want to go inside?" Mickey asked.

"Jesus, yes. I gotta pee like a racehorse. Gimme a hand."

The aluminum beach chair groaned as Patsy stood up. Mickey steadied him.

"How's it feel to walk again?" she asked.

"Like I been to Lourdes," Patsy answered. "The shrine, I mean, not the old hospital in Camden. I tell ya I got that slug they took out from my spine in a jelly jar right next to the one they took out of my lung? I must be pretty hard to kill's all I can say."

"Cleary's never quit," Mickey said as they crossed the sidewalk and into the shade of the overhang. She opened the door to the small apartment. A Sears and Roebuck fan gyrated in the wooden double-hung window frame. Doreen Kuzma, the desk clerk at the Ebb Tide Motel, cleaned the apartment once a week and made sure her father had toothpaste and toilet paper and all his pills. Patsy shuffled to the bathroom. When he finished he came out and sat in the bentwood rocking chair Basil Jablonski had bought him when Basil was the Philadelphia Police Commissioner. Mickey handed him his beer.

"This is the same rocker Jack Kennedy used for his back," Patsy said. Mickey had heard him say it every time he sat down. A cheaply framed Karsh of Ottawa print of the assassinated President hung on the wall along with portraits of Pope John, Pope Paul, Saint Patrick and Frank Sinatra.

"Want the radio on or the TV?" Mickey asked.

"I like the radio – WIP – Wee Willie Webber should be on right now. He's really a very tall guy, did you know that?"

"I think I heard that," Mickey replied, settling him in.

"Can you stay?" Patsy asked.

"Not right now, Dad," Mickey answered. "I got four nuns and seven orphan girls sitting on the beach in Surf City I gotta go check on. I think one of the nuns has probably emptied my beer cooler by now."

"Sounds like my kind'a nun," Patsy said.

"You'd like her. I'll bring her by next time they visit."

"You heard from that soldier boy of yours?"

"Just got a letter today. Says they're treating him well. Hopes he'll be home soon. He asked about you."

"Nice kid. You could do a lot worse, you know. You ain't getting' younger."

Patsy finished his beer and Mickey fetched him another from the old Norge. She set it on the dented metal TV table next to the rocker and turned on the radio, dialing the blue plastic Emerson Solid State to 610 AM.

"Thanks, Michaela," Patsy said. "Your mom would be so proud of you."

"She'd be proud of both of us, Dad," Mickey replied. "We never quit. I'll stop by later before I start my shift, OK?"

"The Chief of Police shouldn't have to work nights, even in Surf City," Patsy said.

"Lead by example," Mickey answered as she moved for the door. "Seems to me you taught me that one."

"Yeah, but I been shot twice when I wasn't lookin'," Patsy said "So what the hell do I know?" He sipped at the Ortleib's. "See ya later, kid."

The afternoon sun was still intense and the town of Ship Bottom's streets were crowded with locals, day-trippers and sunburned shoobies. Mickey had left the Chevy's windows down. As she got nearer she saw a pink paper fluttering under one of the wipers – a parking ticket. The 1966 Chevelle SS police cruiser was almost four years old but Mickey had kept it in prime condition. She'd had it repainted over the winter with new markings so that *Surf City Police* stood out more and *Chief* was less prominent. Now that she had three deputies it seemed to send a better message. The sun and the salt air were taking their inevitable toll, she knew, but thought she could get at least one more summer season out of it. She still loved the sound and the power of the three-hundred-and-ninety six-horses corralled under the hood.

Mickey approached from the driver's side and plucked out the summons – it was blank. Written in black Magic Marker on the back side of it in squat block letters was the message *"Just Kidding"* and the initials DJ. Davey Johnson was one of the Ship Bottom deputies. He'd hit on Mickey once or twice since Ronnie left but she had fended him off gently. She liked Davey but she sincerely hoped he wouldn't become annoying.

She stuffed the summons in her pocket and opened the cruiser's door.

It took her a minute to realize that sitting in the passenger seat was a young girl who was staring at her intently.

"Well, hello," Mickey said, easing herself behind the wheel. "Did you, um, lose your Mommy and Daddy at the beach?" She saw the girl was clenching something tightly in her hand. It looked like an envelope. And she appeared dressed for colder weather with leggings, a long-sleeved top and a front button sweater. Safety-pinned to her sweater was a small square of paper. Mickey looked closer at the words written on it. They were in a woman's hand:

**MY NAME IS BONNE-NUIT TRAN
CALL ME BUNNY**

"Bunny, huh?" Mickey asked. "Is that your name?"

The girl nodded.

"Can I see what's in your hand?"

The girl hesitated. Mickey thought she looked about ten. She was scrawny and pale as skim milk with strong Asian features. Jet-black hair hung just barely to her shoulders.

"Is that for me?" Mickey asked, opening her hand but not reaching over as to avoid a threatening gesture.

"You no done?" the girl asked. Her English was accented but seemed passable.

"No done what, honey?"

"Bunny," the girl corrected. "You no *done*?"

Mickey took off her Ray-Bans and put her hands in her lap.

"I'm done visiting my Dad, is that what you mean?"

Bunny grimaced. "No, no, no," she said, frustration visible on her face. "*YOU* no done?"

Mickey shrugged in confusion. Bunny showed her the plain white envelope but kept it in her hand. Mickey looked at it. Centered neatly on the heavy stock paper were printed the words:

**Pvt. Ronald F. Dunn, U.S. Army
Surf City New Jersey USA
"EYES ONLY"**

Mickey blinked, trying to put the pieces together. Then Bunny spoke.

"Car. You car say Surf City," Bunny said. "Surf City." She pointed to the words on the envelope. 'Surf City. You no done?"

Then it hit her. No, not "you no done." The girl was asking "*You know Dunn?*"

Mickey exhaled loudly and sank back in her vinyl bucket seat. She folded her hands and then leaned toward Bunny.

"My name is Mickey," she said slowly. "But I know Corporal Dunn. He's my very good friend. Do you want me to give this to him?"

Bunny eyed her suspiciously. "You soldier?" she asked.

"No," Mickey said with a tiny laugh. "I'm not a soldier. I'm with the police, the police in Surf City – I'm the Chief in fact. And Ronnie Dunn is my friend. My best friend. Tell you a little secret - he's my boyfriend."

"Married?"

"No, not married. But maybe someday."

Bunny's eyes narrowed. "Where he now? You take me. I give him letter. Only him, Mama say."

"He's not here, Bunny," Mickey said gently. "He's back with the Army for a while."

"Viet Nam?" Bunny asked. She looked panicked at the thought.

"No, Not Vietnam. He's at an Army base in Georgia helping them out with something." Ronnie's location was the one coded message she had figured out from the letter.

"Where Georgia?"

"It's a long ways away. Too far to walk. A few days to drive. You don't drive, do you?"

Bunny looked at her as if roses had suddenly sprouted from her ears.

"Bus go there?" she asked. "I take bus to get here. I take bus there."

"No," Mickey lied. "No bus right now. Where is your Mama?"

The girl shook her head. "Somewhere bad. Bad men take her.

Try to take me but I run. Hide. Mama say if anything ever happen to her to take paper and find Dunn. Dunn know what to do."

Mickey's head was spinning. Bunny was obviously much too old to be Ronnie's Vietnamese love child but what was the connection, she wondered.

"Where is your Daddy?" Mickey asked.

Bunny's expression went blank.

Mickey tried again using a term she'd heard Ronnie say. "Your Papa-san?"

"Papa in bad trouble. That's why men take Mama. That's why I need find Dunn." She pointed a slender finger at Mickey. "You help me find Dunn and he help find Mama and Papa. Make safe."

Mickey noticed they both were sweating so she fired up the big Chevy engine and dialed the AC up all the way. Bunny put her face directly in front of the louvered vent. Mickey recapped the situation in her head: she had a stranded Vietnamese child with abducted or possibly even murdered parents and a letter for Ronnie. The radio crackled.

"Surf City 2 to Surf City 1. Copy, Chief?"

It was Charlie Higgins, her senior deputy.

Mickey plucked the microphone from its silver clip and pushed the TALK button.

"Cleary here. What'cha got, Charlie?"

"Minor beach emergency, Chief," Higgins replied. "Seems like we have a mildy inebriated Mother Superior along with some dehydrated nuns and their female charges. Mother Superior wants to know just what kind of outfit it is you're running here." There was amusement in his voice.

Mickey poked her tongue into her cheek as she considered her reply. She knew that after the brutal events of the 1967 summer, LBI Dispatch in Beach Haven monitored all radio conversations and could record any of them with the push of a button. She imagined that Arlene Shields, a former nurse at a South Jersey hospital who had taken the Dispatch job upon retiring, already had her finger ready and waiting.

"Roger that," Mickey replied. "Advise said individuals to hang loose and that sustenance and liquid refreshments will be arriving shortly courtesy of SCPD. Anything else, Deputy?"

There was a brief pause and a crackle. "Apparently a fresh pack of Virginia Slims and a new lighter are also required. Copy?"

Mickey shook her head. "Yeah, Copy that Surf City 2. Surf City1 rolling, Code 4."

Mickey replaced the microphone and looked at Bunny. "Ever been to the beach?" she asked.

Bunny nodded. "Village on what soldiers call South China Sea. We call *Bien Dong*."

"Well OK, then," Mickey said. "We're going to the beach. But first we have to find you something to wear. Do you have any luggage?"

The blank look returned.

"Any other clothes or belongings? A suitcase or a knapsack maybe?"

Bunny tugged twice at her sweater. Mickey understood.

"May I have the letter?" Mickey asked.

"You promise give Dunn?" Bunny replied.

"I might not be able to give it to him because he's not here. But I can try to tell him what it says. And maybe then we can help your Mama and Papa-san."

Bunny looked torn. "You sure he your boyfriend?" she asked.

"Very sure," Mickey said.

"You do *nhuc-duc* with him?" Bunny asked.

"Nuck duck?"

Bunny sat the letter in her lap and calmly poked the index finger of her right hand into the curled fingers of her left several times.

"Ahhh," Mickey said. "Yes, when he's here. Lots of nuck duck."

Bunny considered this for a moment and then gently picked up the letter and handed it to Mickey, who folded it in half and tucked it into the same uniform pocket that held Ronnie's letter.

She shifted the cruiser into gear, lightly pressed the gas pedal and wondered if she would soon be asking Innocentia to take in one more orphan.

Five

Shamong Township
The New Jersey Pine Barrens

BoDean pulled into the rutted gravel lot outside the Pic-A-Lilli Tavern and parked next to a late model Dodge Charger in a hail of stones. The car was out of place and Billy wondered what he would find inside. Since the old dirt road had become the asphalted NJ Route 206, shore travelers would sometimes mistake the place for a friendly roadside restaurant. It was not. Every other vehicle in the lot was either a pick up or an El Camino flatbed with the exception of a local wrecker which was parked hard against the side of the wooden building.

Piney bars were places of refuge and, when necessary, sanctuaries from pursuing agents of the IRS along with local and state law enforcement. Howard Johnsons' they were not and outsiders were expected to be immediately discouraged by the "**If We Don't Know You Don't Come In**" sign hanging prominently by the centered aluminum entrance door.

BoDean pushed it open and strode inside. He nodded silently to the patrons seated at rough log tables and stood at the end of the bar. His brother Billy's picture hung behind the taps – a nearly toothless grin on his face and a wild turkey in his hand, held by the neck. BoDean regarded the three young men seated on barstools, nearly full mugs in front of them. High school or college kids he figured, with rich parents, by the looks of the car, and usually uppity attitudes. They each wore clean shorts and shirts with collars and banded sleeves. They were trying, unsuccessfully BoDean gathered, to not look scared shitless.

BoDean motioned to Kurt, the bartender. "Three more for our guests." He pawed in his left pocket for some singles. Draws were only a quarter for locals. He walked slowly until he was behind the three boys. Then he reached out his arms and slapped a meaty hand on the shoulders of the ones on the outside.

"Drink up, boys," BoDean said. "If you walk into a man's bar you best be ready to drink like one."

Kurt poured foamy Schiltz's into cloudy chipped glasses.

"We were actually about to leave," the sandy-haired one in the middle said.

"Wouldn't hear of it," BoDean said and shifted his hand to the boy's shoulder, clamping him in place. "I buy you a beer, I 'spect you'll finish it. Otherwise I might take offense."

The three shot each other nervous glances.

"Now drink what's in front of you right quick so my hospitality don't get warm," Billy said.

They downed their beers in single gulps.

The men at the log tables watched in amusement.

"Tha's my late twin brother William in that picture," BoDean said, pointing behind the bar. "He was kilt in a terrible fire at his shack just long on two years ago. Handsome devil, ain't he?"

Kurt delivered the new round.

"Hotter than blue blazes it was," BoDean continued. "Melted him to almost clean nothin'. 'Cept these." Billy fingered the string around his neck. "All I got left to 'member him by. Some little bitty wrist bones I dug outta the sand. Want to feel?"

Three heads shook in the negative simultaneously.

"I'd take it as a sign'a respect to my kin if you did," BoDean said. "But first drink that fresh round I bought'cha. You look like nice college boys. Bet y'all can chug 'em in one swalla."

The boys did as they were told.

"Damn," Billy said. "You boys is practiced drinkers. Set 'em up again, Kurt." He slapped another wrinkled dollar bill down on the bar and held the necklace with Billy's bones out from his dirty shirt. "Feel how smooth they are. Kind'a like throwin' dice."

Each of the boys took a cursory feel and then stared at the fresh brews now resting before them. None of them looked remotely thirsty.

"Thing is," BoDean continued, "Ain't nobody ever figured out how the fire come to start or who started it. Weren't no regular fire either, no sir. Like some kind'a atomic bomb went off. The dirt was still warm when I come around coupl'a days later lookin' for him. A mystery to me, it is." He extended the pinky and thumb of his right hand and wiggled them in the universal sign for "drink up."

The boys each took a deep breath and sucked down the beers. BoDean thought they looked just about ready to puke. He decided he didn't want a mess that Kurt would have to clean up.

"Well, best be on yor way now. Funny things can happen down here after dark." Billy lowered his voice. "Things you wouldn't like very much if they was to happen to you." As they inched back their chairs BoDean said, "Always nice to tip the barkeep. Just good manners. Even Pineys got manners."

Three five dollar bills appeared. BoDean made a face that clearly showed dissatisfaction. Three twenties quickly dropped on top of the fins. BoDean stepped back just far enough so that they had to squeeze past him to get away from the bar. They bee lined for the door without a look back.

"Jersey plate, EVD 422," BoDean said to Kurt after they'd exited. He settled himself at the stool directly across from Billy's picture. "You got the number."

As Kurt dialed the New Jersey State Police to report a drunk driver on Route 206 the men at the table sidled up to the bar with their bottles.

"To Billy," one said and they clinked the cold quart of Iron City in BoDean's hand which had appeared as if from nowhere.

"To you, brother," BoDean said, hoisting the dark brown bottle. "The hunt is about to begin."

Six

Surf City

Charlie Higgins almost blotted out the low angled sun as Mickey approached. A lacrosse star at Rutgers, she had recruited him right out of the Academy to replace Kaylen Fairbrother, her previous deputy. Mickey kept a picture of Kaylen in her wallet and visited his grave at least twice a year. As she navigated the bumpy hillocks of sand she mused that where Kaylen Fairbrother had been thin, ghostly pale and almost painfully shy, Charlie Higgins was the exact opposite in every regard. Mickey dropped the six-pack and a small bag of ice in the cooler which, she noticed, now contained only dead soldiers.

"I see you're what they call an equal opportunity employer," Innocentia said with just the slightest hint slurring.

"Yeah, you could say that," Mickey replied. She pulled the pack of Virginia Slims and a plastic Bic lighter from a small paper bag and handed them to the reclining nun.

"Bible says we're *all* equal in the Eyes of the Lord," Charlie said. Mickey loved his soft North Carolina drawl and the deep register of his voice. She assumed he would have made a great preacher in another life.

"Ha! Don't believe everything you read," Innocentia said, reaching into the cooler. "Pretty sure He plays favorites. Bad people burn. Bad people *deserve* to burn. Ain't enough *mea culpas* in the world to save some of the sons-of-bitches I've seen."

Charlie laughed. "I like someone who calls 'em like they

sees 'em, Sister," he said, employing what Mickey knew was his favorite baseball analogy.

Bad people deserve to burn.

For a moment Mickey was somewhere else, crawling on her hands and knees, being eaten alive by insects in a cloud of choking smoke.

Bad people deserve to burn.

"Left the cruiser running, Chief Cleary," Charlie said.

"What?" Mickey replied, snapped suddenly back into the present.

"Your cruiser. You left it running. You want me to go shut it off?"

Bunny. For an instant Mickey had almost forgotten. "No," she said, still pulling herself free of the memory. "No, Deputy Higgins. Please stay here for just a moment. I have some sodas and sandwiches I want to bring down. And someone I'd like you to meet.

◆ ◆ ◆

Fort Benning, GA

Ronnie sat on the lower bunk and considered his options. His footlocker, the only one in the otherwise unoccupied barracks, contained typing paper and small notebook filled with song titles, lyrics and phrases – each with a cryptic notation next to it. He knew they would read his mail. At least now, he thought, he knew how *closely* they were reading it. He checked his footlocker several times a day and it still appeared undisturbed and hopefully unsearched. The notebook, purchased at Mary T's Notions and Lotions in Surf City, was swaddled in two pairs of boxer shorts and so he doubted it had been gone through. Yet, he reminded himself. He spared a second to amuse himself with the idea that Mary Theresa, the nice lady who owned the shop and who lived in King of Prussia during the winter, had discovered that by simply adding a full line of Coppertone products to her inventory she could double her summer income. When Ronnie had purchased the notebook before shipping out, she had shared that she was considering stocking scented massage oils and maybe some other "unique items" which weren't readily available on the Island. It occurred to him to tell her that it seemed like "Free Love" was becoming increasingly more expensive, but he just paid for the notebook and left.

Across the barracks was a small office desk and the old Underwood typewriter the Quartermaster had provided him for his correspondence. It was black, cast-iron and probably weighed thirty pounds. He'd spent a whole day just cleaning out the dust and squirting in some 3-In-One machine oil so the spider-leg keys wouldn't stick together. The ribbon it had come with was little more than a few tattered black and red threads, long-since devoid of any actual ink. It had taken almost a week to requisition a new one.

He also assumed they were redacting portions of his letters – blacking out words or phrases they deemed to contain "sensitive information." Without the opportunity for even a single phone conversation, which he knew which would be wire-tapped and recorded anyway, his chances of getting information to or from Mickey were close to non-existent. Nope, he decided, it was the undisguisable clack-clack of the Underwood or nothing.

Ronnie rose from the bunk, took four steps and bent down to open the locker. He grabbed the orange cardboard package of Eaton Corrasable Bond and walked to the desk. The metal chair scraped loudly as he pulled it out. Settling himself he slipped in a sheet of the typing paper and twisted the ratcheting roller until the paper appeared. He hit the silver lever on the right of the carriage several times to advance the page and then the punched Tab button. After a quick swig from the Coke bottle he began to peck away.

Michaela E. Cleary, Chief
Surf City Police Department
Long Beach Blvd
Surf City, NJ   **14August,**
1969

Dear Chief Cleary,

Seven

Surf City

"Well, well, and what do we have here?"

Charlie Higgins peered in through the fully retracted passenger side window of Mickey's cruiser.

"You G.I.?" Bunny asked. "You look like G.I."

"I'm sure I do," Charlie replied. "In fact, I'm damn sure I do."

Ronnie had told Mickey, and Charlie had reiterated the fact several times, that the percentage of black soldiers in Vietnam was higher than the percentage of all black people in the entire U.S. population.

"He's a police officer, just like me," Mickey said. "His name is Charlie and we work together. He's a good guy. He's going to help us."

"Still look like G.I.," Bunny said, apparently unconvinced. The clothes she had appeared in were folded neatly on the back seat. Mickey had found her a modest one-piece pink swimsuit and a white terrycloth cover-up that came to her knees and tied in the front. In the cruiser's front seat she kept pulling it down over her legs.

"I thought maybe she could meet Innocentia's girls and play for a while until we figure out what to do next."

"Next?" Charlie asked.

"Yeah," Mickey replied, "As in the next twenty-four hours at least."

"Shouldn't we be looking for Mom and Dad? Maybe a quick

BOLO?"

Mickey put a finger to her lips. "A little more to it than that, I'm afraid. Let me get her settled at the beach and then I'll fill you in. It's a bit...complicated." Mickey bit her tongue, recalling old Doc Guidice using that word when she'd first been on the job and the dead body of young Dante Ragone had washed up on the beach.

"Any ID on her?" Charlie queried.

"Just a note with her name pinned to a sweater. "Bunny Tran."

Charlie laughed. "Well, Tran in Vietnam, and I'm assuming that she's Vietnamese, is like Jones in North Carolina. There's a million of them."

"Dunn her boyfriend?" Bunny interrupted.

Charlie put his muscled forearms on the window frame. "He most certainly is, Bunny. Most definitely her boyfriend."

"She say, she say they do *nhuc duc* all the time."

Before Mickey could stop her Bunny repeated the finger in fist motion. Charlie burst out laughing, a booming sound that filled the cruiser's interior.

"Bunny!" Mickey said with some force. "E-Nough with the nuck duck, OK. No more-" she imitated the gesture while shaking her head. "No. More. Nuck duck. Got it?"

Bunny looked at her.

"You read me?" Mickey said

Bunny nodded. "Five by Five." She pointed to the beach. "We go. *Didi mau.*"

Mickey looked over at Charlie. "She means, well let's go if we're gonna go," he said.

Charlie opened the door and Bunny popped out. He closed it gently and offered her his large open hand. To Mickey's surprise, she took it and began leading him toward the sand.

As Mickey came astride of the pair Charlie looked at her. "Nuck duck *all the time?* Damn, girl," he said. Mickey just rolled her eyes.

◆ ◆ ◆

Innocentia was dozing peacefully and Mickey decided to let her be. Slathering Bunny's pale limbs, shoulders and face with suntan lotion had taken a while, mostly due to entrenched resistance on Bunny's part.

"You'll get a sunburn," Mickey tried to explain.

"Smell like napalm," Bunny said. "Napalm burn you. Burn you bad. Burn you dead."

Bad people deserve to burn.

There it was again, Mickey thought. She wondered just how many horrors this little girl had witnessed.

"It does not smell like napalm," Mickey said, adding a dab of zinc oxide on the tiny nose. "Napalm smells like gasoline. This smells like coconuts."

"Not real coconuts," Bunny countered. Mickey didn't bother to argue.

"I want you to meet some of my friends – they're the nuns in the black robes over there – and the girls they take care of." Mickey pointed to where the Sisters sat letting the wavelets of the outgoing tide wash over their toes. "They're looking for their Mamas and Papa-sans too. You'll like them and maybe you-"

Before she could finish Bunny had doffed her cover up and was running toward the little group. Mickey watched as the tiny girl almost tackled Sister Mary Lambert and wrapped her arms tightly around her the young nun's waist.

"Huh," Mickey said. "Didn't expect that."

"Lots of nuns doing missionary work in Nam. The VC tend to leave them alone. The priests, well, them they usually just kill."

"Serves 'em right, the horny bastards," Innocentia muttered and then went back to sleep. Mickey removed the burning Virginia Slim with its drooping ash from her lips.

"How do you know so much about this?" Mickey asked.

"My brother, Darnell. He spent time in-country. Got wounded during the Tet Offensive. He's in a VA in Omaha right now waiting for an artificial leg."

"I'm sorry, Charlie," Mickey replied. "I didn't know. You never said a word about-"

"He's alive, Chief. And I thank God for that. Trying to get him moved to the hospital in Greenville. Momma and my sisters can visit him easier there. I can drive it from here in a day. We're hoping maybe by September. We tend to keep our family business to ourselves. No offense, ma'am."

"Let me know if I can help," Mickey said. "My little adventure won me some friends in high places. They'd do right by me if I asked."

"Obliged, ma'am," Charlie answered. "But seems to me like folks here are pretty tight-lipped about your little *ad-venture*." He leaned on the word for an extra beat. "Now me, I'd love to hear all about it. When the time is right, of course."

"Little adventure," Innocentia repeated from a deepening alcohol haze.

"One thing you need to learn about life down the shore, Deputy," Mickey said. "If it wasn't something good that happened, then it never happened."

"Read you, Chief. Five by five."

When Mickey looked back at the ocean Bunny was splashing happily in the small surf with the other girls.

"You want me and Rodriguez to split your shift tonight?" Charlie asked. "Been pretty quiet all day. Seems like you got your hands full here. You any good at baby-sitting?"

"I was an only child and I never had a baby-sitting job in my whole life," Mickey replied. "Patsy wouldn't hear of it. Interfered with sports."

"I did a fair bit with my youngers," Charlie said. "Mom and Pop both worked two jobs or extra shifts so we all could go to good schools. I can spell you if you need me to."

"Let me give it a try tonight," Mickey answered. "I still don't know how this girl got here, where she actually got here *from*, and who may or may not be looking for her."

"The little bit you told me leads me to suspect some bad actors are involved," Charlie said. "Lot of possibilities, very few of them favorable for your little friend or her family. I'll be calling Darnell – let me run the scenario by him – no names or ID'ing details of course – and just get his take on it. He was a Poli Sci major at UNC when he enlisted in the Marines and he's still plugged in since he was an LT. It's possible he could help us."

"A lot of the bikers holed up in the Pines are guys back from Nam," Mickey replied. "Might be some intel or connections there. Worth a shot, maybe."

"Stellwag," Charlie said. "Now that dude is a trip. Runs that gang like an Army Ranger Unit. I wouldn't want to skirmish with them."

"Hopefully we never have to," Mickey said. "They seem content to drink beer, ride Harley-Davidson's and plow bevies of underage girls. Probably with a little Gary Puckett on the stereo to set the mood."

"Uh, yeah to the first part, but I think maybe they're starting to go less Gary Puckett and more Rolling Stones, if you get me."

"I don't, Charlie."

"Dark side, Chief. Sympathy for the Devil, Jumpin' Jack Flash. The Stones aren't playing at that music festival up in New York this week. I think they did that on purpose. Peace, Love, even young love and Flower Power – that's not where it's going anymore is all I'm saying." He dabbed his brow with a tan handkerchief pulled from his uniform shorts. His thighs, Mickey thought, looked like twin torpedoes.

"I was a Peace and Love dope-smoking California hippie for a whole year, Charlie. Does that surprise you?"

"Chief Cleary, trust me – nothing about you could surprise me. And I'd be careful around Stellwag – I believe you inspire in him what Pastor Lewis back home would describe as highly impure thoughts."

Mickey thought about the note on her windshield and Innocentia's comment about her old self. "I can handle Stellwag," she said.

"Of that, Chief Cleary, I have no doubt," Charlie answered.

Mickey looked again at the sparkling green water near the shore and the deep blue of the Atlantic stretching all the way to the horizon. Splashing noisily in the breakers, Innocentia's girls had already adopted Bunny as one of their own.

"OK," Mickey said. "I'll take you up on your offer about tonight's shift. But you have to tell me something. You were first in your class at the Academy. You were the equivalent of a number one pick in the draft. Why did you ever choose my little town?"

Charlie folded his arms on his chest and smiled. "That was easy, Chief," he said and took a long look in both directions. "I just really thought this place needed a little color."

Innocentia began snoring.

"Jesus," Mickey said, "I sure as hell hope one of these other nuns has a driver's license."

Eight

Portland, Maine

The contrast could not have been more striking. The woman weighed, perhaps, a hundred pounds but probably less. The two men each went about two-twenty maybe two-thirty, one more thickly muscled and both multiply tattooed.

"Where is it?" the slightly taller of the two men asked. "Last time I'm asking nicely."

"I tell you already. I don't have it. Lost. Lost somewhere on trip."

"Bullshit!" the shorter man shouted.

The woman recoiled as much as she could, her wrists and ankles being zip-tied to the arms and legs of the wooden chair. She was naked and the ice water they'd poured on her was causing her to shiver almost uncontrollably.

"This is next," the taller one said. He lit a cigarette and held the glowing tip close to the woman's face. She reflexively turned away.

"It can be real easy," the shorter man said. "Maybe you don't have it. Maybe the kid has it. And if the kid has it, you'll help us find her, we'll get what we need and let you all go. Don't make this hard for us. We're not bad guys, we just want what belongs to us. What you promised to deliver. *Hieu?*"

There was a scream from an adjacent room.

"Whaddya think?" the shorter one asked. "A car battery hooked up to his balls or... maybe they just went right to the K-Bar and started cuttin' him."

Another scream pierced the air and the woman began to cry.

"You *can* make it stop," the taller man said. He had a bristly mustache and a thick, ugly scar across his shirtless torso that disappeared into a pair of camouflage pants.

The woman's jet-black hair was matted to her neck and back. The classic Asian features were mottled and blotchy.

"You know what a Double Veteran is, don't you?" the shorter man said. He had a brush cut and an incongruous pair of muttonchop sideburns. "Sure you do. All of you gook bitches know what a Double Veteran is. That what you want to be? We'd like that for sure. Even poor Corporal Winston next door wouldn't want you once we were done. Not that he'll be around much longer if they're using the K-Bar already. But – to be honest, it sounds more like an electrified balls scream to me."

"Look," mustache and scar said, "Even if we have to pop you both we'll still find the kid. I mean, she's out there somewhere all by herself." He took the pitcher of ice water and poured a slow trickle on the woman's head. "Only a matter of time. Who out there do you think is gonna protect her?" He stroked the woman's wet hair and traced a finger down her bony spine. He looked at muttonchops. "You sure you searched her *everywhere*?"

"Yeah. I went deep into both tunnels, Sarge. Empty. I suppose she could have swallowed it."

Former Army Staff Sergeant Harlan Brinson paused. He walked to the thin plaster dividing wall and rapped three times. Three raps replied. There were no more screams. "You know, Dickie, for a guy who couldn't make PFC you might have just saved the day."

Former Army Buck Private Richard Robichaux looked puzzled. "You got a pair of X-Ray glasses I don't know about?"

"No, dipshit. But my soon-to-be war bride Miss Tran here is going to very shortly have terrible belly pain and the good doctors in the ER up the road at Maine Medical are going to want to do a real X-Ray - and damn quick. Get that puke syrup out of the medicine chest. And what did you do with her clothes?"

"They're in her bag, in the closet. "

"OK," Brinson replied. "I'll make sure they're presentable. You get her dried off and cleaned up. See if she has any makeup and make sure she puts it on. Let her get dressed but keep a barrel pointed at her. You of all people know how they are." He stood opposite the woman and spread his hands, gripping the edge of the table while Robichaux fumbled in the bathroom for towels. The he brought his face close to hers and spoke softly, almost in a whisper.

"You know, just for the kid's sake, I sure as shit hope you swallowed it. 'Cause like I said, there ain't nobody out there to protect her now if you didn't."

◆ ◆ ◆

Surf City

"Well, do they fit?"

Mickey sat on the side of the double bed facing the closed door to the bathroom.

"Come on, we couldn't have been that far off."

Slowly the warped wooden door opened, creaking on its brass hinges. Bunny emerged, a towel wrapped partially and precariously around her head. She was wearing the blue floral print summer pajamas they'd picked out at the Surf City 5 & 10. Mickey had also sprung for a light flannel robe and a pair of fuzzy pink slippers that Bunny adored the second she saw them. The neck and hem of the pajama top were trimmed in white eyelet lace.

"What these flowers?" Bunny asked pointing to the print top.

"Come sit by me and we'll see," Mickey said.

Bunny shuffled over and climbed onto the bed. Mickey could smell the soap and shampoo and wondered when the last time the girl had had a proper bath before tonight. As Bunny pointed to each one Mickey said its name. "Daisy. Hydrangea. Tulip. Buttercup. Bluebell. And I don't really know what that one is. Did you brush your teeth?" Bunny's blank look returned. Mickey took her finger and rubbed it across her front teeth.

"Yes," Bunny replied. "Boo Coo." She tried to show Mickey all her teeth at once.

"Good," Mickey said. "You must be one tired little girl."

"Where sleep?" Bunny asked, look around the room at the floor.

Mickey patted the mattress next to her. "Right here. This is where Dunn sleeps when he's not away."

"Not floor? Where mat?"

It took Mickey a second but then it registered. "Not floor and no mat. Right here with me, OK?"

"Keep shoes on. OK?"

"Slippers," Mickey corrected. "And yes, you can keep them on if you'd like." Mickey got up and opened the window that faced the ocean. A cool offshore breeze wafted in, fresh and salt-tinged. The surf boomed in the distance as rollers pounded the beach at the moon's behest.

"Sound like *Bien Dong*," Bunny said with a yawn.

"I bet," Mickey replied. She fluffed up the pillows and gently leaned the little girl back. "Covers?" Mickey asked. Bunny shook her head. No.

Mickey turned off the lamp. A tiny blue nightlight in the shape of a television screen and a silvery crescent of moonlight lent a faint glow to the room.

"We look for Mama and Papa-san?" Bunny asked. Mickey thought she was already asleep. "We find Dunn so he help Mama and Papa-San?"

"Tomorrow," Mickey answered, having absolutely no idea how she was going to keep such a promise. "Bunny?" she said next. "What is Papa-san's name?" The girl's breathing had slowed and Mickey figured she was just a few seconds too late. She laid her head on her own pillow and tried to understand how another complicated situation had somehow found her on a skinny barrier island in a town that was slightly less than a mile square.

We're a little drinking town with a big fishing problem. We're not very good at complicated.

Doc Guidice had told her that as they stood in the morning surf next to the mangled body. She had ignored his advice and very nearly ended up dead because of it. She should, she reasoned, just take Bunny to the nearest State Child Welfare Office and be done with it. That would un-complicate things very neatly and very quickly. She wished Ronnie were here. But she knew Ronnie would definitely never hand the girl over to the State of New Jersey. And it was Ronnie and not her that Bunny and her family were counting on. But Ronnie wasn't here. He might come home next week or he might come home next year, she told herself. She didn't think the little girl had time to wait to find out which one it was.

"Mickey-san?" Bunny said, turning slightly and burrowing into Mickey's side. It was the first time she'd used her name.

"Yes, Bunny?"

"Coo-pral Winston."

"What did you say?"

"Papa-san name. Coo-pral Winston. Tomorrow we look for Dunn." Bunny exhaled sharply and then fell deeply asleep. Mickey did neither of these things. She lay awake watching the moonlight dance on the wall and listening to the cadence of the crashing waves

Coo-pral Winston.

Coopral Winston.

Corporal *Winston*.

Papa-san is Corporal Winston. It was a place to start, Mickey thought. But then, she realized, so was the body on the beach.

Nine

The Pine Barrens

One thing BoDean loved about Pineys was the accumulated knowledge they possessed. It was almost tribal, he decided, held tight from outsiders but passed freely among members. The Piney family histories went back so far it was almost impossible not to find someone who had lived through or participated in a major world event. There were World War I veterans and kids fresh out of Nam. A lot of the knowledge was practical but a fair bit of it was criminal. A neighbor had just shared with BoDean a better way to dissolve dead bodies, bones and all.

At the moment he was excited about something new that was actually something quite old. Frannie Leusner, who's lean-to shack was about a mile from BoDean's cabin, had come into the Pic-A-Lilli shortly after he'd sent the drunk boys packing. BoDean had been sharing some ideas about the best way to burn down a small house in the shortest period of time. Leusner had listened for three quick Schlitz draws and then blurted out two words along with a wad of yellowish phlegm.

"Foo Gas."

At first BoDean wasn't sure if Leusner was choking on something or if he was about to puke so he'd clapped him on the back and politely inquired what the fuck it was he was trying to say.

"Foo Gas, ya damned fool," Leusner had repeated. "Used it in WW Two against the Jerries in Europe. Lit 'em up real good, we did. Never seen a body burn like that while still alive. Never heard a man scream like that 'fore nor since."

The last part had piqued BoDean's interest and so he'd spent the next hour picking the atrophying coils of Leusner's brain. The locals called him Loose Nuts for a reason. BoDean didn't think there were any bolts left, truth be told, but he figured it was still worth a shot. The conversation had cost him a few more draws and three fingers of Old Mr. Boston, but it had good gamble.

BoDean lay awake in his bed almost giddy with excitement. He'd have to do some digging, but if what Loose Nuts had described was real, it was exactly what he'd been looking for. Quick, easy, pretty much untraceable and able to inflict maximum agony in a very short period of time. BoDean had a picture dancing in his head and his dick even started to get hard. A small, unapproachable inferno with inhuman screams coming from within. And over so fast the fire trucks and cops would be helpless to even get near it, much as less put it out.

Loose Nuts had been a little fuzzy on the actual technical details by the end of the Old Mr. Boston, but BoDean knew where to find him when his hangover passed so he didn't see this as a particular problem.

BoDean's toes were unconsciously curling and uncurling with anticipation. The other advantage of Piney life, he knew, was that there was literally nothing that could not be obtained by asking, borrowing or stealing, the last being the most common method. BoDean would use a very small barrel. A nail keg, he decided. It would be easy to get and transport. The gel petroleum was the thing he was most unfamiliar with, but someone he knew would know, he assured himself.

Loose Nuts kept saying "but ya gotta ra'member to use the 'nesium," and it now dawned on BoDean that the old sot meant Magnesium. He didn't know much about Magnesium and had never used it for anything before but decided this would be a good learning experience. There would always be more people to be murdered for money and this "Foo Gas" Leusner talked about, if it worked the way he said it did, might just become BoDean's calling card. The Mob families loved dramatic hits – especially gruesome ones that sent a strong message along with eliminating troublesome individuals. Billy had always liked the long, slow torture sessions. BoDean went along with him out of filial loyalty, but he was never quite as enthusiastic and Billy usually ended up finishing the job by himself while BoDean jerked off. But a man alive and on fire, he mused, now that would be something to see. Front page shit, he figured. Maybe even the TV news.

"Never seen a body burn like that while still alive," Leusner had said. BoDean repeated the words out loud. He reached into his grimy boxers and started tugging.

Ten

Surf City

Charlie Higgins sat in the idling cruiser on the street in front of Mickey's house. The sun was several degrees above the horizon and seemed to undulate in the morning sky. Charlie had taken the first half of the Chief's night shift and then conked out. He was still brushing out the cobwebs when he took over for Rodriguez less than fifteen minutes ago. The large coffee from Bill's Luncheonette was helping immensely and he felt himself slowly revving up. He'd wolfed down three TastyKake fruit pies – two peach and one cherry - and the sugar was just now rushing to his head. He checked his watch and kept an eye on Mickey's front door. When he saw it move he turned off the ignition, opened the door and got out.

Mickey approached in her uniform and holding a cup of coffee.

"How'd it go?" Charlie asked.

"Got a name," Mickey replied taking a careful sip from the steaming cup. "Corporal Winston."

Charlie nodded.

"Kid still asleep?"

"Unconscious would be more like it," Mickey said. "I have a dent in my ribs from those bony little knees, too."

"Face it, Chief. You're all she's got right now. Instant motherhood."

"That's a scary thought," Mickey replied. "No one has ever

accused me of being maternal."

"Bet your mom would disagree."

"My mother died when I was young. Suicide, I came to realize much later, although that word was never actually mentioned. I might know what to do with a boy, but a girl – no idea, really."

Charlie was leaning on the roof of the cruiser as he spoke. "I called Darnell last night after I left you. He said he'd make some polite inquiries. Said something funny, though."

"What was that?" Mickey asked.

"They'd just given him some morphine for his phantom leg pains so he was a little all over the place, but he said something about black market families."

Mickey's face showed her confusion. "What the hell is a black market family?"

Charlie shrugged. "That's all I got from him. Ten seconds later he was asking if our daddy had bought that new car yet." Charlie took a large swallow from his cardboard cup. "Our daddy's been dead nigh on ten years now."

"Got it," Mickey said. "Morphine is good shit."

"When it's free it is. I worry they making him a junkie and he doesn't even know it. That's why we want him closer as soon as possible. Make sure he's clean off that good shit before they release him. You see what I mean?"

"He'd still get pain medicine from the VA, wouldn't he?" Mickey asked. "I mean, they wouldn't just cut him off."

Charlie raised his eyebrows. "Tough to match that morphine high, they say," he continued. "Sometimes have to look for alternatives that don't come from the corner drugstore, just from the corner."

"You mean–"

"Chief Cleary," Charlie said in a controlled tone but one that belied alarm. "Don't move. Don't turn around." His hand dropped to his holster

"What's–"

"Don't move, Chief. We got ourselves a situation here."

A girl's high-pitched voice, rising and falling. Close to screaming. Rattling the still morning air.

"Is that–"

"It's Bunny, Chief."

There was a soft pop as he unsnapped the safety strap on

his holster.

"Charlie, what are you doing?"

"It's Bunny, Chief. And she's holding your gun."

◆ ◆ ◆

Maine Medical Center
Portland, Maine

Dickie Robichaux squirmed uncomfortably in the row of attached chairs. The Emergency Department Waiting Room smelled of Pine-Sol, urine and vomit in equal measures. After a few more minutes of gymnastics he found a position that was the least uncomfortable and began the slow descent into sleep. He was almost there when Harlan Brinson slapped him on the soles of his stocking feet.

"-the fuck?" Dickie said uncurling himself from the chairs.

"Where is she?" Brinson asked.

"Still in back with the docs I guess," Dickie answered. "Nobody's come by here."

Brinson looked around nervously. "And you know this because you were not asleep? Christ, Dickie, I was gone for five minutes. She could be in the wind by now."

Dickie rubbed his eyes. "Sarge, I just closed my eyes for a second. I swear. Nobody been in or out past me while you were gone."

Brinson checked his watch. 'Nine hours we been here already. You sure no doc came out?"

"Nobody came out," Dickie replied, scratching lazily at his crotch. "Last thing I heard was that nurse saying they had her in triage. That the big car crash out on 295 had tied up all the docs but they'd get to her as soon as they could."

"Did she say if they'd gotten an X-Ray?"

Dickie shook his head. "Nothin' about an X-Ray."

Brinson lit an unfiltered Camel and paced. "This is takin' too long," he said. "We ain't had eyes on her for almost four hours." A few of the Waiting Room patrons shifted their gaze toward him. "I sure hope she's OK," he said, loud enough for them to hear. He sat down next to Dickie and leaned in. "I'll stay here and act concerned. See if you can slip back there and at least make sure she hasn't run. Anybody asks, tell them you were looking for the latrine."

Dickie got up slowly and bent his back to work out the kinks the hard chairs had put there. Slowly he padded around the chipped and pitted tile floor and then pushed through a door marked "Staff Only."

Brinson marked the time on his watch.

Ten minutes later Dickie returned, holding a vending machine coffee.

"She's back there," he said. "Layin' on a stretcher. Sleeping, looks like."

Brinson breathed out sharply. "Let me see if I can find out what they're doing."

As he finished this sentence an exhausted looking doctor in scrubs stained with what Brinson assumed were various bodily fluids shuffled out from the door that Dickie had gone through.

"Anyone here with Miss Tran?" he asked.

"Right here," Brinson replied. The young man walked over.

"Are you family?" he asked.

"I'm her - I'm going to – we're going to be married next month. So not quite but almost."

"Well, good news," the young doctor said. "Whatever it was has passed. Just a little GI upset, gastritis we call it. Maybe something didn't agree with her. Her belly's soft and her tests are negative. I think you can take her home. Might stick to liquids for the next twenty-four hours, though."

Brinson puffed on the Camel. "That won't be a problem," he said. "Was the X-Ray OK?"

"You know, I almost didn't do one," the doctor answered. "Her symptoms were gone by the time we got to her. Guess you heard about the big wreck."

"Yes," Brinson answered. "Unfortunately, the ambulances started arriving just as we got here last evening."

"Well, at least you're taking her home," the young man said. "Lot of husbands and parents aren't so lucky this morning."

Brinson feigned sorrow. "But the X-Ray? You said it was OK?"

The doctor looked over Brinson's shoulder at an arriving stretcher. "Yeah, yeah. Flat plate was clean as a whistle. Chest too. Little bit of gas in the distal colon. Hardly any stool, though, which is unusual. When's the last time she had anything to eat?"

"Thank you, Doctor…" Brinson said, looking at the name stitched on the white coat. "Doctor Morley. We'll get some liquids in her as soon as we get home. Milk and orange juice OK? Maybe some tea with honey?"

"I think you can start with those. Nothing carbonated, though." Dr. Morley tucked the stethoscope he'd been holding into one of the large side pockets.

"Thank you again. We'll just wait here, then?"

"One of the nurses will bring her out to you," Morley answered. "And," he paused.

"Do you mind a little free medical advice?"

"Fire away," Brinson said.

"I just read two more scientific papers about cigarette smoking. I'd recommend quitting right away. Those things will kill you."

"Thanks," Brinson answered. "But I'm afraid if that's true then they'll just have to get in line."

Eleven

Surf City

"I got this, Charlie," Mickey said. She raised her hands in a surrender posture and slowly turned around.

Bunny had two hands on the Nine Millimeter Glock but it was still heavy enough to prevent her from raising the angle of the barrel much above forty-five degrees.

"What's the matter, Bunny?" Mickey asked.

Tears were streaming down the girl's face.

"You leave me. You go to find men. Men to take me away. I know."

Mickey put her arms down and took a single step forward.

"Bunny, you were sleeping and I didn't want to wake you up." Mickey took another step. "No one is coming to take you away. You are safe with me and Charlie."

"You lie!" Bunny screamed. The shaking barrel of the gun dropped another degree.

"Men who take Mama say I be safe with them. You all lie! Where letter for Dunn?"

Mickey tapped her uniform breast pocket. "Right here where I put it when you gave it to me. I haven't even opened it."

"You show!"

Mickey took two steps, unsnapped the pocket and reached inside. She slowly withdrew the envelope.

"See?" she said. "Just the way you gave it to me." Mickey held the envelope out in front of her and slowly closed the gap between her and the girl. "Do you want it back?" The gun barrel now pointed at the sand in front of Bunny's feet.

"You keep," Bunny said. Her tiny shoulders slumped. Mickey bounded forward and grabbed the gun.

"Do you know how to use this?" Mickey asked.

Bunny nodded. Yes.

"Good," Mickey said. "But you can never touch it unless I tell you to. Read me?"

Bunny nodded again.

"Read me?" Mickey repeated.

"Five by five," Bunny answered and began to cry uncontrollably. Charlie appeared next to her and Mickey handed him the gun.

Mickey lifted the sobbing girl and held her tight.

"You're safe with Charlie and me," she said. "I promise, Bunny. We will protect you. Tell me you believe me."

"I believe you," Bunny answered.

"Tell Charlie you believe him," Mickey said.

"I believe Charlie-san."

"OK, then," Mickey continued. "Now that we've had a whole day's worth of excitement how 'bout we go inside and get you some breakfast."

"Cocoa Puffs," Bunny said, sniffling but no longer shaking. "Cocoa puffs with chocolate milk."

Mickey looked at Charlie.

"On it, Chief Cleary," he said with a wink. "I'll just keep the gun with me for now if that's OK."

Mickey stroked the girl's hair and walked with her into the house.

♦ ♦ ♦

Portland, Maine

Yvette Tran was once again zip-tied, wrists and ankles, to the wooden chair. This time she was fully clothed.

Harlan Brinson sat on an identical wooden chair on the opposite side of the square table. In front of him was a large white enameled basin filled to the brim with cold water. He brought his face closer to Yvette, who kept her eyes downcast.

Dickie Robichaux stretched out on the dirty couch trimming his fingernails with a bayonet. "How's a gook chick get a name like Yvette, anyway?" Dickie asked.

"The French invaded Nam a long time before we showed up. Had fancy coffee plantations, impregnated the locals. Tried to turn Saigon into Paris in the jungle." As Brinson said this he pushed the basin slightly closer to the restrained woman.

Dickie finished scraping at his nails and stuck the bayonet into the faded floral cushion. "Oops," he said. "There goes the security deposit."

Brinson spoke softly to Yvette.

"In Jungle School they teach you that the human body can go without food for three weeks, maybe even a little longer. But now water," he dipped a finger into the basin, "yeah, well now, going without water, that's what you call a whole 'nother story. In cool temperatures you can last maybe five days. If it's warm, like it'll be in here when we shut off the AC, I'd say three'd be more like it. And dying of thirst is slow and, at least I'm told, really, really painful."

He edged the basin closer.

"So here's how this is going to go down. Corporal Winston is in the identical situation you are next door. Except he doesn't have any water."

Yvette trembled slightly.

"We're going to leave here today. We think we can find the kid and hopefully what else we're looking for. We're heading South, but it's a good full day's drive to start. You'll be fine for a few weeks if that's how long it takes us. But Harold, well that poor bastard only has about three or four days. Just to help things along, we've sealed his windows and brought in a couple of heaters to make sure he doesn't get cold. I imagine you'll be able to hear him suffering – he might even ask you to help him out. Maybe he really doesn't know exactly where the kid went. Or even if he does, we know he won't tell us. All that interrogation resistance training the Army gave us. Works both ways. But you do. And you might."

Brinson dipped two fingers in the water and put them to Yvette's lips.

"We've posted a sentry outside Harold's door. So, if and when you finally decide to help us, he'll go get him a nice cold Coca-Cola. Hell, maybe a whole six-pack of them. Or even a beer, who knows? But if it takes us more than a few days to locate the girl and you ain't being helpful, well then the Corporal's slow and miserable death will be on you, not us."

Yvette finally looked up. "You will hurt her."

Brinson pushed back from the table and laughed. He had his shirt off and was stroking his scar. The tattoo on his left chest read "Born To Kill."

"Now," he said, "do I really look like the kind of guy who would harm an innocent child?"

♦ ♦ ♦

Fort Benning, Georgia

Ronnie stood at attention next to his footlocker.

"At ease, soldier," Captain Huilinga said. He pointed to the book on Ronnie's bunk. "What are you reading?"

"'Heart of Darkness' by Joseph Conrad, sir."

"Let's dispense with the formalities for the purpose of this visit, shall we, Private?"

"As the Captain wishes," Ronnie replied.

"Yes. The Captain wishes." Huilinga said. "And my first name is Lucas." His tone was weary. He pulled the metal chair away from the office desk and sat backwards on it, facing Ronnie.

"What happened last year in *Quang Ngai* Province was a shit show of absolutely astronomical proportions. A shit show from which the American military and its mission may, if not handled properly, never recover. And we're off the record here. You have my word as an officer. So please sit down and get comfortable."

Ronnie sat stiffly on the bunk. Huilinga continued.

"I read Conrad in undergrad. 'Lord Jim' and then "Heart of Darkness.' Boston University. Had a great English Lit professor, Dr. Danny Lipinski. Used to sit with his chair up on his desk and zing erasers at people who hadn't read the assignment. Pretty good shot, too." Huilinga loosened his tie.

"Listen. I understand that shit goes south in the jungle in a heartbeat. I understand there are impossible situations. Situations that cannot possibly end well no matter what course of action is chosen. To me, those are givens. I don't need a lot from you, Ronnie. But I need a little. You're basically incommunicado here.

I can loosen that up. But like I said – I need a little from you. I have maybe five hundred dead civilians, many of them raped and mutilated, and I have the Mission Photographer's pictures to prove it. I have a helicopter pilot who trained his machine guns on American soldiers to make it stop. What I don't have is an explanation that will allow us to move forward with the decidedly dirty job of protecting the world."

Huilinga inched his chair forward.

"You don't have to testify. You don't have to appear in open court. A quick sworn and witnessed deposition is all I'm asking for. A sliver of exculpatory evidence to save the entire United States Army all the way to the Pentagon. I've arranged for you to have one long-distance phone call per day. If you were to make said phone call between, let's say, thirteen hundred and fourteen hundred hours local, when the Comms Clerk takes his lunch break, then I will promise you those calls will be completely private. The number you call will be duly noted, but that's it. Again, you have my word."

Huilinga leaned back and put his hands on his knees.

"You were on the Mekong River, weren't you?"

"Yes, sir. Brown water Navy. It was in my statement."

"Then 'Heart of Darkness" should hold special meaning for you. It's about a river trip."

"I've read it several times, actually," Ronnie replied. "Starting in high school."

Huilinga stood up and pushed up his tie. Ronnie started to stand as well.

"As you were," Huilinga said. "Dugoni wants to squeeze you 'til you pop, but I really have no interest in doing that. A little help and you can be on your way back to the beach before Labor Day. In the meantime, I'll have a phone hooked up here. Thirteen hundred to fourteen hundred. Don't forget."

"Thank you, Captain," Ronnie said.

"You're lucky really. You know that, right?"

"How is that, sir?"

"You'll be done with this soon. You'll read about it in the papers and the magazines next year or maybe the year after. I'll carry this abomination with me to my grave."

Ronnie saluted and Huilinga returned it.

"Just look at the picture I gave you. And say hi to your friend,

Chief Cleary. I got a peek at her FBI file, by the way. One tough cookie by the looks of it."

"That she is, Captain. I'll be sure to pass on the Judge Advocate's personal regards."

Huilinga turned and left. Ronnie picked up the book and turned to the opening page where he had underlined a sentence long ago:

"*And this also,*" *said Marlow suddenly,* "*has been one of the dark places of the earth.*"

The dark places of the earth, Ronnie thought. He had been to one of them. He wondered how many more there were to come.

Twelve

The Pine Barrens

BoDean found Frannie Leusner defecating at the base of a scarlet oak tree. Flies buzzed nosily around his recent deposit.

"Need some paper?" BoDean asked.

"I don't think so," Leusner replied and hitched up his muddied blue work pants. He cinched the belt to its last hand-punched hole but still they hung precariously on his hipbones.

"'Member what we was discussin' last night at the bar?" BoDean said.

"Beer?" Leusner answered.

"Foo Gas," BoDean said. "You was tellin' me about Foo Gas."

"Five dollars might help me recollect better," Leusner replied. He began walking toward his rickety lean-to. "And what do you need Foo Gas for, anyway? Shit, those things make a fireball so big it'd bring every dumb ass with a badge or a hose from hunnert miles in every direction. They still got that Fire Tower up in Tabernacle – even a greenhorn spotter wouldn't miss that."

"Don't need it big," BoDean replied. "Just need it hot."

"It sticks to ya," Leusner said. "That's the trick of it. That jelly gas gets on ya and won't come off. Just keeps burnin' ya 'til there ain't nothin' left to burn. Takes a while though. Hotter than bejeezus it is. Watched one Kraut bastard cut his own throat just to end his misery."

BoDean followed Leusner to the parallel strips of corrugated tin that defined his "house".

"Can you make it smaller?"

Leusner held out his thickly calloused hand. BoDean pulled some bills from his coveralls and handed over a ragged five dollar bill.

"Make it any size you want, I s'pose," Leusner said. He tucked the bill in the breast pocket of a faded flannel shirt. "Just gotta get the pur-portions right, is all."

"Is there a formula?" BoDean asked, proud of himself for remembering the term.

"Ain't no fuckin' formula," Leusner said. He spat a wad of green-tinged phlegm on a nearby rock. "Little-a this, little-a that. Jelly gas and the nesium. Gotta figure out how to light it, though. It ain't e'zactly a controlled thing once it gets goin'. I'm still askin' -why the fuck do you need Foo Gas, anyway."

BoDean shuffled his feet. "Got a small job to do. Some old business to take care of. Thinkin' this might do the trick."

"Jesus Christ on A Crutch," Leusner said, reaching for a Mason jar of cloudy liquid. "And I always thought Billy was the sick one in yor fam'ly." He unscrewed the top and sipped. "I hope *I* never piss you off, tell you that much."

"Where do I get the jelly gas?" BoDean asked. "And I don't mean to buy."

"Well, you'll need some tar and some lime, too. Prob'ly best track down Cowboy Jack Barstow. He's with the Public Works Department in Hammonton. Has keys to the yard and all the pumps. I'd imagine they'd have ever'thing 'cept the nesium. For that you might have to deal with them new biker boys – they is way, way into fancy chemicals. I think they use it to make that L.S.D. shit."

BoDean handed over another rumpled bill. "You won't recollect much about this little talk, will you?"

Leusner took a hearty slug from the jar. "Loose Nuts," he said, toasting himself. "Barely remember my own name after a couple more swigs a'this."

"That's what I figured," BoDean replied and began the long walk back to his truck

◆ ◆ ◆

Interstate 95, Mile Marker 25
Cumberland, Maine

The Rest Area was crowded and Dickie Robichaux had to park at the very end, next to a dented blue Plymouth Belvedere station wagon overflowing with dirty-faced children. The car had Jersey plates and badly needed an improved suspension. The back bumper hovered a foot or two from the baking asphalt and only half of the eight children Dickie had counted were in it. He lit a Lucky Strike and waited for Brinson.

Off the roadway the breeze was non-existent and Dickie peeled off his shirt. The woman in the Belvedere smiled at him and he rolled his driver's side window down all the way.

"Family vacation?" he asked.

"How'd you guess?" the woman replied. "Got one to spare?"

Dickie tapped the pack and extended his arm. The woman reached across and plucked the protruding unfiltered cigarette.

"Lucky Strike Means Fine Tobacco," she said.

"Indeed it does," replied Dickie. He watched as she withdrew the dashboard lighter and held it to the cigarette. "Where you headed?" he asked.

"Acadia National Forest," she said. "His idea of a road trip." She pointed to the empty driver's seat. "I wanted to go to the Poconos. You?" She took a long drag, held it and then blew three perfectly round smoke rings.

"Waiting to find out." Dickie motioned to the outdoor phone booth where Harlan Brinson was engaged in animated conversation.

"Trade ya places," the woman said wearily.

Dickie thought she was probably still young but already had the face of an old woman. Maybe it was the eight kids, he wondered.

The woman took another long puff. "The AC quit in Connecticut. Travel is a foretaste of Hell, they say."

"Never heard that one," Dickie replied. He stubbed out his own butt in the flip-out ashtray and withdrew a fresh one from the pack.

"Voltaire," the woman said. "Eighteenth Century French philosopher. I was an English Major in college, believe it or not. 'Til I got knocked up with number one, that is."

"Well it's the language everybody speaks, so that must'a been pretty easy," Dickie shot back.

The woman looked at him strangely, Dickie thought. The she laughed.

"You're in the Army I take it?"

Dickie fingered his dog tags. "I was," he said. "But I'm out now." He decided the circumstances surrounding his Dishonorable Discharge were none of her business.

"Nam?" she asked.

"Two tours," Dickie answered. "You got a problem with that?"

The woman laughed again. "My little brother Mikey was a Marine. So the answer to that, as he would have told you, is Fuck No, I don't have a problem with that."

"When did he get home?"

"May fifth. We met his plane at Dover AFB. Thanks for asking."

Dickie knew what it meant. The coffins of GI's killed in-country arrived back in the U.S. in groups at the Delaware airbase on huge C141 Starlifter transport planes.

"Sorry," he said. "Didn't mean to –"

"Yeah, nobody means to. How about you give me one for the road."

Dickie handed her the pack.

"I didn't really want to go to the Poconos," the woman said. She tapped out another cigarette. When the dashboard lighter was ready, she fired it up. This time she pushed out a thin jet stream of blue smoke. "I *really* wanted to drive down to D.C. and shoot Nixon, Kissinger and McNamara in the head." A child wailed in the far back section of the wagon. "But, you know," she said nodding toward the rear, "Duty calls."

Dickie was thinking of something to say when Harlan Brinson opened the passenger side door.

"New Jersey," Brinson said. "Some island, I guess. Seven hours if we don't stop for anything but gas, food and coffee. Just stay on I-95 South. We'll grab an Esso road map when we get closer."

Dickie turned the key in the ignition. As he backed out he saw the woman changing a screaming infant's crap-filled diaper on the Belvedere's flip down tailgate.

Yeah, Dickie thought. Duty calls.

◆ ◆ ◆

Fort Benning, Georgia

Ronnie looked at the phone for several minutes. It was old, black and had a rotary dial. The phone jack was on an inside wall and a yellowing flat plastic cable connected the two, snaking across the polished floor and crawling up the table leg.

He checked his watch, a new one they'd given him at Intake. The ribbed olive green band was still stiff but the matching color plastic case already had a chip in it. The face was black with white numbers. Large ones for One through Twelve and smaller ones directly underneath for Thirteen through Twenty- Four, denoting military time. The small hand was not quite midway between thirteen hundred and fourteen hundred hours. Ronnie had been mulling the problem over since before lunch. He really wanted to make the call to Mickey. But Huilinga and Dugoni had now switched to the good cop/bad cop routine. It was an old and fairly reliable interrogation technique. Some of the Air Force and Navy guys he knew had been subjected to all manner of mental and physical abuses that they were told they could expect if they were captured by the VC or stranded in hostile territory. The school was called SERE – Survive, Evade, Resist, Escape. Those guys just called it Jungle School, even though the Army had similar jungle warfare training in Panama. Ronnie pondered the acronym. He couldn't easily escape nor did he need to, and short-term survival wasn't an issue. That left only evasion and resistance. But what exactly, he asked himself, was he evading or resisting? They had his statement and it was the stone truth. He could testify to hearing some drunken soldier sharing violent fantasies and him losing his temper over it. They'd already punished him for that. Then they un-punished him. Now they said they needed his help.

"And the Mission Photographer's pictures to prove it," Huilinga had said.

Ronnie put his hand on the receiver and then drew it back.

There was definitely something they weren't telling him.

Thirteen

Portland, Maine

Yvette Tran was as tight to the table as she could make herself. She stretched her neck until it felt like it would pop. The scarred one had placed the basin just beyond her parched lips. She could feel the coolness of the water in the already warming room. The trick was going to be, she realized, using either her teeth or her chin to slide the basin close enough to her at least lap up some of the water like a cat.

For a moment she thought of Bunny and wanted to cry but squeezed her eyes tightly to dam the flow. Tears were water she couldn't afford to waste.

Yvette settled on the bite strategy. She was afraid her chin might tip the basin and spill its contents if she didn't drag it exactly straight. She extended her lower jaw until she felt the incisors engage the underside of the rolled edge. Then she slowly closed her mouth, bringing her carious upper teeth down gently but firmly. Her neck ached and her head was pounding but slowly she inched the heavy vessel toward her. It was agonizing.

She released her jaw and measured the progress. A few millimeters at best. She wondered how many attempts she had left in her and whether her strength would give out before she could even taste the precious liquid right in front of her.

Yvette thought again of Bunny. Her little Good Night. She had chosen that name right after delivering the child. The black sky overhead had been filled with stars. After hours of pushing, they all seemed to glow with bright haloes, she remembered. They had seemed even brighter than the half-moon. Waves were crashing on the beach at *Bien Dong*, but softly somehow, as if they were singing to her. The newborn was on her chest.

"*Be' gai'! Be' gai'!*" the old midwife had said. "Baby girl!"

Baby girl, Yvette remembered thinking. Baby girl on a beautiful night.

Yvette's Papa had spoken French. Beautiful night. She had reached for the words and then found them.

Belle nuit. Belle nuit. No, she had thought, not *Belle.* That wasn't quite right. It was more than just a beautiful night. It was a *good* night. A good night for a baby girl. She reached for the word.

Bonne. Papa had said it often as he patted her on the head or stroked her hair. *Bonne.*

"*Ten? Ten?*" the midwife asked. *Name?* Her wide grin revealed red-stained, barren gums.

"Bonne Nuit," Yvette had replied. "Bonne Nuit."

The old woman clapped. "*Bonne! Bonne!*" Without teeth to help phonate it came out, "*Bun-nee! Bun-nee!*"

Bunny.

At the table, Yvette drew in a breath and then exhaled slowly, emptying her lungs. She leaned out again and clamped down on the rim. When it came to Bunny, her strength, she knew, her strength would never give out.

◆ ◆ ◆

Surf City

Bunny was bouncing around the station house like a *Wham-O* Super Ball.

"Seriously?" Ricky Rodriguez said, his feet up on his desk. "You fed this child two bowls of Cocoa Puffs *and* two bowls of Sugar Smacks? With *chocolate* milk no less?"

Mickey knew her deputy had three children of his own whom he referred to never by name and only as "the rug rats."

"She was starving," Mickey replied, plopping down in her wooden swivel chair. "Who knows how much she's had to eat in the last week?"

"Let me get this right, Chief," Rodriguez continued. "You

loaded her up with all this sugar *after* she pulled your piece on you?"

Bunny was swinging on the jail cell door. "Sugar smacks! Sugar smacks!" she bubbled with each squeaking metallic to and fro.

Rodriguez got up and walked over to where the shotguns were racked and theatrically checked the padlock. "You know. Just in case you decide to give her a Turkish Taffy or some Jujyfruits next," he said. "Oh, and Mayor Billy called. Said to drop by this morning if you can.

"OK," Mickey answered. "Anything criminal cooking so far in our fair borough?"

"Some early arrivers on the beach down by Fourteenth and Ocean. South Philly guys, I'm guessing. Pretty greasy. Looks like they got off the graveyard shift at the factory and barreled straight for us."

"You talk to them?" Mickey asked.

"I introduced myself is all," Rodriguez replied. "Told them they'd need beach badges."

"Beach badges," Mickey said with a sharp exhale. "When Mayor Billy first said that I thought he was crazy. Now he's a goddamn visionary, according to the papers. He's going to be Mayor for Life at this rate."

"Say what you will," Rodriguez replied. "We got a Chief and we got three deputies and we got money in our budget for pizza from Emil's."

"Pizza!" Bunny chirped from inside one of the cells. She was trying to bounce on the thin bunk mattress. "Pizza!"

The mention of pizza from Emil's Tavern, across the causeway bridge in Somers Point, took Mickey back to Ronnie and their night of soul-sharing in front of a beach fire during the Summer of Love. The pizza had gotten cold and the beer had gotten warm. It all seemed like a lifetime ago.

"What did they say about the badges? No, wait. Please say they didn't-"

"Yep," Rodriguez replied. "Although I'm sure it was intended as a respectful nod to my heritage." He struck a theatrical pose. "Badges? Badges? We don't need no *steeenking* badges!"

Mickey laughed out loud.

"Badges!" Bunny cried, flushing the cell's commode repeatedly.

"And you reacted how?" Mickey asked.

Rodriguez pulled on his gunbelt and holster. "Like the seasoned law enforcement officer you've taught me to be over the last twelve months, Chief Cleary." He reached for his hat. "I told them I would personally purchase badges for all of them if they could tell me what movie that line was originally from."

"'The Treasure of the Sierra Madre'," Mickey shot back.

"Well, yeah, you and I know that."

"And I take it they didn't," Mickey said.

"No they didn't. Close, though. They said it was Mickey Dolenz on 'The Monkees' TV show. Said they remembered because Dolenz was a Spic name like mine."

"It is?"

"No, Chief it isn't."

"They actually said Spic to you?"

Mickey looked at Rodriguez who stood six-foot-two and had been an All-State middle linebacker at Salesianum High School in Delaware.

"It's a term I'm familiar with so pretty sure I heard it correctly. But I retained my professional demeanor and said I'd return in an hour to make sure they were badged up." Rodriguez checked the oversized dive watch he favored on duty. "'Bout time to go," he said.

"Take Charlie with you. Sounds like they might benefit from a Civics Lesson. You know, expand their intellectual horizons a bit." She tapped her nightstick. "Then you go home and get some sleep. Thanks for covering for me."

"Pleasure, Chief."

"What do *your* kids have for breakfast?" Mickey asked as he moved for the door.

"Oatmeal with a dash of brown sugar," Rodriguez answered. "Maybe a banana or an orange to go with it." He paused. "Cocoa Puffs and Sugar Smacks – might as well have just given her heroin. I don't want to be here when she comes down."

"I'll take her with me to see His Honor," Mickey replied. "He loves kids. At least that what he says. Maybe he can watch her for a few hours. Do you want me to take your shift tonight?"

"No, you don't need to do that. I'll use the OT to take the rug rats over to the amusement park in Seaside Heights. They love that roller coaster that goes out over the ocean." Rodriguez tipped his hat and left.

Mickey noticed that Bunny was crashed out on the cell bunk. She looked around the station. After the bloody shootout they had razed the old one and it still remained an empty lot two years later. She thought about Kaylen and how quickly even a seemingly small and normally routine situation could spiral totally out of control. A traffic accident. And then - Dante Ragone, Artie Petroni, Shots Caputo, Kaylen Fairbrother, Steve Speziale, Charlie Sesso and the sub-human Billy Bowker – all dead within three days. And with the exception of the Ragone boy, Mickey knew she was the common denominator. She thought again about old Doc "Juice" Guidice. She didn't know if he was alive and in hiding, or rotting deep in the muck of one of old Danny Rags' landfills or perhaps lying entombed in the concrete that was still being poured for her beloved Philadelphia Phillies new stadium out by Broad and Pattison, where the gasoline storage tanks bloomed like mushrooms and the gas flares gave the night sky and an infernal glow.

She reached for the push-button phone and punched in the number for Mayor William P. Tunell.

Fourteen

Atlantic County Public Works Department
Hammonton, NJ

"Cowboy" Barstow was pulling the big ELGIN Pelican street-sweeper past the chain link fence when he spied BoDean Bowker's truck pulling in behind him. Barstow didn't much like BoDean – didn't really know anyone who did. BoDean had always ridden on the coattails of his twin brother Billy who, Cowboy thought, was just stone cold crazy. BoDean was sort of crazy-by-association and so feared almost as much. But with Billy reduced to nothing but ash and bone, or so the story went, BoDean's stature was now somewhat diminished in Cowboy's way of thinking.

BoDean's horn tooted. Cowboy stuck his arm out of the Pelican's high cab and waved in acknowledgement. Then a "follow me" gesture as he pulled around the back of the giant multi-bay garage that housed all the heavy equipment. Cowboy shut down the big John Deere engine, popped open the cab door and clambered down the ladder. BoDean met him at the bottom.

At only about five-foot-five in his hand-tooled boots, Cowboy was almost a full foot shorter than BoDean. He thrust out his arm to shake hands but BoDean ignored it. He had a slip of paper in his hand and was studying it intently.

"Need some s'plies," BoDean said.

"They count everything here these days," Cowboy replied. "Hope it ain't too much of any one thing."

"It ain't," BoDean answered. "You got jelly gas?"

"Jelly what?" Cowboy asked.

"Jelly gas. Loose Nuts said you'd have jelly gas. Need about a gallon."

"I don't know what you mean."

"Said it sticks to stuff and burns like blue blazes. Called it jelly gas."

"What 'm guessin' you're talkin' about don't come out of no Sunoco pump, ya dumbass. Jesus, BoDean, what you're wantin' is fuckin' Napalm. Like they use in Nam. That shit you got to make yourself 'less you got a friend at Dow Chemical."

"Can *you* make it?" BoDean asked.

Cowboy tipped back his oversized Stetson. He'd been born in Delaware, never roped a calf or ridden a horse, but had purchased the hat one humid night at the Cowtown Rodeo when he went to see Chief Halftown perform. Boots soon followed and then the moniker. Cowboy Barstow was obviously no cowboy, but the name had stuck tight to him anyway.

"No, I ain't gonna make it," Cowboy replied. "I can get you the ingredients but I ain't mixin' that shit myself. Too dangerous."

"What ingredients?"

"You need some palm oil and some naphthalene to thicken the diesel fuel. It's tricky stuff, though. What the hell did Loose Nuts tell you?"

"Foo Gas," BoDean said, growing impatient.

"*Fougasse*," Cowboy corrected. "That old alky is talkin' about a flame *fougasse*. Basically a gasoline bomb. Been around since the First World War." Cowboy was trying to remember in which of his library-worthy collection of books on war and armaments he had read about it. "What are you fixin' to use it for?"

"None a yor business," BoDean said.

"Got that right. And I don't want it to be none of my business. You get yourself a gallon of diesel somewhere else. I'll scrounge up the thickeners. Rest is up to you."

"How about the magnesium?" BoDean asked, looking at his paper.

"Oh for Christ's sake," Cowboy said. "You don't need no magnesium. Why the fuck would you listen to Loose Nuts anyway? He's half in the bag by sunup most days."

"How do I light it?"

"Like I said. Tricky shit. You got to find yourself somethin' that'll let you be far enough away. That ain't my department."

Cowboy watched BoDean step closer and wondered if he was about to get clocked.

"When can I pick it up?"

"Come back after six when the yard closes. I'll leave the stuff by the cyclone fence, southeast corner where the trees are. Get a gallon of diesel like I said. I'd give it to you but now I gotta punch in a code on the pump that 'dentifies me and they count every last drop. I'll measure out the other stuff. Mix it slow and not near anything that'll spark. You'll be a crispy critter otherwise. Mix it in a little bit at a time 'til it's like a thick pudding. You got something for the diesel?"

"I got somethin'," BoDean replied. He turned to walk away.

"A little thanks would be nice," Cowboy said.

"Maybe I won't use it on you," BoDean said. "Good enough?"

"You're welcome," Cowboy replied and tipped the Stetson's soiled brim down to shade his eyes. He watched BoDean climb into his truck and drive off. When you're short and skinny you need big friends, he told himself. He might need BoDean to do something for him someday. All he was providing were some common household chemicals. Cowboy kicked the dirt with his boot tip. He just wished BoDean hadn't said maybe.

♦ ♦ ♦

Surf City

On the checkered linoleum squares of the City Hall lobby Billy Tunell was dancing a jig in his Thom McAn penny-loafers.

"Did you read this?" he chirped, holding aloft the latest issue of *The SandPaper*, the free weekly newspaper based in Surf City that served all of Long Beach Island and several of the surrounding seashore communities. Mickey knew the rag was about ninety-percent ads and pictures and only ten-percent written news and that it was in no danger of ever winning a Pulitzer Prize, but she gave the mayor his moment. "Visionary! Visionary!" He smacked the thick, folded tabloid against his thigh.

"I did read that," Mickey said. She realized the mayor was not registering the sleeping child she was carrying like a sack of russet potatoes.

"Ship Bottom's next. Even that haughty haven of the high and mighty, Ocean City, has beach badges on their Council agenda next month. Except they want to call them 'beach tags' as if there were any living difference. Ha! Who needs blood in the water when you've got money in the air?" He smacked the paper against an open palm. "Visionary!"

Then Mickey saw his expression change.

"My dear Chief," Tunell said. "What do you-"

"It's a long story, Mayor Billy," Mickey replied, shifting the child's head to her other shoulder. "Meet Bunny. She's been separated from her family and sort of appeared in my cruiser out of nowhere yesterday."

Tunell let the paper hand by his side. "Not to fear," he said. "I know everybody at Child Welfare – they'll take her off your hands, literally, in two shakes of a lamb's tail, as my sainted mother used to say."

Mickey shook her head.

"It's a *really* long story and I don't have time to tell you right now. She showed up here all alone with a letter for Ronnie in her hand."

Tunell's gaze narrowed.

"I need to leave her with you for a little while, if that's alright," Mickey continued. "We've got a commotion on the beach at Fourteenth and Ocean I need to go see about. I was wondering if maybe Loretta-"

"Did I hear my old upstairs neighbor just call my name?" The voice came from Tunell's office and seconds later his door opened. Through it walked Loretta LaMarro.

"Well, I-" Mickey said.

Loretta was dressed in crisp white linen shorts and a print top which, Mickey noticed, she had on inside out. White espadrilles tapped the tiles as she walked with her arms outstretched.

"Give her here," Loretta said, wiggling her fingers. "You go see about your commotion."

♦ ♦ ♦

Interstate 95 South
Mile Marker 45.9
Peabody, Massachusetts

"Get off at the next exit," Harlan Brinson said. His hands were refolding a creased and stained page he'd torn from a Rand-McNally Road Atlas at the Service Plaza in Rhode Island.

"Why don't we just get south of Boston first and then stop?" Dickie Robichaux flicked his cigarette out the window. The orange and black '69 Plymouth Road Runner was doing a steady sixty-nine miles an hour, four above the posted limit.

"Heard a guy at the last rest stop saying the Red Sox had a double-header at Fenway today. Means we'll be snarled for a little while. Best get what we need now. I'm getting hungry anyway." Brinson tapped out a Camel and lit it.

"Peabody," Dickey laughed. "Pea-*body*. Like that cartoon, Sherman and Mister Peabody. I love that show. That and 'Underdog.'"

Brinson rolled down the window to let the smoke slipstream out on the Venturi Effect. "You are a connoisseur of the dramatic arts, Dickie. I'll give you that." Brinson reflected on the fact that the Army had offered him a free ride to college if he re-upped after two tours in the shit, based on his top-percentile scores on every aptitude test they gave him. But once he discovered "the trade," as he liked to call it, he realized he could make enough money in four years to buy himself a college, so he had declined the offer.

"Pea-*body*," Dickie said again for no reason as he slowed slightly for the upcoming exit for Massachusetts State Highway 128.

"That's not how they pronounce it," Brinson said between puffs. "They say it like 'PEEbuhdee', but all run together real quick." He put the emphasis on the first syllable.

"How do you know that? Ain't you from Buttfuck, Iowa?"

Brinson pushed his boots against the footwell to straighten his legs, forcing the back of his bucket seat to groan. "Dated a girl from Peabody for a little while. A Spec 4. Loved the way she talked, man. Called water coolers 'bubblah's' and milkshakes 'frappes.' And she was a looker. Dark hair, dark eyes. She was actually from Lynn, which is the town right next to Peabody. I remember because her name was Linda. I called her Lin from Lynn."

"You tap her?"

Brinson bent his knees. "No, Dickie, I didn't tap her. Her ETS arrived and she was gone. I heard she got married to a guy who was going to medical school New Jersey."

"Doctors are all rich pricks," Dickie replied. He tapped the turn signal.

"If you're rich, Dickie, then you get to *be* a prick. That's how it works. We do this right and we get to be pricks for the rest of our lives. Try and remember that." Brinson rolled up the window. "State Police car on the shoulder," he said. "Watch your speed and don't look over."

Dickie Robichaux tapped the brakes and eased into the exit lane. The 383 cubic inch V-8 engine throttled down as flow through the fiberglass Air Grabbers under the raised hood intake vents diminished. Brinson stared straight ahead.

Fifteen

Surf City
14th St. & Ocean Avenue

When Mickey pulled up in the Chevelle cruiser two of her deputies' cars were parked hard by the beach access that cut a sandy, shell-strewn path through the dunes. Both vehicles had their flashers and cherry-tops going. She could hear shouts and what surely sounded like threats wafting on the offshore breeze. She flipped on her own blue and red light-bar and whooped the siren several times to let the troops know she was there.

Mickey passed through the lane, lined with sections of fractured and faded wooden snow-fence, that opened out onto the expanse of brilliant white beach. A crowd had gathered about midway between the end of the dunes and the curling waves. Four husky men who appeared to be in their early twenties were standing almost shoulder to shoulder with their backs toward the mirror-like ocean.

They appeared to be, Mickey thought, something beyond intoxicated. "Hopped up," was the expression she'd learned when she walked a beat as one of Philadelphia's PD's first rookie policewoman. And hopped up, she knew, was for more dangerous than drunk and disorderly and far less predictable than bellicose and belligerent. And these guys were not small, she realized. She doubted any one of them went less than two-hundred. They all wore cut-off work pants and white, grease-stained U-shirts. They were muscled and dirty and Mickey figured either a South Philly tire plant or a foundry night shift had been their port of origin.

"Check it out," one of them yelled as Mickey approached. "An eggplant, a Spic and now a twat. Shit, what's next ya think – a Chink or a cripple?" They all laughed but there was a strange, almost cackling quality to it. They were starting to get a wild-eyed look as well. Whatever they'd ingested or shot up it was something new to the beach, she decided. But maybe not something new.

During the second half of the one year she'd spent "decompressing" as the commune's car mechanic on a marijuana farm in Northern California, a new drug had made its way up from the streets of San Francisco. It had several names but the one she remembered clearly was "Angel Dust." A few of the north-migrating Haight-Ashbury hippies had called it the "Peace Pill," but its effects were anything but peaceful in her experience. Anyone who used it seemed to become at first anxious followed by a fairly rapid progression to near-psychosis which usually manifested itself as aggression, paranoia and often unprovoked violence. And, she recalled, it seemed to temporarily imbue the user with near-superhuman strength. If this crew was on Angel Dust, as Mickey feared, she and her deputies were already overmatched.

"Think it's crystal meth, Chief?" Charlie Higgins asked.

"It ain't meth," Rodriguez said. "Definitely not meth. I think it's that really bad shit that was on the flyer we got last week. The one from the DEA."

"PCP?" Charlie asked.

"Yeah," Mickey said. "I think this could be Angel Dust. Probably sprinkled it on some weed. Where's Dip?"

Denny Dippolito was Mickey's rookie Deputy, into the job less than three months and the physically least-imposing of the trio.

"Runnin' some papers up to Toms River for the Mayor," Rodriguez answered. "Should'a been back by now."

The crowd of rubberneckers was growing, Mickey noticed. She had a sinking sense things were about to get out of hand.

"I say we pull on them and put them down like dogs right now," Rodriguez said out of the side of his mouth.

"We are not shooting four Southwark shitheads in front of a crowd of vacationers," Mickey replied. Onlookers had unwisely started to encircle the group. The beach was quiet for a moment as if everyone were waiting for something to happen. Then a voice yelled out.

"Death to Pigs!"

The squeaky shout seemed to take everyone, including the four miscreants, by surprise. In another situation it would have been funny, almost absurd, Mickey thought. It had come from a freckled girl of about fourteen in a frumpy two-piece bathing suit and a bucket hat standing in the second ring of the crowd. She had a pale, bony arm with a clenched fist raised defiantly above her head.

"Ah, shit," Mickey said. An adult hand clamped down over the girl's mouth with an audible smack but the damage had been done. The four men started swaying slightly. They were now covered in a drenching sweat and their eyes appeared menacing but unfocussed. They seemed to lick their lips obsessively.

"Death to fuckin' pigs," one repeated.

"Sticks," Mickey said. They all slipped heavy, illegally leaded nightsticks out of their belt rings.

"Death to fuckin' pigs," another one chimed in.

The girl who had shouted was now crying hysterically and the crowd began to inch back.

"Down on the sand, motherfuckers. *Now!*" Mickey commanded.

A siren wailed behind the dunes.

Dippolito, Mickey figured.

"I *said* - get down on the sand and I mean right–fucking-*now!*"

The four had malicious grins on their faces and had started to move rhythmically. They were making unintelligible sounds.

"Chief?" Rodriguez asked.

"Wait 'til they rush us," Mickey said. "They won't have any balance on the sand. "Sticks to the head first. Get them on the ground and then just start wailing 'til they stop moving."

"Oh, holy shit!"

A voice behind her.

Mickey turned her head to see Denny Dippolito emerging from the dunes with his 12-guage shotgun racked and pointed several degrees above the horizontal.

"Dip, no. Don't -" Mickey said.

A blast followed. The crowd, which had been transfixed by the unfolding drama, screamed and began running.

Mickey felt a few buckshot pellets tickle her neck like hot raindrops.

Then it all went straight to hell.

♦ ♦ ♦

Beach Haven, NJ

The schooner *Lucy Evelyn* had begun life in 1917 in the busy shipbuilding town of Harrington, Maine, not quite two hundred miles northeast of Portland where the Gulf of Maine mingled with the Bay of Fundy and Nova Scotia filled the horizon. A hundred and forty feet from spit to stern, with a thirty-two foot beam and a ten foot draft, she was a three-masted windjammer of elegant lines, plying mainly the Atlantic coastal waters from New England to South America, her holds loaded with timber, coal, gypsum, molasses and tobacco. She wasn't afraid to wander, though, and had ports of call from Liverpool all the way to the Cape Verde Islands and Barbados. She was even shelled by the German navy during World War II.

Loretta LaMarro knew ship's the history by heart.

Bunny was somewhat less interested.

"These bite you?" she asked, holding up a speckled and polished Cowrie shell the size of a small hen's egg. She was inspecting its serrated white aperture.

"No, honey," Loretta said. "They don't bite."

"Bunny." It was the fourth time the child had corrected her.

Loretta laughed. "OK. But from now on you are Honey Bunny. Is that better?"

Bunny smiled. "Better," she replied. "*Boo coo* better."

There was a freshening offshore breeze and brightly colored pennants snapped overhead in the ship's rigging. An American flag stood straight out from the stern rail. A few locals and day-trippers milled about the wooden deck, often stopping to look straight up the tall masts. Every few minutes one or two would enter or emerge from a companionway that led to the gift shop below decks.

Bunny rooted in the little bag of treasures Loretta had purchased for her.

"How they get boat in here?" she asked, pulling out a ship-in-a-bottle.

Loretta looked at the green-tinged glass and the seam running longitudinally from wax- sealed tip to bulbous bottom.

"Tiny little men climb in and build it," Loretta answered, doing her best not to laugh. "They raise the sails and then have to run very fast to get out of the bottle before the cork goes in. Sometimes one of them gets stuck and has to stay in the bottle forever." Loretta raised her eyebrows for emphasis.

Bunny held the bottle up to the mid-morning sun. The tiny replica schooner with its triple toothpick masts and paper sails was held fast to the inner glass by what looked like blue chewing gum that had been molded into a faintly wave-like shape.

"You lie," Bunny said pleasantly.

Loretta touched the top of Bunny's head which was covered by a stiff white sailor's cap. "Bunnee" was written in cursive silver glitter, some of which had drifted down and clung to the child's nose and cheekbones. "I do lie," said Loretta. "But just for fun. I have no idea how they get it in there."

"Why ship not sail?" Bunny asked, turning the bottle this way and that.

"Oh, it sailed a long time ago," Loretta replied. "All over the world. But when it got old, instead of wrecking it or sinking it they sailed it here. Then they put stones and big rocks all around it so it would be safe and so people could come visit it whenever they wanted."

Bunny leaned on the Port rail which faced Little Egg Harbor Bay.

"I go for ride on gunboat once," she said in what sounded to Loretta like a far away voice. "Coopral Winston take me. Let me fire machine gun. Fifty cal. Very loud but *boo coo* fun. *Boo coo* loud. Hurt my ears. Fifty cal."

Loretta pondered the situation. A pre-teen girl from Southeast Asia was reminiscing about firing a machine gun while standing on a cheesy New Jersey tourist trap. It made her think for a moment of when she had read sections of Lewis Carroll's *Alice in Wonderland* to her third-grade class at the little Catholic school in Riverside.

"OK," Loretta said with a clap. "As soon as Mayor Billy's back we'll –"

"Able-bodied seaman William Tunell, reporting," the mayor chirped. "There was a line for the bathroom. Just letting loose over the side would have been frowned upon by the good citizens of Beach Haven, I assumed." His mouth formed a twinkly grin.

Loretta rolled her eyes.

"You married?" Bunny asked. She wiggled a bony index figure back and forth at Loretta and the mayor.

"Well we were," Tunell replied. "But we were married to other people and for a long time. But they died. And so now Loretta and I are, well, we're very good friends."

Bunny cocked her head. "You old. You still do *nhuc duc?*" Even with the bag of trinkets and the bottle in her hands Bunny managed to make the finger-in-fist gesture again.

"Bunny!" Loretta cried.

An elderly shoobie couple looked over. Loretta put her hands over the girl's.

"Who taught you that?"

"Soldiers," Bunny said as if the answer were obvious. "Soldiers teach everything."

"I'm sure they did," Tunell interjected.

"Where your kids?" Bunny asked, looking at Loretta. "Why they not live here with you?"

"I don't have any children," Loretta answered. "But I was a schoolteacher for a long, long time. So it was like I had lots of kids."

Bunny seemed to consider the information.

"I think we need to burn off some energy," Loretta said. "*Lots* of energy". She looked at Tunell.

"Trampoline Park," they said almost in unison.

Loretta put a hand on Bunny's shoulder. They walked toward the companionway that would take them below deck and then out through the door that had been cut in the hull on the schooner's starboard side on the boardwalk level.

"Nuck duck?" Tunell mouthed the words at Loretta.

"After trampoline," Bunny said as they walked, the mangled word coming out like *cramporeen*, "then we go see Mickey-san and tell her we look for Dunn."

Tunell gave Loretta a quizzical look. For just a moment she saw the circle of small, upturned faces, the classroom's plaster walls and peeling paint, the dusty blackboard with the cursive alphabet letters above it. She saw the portrait of President Kennedy by the door and tasted the tears from the only time she had ever cried in front of her students. She felt the book in her hands, the smooth vellum pages and the hard cover with the bent corners.

"You know, Billy," she said, "This whole thing just keeps getting curiouser and curiouser."

Sixteen

Surf City

Mickey was the last one up the beach path.
She thought her teeth were all OK but she still had the hard metallic tang of blood in her mouth. Dippolito had gotten the worst of it, the shotgun being a poor defensive weapon once discharged.
The centralized dispatch system had worked beautifully. Arlene had called the Cavalry and then some. The only thing missing, Mickey thought, was air support.
The Ship Bottom officers had arrived first and just in time. The four dipshits each had the strength of Massa, the huge silverback gorilla at the Philadelphia Zoo. Charlie and Rodriguez had held their own but Dippolito was like a high-school kid at a heavyweight prizefight.
"Motherfuckers," Charlie said. He was using one hand to furiously rub sand out of his short-cropped Afro. It was the first time Mickey had heard him use such language.
Rodriguez still looked woozy. He'd taken the stock of Dip's shotgun to the back of his head in the melee. He was sitting on the trunk of his cruiser holding a bloody rag to what Mickey figured was a none-too-small and probably deep scalp laceration.
"Might need to get that stitched up," Mickey said as she came abreast of the deputy's car.
"I'm OK, Chief," he said. "It'll stop in a minute. Hey, where'd you learn that move?"
"Wrestling," Mickey replied. "Called sweeping the leg. They'd

never let me compete because I was a girl but I could still practice. I'm not sure it helped that much in the long run."

"So you weren't into the whole dolls and dresses thing growing up? That's all my rugrats care about most days."

Mickey laughed. "Rodriguez. Seriously. Do I look like a dolls and dresses kind of girl to you?"

"No, Chief, you do not," Rodriguez answered.

"We good here, Chief?" The question came from Lieutenant George Joo of the New Jersey State Police.

"I think so," Mickey said. "Thanks for bringing the extra muscle."

"Our pleasure, Chief Cleary," Joo replied. Mickey knew he pronounced his last name like "Joe" and made sure all the deputies knew it as well. "Most fun we've had all summer, to be honest." He smiled at Mickey. "Remember when we first-"

"Hard to forget," Mickey answered. "Weren't you holding me in my own station house on suspicion of murder?"

"Actually, that was Captain Hernandez. I believe *I* was keeping Mr. Dunn company in the back of a squad car." He squared his cap and straightened his Sam Brown leather belt. "You know we can never-"

"Yeah, I know," Mickey replied. 'Never, they said. And I do believe they mean it."

"They most *certainly* do, Chief," Joo said. "They most certainly do."

"Mantle retired, you know," Mickey said.

"Yes, too bad," Joo replied. "Guess I can get rid of his baseball cards now."

"Ah, maybe save one for old-times' sake," Mickey replied.

"OK, I'll hold on to his rookie card. Who'd want that, right?"

"I guess. So what are you going to do with the four assholes of the apocalypse," Mickey asked.

"They're on their way to our little Welcome Center in Hammonton," Joo replied. "They willfully assaulted several law-enforcement professionals today. That will turn out to be a very poor choice on their part. Let's just leave it at that."

"Where'd they get the Angel Dust, do you think?"

"Probably stopped by one of the biker's places in the Pines," Joo said. "Angel Dust is the old hippie name. Now it's Animal Trank, Trank or – and I just heard this one – Rocket Fuel. Scary shit. If it's one of them on it and just one of our guys on a lonely road some night, they get a bullet. No questions asked."

"Don't tell me Stellwag-"

Joo shook his head. "No, not the LT. Not yet, anyway. They've got their little criminal enterprises, for sure. But it's still mostly old school stuff. There's a newer, darker element moving in there now. Way deep in the Pines. It's not the vets looking for the comrades-in-arms days anymore. Now it's real career criminals - murderers, rapists. Graybar-to-Barrens is what they say. Even the Pineys are scared of them."

"No Sympathy for the Devil," Mickey said.

Joo laughed. "I'll have to remember that." He brushed sand off his tunic. "I'll need copies of your and your deputies' reports. And did someone really yell 'Death to Pigs?'"

Mickey shook her head. "Some young girl. Watched one too many episodes of *The Mod Squad* is my guess."

"Or maybe the Evening News," Joo replied.

"We'll mimeograph the reports as soon as they're typed up and have one of the guys run them up to you. Twenty four hours, OK?" Mickey spit a bloody wad onto the sand-covered asphalt.

"No rush," Joo said. "You really need to get a teletype machine. Save you a lot on time and gas." He looked over to a small convertible sedan parked just up the street from the beach access. A middle-aged man in a rumpled khaki suit stood by it holding a pen and what looked like a small notebook. "Huh. *The SandPaper* have a Crime reporter now?" Joo asked. Then he turned and left without waiting for an answer.

Mickey scraped dried blood from her chin. As Joo departed the man in the rumpled suit began walking toward her. She did not have a good feeling about why he was there.

◆ ◆ ◆

Interstate 95 Mile Marker 29.6
Coventry, Rhode Island

Harlan Brinson looked at his watch.

He assumed Corporal Declan Winston was starting to get a little bit parched right about now. The two shabby rooms they'd rented on India Street in the East Bayside neighborhood of Portland didn't have thermostats, just ancient radiators. He'd cranked the heat all the way up in Winston's room and sealed the windows with heavy tape. He'd wanted space heaters to hasten the dehydration process but the moron Dickie, who was now snoring loudly in the passenger seat, had bought kerosene ones. Even if they didn't catch fire, Brinson knew, they'd produce enough carbon monoxide to quickly kill at least Winston and maybe the woman, too. Brinson was figuring the child didn't have the key, but she was their one bargaining chip. Winston could croak for all he cared. He'd been through Jungle School just like the rest of them, plus he was a Marine. He wouldn't talk. If *she* knew they really had the kid, though, the woman would give up the information in a heartbeat. He was certain of that. He tried not to think of what would need to be done next. Harlan Brinson had never killed a child intentionally or accidentally. Not even in-country. He'd had a few double-veterans, but rape and collateral damage were a part of warfare since wars had begun. What the peaceniks he and Dickie had seen marching outside The Little Depot Diner in Peabody would never understand is that what the VC did was just so much worse.

Brinson was also not sure how he'd deal with Dickie once they recovered their property. He'd have to think on that a little longer

Dickie Robichaux began listing to port and Brinson shoved him back toward the car window where his head connected with a soft thud. Dickie continued to snore as if nothing had happened. No sense, no feeling, Brinson mused.

The Road Runner was cruising south at the same safe sixty-nine miles-an-hour they'd agreed on since crossing out of Maine. The long horizontal speedometer was bracketed by a few idiot gauges that bounced occasionally but otherwise remained boringly dead center in the normal range. He looked at the gas gauge. They'd filled up at a Sinclair station outside Lynn that was giving away plastic dinosaurs as promotional items. Dickie had taken two, one of which sat on top of the dashboard at the moment.

Brinson did the arithmetic in his head again. The four bricks were worth about six-hundred-thousand dollars on the street. His share was four hundred of that six hundred thousand. He looked over at Dickie. An empty passenger seat was therefore worth almost a quarter million, he realized. But Dickie had been a tunnel rat – killing VC with his bare hands, a knife or a sidearm in dark, confined spaces. The .38 Special he'd carried with him in-country was at present in the glove compartment. Dickie had survived not only enemy combatants but giant rats, venomous spiders, scorpions, *punji* sticks and poisonous snakes. If he wanted that two-hundred K, Brinson thought, he was going to have to earn it. Probably the hard way.

An old lady in a shit-brown Ford Futura drifted into Brinson's lane. He leaned hard on the horn and swerved onto the left shoulder to avoid her.

"S'goin on?" Dickie asked, awakening sluggishly. He'd ordered two full meals at The Little Depot and then topped them off with two pieces of pie and a strawberry frappe.

"Nothin'" replied Brinson. "I was just thinking about how rich we're both going to be." He reached forward to turn on the radio. Joe South came out of the small speakers embedded in the dash. "Games People Play." Brinson had read somewhere that the distinctive opening riff was actually played on electric sitar and not a guitar

"Turn it up," Dickie said.

Two hundred thousand, Brinson thought, and twisted the volume knob.

◆ ◆ ◆

Fort Benning, GA

Lucas Huilinga tapped his fingers on the table.

"I don't think he's going to call her," Dugoni said.

"Maybe that's because he doesn't trust us," Huilinga replied. The Comms Clerk was obviously trying to suppress a smile at the irony of the comment.

"Okay," Dugoni said. "It's fourteen-o-five. We'll see what he does tomorrow."

The Comms Clerk, a straw-thin kid from Dallas named Tuggle, took off his headset.

"That'll be all," Huilinga said. "One of us will be here at thirteen-hundred tomorrow."

The clerk rose, saluted the two Captains and left.

"We really don't need him for anything," Dugoni said wearily. "I say we send him home."

Huilinga rubbed at his shaven temples. "Not yet. He might

give us something useful yet."

"We're on thin ice here as it is, Luke," Dugoni replied. "His testimony won't help us at all. We need to bury it so deep in Discovery it never sees the light of day. It's not exculpatory and it's questionable whether it's even relevant at this point. Let's classify his information so he can't yak about it and cut him loose. Unless there's something you know that I don't."

Huilinga said nothing for a long minute. Then he reached for his briefcase.

"You know how sometimes if you try to pull on one loose thread the whole sweater starts to unravel?" He produced a thin folder with the JAG Corps seal on it and slid it toward Dugoni who flipped it open.

Dugoni looked puzzled.

"So what is Operation Hip Pocket?" he asked and peered at the folder again, adjusting his glasses. "And who the hell is Declan Winston?"

Seventeen

Surf City

Mickey thought the man in the khaki suit looked about forty. He wore a wide, Paisley print tie but it was loosened and his collar was unbuttoned. He walked with an easy but determined gait.

"Chief Cleary," he said when he was about ten yards away. "Do you have a minute?"

The door to Mickey's Chevelle cruiser was open. She had one foot on the running board and her arm on the roof. She could still taste blood in her mouth.

"Do I know you?" Mickey asked. He was clean-shaven and his reddish-brown hair was already thinning on top, creating what Rodriguez humorously referred to as "power alleys," marooning a lonesome thatch just above the middle of his forehead. It tousled slightly in the breeze.

"No, Chief, you do not," the man replied. "I'd like to reach into my jacket pocket for my card with my left hand now if that's alright." He held the pen and notebook with his right and with deliberate, almost exaggerated movements Mickey thought, slipped his fingers inside the khaki suit coat. She decided he'd spent considerable time around cops or other armed individuals.

He fumbled for a few seconds then withdrew a business card and held it toward her.

"Mike Gannon," he said. Mickey glanced at it and then at his car parked up the road. It had a dirty blue-on-yellow Pennsylvania front plate.

"I write a column for the *Philadelphia Inquirer* every now and then."

Mickey took the card. "No offense, but as they say, funny, you don't look Irish," she said, holding on to it while closing the cruiser's door.

"Indeed, not," Gannon replied. "Family name is actually Ganon." He pronounced it like Ga-NON. "Jewish right down to the matzos and brisket. North Jersey. But every editor, copywriter and linotype setter on earth thinks it's a misprint and makes it Gannon so I finally gave up and changed it myself. Has a better ring to it, I suppose. Like Mickey Spillane. Or Mickey Cleary. Now that would be a good name for a writer – or maybe even fictional character."

Mickey palmed the card. "Do you write fiction, Mr. Gannon?"

"No, Chief, I do not. I usually write about crime. And politics." He wiped a few beads of sweat from just above his eyebrows. "Not that there's much difference anymore."

Mickey nodded toward the beach. "Our little skirmish hardly qualifies as the kind of crime a reporter for a great metropolitan newspaper would find interesting."

"An interesting sidebar, perhaps," Gannon replied, "And I did get the Superman Daily Planet reference, by the way. But it's not why I'm here. Buy you a cup of coffee if you've got time."

"No doughnut?"

Gannon laughed. "No, no doughnut. I hate cliché's. And you, Chief Michaela Eileen Cleary, are anything but a cliché."

Mickey eyed him warily. "Done a little research already, I presume."

"A little," Gannon said. "You wouldn't think much of me if I hadn't, now would you."

"No, no I would not, Mr. Gannon," Mickey said, unconsciously miming his previous responses to her.

"I'm sure you've got a report to write and paperwork to file. Anytime the New Jersey State Police are involved that only multiplies the misery. Did I recognize Lieutenant Joo that you were speaking to a few moments ago?"

Mickey's mouth opened but nothing came out.

"I remember seeing his name on a report I was shown. Maybe a couple of summers ago? He was a Trooper back then, I believe. The report was heavily redacted, unfortunately. Not much help to an investigative reporter, really."

Mickey opened the Chevelle's door again. "Why don't you tell me what it is, exactly, you've come to investigate, Mr. Gannon, and I'll see if I have time for coffee."

Gannon took two steps forward and set his notebook down on the cruiser's hood. He clipped the pen in the breast pocket of his wrinkled white shirt.

"Like I said. Crime," he said. "It's my specialty. It's what intrigues me. The things people do and they reasons for which they do them. Crime is as old as Adam and Eve."

"I thought it started with Cain and Abel," Mickey replied.

"Touché. Adam and Eve's transgression was a mere major misdemeanor not a 187," he said using the California Penal Code's numeric designation for murder. "They got a hanging judge, unfortunately." He turned and rested against the Chevelle's front fender. "There's a story here, Chief Cleary. I know it the way a dog knows there's a bone. Now it's just about the digging."

Mickey crossed her arms in front of her. "Surf City is one square mile in total area. Long Beach Island is eighteen miles long and only a half-mile at its widest point. It's got a lighthouse at one end and a marina at the other. It's a ghost town after Labor Day until the next Memorial Day. There's no story here, Mr. Gannon."

Gannon smiled. "Your father's beat was only sixteen city blocks."

Mickey felt the surprise register on her face and knew Gannon saw it.

"I'm not here about your dad, so don't worry. But things are changing. In Philly, down here, all over. Casino gambling will be in Atlantic City much sooner than anyone thinks. Biker gangs are taking over the Pine Barrens. Young guys are challenging the old Mafia *dons* in public in the heart of the Italian Market. Drugs are everywhere. Somehow, whatever happened here in 1967 is at the heart of that story. And I believe you, Chief Cleary, are the key that unlocks it all."

Mickey forced a laugh. "Well, just make sure that when you write this highly fictional account, Mr. Gannon, that my character has blonde hair, big tits and dead aim."

Gannon grinned. "I've found that truth is always stranger than fiction," he said. "I'm checked in at The Ebb Tide Motel for the week. A working vacation, so to speak, as far as my editor is concerned. The desk clerk is a lovely woman named-"

"Doreen," Mickey interjected. "I know her very well."

"Yes, I'm sure you do," Gannon replied.

Mickey paused. "I'll make sure she keeps an eye on you," she said.

"Yes, I'm sure you will," Gannon replied. "Anyway, leave word with Doreen when you've got a few minutes to talk. Completely off the record, of course." He retrieved his notebook from the cruiser's hood and straightened his back. "Chief," he continued, "I also believe you are tough, honest and committed to protecting your one square mile from every and all manner of evil. But I also believe the kind of journalism I practice is like a fire you light in the deep woods – it burns to keep that evil at bay. I really do hope you'll call me."

Gannon nodded to her and began walking the sand-strewn asphalt back to his car. Mickey noticed it was a white Dodge Dart 440 convertible with a faded red interior. Probably a '62, she guessed, which would mean a 3-Speed Slant 6 engine. A honey when it was new but, like Gannon she assumed, it was starting to show some wear.

Mickey slid into the Chevelle's front bucket and brought the big engine to life. The high idle and the vibrating thrum of the chassis always seemed to put her at ease. She watched Gannon execute a quick K-turn and drive off toward Surf City's little downtown.

The letter for Ronnie was still in her pocket. She decided she'd check on Bunny first and then open it. An abandoned child, she thought, beachgoers high on animal tranquilizers and now a city paper reporter sniffing around a past she'd thought she'd buried. She put the cruiser in gear and peeled out, hoping things couldn't get any worse.

Eighteen

Fort Benning, GA

Huilinga chose a private booth at the Officer's Club that was out of, as far as he could tell, most sightlines. He tucked himself in behind the table and waited for Dugoni who arrived less than a minute later.

"All this cloak and dagger really necessary?" Dugoni asked as he settled in. "I mean, all that's missing is Maxwell Smart's Cone of Silence."

Two Scotches, neat, arrived on a tray carried by a pimply Corporal who set them on the table.

"Enjoy, Captains," he said before disappearing.

Dugoni rasied his glass. "To justice for the undeniably guilty," he said.

Huilinga picked up his own glass and drank.

"Given any more thought to kicking Dunn loose?" Dugoni asked.

"I have," Huilinga answered. "And you're right, we should." He took another sip of the Scotch. "But not for the reasons you think."

Dugoni drained his glass and dabbed his upper lip with a curled index finger. "What other reasons are there?" he said. "We're defending a hopeless case and his testimony is useless."

Huilinga checked his watch. "There may be one or two things I haven't been able to share with you," he said. "Things that are not, shall we say, exactly germane to our pending Court Martial proceeding, for instance."

"OK, Lucas," Dugoni said and brought the glass to his lips. "Exactly what the fuck is going one here and how much more Scotch am I going to need to process it?" He downed the smoky liquor in one swallow, grimaced and then leaned his head out of the booth looking for their NCO waiter.

"You're going to want to listen carefully," Huilinga replied. "And with a reasonably clear head to what our guest has to say. Then we'll order some more."

Dugoni appeared confused. "Guest, what guest?"

Huilinga looked down at his watch again. When he looked up a burly man with a buzz cut and wearing a crisply pressed Army Combat Uniform had appeared. Huilinga motioned for Dugoni to slide in.

"Meet Warrant Officer Cole Prejean, Criminal Investigative Division."

"CID?" Dugoni asked.

"Yes, sir," Prejean replied. "Although scuttlebutt has it DoD will soon be changing the name to Army Criminal Investigation Agency. Always wanted to say I worked for the CIA."

"Drink?" Huilinga asked.

"No, thank you, Captain," Prejean replied. "I do not imbibe. But don't let that stop you gentlemen from enjoying yourselves a little." He placed his two large hands on the table and interlaced his fingers.

"Maybe later," Huilinga said. "I'd like you to bring Captain Dugoni up to speed on your investigation and its relation to our witness."

Prejean looked around. "Here, sir?"

Huilinga nodded.

"I was assigned to the CID Far East Region," Prejean began. "Only been stateside about thirty days. Been tracking two dischargees whom we suspect are part of a ring smuggling contraband out of American installations in-country on Freedom Birds and using Vietnamese civilians either as cover or as part of the operation."

"And now you're going to tell me Ronnie Dunn is one of these dischargees?" Dugoni asked

"No sir," Prejean answered. "But he has a connection to a service member who was assisting us in our investigation, that is until that service member abruptly disappeared from our radar screen."

"Declan Winston," Dugoni said.

Prejean looked over at Huilinga.

"It's OK," Huilinga said. "He needs to know."

Their NCO waiter poked his head in. "Refills, sirs?"

Huilinga was about to decline when Dugoni interrupted.

"I'll take a double" he said. "Put it on Captain Huilinga's tab. The price for withholding evidence, counselor."

♦ ♦ ♦

The Ebb Tide Motel
Surf City, NJ

Mike Gannon stared at the blank page peeking up above the Royal portable's silver paper bail. It was an odd quirk, he knew, but he could never start a piece without a working title. Several had come to mind but he had quickly dismissed them as too cute or too reminiscent of the potboiler novels he'd devoured as a kid in Avenel.

"Blood and Sand: Murder at the Shore," was still in the running, as was "Crime Waves: Murder and the Mob on Long Beach Island." A half-empty bottle of Miller High Life sat next to the blue and cream colored plastic typewriter on the wobbly motel writing desk. A smoldering Chesterfield balanced precariously on a green glass ashtray. The room had a sliding glass door that faced East. A bent and holey screen stood guard with the door now open. Gannon could hear the sounds of the ocean and people on the beach. The tangy scent of the salt air was strong but not unpleasant. He rose from the thinly padded chair, grabbed the beer bottle and walked up to the screen. The Atlantic Ocean glowed in the fading rays of the late-day sun. The tide was going out, exposing long stretches of flat, wet sand that sloped gently toward the horizon. Blankets and umbrellas still dotted the beach but not at the wall-to-wall level he'd seen when he had checked in. A single engine plane towed a banner out past the far breakers.

"DUNES 'TIL DAWN," it read, fluttering in what he assumed must be a strong northeasterly headwind.

Gannon had always like alliteration and worked it into his

stories wherever he could.

"She sells sea shells by the sea shore," he said to the empty room. Then, a little louder, the second, lesser known-verse: "So she's sure every shell she sells is a sea shell."

But "S" was too soft, he thought. This was a hard story and it needed hard consonants. "Dunes 'til Dawn," kind of consonants. Gannon sat back down at the desk.

"Death on the Dunes." No, but close. He positioned his hands above the keys. "Crime and Coppertone." Almost. His fingers fluttered. Then it came to him and he began to type:

CRIME WAVES:
Death and Drama Down the Shore
Part One

The sight of the spider-leg typebars rising from the bowl and the familiar clack-clack of keys simultaneously striking inked ribbon and paper was like a jolt of adrenaline. He hit the Carriage Return lever on the platen, advanced the paper a few lines and looked at the words. He decided it was exactly what he wanted and went immediately back to work.

The beer would be warm before he took another sip.

♦ ♦ ♦

Mickey pulled into the vaguely oblong parking lot that served the little building she had called home. The asphalt, she noticed, had been replaced by crushed sea shells and pebbles. It crunched and popped beneath her tires, Loretta LaMarro's apartment was still on the first floor. For more than a year Mickey's had been right above it, graciously provided rent-free by Mayor Billy and the Borough when she'd first arrived to take the Chief job two summers earlier. Loretta had been her first real friend on the Island and remained a surrogate mother of sorts.

She looked at the two other cars parked side-by-side. Mayor Billy had traded in his Kelly Green Lincoln for a new Buick Riviera and then immediately procured an ill-advised $29.95 Earl Scheib paint job in Camden that matched perfectly, or at least he claimed it did, the Golden Dome at Notre Dame, his beloved alma mater. Having triumphed with beach badges, his next stated "vision" was the branding of Long Beach Island as "America's Riviera." His request to have the borough purchase the car as advertising had been quickly rebuffed.

Loretta's candy apple red Mustang convertible had been bought for a hundred dollars, a *quid pro quo* from Debra and Tony Iannuzzi for keeping their teenage son's name out of any official reports generated from the tangled events of 1967. A year later, the Iannuzzi's had sold their small beach house to Mickey and Ronnie, although Mickey had insisted on paying a fairer market price. Ronnie's dilapidated beach shack, a place with great sentimental value to both of them, had turned out to be worth a mere fraction of the beachfront real estate it occupied. They went to Ocean City the day the developer bulldozed it flat.

The radio was playing "Only the Strong Survive," and Mickey turned it up. Jerry Butler's soulful baritone reminded her that she'd survived without her mother and that perhaps Bunny might need to as well. She let the song finish, tuned off the ignition and pulled the letter from her pocket.

♦ ♦ ♦

<u>SURF CITY, NJ</u>: Make no mistake, Police Chief Michaela "Mickey" Cleary is tougher than she looks. And she looks pretty tough – even for a strikingly attractive young woman. Two years into the job, busting stereotypes along with occasional heads, this Chief is no shrinking violet when it comes to enforcing the law. Don't let the short-cropped reddish hair, the rash of freckles and facial features like a map of Ireland fool you – this babe is as hard as nails when she needs to be, transcending not just her gender but the idea that being a "beach cop" is somehow easier than being a beat cop. And here's a little secret: Mickey Cleary has been both.

The latest in a family of peace officers that stretches back three generations and across the Atlantic to County Kildare on the Emerald Isle, Chief Cleary was one of the first female Philadelphia Police Officers to ride more than a desk and take more than dictation. She's shown courage under fire, being wounded in the horrific shootout at a drug house down at K & A that's still talked about in every police precinct under Billy Penn's hat.

Surf City's mayor, the Hon. Bill Tunell, whom the local press hail as a visionary, made the bold move of hiring this lovely lass of The Law as his Chief in the Spring of 1967, replacing Pete Graham who departed silently under uncertain circumstances and rumors of irregularities that remain unsubstantiated.
But who is Mickey Cleary? That depends on who you ask.

Gannon paused. He hadn't asked anyone anything yet, but he had a whole week. He'd start with some platitudes from Hizzoner Tunell and then something from the deputies – the ones still among the living, anyway. Kaylen Fairbrother, who'd been Mickey's Deputy when she hired on, had died in one of the two adjoining rooms he'd rented down the long second-floor hallway from Gannon's current digs at The Ebb Tide. The case files were sealed tighter than a drum and he didn't qualify for the "Need to Know" restriction placed on them by the local and state agencies and even by the FBI. Doreen, the Ebb Tide's desk clerk, had gone pale when he mentioned the subject so Gannon figured he'd start to work on her in a day or two. The motel's owner, one Eddie Giacometti, would not return his calls and Doreen claimed he was out of town on business.

Gannon pondered the minor introductory falsehood he had related to Mickey Cleary about his press credentials. While it was true that he *had* written a couple of pieces for the stately *Philadelphia Inquirer* when he was fresh out of St. Joe's with a Bachelor's in English, they were puff pieces about a schoolboy catcher from the little town of Oley, Pennsylvania who some thought had Major League potential. The *Philadelphia Daily News*, his actual employer, was a newspaper much more suited to his style and demeanor. A detractor at the *Evening Bulletin*, Philly's other major daily, had once described Gannon as "a Jimmy Breslin wannabe – Yellow Journalism suffused with Purple Prose." Gannon had taken it as praise of the highest order, even though the wag had gone on to point out that "yellow and purple combine to make brown – certainly the appropriate color for such literary Shinola."

The *Daily News* had never won a Pulitzer Prize and had no real ambitions in that direction as far as Gannon knew. It was being called a tabloid, printed in a squarer and shorter format that could be easily read by subway and bus riders, even while standing. The

Inquirer began publishing in all the way back 1845 but the *Daily News* had come along in 1925 so it had some palpable history of its own. Gannon's editor had once described the *Inquirer* as "the girl you take to the Prom" and the *Daily News* as "the girl you take to the back seat." But sometimes, Gannon knew, the leeway he had in writing for a less prestigious rag gave him an edge when it came to digging up dirt. Whatever had happened in 1967 was worth looking into, he figured, if only because so many people were trying hard to make it look like nothing ever happened in 1967.

The Chesterfield was now more ash than butt so Gannon took a quick drag and stubbed it out. He hit the Paper Release tab and pulled out the sheet, leaving the blank space for as yet unprocured and possibly fabricated quotes and backstory. He slipped in a fresh sheet of Eaton Corrasable Bond, twisted the ratchet on the platen until the lip of the paper appeared under the bail and then went back to work.

Nineteen

Fort Benning, GA

Dugoni's double Scotch remained untouched.
Prejean looked at both Captains. "So as you can see," he said, "our window of opportunity is closing rapidly."

"How much did you say the heroin was worth?" Dugoni asked.

"Depends on where it lands, who cuts it and how," Prejean answered. "On the street, half a million would be a conservative estimate. Cut it light and it could be as much as three-quarters."

"Seven hundred and fifty thousand dollars," Dugoni said. He picked up his glass and downed half the contents. "Split how many ways?"

"Just Brinson and Robichaux once it gets stateside, as far as we know," Prejean replied.

"Until one of them eventually does the math," Huilinga interjected.

"Yes, sir," Prejean said. "And they're certainly much easier to track as a pair. One guy with that much money? We'll never find him."

"Tell me again how Dunn got involved?" Dugoni asked.

"He never really got involved, Captain," Prejean answered. "He and Winston were buddies – same boat crew. Winston was the deck gunner. Fifty caliber machine gun. You can kill a lot of cocoanuts with that. Dunn was a sniper – apparently one hell of a shot. Took out a VC hiding in a palm tree on the banks of the

Mekong RIver who had a bead on Winston's Six."

"If Winston needed help stateside," Huilinga said, "he'd go looking for Ronnie Dunn. They were that tight."

"Did – or maybe I should say *does* Winston know where Dunn is?" Dugoni asked.

Prejean rubbed at his chin stubble. "They had some correspondence after Dunn's double D, so the only LZ Winston would have for Dunn is this little beach town in New Jersey. So either Winston's headed there or, more likely, Brinson and Robichaux are."

"What about the civilians?" Dugoni asked.

"Mother and daughter," Prejean said. "Winston planned to marry the mom stateside so she'd get automatic citizenship and then adopt the little girl. Hope you like irony – they're survivors of your client's little party. They were out gathering wood when it went down."

Dugoni drank the rest of the Scotch.

"Our boy killed the husband then, I take it?"

"No, sir. About six months before that action the VC swept the village. They said the father was helping the Americans which, as far as anyone can tell, was not true. They lined up the locals and bayoneted him in front of them as a warning. Our guys get a bad rap and sometimes they deserve it. But if you saw what Charlie does to his own people, you'd look at things a bit different. The locals are the true victims. There aren't any heroes in this one, unfortunately. Except maybe that helicopter gunship pilot. That took guts and he's paying the price for it right now from what I hear. I don't envy you your assignment, sirs. Dunn does understand you're *defending* the accused, right?"

The officers looked at each other.

"He may have made an incorrect assumption which we've decided not to clarify at this time," Huilinga said.

Prejean considered the statement. "Understood, Captains," he said.

"So how did Winston connect with these two drug runners?" Dugoni asked.

"Winston's deal was he'd carry the bricks in his duffel. Nobody checks them on the Freedom Birds. Then he'd stash them in a locker at a bus or a train station. In return Brinson greased the wheels to get the woman and the kid out with him *didi mau*.

Through channels it would have taken months and the situation in-country is deteriorating no matter what Westmoreland or Kissinger say."

"And Winston had second thoughts?"

Prejean nodded. "Guess he got some better intel on the guys he was dealing with and decided he and his new family were safer with CID."

Dugoni ran his finger inside his glass and touched it to his tongue. "What kind of intel?"

Prejean sat back in the booth. "That none of Brinson's previous clients were ever heard from again."

♦ ♦ ♦

The Pine Barrens

BoDean was not accustomed to regular bathing and so his supply of soap was running low to begin with. Even though he'd done all his mixing and measuring fifty yards from his shack he couldn't seem to escape the smell of aromatic hydrocarbons. The jelly gas had been harder to work with than he anticipated but he'd managed. The nail keg would do fine for his primary job, he'd decided. But he wanted a little test run first, so he'd mixed a much smaller batch in a coffee can Kurt the bartender had picked up for him at the Acme in Beach Haven. BoDean had left a portion of the lid attached so he could cold-solder it shut when it was full. He drilled a small hole in the side for the fuse and sealed it with paraffin inside and out.

He'd tracked down Cowboy Barstow a second time to get advice on the fuse, the part BoDean was most worried about. He was also worried about Cowboy but it was more of a long-term concern at this point, BoDean figured, one that could be handled later.

For someone who bought his clothes in the Boys Department at Sears, Bo Dean was impressed at Cowboy's knowledge of weapons of all sorts, especially those that exploded or burned. He knew Cowboy had no wife or children and few close friends, so it was unlikely he'd be disposed to blabbing.

BoDean wanted to see how the test run turned out before asking Cowboy any more questions. He had begun lining and caulking the nail keg, but he'd need a different way to set it off than the one he was using at present. Proximity, Cowboy had told him, was the thing he needed to worry about most. "Fu'ther the better," was his advice. BoDean knew the State was doing some demolition work out by the Parkway near Waretown. The boys at the Pic-a-Lilli were getting some steady day labor and even some overtime. There was talk of a new Toll Plaza and maybe even a new Parkway Exit in the distant future. BoDean figured there might be blasting caps and maybe fuse-wire to be had. He didn't know much more about demolition but figured all he needed was some way to get a spark from one place to another.

He plopped down bare-ass on the old rocker that which sat on the splay of undulating boards that constituted his front porch. The breeze was up and the scent of the pines was strong. In the distance he could hear the sound of motorcycle engines revving and then trailing off. His newest neighbors were a little over a mile away but sound carried in the Barrens. He always knew when they were coming or going.

Billy had once hiked out to their shack – they insisted on calling it a clubhouse – to give friendly notice about where the Bowker clan property began and ended. He'd brought two jars of Leusner's high-test shine as a goodwill gesture. A kid with a scarred face, a tattooed neck and what BoDean recognized as an automatic rifle had met him five hundred yards out. The kid wore a leather jacket that had a tag that read "Prospect" crudely stitched to it.

"What do you fellas call yor-selves again?" BoDean had asked in all sincerity.

"They're the fuckin' Druids, there, Jethro," the kid with the facial scars had answered. "Don't even think about fucking with them. Put the jars on the ground, turn around and go back home. They want something from you, you'll know it soon enough."

BoDean remembered setting the jars down but little else. Ever since *The Beverly Hilbillies* had showed up on the TV in 1962 BoDean had been infuriated when anyone called him Jethro, his first name a homonym to the dumb-ass cracker character's last name. The only time he ever hit Billy had been occasioned by use of the name. On his walk home he imagined the clubhouse in flames, it's doors blocked shut and an unholy chorus of howls swelling from within. BoDean knew how to eliminate threats.

He leaned back in the rocker. It was all so much harder now without his brother. He fingered the necklace of bones and decided that if there was work to do then he'd best be getting to it.

♦ ♦ ♦

Loretta's apartment was deliciously cool and Mickey felt instantly at home.

"Asleep?" she asked.

"Unconscious is more like it," Loretta replied. "How about a beer for old times' sake?"

Mickey shook her head. "On the clock at the moment. Where did you take her?"

"A better question is where *didn't* we take her?" Loretta opened the door of the Frigidaire and pulled out two brown bottles. "Don't worry," she said, "They're both for me. Mayor Billy is snoring in the spare bedroom. Your prodigal child is sprawled out on my bed." She crossed the room and sat down. Mickey noticed that the clear vinyl slipcovers which had been present when she first met Loretta were now gone. "Sit for a minute."

It had been more than two years since Mickey had first set foot in the cozy apartment. She recalled that she had been sweaty and dirty from working underneath the Chevelle and that she and Loretta had drunk Ballantine's from glass bottles. She and the mayor had been a quiet item back then – "keeping company," as they each put it. Although both widowed, they now seemed the picture of an old married couple in every way but their living arrangements.

Mickey sat down. "Why don't you two lovebirds just get your own place?" she asked.

Loretta poured her beer – a Ballantine Mickey noticed – in a glass and took a long sip. "We're too old and much too Catholic to live in sin," she replied. "And Billy's mother is still alive and kicking at ninety-one, you know. Loretta laughed and took another swallow. "I refuse to be the death of her."

"You're too old *not* to live in sin," Mickey said. She knew that Loretta was sixty-three and Mayor Billy was sixty-five, although Loretta dyed her hair a shimmering shade of Clairol blonde while Billy had let what remained on his head go grey. "Really, who cares what anyone thinks?"

Loretta emptied her glass and poured the second bottle in immediately.

"We're a different generation," she said. "Free love and cohabitation is for you young people, dear. Plus we're both sure that our respective spouses, departed as they may be, are indeed keeping watch over us from above. Oh, and I've been meaning to tell you I love your new hairdo."

Mickey reflexively touched her head. "Hides my war wound pretty effectively, doesn't it?" With her right hand she pushed back the hair to reveal where a bullet had taken part of the outer ear with it.

"I tell everyone a dog bit you when you were a child," Loretta said.

"People *ask* you?" Mickey replied.

"Oh, my, yes. This is a very, very small town. People ask a lot of things."

"Like what else?" Mickey leaned forward.

Loretta smiled. "Things that are none of their business," she said. "And certainly none of mine. Did your Sisters enjoy their day at the beach," Loretta said, deftly changing the subject.

"I'm sure Innocentia had a major league hangover but other than that they had fun."

"What are you going to do with Bunny? We distracted and exhausted her today but I think that's only going to work once."

Mickey paused in thought. "The Mayor says he knows some people in Child Services just in-"

"Don't you dare even *think* about it," Loretta said, reaching for a pack of Winston's. "I'll kidnap her and hide her myself before I'll let you do that." She tapped out a cigarette and took a tarnished silver pedestal lighter from the coffee table. Mickey noticed Loretta's hands were trembling slightly as she struggled to light it. Once she did, she took a long draw and slowly exhaled blue smoke.

"It's not really my plan," Mickey said. "But it's not like I can watch her all the time. And I can't keep asking you and-"

"Yes you can and yes you will keep asking. Us and anyone else you need to ask. This child's been exposed to things I don't think either of us can quite imagine. Did you know she once fired a machine gun? A machine gun, for God's sake. We all must do whatever it takes to keep her safe. She's not some Pagan Baby you shill out five bucks for and then forget about." Loretta took two quick puffs and stubbed out the cigarette in a tiny glass ashtray.

Both women were silent for several minutes. Loretta spoke first.

"I'm sorry dear. But I spent most of life around children and I guess I'm just protective. Is she in any real danger?"

"I don't know," Mickey answered. "I think she could be. But I'm not sure. I think her parents – or at least her mother and her mother's boyfriend or maybe he's her husband – I think they're in trouble. How she managed to get herself here on her own I don't know, but she did, and with a note to give to Ronnie. Only the Army has him tucked away tighter than a Mob witness before a big trial. She says he'll know what to do."

"Isn't there anyone you can ask or petition or whatever? Tell them a child's life may be at stake."

Mickey rocked in her chair. "Kaylen's sister JoLynne worked for a State Senator from Atco – I think he might be in Congress now. Maybe I could-"

Loretta stood up. "Get me his name. I'll have Billy call his office first thing in the morning. If he was a State Senator for any length of time Billy will have something embarassing on him, you can bet your boots on that."

Mickey rose from her chair. Loretta handed her a ragged book of S & H Green Stamps. "Write it down on the back," she said.

"You really think he can-"

Loretta's face broke into a big smile. "I know he can. And I know he will. Or no more nuck-duck."

Twenty

Mile Marker 53 I-95 Southbound
Branford, Connecticut

  Kenneth Pham had not thought much about his travel attire when he'd gotten dressed. His housing complex in Old Lyme was having problems with its air-conditioning system and his studio apartment had been sweltering. A high-pressure system had parked itself over Long Island Sound and the sea breeze was nonexistent. He had chosen the black tunic-style shirt at the last minute, concerned about sweat stains being visible on anything lighter. The interview at Yale was an informal one – he'd already been promised the Graduate Assistant spot in Biochemistry – and he expected the drive to take no more than forty-five minutes even with summertime Interstate traffic.
 Pham decided the pressed shorts and thong sandals bespoke a confident yet relaxed demeanor appropriate for an August day. He wasn't interviewing for a professorship, after all. He wished he hadn't agreed to meeting so late in the day but decided he'd grab dinner in New Haven after the meeting. He hoped to get at least another year out of the '66 Volkswagen Beetle he'd purchased from a doctor in upstate New York two years ago. It was a nondescript light blue and the door handle on the passenger side was finicky but that was only a problem on dates. He liked the sound of the small, rear-mounted engine. The "Teutonic clatter" he called it, thinking himself quite clever. It was a discernible change in that same clatter which caused him to pull off I-95 and into the

Rest Area in Branford. He saw only one other car parked outside the little building which housed the restrooms. The VW engine was air-cooled and Pham thought he'd let it sit for a few minutes and see if that helped. The sparse array of dashboard gauges all read normal but he had never trusted them, relying on his ear to troubleshoot instead. Having brought along nothing valuable that wasn't in his pockets, he rolled down both windows, turned off the engine, jammed the stick into the second gear position and pulled on the parking brake. He hadn't really needed to pee until he started thinking about it. The Rest Area buildings were usually air-conditioned, he knew, and he was already moist. It would be a worthwhile stop.

The door to the Men's Room squeaked when he pushed on it. He didn't see anyone else at the urinals and a quick sweeping glance at the stalls revealed no shoes or sneakers. The air smelled like Lysol.

When Kenneth Pham swung open the stall furthest from the door he was more than startled. He was shocked. A shirtless man was perched on the toilet seat staring intently at him. It took Pham a second or so to realize just exactly what he was holding in his hand.

♦ ♦ ♦

Ft. Benning, GA

The evening air was still and the humidity was stifling. Ronnie passed under one of the base streetlights and listened to the noise from the new recruits' barracks. He was about to turn back for his own billet when a voice called to him from behind a stack of gasoline drums.

"Dunn," it whispered. "Dunn. Hey, over here."

Ronnie tensed. He hadn't made any enemies that he knew of, but his status as a witness to a possible war crime was probably not a well-kept secret. He'd knew of soldiers who'd been fragged for less.

"Step out," Ronnie said.

A thin soldier with light colored hair came into view.

"It's just me," the soldier said. "Nothing funny. I promise."

"What do you want?" Ronnie asked, "And how do you know me?"

The soldier put his hands out in front of him. "I come in peace, man. I can do you a favor if you want."

"What kind of favor?"

"I'm the 3C, Communications Clearance Clerk. Name's Clay Tuggle. I'm from Texas. Denton, Texas. I know you want to call your girl. And I know you know they're listening in, no matter what they told you."

"That's what I figured," Ronnie said. He took a stride toward Tuggle and could now see he was indeed alone.

"So why do you want to help me, Corporal Tuggle?"

"Cause I hate lawyers and I hate officers and I hate the fuckin' Army. Those two dickweeds especially. They're not your friends and they're not here to help you."

"I figured out that much on my own. I'm not an FNG, you know. I've been in the shit."

"I'd rather be in the shit for a year than here for one more fuckin' day," Tuggle replied. "This ain't why I joined up. To be a fuckin' telephone operator. Or a snitch."

"You smoke?" Ronnie asked.

"Nah," Tuggle answered. "I got the asthma."

"Me neither," Ronnie said. "I got a carton of Lucky's they gave me but that's all. Sorry."

"I'll take 'em," Tuggle said. "Always negotiable, smokes are."

"I'll leave them behind the door. What are you offering?"

"I take a supper and shitter break at 1800 hours. There's no relief and the night clerk doesn't report until 1900. I'd say that might provide a window of opportunity for someone that might want some conversational privacy."

"A very open window," Ronnie replied. "Aren't you taking a big risk?"

"Shit, no," Tuggle said. "Who you think it is types up the fuckin' call logs in the morning? If I don't type there was a call then there wadn't no call, now was there?"

"Guess not," Ronnie replied. "But how do I know-"

"Gotta trust somebody, Dunn," Tuggle answered. "I got no reason to screw you over. I heard 'em say you were a sniper. You was, wadn't you?"

"I *was*," Ronnie said.

"How smart you think it'd be to fuck over a guy who can blow your fuckin' head off from a thousand fuckin' yards."

"Not very smart," Ronnie conceded.

"One other piece of advice," Tuggle said as he receded a bit into the shadow of the stacked drums. "Make a bullshit call at thirteen hundred hours tomorrow. Just don't say nothin' you don't want Abbott and Costello to hear."

"Got it. Listen, Clay - it'll sound like bullshit but if you ever get north we've got a hell of a beach back home. You'd be welcome to-"

"I got your name, Dunn," Tuggle replied, smiling. "And pretty soon I'll have your girlfriend's phone number, so you best be careful, pard."

Ronnie gave the boy a quick salute.

"Yeah. Fuck that shit," Clay Tuggle replied. Then he returned the salute.

♦ ♦ ♦

I-95 Rest Area
Branford, CT

"Drive," Dickie said, pulling the car door shut with a bang. He was sweating profusely, Brinson noticed.

"Dickie, what the fuck happ-"

"Just fucking drive, Harlan," Dickie said through gritted teeth. "We need to get back on the fucking road right fucking now."

Brinson shifted the Dodge into Reverse, backed up a few feet, put it in Drive and then pulled slowly toward the rest area's long exit road.

"Hurry up, Harlan. We got to get out of here."

Brinson saw the blood on Dickie's arms. There was more on his chest.

"Where's the knife?" Brinson asked.

"In a toilet tank. In the Ladies Room."

"Where's the body?"

"Just fucking drive, will you?"

"Dickie, we have to think this through right now. We aren't in the jungle anymore. We're on a goddamn U.S. Interstate Highway with Hot and Cold running cops. We have to deal with whatever happened back there or we're fucked."

"No witnesses. Nobody else in the building or that VW so he

was traveling alone. We're good. Trust me, Harlan. We're good here."

Brinson remained quiet. This had happened before. Twice. Dickie would, for no reason Brinson could figure out, suddenly find himself back in a jungle tunnel. He'd received commendations for what he'd done in those tunnels in-country. Nobody ever asked what the tunnels had done to him. Each of the previous times Harlan had been close enough to prevent mayhem from transpiring. Apologies and wads of cash had taken care of the near misses.

"Was he-"

"Yes," Dickie replied. "First I heard the thongs. Then I saw a black shirt and then the face. Next thing I know it was all over. I cleaned it up real good, though. Sat him on the head with his feet on the floor. Who's to know? At least not for a while."

"Did he shit himself?"

Dickie looked at Brinson. "Of course he shit himself. They always do. It's a fucking highway restroom, Harlan. They're supposed to smell bad."

"We have to get you cleaned up," Brinson said. "You going to be OK 'til we get past New York?"

"I'll be fine," Dickie Robichaux answered. "We don't have to drive through any tunnels, do we?"

"No," Brinson replied. "There's one in Baltimore but we aren't going that far."

"Then I'll be fine," Dickie said. He rolled down his window and put his hands out to dry the blood on them. Then he rubbed them until the congealed flakes started to peel off and blow away.

Brinson knew any further conversation was a waste of time. He needed Dickie functioning until they had the bricks in hand. Until Winston, the woman and the girl were all dealt with. After that, Brinson now figured, Dickie would be nothing but a liability. And a highly dangerous and unpredictable one at that.

Twenty-One

Ship Bottom, NJ

    Patsy Cleary was snoring on the sofa. Mickey could hear him through the screen door, Patsy having left the inner wooden door wide open. The new GE air conditioner she'd bought him rattled ineffectively in a side window, trying in vain to counteract the warm air rushing in. She opened the cheap aluminum outer door and stepped inside. The snoring stopped.
    "Dad, wake up," Mickey said gently. She moved toward the sofa, a relic from her childhood home and, more recently, Patsy's tiny apartment on Cottman Avenue in Philadelphia's Great Northeast.
    "Wake up, dad," she said again and glided past him on her way to the tiny kitchen and the cold beer in the fridge she knew he'd want.
    The kitchen was separated from the larger front room by a plaster wall with a curving arch and the refrigerator sat behind it. Mickey opened it and pulled out a Miller High-Life, one of a six-pack of bottles she'd gotten a week ago at Little Willie's in an attempt to broaden her father's brewed hops horizons. All six, she noticed, were still there. She opened what Patsy called his "junk drawer" and rifled through it until she found an opener, then popped the cap and headed back through the arch.
    "Here, Dad," she said, "Time to try the Champagne of Bottled Be-"
    "Don't move a muscle, punk."

Mickey saw that Patsy was sitting up but yet somehow she didn't think he was actually awake. This wouldn't have worried her were it not for the service revolver in his right hand.

"Dad, it's me. Michaela. Dad, wake up. It's me."

Patsy blinked several times. "I seen you watching me. I was a on the job for sixteen years. You think I didn't see you?"

"*Dad*," Mickey said in a louder but what she hoped was a non-threatening tone.

Patsy's right hand was trembling. It looked like his finger was on the trigger but Mickey couldn't be sure. The refrigerator kicked on and it seemed to bring Patsy back into the moment. He looked at Mickey and leaned forward.

"Eileen? What are you doing here?"

The mention of her mother's name startled her. She wondered if Patsy was in the throes of a stroke.

"Dad, it's me, Michaela. Mickey. We're in Ship Bottom, New Jersey now, remember, Dad? Everything's OK. You maybe want to give me the gun?"

Patsy looked down at his right hand as if it belonged to someone else. Tears welled up and Mickey stepped forward to place her hand over his.

"Jesus, Michaela," he said. "What just happened to me?"

"Nothing, Dad. You weren't just quite awake." She eased the .38 Police Special out of his hand and snapped on the safety. "Not sure napping with a loaded piece is such a great idea, though."

"I know that guy was watchin' me yesterday. I ain't never gonna be taken by surprise again. Not after Shots Caputo and then that dirtbag Sesso tried to take me out. Never again, I promise you that."

"Yeah," Mickey said, placing the gun on the small coffee table, "Well, you're still breathing and neither of them are, so you win. How about instead of sleeping with a gun in your hand you let me have the Ship Bottom boys run some drive-by surveillance on this place for a week or so. I'll have Davy Johnson stop by – you give him the lowdown on the truck and this guy you saw and they'll be on the lookout. Anyone driving on or off Long Beach Island has to come over the causeway bridge and through Ship Bottom."

"You met their new Chief?" Patsy asked. He rubbed at his eyes.

"Interesting fellow," Mickey said.

"He's a pipsqueak," Patsy declared. "Don't look like no

California motorcycle cop to me. What do his deputies tell you about him?"

"They like their jobs, so, not much. You know how it is."

"Johnson. He the one with the blond hair looks like the Dutch-Boy Paint kid?"

Mickey laughed. "Yeah, that's Davey. He's a good guy. He won't mind."

"You know how he looks at you right? He'd never make it undercover. But I'd sure like to play poker with him."

Mickey sat down next to Patsy and handed him the beer. "How would you feel about me hanging on to your gun?"

"How about I promise to keep it between the mattresses?"

Mickey pondered the offer.

"How about the drawer in the nightstand? Seem like a fair compromise?"

"Yeah, OK, kid." Patsy sipped the beer. "Champagne beer, huh?"

"I didn't say it, they did," Mickey replied.

Patsy drank again. "Not bad. I'll give it a fair shake."

Mickey got up. "I'll be back later. I'm kind of looking after a little girl who's gotten separated from her parents. I'll bring her by so you can meet her. Her name is Bunny." She took the gun. "Nightstand drawer. That's where I'm putting it. And that's where it stays. Promise?"

"Promise," Patsy answered.

"You, OK?"

Tears came again and Patsy wiped them away. "You look just like your mother, God rest her soul. I should'a been a better husband to her and father to you. I should'a been-"

Mickey put a hand on his shoulder.

"You did great job, Dad," she said. "Mom loved you. She loved us."

Patsy stared at the floor. "It wasn't no suicide, Michaela. It was a pint of Four Roses and a bottle of sleeping pills."

"I know, Dad. I've known it for a long time. It wasn't your fault. She had a disease – they have medicine for it now. She had a disease and it killed her. Mikey had a disease and it killed him. Neither one was your fault."

Inside, Mickey felt the nuclear reactor of emotions she usually so successfully managed threatening to melt down. The older brother she never knew, dead from lymphoma at seven, a year before Mickey was born. The mother she adored, gone when Mickey was only a teenager. She leaned her lips close to Patsy's ear.

"They would want us to live our lives and be happy, Dad. Let's do that, OK?"

Her father had never been particularly demonstrative or affectionate and so she was surprised when she felt his still muscular arms encircle her. She stroked the gray buzz cut on the top of his head.

"Ain't you gonna say it?" Patsy asked.

Mickey leaned back.

"Cleary's don't quit and Cleary's don't cry," she whispered, struggling herself for control.

"Eileen came up with that," Patsy said and released his hold. "Just so you know."

Mickey stepped back. She took the gun into the little bedroom and tucked it in the hand-carved nightstand that had come from her grandmother's home in County Kildare. On top of it, in a tarnished silver frame, was a picture of her mother. Mickey looked at the fading photograph and then at herself in the mirror on the near wall. The same rash of freckles, the same dark eyes and dark hair that shone like copper in the sun. She was, she knew, her mother's daughter. Her father's only sin was trying to make her a replacement for the little boy whose death had ruptured his heart. But she had long ago forgiven him, come to understand him. She was never a dolls and dresses girl, she'd told Rodriguez. Without Patsy, she knew, she would probably be working the perfume counter at Bamberger's at the Cherry Hill Mall. Instead, she was a cop – one that everyone liked and respected. She owed that to her father.

Mickey drew in a couple deep breaths and walked back out toward the front room. Patsy had the television on. KYW's *Eyewitness News* was running a story on the Apollo 11 astronauts finally being released from quarantine after their historic landing on the moon more than three weeks earlier.

"You want me to change it to Channel 10 so you can watch John Facenda?" Mickey asked.

"Nah, leave it there," Patsy replied. "Vince Leonard's OK but I want to watch this Tom Snyder guy. He's gonna be somebody big one of these days, I think."

Mickey was almost to the door when Patsy's phone rang.

♦ ♦ ♦

Yvette Tran had managed to pull the bowl toward her, millimeter by painstaking millimeter, until she could use her chin to tip it until the water touched her tongue. She had been able to slurp enough of it that her vision, which had gone fuzzy, was starting to clear.

As she drank more, she realized that she must have been very close to unconsciousness, for the room around her was also starting to come back into focus. She gave another tug with her chin and the bowl scraped on the wooden table to a point where she could dip her face in the now lukewarm water. Her fingers were numb and useless. She had lost feeling in both feet, so tight were the plastic ties that bound them.

She thought again of Bonne-Nuit and a single tear meandered down her cheek.

Yvette had been vaguely aware of a commotion in the adjoining room but in her weakened state could not be sure she hadn't imagined it. She wondered if Declan was already dead. She wondered if the sounds had been him being killed or perhaps, without the water that now dripped from her chin, he had died and what she'd heard was his body being dragged out.

It was so hard to think.

She lowered her head sucked in as much as she could, although swallowing now hurt tremendously.

She thought she heard something outside the door. If Declan was dead, she knew her time was running out. If they'd found Bunny, it was even shorter.

The door burst open in a crash of popped hinges and splintered wood. It was only her near vision that was clear, Yvette quickly realized. She could see the outline of a large man moving toward her. Each step seemed to last for minutes. There was something in his hand. She focused on it. K-Bar, she knew. It had blood on it.

A shadow brushed by and then the man was behind her.

She tried to scream but only a parched whistle emerged. Yvette now tucked her chin down as far as she could. She didn't want him to cut her throat. She gritted her teeth and waited for the blade in her back. Her chair was being dragged away from the table and he was speaking to her. Shouting but somehow whispering at the same time. A hoarse, angry sound. She hunched her shoulders up to try and further protect her neck. His smell was rank. She convulsed when his hands fell on her shoulders.

"Yvette," he said. It was like a dream now, the waiting. Why was he saying her name, she wondered.

Her chair spun roughly around. She saw the wet blood on his hands, smeared on his arms.

"Yvette," he said again. The big knife glinted. She squeezed her eyes shut and made herself think one last time of Bunny, the singing waves and all the stars glowing in the deep black sky.

Twenty Two

Ship Bottom, NJ

Patsy drank two bottles of High Life during the call.

"Well, what's going on?" he asked. "How the hell did he know to call here?"

Mickey looked at the notepad she'd pulled from her pocket, the one she used on police calls to record details or statements. The one blank page that had remained was now full of doodles, numbers and sentence fragments.

"He didn't." Mickey replied. "But if I wasn't here he figured you were the safest person to leave a message with."

Patsy sat the empties next to his rocker.

"You don't look so good, Michaela. What's goin' on?"

Mickey looked at the pad then snapped it shut and put it back in her uniform shorts. "He's OK. He thinks maybe he won't be there more than another week or two. That's the good news."

"Should I get another beer for the bad news?"

"I'll get you one before I go," Mickey replied. "But I'm going to repeat what he told me while it's still fresh in my mind and so we'll both have it."

Patsy sat forward and the rocker creaked a little on the floorboards.

"I think we might be looking at real trouble, Dad," she continued. "The letter that Bunny – that's the little girl I mentioned – the letter she gave me was from a soldier Ronnie served with in Viet Nam. Guy named Declan Winston. They were pretty tight and I know he and Ronnie were in touch a time or two. Ronnie told me once that Declan was convinced Ronnie saved him from being picked off by a VC sniper while they were on river patrol. Anyway, Declan stayed in the Army. Ronnie said he was planning on marrying a woman, a widow he'd met and bringing her and her little girl home to the States to live."

"Wait," Patsy interrupted. "You're babysitting a Vietnamese kid?"

"Yeah, sort of," Mickey answered. "Although I don't think babysitting quite covers it."

"So what's this real trouble you're talkin' about?"

"Ronnie said that usually it would take months or years to make that happen if a soldier went through official channels. But there were quicker ways that came with strings attached."

"Like?"

"Like packing drugs, usually heroin, in a duffel bag. They never search the solders' personal stuff when they're on their way home. Ronnie brought back-"

Mickey stopped herself.

"Ronnie brought back some things you can't find in Ricky's Army-Navy store, let's put it that way."

"Not drugs?"

"No, not drugs, obviously. Ordnance," Mickey countered. "Came in handy a time or two a couple years ago."

"I think I'll have that beer now if you don't mind," Patsy said. Mickey got up from the sagging sofa and went to the refrigerator .

"Want another High Life?"

"Sure. Champagne in honor of your first babysitting job."

Mickey shot him a look and came back with the beer. She paced back and forth on the oval braided rug while she continued.

"All Ronnie can figure is that things must have got sideways somehow and the two names in the letter are the stateside dealers. He thinks Bunny can either lead them to the drug stash or they'll use her as a bargaining chip – that is if Declan and her mother are even still alive at this point. Bunny said she ran away from two bad men – I'm assuming they're the guys mentioned in the letter."

Patsy took a drink and pondered. "You run their names?"

Mickey nodded. "Charlie Higgins is doing that for me right now. But we don't have access to federal or military records, so unless they got a DL or got collared in the Delaware Valley in the last two years they might as well be on the moon with those astronauts."

"They're back now, kid. They been back about a month. You should watch the news with me more so you'd know what's going on in the world."

"You know what I mean," Mickey said.

"How about that FBI guy? Thought of asking him?"

"J.J. Durkin?"

"No," Patsy answered, "the young guy. The one's always giving you his card. The one wants you to be the first girl FBI agent. Him."

"Evan Driscoll," Mickey said. "He thinks FBI stands for Female Body Inspector, apparently. I do not want to owe him a favor."

"10-4 on that," Patsy said with a small chuckle.

Mickey rubbed her chin. "Maybe we could go through Uncle Basil." Her "uncle" Basil P. Jablonski had been Patsy's first partner in uniform, Mickey's godfather and, more importantly, the recently retired Philadelphia Police Commissioner. He had a small house in Margate but had suffered a light stroke in the spring and recuperation had been slow. "How's he doing?"

"He's about ninety percent, I'd say," Patsy replied. "Remembers things that happened long ago better than things that happened an hour ago. Might be worth a shot. He still feels guilty about The Troubles. Like it was his fault, so you got guilt working in your favor."

"Guilt is the gift that keeps on giving," Mickey said. "I should go see him."

"I'll go," said Patsy. "I still like drivin' my old Chevy. I ever tell you what your mayor offered me for it?"

"Yeah. You should have taken it."

"Nah," Patsy said. "That '57 Bel-Air is a classic. I'm keepin' it. So what's your plan?"

Mickey crossed her arms. "I've got to keep this little girl safe until her parents show up. That's job one."

"*If* they show up," Patsy interjected.

"Yeah, I've considered that possibility."

"But if the two creeps show up first, one little Asian girl ain't exactly going to be hard to find, you know," Patsy said.

"I've considered that, too. Just haven't figured out what to do about it."

Patsy cradled the beer bottle in both hands. "If it comes to it, if things really do get dicey, we could maybe hide her with Basil and Etheldra over in Margate. They have a couple of extra rooms in case their kids and grandkids come down. I could take her."

Mickey crossed the floor and touched him on the arm. "Well then maybe you should meet her, just in case."

"Her name really Bunny? Like a bunny rabbit?"

"Close enough for government work," Mickey answered. "I'll let her explain it to you when I bring her over." Mickey patted her holstered gun. "I gotta check in at the station and make sure I haven't missed a crime wave. The deputies are taking my night shifts but I can't ask them to do that forever. I'll see if Charlie came up with anything. I'll try to swing by on my way home." She walked to the door and turned around." Hey, Dad?"

"Yeah, kid?"

"Leave the gun in the drawer, OK?"

She didn't wait for Patsy to answer before leaving.

◆ ◆ ◆

The Pine Barrens

The sun was finally down when BoDean arrived at Harry Leusner's place.

"You come bearin' gifts?" Leusner asked.

The few teeth he had left were all gold-capped and BoDean made note of this for future reference. Leusner was splayed comfortably on the 40 section of a 60/40 front bench seat salvaged from an old Buick LeSabre. The tip of an odd spring or two poked through the fabric upholstery at its base and two halves of an unbuckled seatbelt hung loosely from either side.

"Little token of appreciation," BoDean said and set the can down carefully. He placed it several feet from Leusner's chair in a shadowed recess. Light from the kerosene lantern illuminated only the metal top and the Acme logo.

BoDean could see that Leusner was in his usual state of perpetual inebriation but he knew from previous encounters that the old rummy could go on for hours just this side of consciousness. BoDean wanted to hurry the process just a bit.

"I did a new batch of shine," BoDean said. "Real white

lightning – prolly best I've made this year. I'll fetch it if you'd like."

"I'd be much obliged," Leusner answered.

BoDean leaned forward and feigned tying the lace on his boot. "Is that a buck I saw out yonder when I was walkin' up."

Leusner squinted into the gathering gloom. BoDean used the short but diverted span of attention to unspool the fuse wire concealed on the underside of the coffee can. Shielding Leusner's view with his bulk, he turned and walked toward his truck, letting the wire play out as he went. He opened the driver side door. The Mason jar shook as he attached the cord to an ignition wire with a Marette thimble connector. He left the door open, grabbed the jar and walked back to Leusner's lean-to.

"'That's all you brung?" Leusner asked.

BoDean set the jar down on the wooden cable spool that served as a makeshift table.

"All we'll need," Bo Dean answered. "And all for you."

Leusner rubbed at his stubble. "You want the jar back?"

"Yors to keep," BoDean said as he unscrewed the cap and slid off the seal. He handed it to Leusner who grabbed it in one filthy hand and put it immediately to his lips.

"It's Hi-Test," BoDean chided. "Go easy there, Loose Nuts."

Leusner took a hearty swallow and blinked. The he took another.

"I've had stronger," Leusner said.

"Well I ain't tryin' to kill ya with it," BoDean replied.

"It'd take more than this," Leusner said. Then he finished off the remainder. "It's smooth, I'll give you that. Billy never did get the hang of shine makin'. His shit always tasted like kerosene – 'course nobody was ever brave enough or stupid enough to tell him that." He set the empty jar down. Lamplight played on the glass and the rivulets of liquid and saliva coursing down it. "D'ja find the jelly gas alright?"

Leusner's eyes were half closed now. BoDean didn't answer right away, waiting to see if the old man would rally or succumb to the potent dose of nearly pure ethanol.

"I found it OK," BoDean said and stepped back. The blackness of the night now enveloped them. Critter and insect noises rose and fell. BoDean moved the lantern until it was right next to the fabric of the bench seat. He watched Leusner for a few moments. The old man was talking quietly and pointing at something only he could see. BoDean carefully lifted the two halves of the seat belt, pulled them across Leusner's lap and quietly slipped the metal tongue into the buckle. Leusner flinched when it clicked but quickly returned to mumbling which eventually grew too faint to understand.

BoDean retreated to his truck as quietly as his large frame would allow. He gauged the distance at about fifty yards. Once he squeezed into the driver's seat he rolled up the window but left the door open at an angle that he figured would deflect anything in the air. Then he slipped the key into the ignition.

♦ ♦ ♦

Surf City

When Mickey arrived at the station, all three of her deputies were at their desks. Charlie Higgins was bent over a stack of papers. Dippolito and Rodriguez were in hot debate about something.

"OK," Rodrguez said, acknowledging Mickey with a quick salute. "Chief Cleary is obviously a woman – we'll see what she thinks."

Mickey walked to her desk and sat down. It was old and wooden, in contrast to the newer model metal and Formica ones the deputies had, but she had insisted it be salvaged from the old station house. There were faded spots and divots where blood spatter had been either bleached out or sanded down. "The Troubles," her father had called the events – like it was Northern Ireland, which, she thought, maybe it was: A war that never ended, innocents dead alongside combatants and not a just or noble cause in sight. She thought of Ronnie and then of Bunny and what they'd seen, what they'd endured. Police, soldiers – the thin line they defended that kept it all from descending into chaos. She hoped it wasn't what Rodriguez and Dippolito were arguing about.

"Well, which one?" Dip asked. She had obviously missed the question.

"Which one what?" Mickey said. She pushed her chair back.

"Tom Jones or Engelbert Humperdinck?" Rodriguez chimed in. "Which one's a bigger turn-on for women?"

"Seriously?" Mickey said. "This is the burning question of the day?"

Dippolito looked puzzled. "Well, yeah. They're both coming to the Latin Casino in Cherry Hill. Both are already sold out with most of the tickets bought by women. Which one would you go to see?"

"Neither," Mickey replied. She gave a dismissive wave. "Now can we-"

"All I'm saying," Rodriguez intoned, "Is that grown women throw their panties and their hotel room keys on the stage when Tom Jones is up there. The only step after that would be solicitation."

"Well, Engelbert sells more records. You can check it out," Dippolito responded.

"Yeah but his name is still freakin' *Engelbert*," Rodriguez countered.

"His name is Arnold."

Mickey, Rodriguez and Dippolito turned to look at Charlie Higgins who was holding a pencil with both hands and staring at them with a barely perceptible smile.

"His name is Arnold," Charlie repeated. "Englebert Humperdinck was a German composer. He wrote *Hansel and Gretel*, which was a famous opera. The singer's real name is Arnold Dorsey. But there ain't no woman I know going to throw her dainties at a guy named Arnold even if he is wearing a tuxedo."

"You made that up," Dippolito said. "How would you even know that?"

Charlie laid the pencil down. "I needed three more credits for my degree at Rutgers so I took a Music Appreciation course. Taught by a lovely professor named Rita Fitzpatrick. I thought it was a puff course. Turns out she damn well wanted to make sure you appreciated music. Two papers, mandatory class attendance, a two Blue Book final *and* you had to attend a concert. And I don't mean going to the Spectrum or the Tower Theatre to see Janis Joplin or James Taylor. I went to the Academy of Music and watched Eugene Ormandy conduct the Philadelphia Orchestra. They performed *Hansel and Gretel* by my man Engelbert. Any questions?"

No one said anything. Then Rodriguez rapped his knuckles on his desk.

"OK, but I still say panties don't lie." His body language made it clear that this was his idea of the last word.

Mickey shook her head. "Does anyone have anything remotely

related to law enforcement in our fair borough?"

"Dippolito raised an index finger. "Mr. D from the Surf Shoppe complained again that parking by shop owners on Long Beach Boulevard was interfering with his customer flow. And little Willie wants to know when he's going to get reimbursed for the damages he says you caused at his liquor store – get this – in 1967."

"Noted," Mickey said. "Tell Mr. D I'll have the Chamber president remind store owners they should leave ample parking for customers on our main thoroughfare. But do not tell Mr. D that the Ron-Jon in Ship Bottom is expanding their parking lot to twice its size. As for Little Willie, tell him I said the check is in the mail."

Rodriguez spoke up. "The guys we tangled with on the beach all tested positive for PCP according to the State Police. They said someone way back in the Pines is the source."

Mickey looked at Dippolito. "You fill out a report on discharging your weapon?"

Dip looked at the floor. "It's there on your desk. Are you going to –"

"I'm going to file it away. And we all need to think about situational awareness when the public is present. Anyone complain?"

"Complain? No," Rodriguez said. He shuffled the papers in front of him. "But the 'Death to Pigs' kid came in with her parents to apologize. She left this." He held up a sheet of lined loose-leaf paper covered in neat cursive. "Want me to read it, Chief?"

"Just the highlights, maybe."

"OK. 'Dear Marshal Cleary and Surf City Deputy Marshals,'" Rodriguez began. Mickey smiled at the misnomers. "'I'm really sorry, blah, blah blah… Appreciate the work of law enforcement… didn't understand the seriousness of my actions…bunch more about how sorry she is and hopes we can forgive her immaturity. Signed, Susie Joyce, Age 12."

"Think she *wrote* it?" Mickey asked.

Rodriguez studied the paper. "Well, all the i's are dotted with tiny hearts so, yes, I think she *wrote* it but dear old Dad's an attorney in Jenkintown, soooo…"

"Take a letter, Maria," Dippolito quipped.

"Exactly. R.B. Greaves –pretty sure that dude is Chicano. Got that Mariachi vibe going." Rodriguez snapped his fingers to an imaginary tune.

"You think everyone is Chicano," Dip added. "You said Paul Anka is Chicano. You think Sam the Sham is Chicano."

"Sam the Sham is definitely Chicano," Rodriguez. "A Tex-Mex."

"Who's next, the Singing Nun?" Dip complained.

"Sorry, Dip," Charlie said. "She was actually born in Spain. You should quit while you're ahead, man."

"All right," Mickey said. "How long is the Joyce family here for?"

Rodriguez checked his notes. "Their place rents by the week so they need to be out Saturday morning."

"How many stitches did you get," Mickey asked him.

"Six. And no Novacaine. I am one macho *hombre*."

"Good. You can stop by and tell her all is forgiven but how she needs to stay on the straight and narrow and be respectful of the people who are here to protect her. You can lay it on a little thick if you want. How old is your oldest?"

"Eleven," Rodriguez replied. "What's that got to do with-"

Mickey pointed a finger at him. "Right now you're telling yourself no child of yours would ever do such a thing. Never say that out loud. Kiss of death. Just ask my Dad."

"Your dad looks like he could still bust heads if he wanted to," Dippolito opined.

"Thanks for reminding me of something," Mickey said. She swiveled her chair to face the younger deputy. "Dip, ask the Ship Bottom patrols if they'll cruise by my dad's place during their shifts. He's convinced a guy in a pickup was staking him out yesterday."

"He's been off the job *how* long?" Dippolito asked.

"Long time but across the river it's easy to make enemies."

"I'd say we probably made some today," Charlie interjected.

Mickey leaned back in her chair. "And I think if we go poking around the source of the PCP we'll probably make some more. I may need to drop in on Lieutenant Stellwag and his band of easy riders. See if he knows what his new neighbors are up to."

"Want one of us to go with you?" Dippolito asked.

Mickey smiled. "The LT and I go back a few years. I'll be OK. They always provide an escort."

"I think I heard something about that escort once," Rodriguez said. Mickey's look told him there would be no follow-up conversation so the deputy quickly shifted gears. "Where's your new little friend?" Rodriguez asked.

Mickey looked at her watch. "Right now? Probably having after-dinner ice cream with Hizzoner and Loretta at Loretta's place. I'm headed there next to pick her up."

"Chief," Rodriguez said. "My wife says she's welcome at our house. She might have fun with the rugrats – watching four little girls isn't much different than watching three."

Mickey pondered the idea. "I'll talk to her about it. She's a girl on a mission right now. We've been able to distract her for a day but I'm guessing that's all. Charlie?" She looked over at Higgins. "Anything pop on those names?"

He had the phone to his ear and held up two fingers.

"Who's got tonight?" Mickey asked.

"I do," answered Dippolito.

"OK," Mickey said. "Anything funky, I want to know about it. Got it?"

"Define funky, Chief," Dippolito replied.

"Anything or anybody that looks out of place. Especially anybody looks like they don't belong on the Island. Any rough trade. That kind of funky."

Dip nodded. "Copy that, Chief. Anything funky."

Charlie Higgins hung up his desk phone and stood. "Chief Cleary," he said. "Mind if I walk you to your cruiser?" Mickey noticed he was already in motion. She gathered up her keys, patted her revolver and stood to meet him. He passed by her and went to open and hold the door. "See boys?" he said. "Chivalry is not dead."

Mickey slid by him and into the soft night air. The sound of the surf was loud. The moon was still in its first quarter and some scudding clouds made it look like a silver smudge in the inky black sky. The town whole seemed darker, she thought. Mickey had begun to feel at home with the natural rhythms of a beach town; the ebb and flow of tourists downtown, the cyclical influx of day-trippers and weekenders, the subtle change that August brought as Fall loomed within reach. The retailers tried to squeeze every penny out of every day before Labor Day. Mary T from King of Prussia had once told her that sales "fell off the cliff" once school started in the city and the suburbs. Shelves that once held sunglasses and squeeze bottles of Coppertone would soon be stuffed with pencils, protractors and packages of paper and spiral-bound notebooks.

Charlie opened the cruiser door for her and closed it gently once she was behind the wheel.

"OK," Mickey said, "What is it? I know you're a gentleman but this is something else, right?"

Charlie gazed at the ocean just two blocks away and then spoke.

"I talked with my brother Darnell tonight," he said.

"The one in the VA," Mickey replied.

"Yes." Charlie paused. "Chief Cleary, it pains me to admit this but I have not been completely honest with you about Darnell. I lied to you, to put it bluntly." Mickey heard his feet shuffling on the asphalt. She knew he was clearly uncomfortable with the admission.

"Charlie," she said. "Whatever it is—"

"Chief," he continued. "Darnell was injured in Viet Nam but not during the Tet Offensive as I told you yesterday. That was a convenient falsehood. The sad truth is that he was fragged by one of the men in his company. While he was sleeping in his tent. You know what fragging is, I assume."

When Ronnie had first explained it to her Mickey had been horrified. A live grenade rolled under a cot was the most common method she remembered him describing. But Ronnie had told her that white phosphorous and even mortar rounds had been employed. In one particularly heinous instance, a flame thrower had been the agent of destruction. Often, he'd said, the attacks were occasioned by petty disputes with enlisted men but, he'd said, racial divides were often at fault. Mickey recalled Charlie telling her his brother was a lieutenant. Ronnie said there were very few black officers in-country and that commanding a predominately white platoon or company could spell trouble.

"Ronnie explained it," Mickey said. "I think it's horrible. I just can't imagine someone doing that. Was it because—"

Charlie shook his head. "No. It had nothing to do with color. Darnell said he stumbled across some bad shit some of the enlisted guys were into. High end criminal shit, he said. Running ordnance and drugs stateside on government birds with returning servicemen or heavy equipment going back."

"Did he report it?"

Charlie gave a chuckle. "Darnell's smart, Chief. Smartest one out of all of us. He said he made it clear it was none of his business and he thought that would be it. One night, they waited until there was a thunderstorm. He hears a funny sound outside his tent. He was rolling out of his cot when the grenade exploded. If he'd rolled the other way it would have blown off his head instead of his leg."

"Didn't they investigate?"

"They said they did. But Darnell said it was hard to know how far up the chain the rot went. If it's discovered and, more importantly, if it's reported, it's the kind of thing that ruins the careers of full bird colonels even if they weren't directly involved. So you know they didn't look too hard. They took his leg off at a field hospital in *Nha Trang*, sent him to Saigon and then Hawaii for a month. Then they shipped him to the VA where he is now. They gave him a medal and awarded him100% disability so he'll get full pay for the rest of his life. But they keep him stoned on morphine all the time now. It does make me wonder if the fix is still in. Neutralize him by keeping him high constantly or turn him into an addict. That's why we want him moved."

"Did you ask him about our situation?"

"I did, Chief. And that's what worries me. He'd just gotten a dose so he was a little in and out but he reacted, shall we say, quite strongly when I mentioned one of the names."

"Which one?" Mickey asked.

Charlie withdrew a sheet of paper from his shirt pocket and unfolded it.

"Private Richard Robichaux," he replied.

◆ ◆ ◆

The Pine Barrens

Loose Nuts had been right about one thing, BoDean thought. The screams were right out of one of the horror movies that played frequently at the Drive-In Theatre in Manahawkin. BoDean listened with a detached curiosity. The fireball had been neat and almost compact. The various containers of shine, kerosene and propane scattered around the lean-to had gone off with measured pops. The heat was intense but short-lived and BoDean was able to roll down the window to better take in the sound of Leusner's prolonged suffering. When the screaming stopped and the flames died down BoDean ventured back to assess the carnage.

What he saw both pleased and horrified him.

Leusner, or what had once been Harry Leusner, was charred and contracted and fused to what remained of the metal frame of the bench seat. The skin and underlying flesh of the skull were completely burned away and the gold caps stood out in high relief. Leusner had kept his immediate environs cleared of brush and pine straw and so the fire, thus deprived of fuel, had remained surprisingly self-contained. BoDean figured this would also be the case for a wood-frame house on a concrete slab. He debated pulling the gold teeth and melting them down but then decided against it. If someone came upon the scene they would certainly harvest the gold - an act, BoDean figured, which would discourage any early reporting of the deed. He doubted the flames had been spotted by the Tabernacle tower, the corrugated tin having hemmed them in. He reached into his pocket and withdrew the badge, its sharpened edge now sheathed in a strip of deer hide.

BoDean remained for quite some time, walking the perimeter of Leusner's property and then returning to gaze upon the barbecued corpse. It was more than he could have hoped for – all he needed now was a way to rig a delayed fuse. He figured he could still lean on Cowboy for that.

Cowboy was another loner, Billy thought. Not quite as reclusive as Leusner, perhaps, but still one whose absence would not be noticed immediately. But first he needed him to come up with the fuse.

BoDean walked to his truck, almost reluctant to depart the infernal scene. He could relieve himself right there, he knew, his aloneness in the Pines was so complete. He decided to wait, wishing to replay the entire event in his mind several more times before allowing himself the pleasure of well-earned release.

Twenty Three

Surf City

"When Dunn get here?" Bunny asked.

"Soon, he hopes," Mickey answered. The girl was curled next to her on the bed in her floral pajamas and her fuzzy slippers. Mickey had on a ragged t-shirt with a barely visible Property of Philadelphia PD and a pair of red OCBP gym shorts one of the lifeguards had given her. "You can take off your slippers," Mickey said.

"I keep on," Bunny replied, turning her feet inward and outward to admire the high fashion footwear from varying angles. "Dunn come tomorrow?"

"I don't think tomorrow. But he told me some things we can do to try and help your mama and papa-san."

Bunny's feet stopped moving.

"Coopral Winston not real papa-san," she said.

"I know," Mickey said. "Dunn told me what happened. "I'm sorry, Bunny. I don't know what else to say." The child looked straight ahead. Ronnie called it the "thousand-yard stare."

"Everybody mad at us all time," Bunny said. "Viet Cong come to village, say we help Americans. Americans come, say we help Viet Cong. If we help, they kill. But no help, they still kill. Mama say men just do war so they can hurt and kill. Papa-san have brother who fight for NVA. But we all same people, Mama say. ARVN, NVA, VC all same people. All Vietnamese people. GI's say they protect us. VC say they protect us. Then VC kill Papa-san.

Make 'Mama watch. One day I go with Mama. We walk far to get wood for fires. Come back *So'n My* see everybody dead on road. Soldiers still there. I think they will shoot Mama but then chopper land right behind us. Not Huey. Clear head and long tail. Look like big flying bug. Soldiers point with machine guns – point at own GI's. Tell us go behind them. More choppers land. Hueys. Take us away. We never go back *So'n My* again."

Mickey noticed that Bunny spoke evenly and without emotion, as if she had somehow detached herself from the horror. Mickey also noticed that her own mouth had gone cotton-dry listening to a child tell a war story.

"I need a drink of water," Mickey said. 'Would you like some?"

"Soda. You got Coca-Cola?" Bunny asked with a smile. She was back to admiring her slippers.

"No Coca-Cola," Mickey answered, pushing herself off the mattress. "I do have some Tab."

"What Tab?"

"Soda. Kind of like Coke. Sweet but no sugar. Not that you need to worry about getting fat."

"Coopral Winston say Mama and me get fat like American women. Mama laugh and say only if we eat *bon-bons et chocolat*. Then we get *tres, tres grosse*, Mama say."

"Hey, now," Mickey said as she moved for the bedroom door. "I'm an American woman."

"You too skinny," Bunny replied. "You get fat maybe Dunn marry you."

Mickey padded toward the kitchen and the new Kenmore refrigerator. She passed the empty guest room with its bare plywood floor. The room had possessed a lingering odor which repainting and repeated rug shampooing had failed to dispel. The Ianuzzi's apologized but said they couldn't explain it. Only tearing out the carpet had seemed to work. Ronnie had been planning to lay the new rug himself when he was mustered back in.

The ship's wheel clock in the hallway said it was just after eleven. The kitschy timepiece was one of several things the Ianuzzi's had insisted stay with the house. It seemed to Mickey as if they wanted to leave not just the structure but some inhabiting presence or memory behind them. They'd bought a place in Stone Harbor, she knew, but since that ritzy little enclave wasn't on Long Beach Island she had not crossed paths with them since the sale.

It was probably better that way, she mused. Two less people who recalled the Troubles, as her father had coined her experience.

The Kenmore ran considerably quieter than the wheezing, rattling Norge they'd originally hauled out of Ronnie's beach shack. She pulled on the door. It opened with a sound like a wet kiss. She grabbed two bottles of Tab, pulled the magnetic can/bottle opener off the side of the appliance and popped them both. As she closed the door she laughed at Bunny's assessment of her. Then she pulled open the bottom freezer door and slid out the white enameled rack. She shuffled a few items in it until she found the box of Sealtest Ice Cream Sandwiches. She slid two of them out, pushed the rack back in and kneed the door shut. Heading back toward the bedroom she tried to formulate some semblance of a plan for the next twenty-four hours. The weekend was fast approaching and, if the weather stayed good as was forecast, the crowds would be big and both she and all three deputies would be busy. Unless Ronnie Dunn magically appeared, she realized, she'd have a hard time juggling her duties while keeping Bunny close by. Loretta and Mayor Billy had volunteered to watch her again but if Bunny was at risk, she reasoned, they would be as well. She couldn't see them fending off two potentially armed and dangerous ex-soldiers. Ronnie hadn't recognized either of the names in Bunny's note but he'd vouched for Declan Winston's integrity and said to assume the parties named were "bad actors with lethal intent" until proven otherwise. He was supposed to call again between one and two o'clock tomorrow but warned her that that conversation would be wiretapped and recorded and so he wouldn't be able to say much.

When she got back to the bedroom Bunny was fast asleep.

Mickey sat on the edge of the bed. The radio was playing softly, something she hadn't noticed, so rapt had Bunny's story kept her attention. The radio was one Ronnie had bought her and it pulled in not only the AM stations but the new "FM Stereo" ones that were popping up in Philadelphia. Mickey still listened to the WFIL Boss Jock's on the Chevelle cruiser's dashboard radio. Charlie's cruiser had come with an AM/FM radio which he had permanently tuned to WDAS on the far right end of the dial. The rectangular Realistic Model 12 on her bedside table had a fake-wood case and a vertical tuning bar. The sound was certainly better than the tinny RCA AM-only she'd brought with her form

California but she wasn't sure the sound was all that stereophonic. Ronnie had set the tuner to 94.4 FM and Mickey had only moved it once. WMMR was one of the newer stations in Philadelphia and Dave Herman was their nighttime DJ. He had a soothing, almost entrancing delivery. She'd come across a station that broadcast out of Camden, New Jersey with a motor-mouthed DJ who dubbed himself the "Geator with the Heater." She had no idea what a Geator was. Ronnie preferred Dave Herman and so Mickey left it tuned there while he was gone. Now she listened as he introduced and then cued up The Zombies' hit from 1964, "She's Not There."

Mickey unwrapped and scarfed down both of the melting Sealtest ice cream sandwiches, licking bits of clinging chocolate wafer from her fingertips. She drank one of the Tabs, checked to make sure Bunny was still asleep and then turned out the light.

As she lay in the dark, she felt the soft, feathery touch of unconsciousness but tried to resist. She wanted to hear the end of the song.

They won't find her, Mickey thought just before she closed her eyes. They won't find her. Not if she's not there.

♦ ♦ ♦

Ebb Tide Motel

Gannon felt bad for taking advantage of Doreen Kuzma, but only briefly. The clack-clack of the keys and the sloshing contents of the nightcap on the flimsy desk had taken care of that in short order.

Doreen's husband was an over-the-road trucker and so often away from home for days at a time. She didn't long for romance or even sex, he'd quickly surmised, just company and conversation. He was happy to supply both. He'd suggested they meet at the Acme Hotel and Bar on Dock Street in Beach Haven. The hotel aspect of the business seemed to be on shaky ground but the bar was busy and they'd sat on an outside deck overlooking Little Egg Harbor Bay. Doreen held her liquor surprisingly well and Gannon wondered if perhaps chronic imbibitions helped pass the lonely hours at home.

By the time they'd walked to Zorba's, the all-night Greek

greasy-spoon on Bay Avenue, he'd confirmed a few hunches and found a few tantalizing leads he needed to run down. He figured he'd try Chief Cleary again in the morning. For the moment he wanted to ink the rest of what was in his head onto the paper in front of him.

PART TWO
What Happened in the Pines?

The forest primeval-that's what it is. Whether you want to get to the shore or get away from the shore you have to go through the New Jersey Pine Barrens. The home of the Jersey Devil, they say. Dark, foreboding and populated by those who'd rather you didn't intrude on their solitude or their unenforced isolation. Call them "Pineys" at your own risk. Even officers of the law hesitate to turn off the gravelly roads and enter the hamlets and scattered shotgun shacks. So how does the police chief of a sleepy beach town find herself, beaten and bloodied, emerging from this wasteland escorted by members of an outlaw biker gang? What happened in the hours leading up to her escape? Why is there no record of arrests or prosecutions? Why was her original police station demolished soon afterward? Who has escaped punishment? And why have mobsters, police officers and even former P.C. in the City of Brotherly Love closed ranks to fend off any questions? Was the FBI really involved? This reporter will address these questions in this series investigative of reports. You may find the answers hard to believe but, then, in this reporter's experience, truth is always stranger than fiction.

Gannon realized he had none of the actual answers. But, he thought as he sipped at the highball, it had never stopped him before. He went back to typing.

◆ ◆ ◆

Fort Benning, GA

Ronnie was wide awake even before he heard the barracks door open.

"On your feet, Dunn," a voice commanded.

Ronnie sprang from the bed and stood at attention by his footlocker. All he wore were boxers, a white t-shirt and his dogtags. The night air was humid and only ambient light from pole-mounted lamps outside filtered through the interior darkness.

The silhouette in the doorway moved toward him. It did not turn on the light.

"At ease, soldier. You ship out at zero-dark-thirty. Deadheading on a transport bound for McGuire AFB. An MP will escort you and you will report to Fort Dix where your ETS will be processed. You're on your own from there. JAG captain said to remind you all conversations here remain Classified."

"Sir. Thank you, sir," Ronnie replied.

The silhouette moved forward and Ronnie could now see it was a Staff Sergeant dressed in combat fatigues.

"Don't call me sir."

"Yes, Sergeant," Ronnie answered. "Couldn't tell in the dark." He tried to read the name stitched above the left breast pocket but couldn't make it out.

"Dunn," the Sergeant continued in an even but clearly displeased tone, "I don't know who the fuck you are, what the fuck you know or why the fuck these tightasses from the Judge Advocate are taking up an entire barracks with you, but this much I do know. The shit is about to hit the fan around here and when it does a lot of good men are going to pay the price for being soldiers in a war not of their making against an enemy they cannot always identify. If you are any part of bringing those good men down I can assure you that you will be looking over your shoulder for the rest of your miserable civilian life. Do I make myself clear, soldier? Do you read me?"

"Five by five, Sergeant. Permission to contact home in the morning to notify family members of my unexpected arrival?"

"Permission denied," came the answer followed by a low chuckle. "It'll be a big surprise. And you should expect to find your wife or your girlfriend exactly the way you left her."

Ronnie knew what came next.

"Freshly fucked."

The sergeant became a silhouette again then turned and left. Ronnie counted to twenty. The he walked to the door, turned on the overhead fluorescents and went back to his bunk to pack his duffel. He had the feeling that his journey into the heart of this darkness was only beginning.

♦ ♦ ♦

Manahawkin, NJ
Intersection of Routes 9 & 72

Dickie Robichaux wanted popcorn.

"I'll go get it," Harlan Brinson said. "You just stay here."

They were parked in the center of the Manahawkin Drive-In's undulating gravel lot. The evening's promotion was billed as "$5 A CARLOAD!" but a pimply kid with a flashlight said they had to pop the trunk first.

"We'll just pay regular price, then," Harlan had told him as the flashlight bounced over Dickie's face. Dickie had leaned over and stared right into the beam.

Whatever the kid saw unnerved him enough that he had waved them through without taking the ten-spot in Harlan's extended hand.

On the screen Cliff Robertson was portraying Lt. j.g. John F. Kennedy in the last few minutes of "PT 109." The film was several years old but Warner Brothers had trotted it out again following the assassination of Bobby Kennedy in Los Angeles the previous year, riding a rolling national wave of Kennedy nostalgia and a renewed Camelot mystique. The picture was the first half of a double bill. The main feature was "Satan's Sadists" and the lurid poster suggested that its meager plot revolved around biker gangs and naked women.

"They could'a used PT Boats in-country," Dickie opined.

"They had PBR's for that. PT Boats were made of plywood. Besides, what're you going to do with a torpedo on the Mekong?"

"All you'd have to do is light up one or two of those *sampans*," Dickie replied. "Send a stronger message than just machine-gunning them at close range."

"You want a pop?" Brinson asked.

"No, I want a soda. Biggest size they got. Quit callin' it fucking pop. We ain't in Iowa no more, Dorothy."

"Toto," Brinson replied. "And it's Kansas. The line is 'we're not in Kansas anymore, Toto. Toto's the little dog."

"Just get me a fuckin' soda, OK? And a couple of burgers and fries with as much ketchup as you can carry."

Dickie's ignorance was really wearing on him, Brinson thought as he trudged toward the brightly lit Concession Stand. Around him the screech of the corroding metal speakers hanging on their poles or from driver's side windows grated on his ears and his patience. He knew he needed him to complete this mission, but beyond that Brinson wondered if Dickie had outlasted his usefulness.

The concession stand smelled of French fries, popcorn and months-old grease. The two kids working behind the pock-marked counter didn't look they were much older than sixteen.

Brinson bought burgers, fries and the largest Cokes they had. He didn't want popcorn all over the interior of the Road Runner. The ketchup had to be squirted into an array of tiny paper cups that it was already leaking through. Dickie had balked at spending a night in the car but Brinson wanted to see the morning papers to assess whether Dickie's indiscretion at the rest area had caught up with them.

After paying, Brinson asked the kid behind the cash register if he had a screwdriver he could borrow. "Our speaker's bent but I think I can fix it. I promise to bring it back."

The kid looked perplexed but pulled open a drawer behind the counter.

"Phillips or slot?" the kid asked.

"Slot head," Brinson replied. "Biggest one you got."

The kid pulled out a long one with a chipped amber plastic grip.

"That'll work," Brinson said and reached out to take it.

He'd gotten the food. Dickie, he figured, could get them new license plates.

Twenty-Four

The Pine Barrens

    The Breakfast Special at the Pic-a-Lilli cost three dollars. The hand-lettered said it included two draw beers sunny side up and a full shot of Old Crow Whiskey over easy.
    BoDean, the tavern's only patron, sucked down the first draft and held the shot glass up to the light. Small amounts of particulate matter floated slowly to the bottom.
    "Heard there was a little excitement last night," Kurt the bartender said.
    "Do tell," BoDean replied. He put the shot back on the bar without drinking it.
    "Old Loose Nuts finally burned himself up. Looks like his shine must'a caught fire. He was passed out on that old car seat he used as a couch. Guess all that's left is bones, springs and a seat belt buckle. The old fool had clicked himself in with it, if you can believe that."
    "I can believe that," BoDean said. He picked up the shot and downed it. "Buckle up for safety, like they say on them commercials. So who found him?"
    "Stellwag and one of his guys. They're not all that far away."
    BoDean considered the information.
    "Cops yet?"
    Kurt shook his head. "Not far as I know. Doubt the LT wants to report it. He's got his hands full with the Druids."
    "Think they done it?" BoDean asked, reassessing the whiskey.

"Could be. Maybe Loose Nuts saw something he wasn't supposed to." Kurt reached behind his head and retied his greasy ponytail. "Them boys, the Druids, they play by their own rules."

BoDean thought about his peace offering and the Prospect with the heavy artillery. The Druids, he considered, might take credit for the carnage just to beef up their reputation as badasses.

"Prol'ly just an accident," BoDean said. "Harry had more flammable liquids crammed in that shithole than a damn oil refinery. Any kin?"

Kurt grabbed a pink flyswatter and dispatched two big greenheads buzzing lazily around the taps. He flipped them onto the floor in front of the bar. BoDean stretched out a foot to squish them.

"I doubt it. I was thinking maybe we should get him buried but Stellwag said there wadn't even enough left for the critters to gnaw at. He said he wadn't touching it."

BoDean licked the empty shot glass.

"I knowed him a long time," BoDean said. He hoped the gold teeth were still in the charred skull. "I'll put him to rest." He tapped the shot glass on the bar. "Sounds like I'll need some fortification, though."

Kurt refilled the Old Crow.

"Burial expenses," Kurt said, pouring to the rim. "Must be a god-awful way to go. Burning up like that."

BoDean looked at the picture of his brother Billy. He sucked down the second whiskey and touched the glass to the necklace of bones. Then he picked up the other glass of beer.

"You see Stellwag, you tell him I got it took care of. Old Loose Nuts probably slept right through it. I doubt he felt a thing."

Kurt cleared the two mugs and the shot glass and then wiped down the bar with what Ma Bowker had always called a tea-towel. When he was finished he draped it over his shoulder.

"I sure hope so," Kurt said. He put both hands on the bar. "Funny thing, though. The LT said his jawbone was stuck wide open."

"So?"

"Stellwag said he seen it before. Back when he was in Nam. When they lit up the VC tunnels with flame throwers. Said you knew they'd been screaming when they died."

♦ ♦ ♦

Surf City

Don Cannon, one of WFIL-AM Radio's cadre of Boss Jocks, was hosting the 6 to 10 a.m. slot with caffeine-fueled enthusiasm. "I hate to do it," he said with mock sorrow, "but I only play the records. Management picks the songs. So let's get it out of the way while we can. At Number Two on the Famous 56 Boss Sound Survey this week with "Sugar, Sugar," the top completely fictional musical group of the summer, The Archies."

"Turn it off, would you please?" Mickey pleaded. "Or at least switch to WIBBAGE."

"You leave on," Bunny said. "I like sugar song." She was sitting on one of the cell bunks busily scribbling in a "Beany and Cecil" coloring book Rodriguez had brought from home. "What color I make dragon?" A large box of Crayolas was open next to her.

"Green," Rodriguez answered. "And Cecil is a sea serpent, not a dragon. A seasick sea-serpent at that."

"Puff a magic dragon," Bunny replied. She looked over at the box. "Too many greens," she said. "I do blue."

Rodriguez caught Mickey's eye. "And we all know what *that* song is about, don't we Chief?"

"It's just a kids' song, Deputy. Like a fairy tale - Peter, Paul and Mary all swear it." Mickey finished typing. "Can we at least turn it down?"

"NO," Bunny exclaimed. "You leave on. Candy girl. Sugar, sugar."

"You sure your wife's OK with this?" Mickey asked.

"She's fine," Rodriguez answered. "I'll drop her off as soon as I finish this paperwork from last night. How long are you going to be?'

"Couple hours," Mickey said. "But call me if it doesn't go well. OK? And I'll come pick her up."

"It'll go fine, Chief. Girls get along until they get to Junior High. Then something weird happens. Right now they think she's some kind of foreign princess coming to visit. Between Barbie's and some Easy Bake Oven brownies – which I will bring back for *you* to eat, by the way, she may not want to leave. If that doesn't work there are always Colorforms and paper dolls. Would you believe there's Apollo 11 Coloforms already?"

"I think Dip still has his old Outer Space ones," Mickey said as the station house door opened.

"I have what?" Dippolito asked. He took off his patrol hat and closed the door behind him. "What do I still have?"

"Nothing," Rodriguez said with a laugh.

Dippolito sat at his desk. "Chief," he said, "There's a guy out front say he needs to talk to you. I told him to come in but he said he'd rather talk outside."

"Who is it?"

"Motorcycle dude. Pretty scruffy looking. Says he knows you, though. I don't think he's armed but you want me to come out with you?"

Mickey suppressed a grin. "I got this one, Dip," she said rising from her squeaking wooden chair. "I know who it is. It's cool."

Dippolito looked disappointed so Mickey continued, "Keep watch out the window, though, would you?"

Dippolito shot up. "Yes, ma'am. I mean, yes, Chief."

Mickey patted her gun and nodded at Dippolito. "Just in case things go south," she said. She grabbed her Ray-Bans and walked out the door.

The bike was bigger than the one she remembered. Stellwag slouched on it. A slouch truly worthy of James Dean or Marlon Brando, she thought.

"Morning, Chief Cleary," Stellwag said with a grin. He always had perfect teeth she recalled. "Sorry to show up unannounced. If I remember right you once told me I should always call first." The dog tags around his neck clanked as he scratched his chest.

"I'll let it go this time, Lieutenant," Mickey said. She smiled and gave a quick salute. "What brings you out from the deep, dark woods on such a beautiful day? And where's your unit?"

"Just me today." Stellwag dismounted the Harley-Davidson.

"Nice bike." Mickey said. "You've upgraded. I like the Blue."

"Electra-Glide. 1200 cc Shovelhead. You ever think about a motorcycle patrol for your little town? I think you'd look damn good with this between your legs."

Mickey kicked at the sandy crushed-shell parking lot. "I assume you're referring to the bike."

SHIP BOTTOM BLUES 153

"Why, Chief Cleary," Stellwag said, flipping his sunglasses to the top of his head. "What else would I be referring to?"

Mickey rubbed at her chin. She had first encountered Stellwag and a couple of his gang during her first month on the job. She always thought of him as dangerously attractive and despite what he'd done for her and Ronnie, she'd felt it best to keep him and the rest of the Sons of Satan at arm's length.

"I really like my Chevelle," she shot back. "It's got more horses."

"I don't know," Stellwag said. "I hear the new Chief in Ship Bottom is looking at putting two bikes on his streets by next summer. Word is he was a motorcycle cop in California."

"That's what he says," Mickey replied. "Confirmation of that is still pending."

"Word is also that he's pushing for a single Long Beach Island Police Department instead of all these independent units. Makes a little bit of sense, I suppose."

"It does to Jim Justus," Mickey answered. "Since he's, of course, proposing that he'd be in charge of it. The Mayor says it's not happening."

"Well he is a visionary, your mayor," Stellwag said. "Chief Justus. Like the Supreme Court. Has a ring to it, you have to admit."

"My dad called him a pipsqueak," Mickey said. "I like the ring to that better."

Stellwag took a step closer. "I think your dad's a good judge of character. But that's not why I'm here."

Mickey took off her Ray-Bans and hung them on the breast pocket of her uniform blouse. "Must be something up for you to come all the way from your lair in the Pine Barrens just to see me."

"Let's go sit over there," Stellwag said. He pointed to a city bench that bordered Long Beach Boulevard, the asphalt spine that ran the length of the island. "How's Dunn holding up?" he asked as they walked.

"Hopefully home soon," Mickey said. "Isn't that what all the protestors say they want to do? Bring the troops home?"

They passed the converted garage that housed Farias Sales and Rentals at the corner of 5th Street.

"That's a genius idea," Stellwag said pointing at the beach umbrellas, chairs and inner tubes. "Are they locals?"

"Schoolteachers from Edgewater Park, actually," Mickey replied. "So they have the summer off. Cars are getting smaller, you know. No room to haul all that beach gear from home like the old days. My bet is they're going to make it. Ship Bottom has the Ron-Jon but that's geared more toward the surfing crowd. This is for renters and day-trippers alike. Genius, like you said."

When they got to the bench Mickey sat down. Stellwag remained standing.

"Things are changing out there," he said, squinting.

"Out there, you mean like in the country or what? It is the Age of Aquarius according to the song."

"In the Pines," Stellwag answered, "In the Pines it's still the Dark Ages. I mean, the Barrens have always been a mix of the Wild West and the deep backwoods but our neighbors are upping the game."

"The Druids?"

"For starters," Stellwag said. "They represent something new, Chief."

"And what's that?"

"Absolute disregard for any sort of code."

"No offense, Lieutenant, but is there a code for banging underage girls?" Mickey said. "You guys aren't exactly altar boys."

"No we're not. But we all served. You don't get to join SOS unless you saw action and you were honorably discharged. No offense to Dunn, although I guess that's all been straightened out now. And, you know, we do what we do to get by but there's a line we don't cross. These guys, these guys are different. Way different. Law of the Jungle."

"You scared of them, LT?" Mickey asked. "I don't believe that. Not the Sons of Satan."

"Chief, you can't see what we've seen, do what we've done in the name of our country and ever be scared of anything again. But this is like a pack of rabid dogs. And new dogs show up every month. There's no DMZ in the Pines, Chief. It's gonna come to something. Sooner than later."

"If you give me information about a crime I have to act on it. You know that, right?"

"I'm just giving you a heads up is all," Stellwag countered. "They're hiring themselves out as muscle for the mob and some of the unions. If they start to make inroads there they'll make Murder

Incorporated look like the Little Rascals."
Mickey gazed out at the busy street.
"They're dealing PCP," Mickey said. "I'm sure that's not a news flash to you."
Stellwag dropped his aviator sunglasses back down on the bridge of his nose. "Like they say in the military," he answered after a pause, "I can neither confirm nor deny that."
Mickey chuckled. "If it's OK to ask, what did you do in-country?"
"Little bit of everything," Stellwag said. He sat down next to Mickey. "I started out in demolitions. Then I went to helicopter school. I have what they called 'exceptional spatial awareness' which helps if you go into a spin in a Huey with a platoon or with wounded on board."
Mickey thought about Bunny's story. "Did your helicopter look like a big bug with a glass head?"
Stellwag laughed. "No, like I said, I flew a Huey Iriquois. The Huey's are the ones you see on the TV news all the time. Grass blowing in the rotor wash and Dan Rather or Morley Safer jumping out while they film. I did a few of those missions. We'd drop the cameraman off first and then circle back for the action shot. No, the bird you're describing is a Hiller Killer."
"Hiller Killer?"
"Technically a Hiller OH-Twenty-three Raven gunship. Three man crew. Two thirty-caliber machine guns on the combat version but you could mount stretchers on the skids. That's what we did for med-evacs."
"Pretty deadly?"
"Mostly to the crew. The nickname came from Army Aviation School. It had its share of accidents with pilots in training."
"Could you still fly one?'
"Like riding a bicycle, Chief. Believe me, if I could figure out a way to hide one at our place I would. There's no high ground in the Pines, so air superiority would be key."
Mickey noticed that passersby were looking in their direction.
"It won't hurt your reputation to be seen talking to law enforcement?" Mickey asked.
"Not if it's you," Stellwag replied. "Anyone else, then, yeah, there might be a problem."
"You came here to tell me something," Mickey said. "Let's

walk back."

They stood up and headed toward the station. A young mother with several children in tow was struggling with a beach umbrella, a squalling toddler and a boy in the throes of a temper tantrum.

"I want a boogie board," the child was screaming. "I don't want a raft. Rafts are stupid."

"You heard your dad," the mother said as the umbrella began to open.

Stellwag quickened his pace a grabbed the umbrella just as the wind began to drag it and the woman toward the traffic on the Boulevard.

"Thank you," she said as he folded the fabric back down and secured the tie.

"My husband has been looking for a parking place for an hour." It took her a moment, Mickey noted, to realize that her help had come from an imposing man in motorcycle chaps and a leather vest over a bare and tattooed chest. Mickey quickened her pace to catch up with them.

"Don't be afraid. He's not as dangerous as he looks, ma'am," she said. The relief on the woman's face was obvious.

"Is that a real gun?" The disappointed child had stopped his tantrum.

"Yes it is," Mickey said, placing her hand over the stock of her sidearm.

"You ever shoot anybody?"

"Only if they didn't listen to their mother," Mickey replied. The child's eyes widened.

Mickey heard running footsteps. A small man in a loud print shirt and way-too-short tennis shorts came up to them. His black socks and leather sandals completed what Mickey had come to know as the "Full Shoobie," right down to the plastic Foster Grant clip-on sunglasses.

"Is their trouble officer?" the man asked, decidedly out of breath. "Was this guy bothering my wife?"

Stellwag took a step back and held his hands up.

"No sir," Mickey said. "Everything's fine. The lieutenant was just helping your wife, actually. The beach umbrella was trying to take her for an unplanned ride."

"You really need better parking in this town," the man said, turning to Mickey. "First it's tags just to step on the sand. Then highway robbery for beach equipment. Why, I've a good mind to-"

"Calm down, honey," the woman said. "Remember what Dr. Harman said about your blood pressure."

Mickey decided to intervene.

"I apologize for the parking, Mister –"

"Nepp," the man said, regaining a bit of composure. "Mark Nepp. This is my wife Nancy. We're from Palmyra."

"New Jersey or Pennsylvania?" Mickey asked.

"Pennsylvania. Up by Hershey. What does that-"

Mickey took a conciliatory tone. "We'll you've had a long day on the road already, then. First the Schuylkill Expressway, then traffic on the Walt Whitman bridge, the Parkway and finally the bottleneck at the Causeway. It's a wonder anyone drives here anymore, especially with a car full of kids. I can understand you're being a little frazzled. But Surf City is only one square mile – so unless we start letting people park on the beach I'm afraid there's not much we can do."

"We understand, Officer," Nancy Nepp said. "Thank you for your help, sir."

Stellwag tapped his forehead in a little salute. "She's the Chief of Police, actually," he said. "So you're getting it from the top of the chain of command."

Mickey nodded. "Do you need further help with anything?"

"We're fine," Mark Nepp said. He grabbed the umbrella. The pointed aluminum extension tube promptly fell out and clanked on the pavement.

"I'll get it," said Mickey. She picked it up and handed it to the young boy. "You can use this to fight off sea monsters." The boy reached out with both hands. "Ask the lifeguards for help getting set up," Mickey advised the couple. "Gives them something to do besides talk to girls."

Nancy Nepp mouthed a thank-you and the family toddled off toward the beach.

Mickey and Stellwag resumed walking.

"So?" Mickey asked.

"I'm not sure what it means, if anything," Stellwag answered. He had the confident, unhurried gait of an athlete, Mickey noticed. "But I came across one of the squatters out in the Pines. Old guy I've see poking around junk piles once in a while. Him and his little lean-to were all burnt up. Ashes and bones is all that was left."

"Accident?"

Stellwag stopped about ten feet from his bike.

"Maybe," he said. "Looks like he had moonshine, kerosene, gasoline, paint thinner - all of them what we called 'accelerants' back in my demolition days."

"But?"

"He had this old car seat he must have pulled out of some junker. Used it like a sofa, I guess. Even had seat belts. Not much left of him or it. But funniest thing – I'd swear he was buckled up when he burned."

Mickey considered the information. "What are you telling me?" she asked.

"Something not quite right about it. It was too neat," Stellwag answered. "Too contained. And this guy wasn't just burned, he was incinerated."

"What would do that?"

"Flame thrower, maybe. Napalm would, if it dropped right on you."

"A Willy-Pete grenade?"" Mickey asked, using military slang for white phosphorous.

"I didn't see a crater or any casing fragments," Stellwag said. "But it did cross my mind. Given the past history out there. That's why I thought you should know."

Mickey brushed her hair down over her ear.

"It's not my jurisdiction and unless somebody reports it-"

"Nobody's going to report it," Stellwag replied. "Mention it to Dunn when he gets back. And tell him he owes me a beer."

Mickey looked at her watch. "He's supposed to call me today between one and two o'clock. Hope it's to tell me he's coming home soon."

"They'll be listening, you know."

"Yeah. That's what he said. This'll have to wait until he's back, I guess." She looked at the big Harley. Something about it tickled at her brain. Stellwag spoke again.

""The other thing about this guy," he said and then paused. "His jawbone was stuck open. Means he was screaming when he died. Buckled up and screaming. You know what feeling the vibe means?"

Mickey nodded. "Ronnie talked about it."

"OK, then," Stellwag said.

"OK, then," Mickey answered. "Thanks for the info. And you need to wash your bike. Nothing cool about an ElectraGlide in Light Brown."

"That storm couple days ago turned a lot of trails in the Barrens into pure mud," Stellwag said. "They're just now starting to dry out." He mounted the Harley and kick-started the engine, twisting the throttle until it reached an ear-splitting roar. Pedestrians stopped and stared. He gave Mickey the peace sign and then peeled out in a hail of sand and shells.

It was mud that had caught her eye, she realized. Dried mud on the fenders and the gas tank. What was it Patsy had said about the phantom pick-up truck? It had a funny kind of mud on it. A lighter mud.

There are no such things as ghosts, she told herself.

But now, she realized, Stellwag wasn't the only one feeling the vibe.

Twenty-Five

Somewhere over North Carolina
Altitude 7,280 ft, Speed 320 mph
Heading NE 3

The Douglas C-124C Globemaster II was built, Ronnie guessed, only a few years after he was born, a thought which he found not at all comforting. He was strapped into a cargo net strung against the starboard fuselage and was sure that all his dental fillings had come loose in the roughly forty-five minutes they'd been airborne. With the exception of a battered jeep, Ronnie and his escort, it appeared, were the only cargo in the cavernous hold. There were windows on both sides and a cold, gray light filtered in.

They had, as promised, awakened him at zero-dark-thirty but only, it appeared, so they could spirit him off the base-proper before reveille. He'd spent the bulk of the morning drinking lukewarm coffee in a dingy hut at Lawson Army Airfield.

To his amazement, the Military Policeman assigned to accompany him back to New Jersey's McGuire Air Force Base was blissfully asleep next to him. The M.P. had introduced himself as Staff Sergeant Dale Gibson from Prophetstown, Illinois. Ronnie had started walking toward the giant C-141 Starlifter cargo plane, the familiar "Hanoi Taxi," back at Lawson when Gibson redirected him.

"No such luck," Gibson had said on the steaming tarmac. ""We're booked on Old Shaky. At least it's got a heater." The Globemaster was still huge but it lacked the sleek, sweptback lines and, more importantly, the jet engines of the Starlifter. He thought the black thimble that housed the avionics on the Globemaster looked like the nose on the cartoon dog Snoopy.

In the few minutes they'd had to converse, Gibson had been pleasant. His brother, he'd told Ronnie, was going to school to learn how to operate some kind of heart-lung pump at a big hospital down in Texas. Gibson said he was planning to do the same when his hitch was up. He said his brother had told him running the machine wasn't all that hard to figure out but that the heart surgeons were all "complete fucking assholes." Just like officers, he'd added for good measure.

Ronnie shared how his two years at Ocean County College and his prior military service had recently gotten him a job with the New Jersey Forest Fire Service and how he'd been assigned to Division B in the Pine Barrens. He was working to qualify as an Incident Commander and the State had promised him his job would still be there when he returned from duty. His employment had put him and his agency squarely in the middle of an ongoing and pitched battle between heavily moneyed real-estate developers who wanted to build a supersonic jetport in the Pines and a group of people who started calling themselves conservationists and who saw the vast wilderness as something more than just a million acres of wasted, non-arable land. Fifty square miles of asphalt seemed to be a smart solution, the developers argued to the Port Authorities of New York and New Jersey, and the complex they envisioned would be bigger than the John F. Kennedy, LaGuardia and Newark airports combined. They predicted the project would span a new city of a quarter-million people smack-dab in what was now the real middle of nowhere. Ronnie told Gibson he was squarely on the side trying to preserve the area but his main interest was in the role forest fires played in the natural life cycle of the Pines. The other book in his duffel bag was a tattered and well-thumbed copy of Rachel Carson's "Silent Spring."

"You some kind of ee-cologist, then?" Gibson had asked him.

Ronnie had said no. He tried to explain how he'd come to believe that the seasonal wildfires were the forest's way of renewing itself by burning off the deadfall and ground debris that inhibited the growth of saplings and of new plants by preventing sunlight from reaching the forest floor. Gibson had seemed unimpressed.

"You need to get a job in Watts, baby," Gibson had chided,

referring to the riots and arson in Los Angeles in 1965. "Burn, baby, burn. That's your gig. Shit, man, you tell people you want to stand by and watch a fire burn and I bet Smokey the Bear will show up and personally beat your ass with that motherfuckin' shovel of his."

Before Ronnie could answer the four big turbo-prop engines, each capable of generating nearly four-thousand horsepower, had started churning. The noise and the vibration put a rapid end to any further conversation.

As the plane lifted off he'd thought about how he'd handle his arrival, since no one knew he was homebound and there was no one at the Air Force Base, where they would touch down, nor at nearby Fort Dix, where he'd be processed out of the U.S. Army once again, to meet him. It would normally be about an hour's drive to Long Beach Island. He figured he could hitchhike if he had to.

The multiple cups of coffee had not been a great idea. He scanned the vast cargo deck but did not see any sign of a latrine. His bladder felt like it was the size of a basketball. He tapped Gibson on the shoulder and tried to mouth that he needed to pee. Gibson shook his head, not understanding. Finally Ronnie mimicked holding his joint with one hand a flushing a urinal with the other. Gibson grinned and reached to his right, producing an empty coffee can.

Acme Eight O'Clock brand, Ronnie noticed.

He was going home.

♦ ♦ ♦

Mud City
New Jersey Mainland

For once Dickie had proven to be smarter, Brinson thought. Dickie had chosen to bivouac in the weeds off what the bent and rusting sign said was Bay Avenue. Brinson had gotten the Road Runner's passenger seat to recline almost all the way back and actually fallen asleep quite quickly. Whatever position he'd been in had played havoc with his neck and now he noticed he had trouble turning his head to the left.

"Jesus, this place stinks," Brinson said trying to rub out the crick.

"Smells like home to me," Dickie replied, rinsing his mouth with the remnants of the Giant-Sized Coca Cola from the drive-in.

"I didn't know New Jersey had a bayou."

"I don't think that's what they call it," Brinson said.

Brinson went to the car and pulled out the road map they'd picked up at a grimy Atlantic station with two pumps and a one-lift garage run by, according to the sign, the Yansick brothers.

"How come we ain't heard from that dipshit Hopwood? Christ, Harlan, what if one of 'em broke down and told him where the shit was and how to get it? He could to go into business for himself. Then we're screwed."

"Harry'd never try it. He knows how it would end for him," Brinson said. "Besides, we haven't exactly been in radar range. You don't happen to have a phone that would let us call from the car, do you?"

"Only James Bond has one of those."

"Well, you aren't James Bond and neither is Harry."

"And neither of them rooms in Portland had a phone," Dickie said.

"There was a pay phone in the lobby. I got the number before we left. I told him to be near it at oh-nine- hundred." Brinson looked at his watch. "That's an hour. Let's get some chow and check out this island. Maybe we'll get lucky. Now let's see where we are."

"We're in Mud City," Dickie said. "At least according to the kid at the drive-in. Said down this road there's a bay and an old wooden bridge that takes you across to an island." He pointed into the climbing sun. "And I bet that there bay is just chock full'a crabs and crawdads. Man, if I had my pirogue, some line and a few fish heads we could eat for a week." He walked behind the car and opened the trunk.

"What plates did you get?" Brinson asked.

"Wadn't a lot to choose from, exactly. I got a Jersey one for the front and a Pennsylvania one for the back. Figgered cops only ever look at your plates comin' or goin', not both."

Harlan Brinson had aced every test he'd ever taken and so it pained him to admit, even if it was only to himself, that Dickie Robichaux might not be as dumb as he was counting on. It was not a comforting thought.

"They ain't all going to fit in this trunk," Dickie said.

"Just the woman and the kid need to," Brinson answered. "Winston will have to – what's it say in that book about the Mafia – sleep with the fish?" Brinson studied the map. "Where'd you put our supplies?" They had stopped at a Two Guys Department Store in Newark and picked up rope, heavy duct-wrapping tape, plastic tarps, two hunting knives and a gallon of bleach.

"I put 'em in the well with the spare," Dickie answered. He slammed down the trunk. "You know, maybe with my half of the money I could open a little place right here. "Dickie's Crab Shack or maybe Chez Robichaux. Plant some cypress trees. Hire a few of my coonass cousins to shrimp and fish and go crabbing. I would cook it right off the boat, right out of the crab pots. Chez Robichaux – I kind'a like the sound of that. Maybe even bring mee-maw up from the parish. If there's only one way on and off, I'd get the tourists comin' and goin'."

"First we get the bricks. Then we get the money. Then you can get the tourists."

"Where are they? The bricks?" Dickie asked. "Do we even know for sure?"

"Winston flew into Philadelphia on a Hanoi Taxi. That's where he was supposed to stash them, remember? At the airport or a bus or a train station. Then he drove up to Portland and was supposed to bring us the location and the key or the combination and get the woman and the girl in return."

"I got all that, Harlan. But there ain't no *garontee* that he didn't deal them on his own."

"That's why we need the kid. That little gook brat is the key, whether she has the actual key or not. Winston will give us the bricks if it means saving her and the woman."

"You was the one s'posed to be watchin' her when she went MIA."

"You don't need to remind me, Private."

"And don't pull that rank shit with me anymore, Harlan. Those days are done. I killed *beaucoup* people with my bare hands and you ain't. So when it comes time you know I'll be the one getting' wet, not you."

Brinson decided to let it go. Dickie came around, unzipped himself and started to take a leak on the asphalt not far from Brinson's boots.

"How do we know the kid's on this island again?" Dickie

asked, shaking his member several times.

"Hopwood found part of a phone number in one Winston's pockets. Called the Bell Telephone Operator and asked where the area code was. He only had the word after that which was Hyacinth. The Operator told him it was Southern New Jersey and Hyacinth meant the first two numbers had to be four and nine. That meant somewhere on this place called Long Beach Island."

"We know who he was trying to call?"

"No. Winston's from Virginia so it's not family. But it has to be where they sent the kid. Maybe to let someone know she was coming."

"Let's hope so," Dickie said. "How far to this island?"

"Just a few miles," Brinson replied. "If this is Bay Avenue then we just keep heading east. It'll turn into Route 72 up ahead and take us into some town called Ship Bottom."

"What the fuck kind of name is Ship Bottom?"

"Well, the other ones are Harvey Cedars, Loveladies and Barnegat. Looks like Barnegat might have a lighthouse. Ever been to a lighthouse, Dickie?"

"Never. Let's go there first and recon from the high point like they always taught us to do. Get some chow, maybe."

Brinson was still looking at the map. "There's a town called Surf City. Wonder if it's the same one in that Beach Boys song."

"Ain't the Beach Boys from New Jersey?"

"No, Dickie, that's the Four Seasons. The Beach Boys are from California."

"Yeah, well, I don't think either of them are even around anymore, are they?"

"I think they still are," Brinson said.

"Well, I'm bettin' not for long," Dickie said, zipping up. "I'd go see The Monkees, though."

"The Monkees? Seriously."

"Shit," Dickie said. "You know much young tail there is at a Monkees concert?"

"OK. Now it makes sense," Brinson replied. He refolded the map and rubbed at his neck again. "Let's find a place to eat. I didn't hear anything on the Philly radio stations about your little indiscretion. There's a station out of New York City, WABC, but the reception was really bad. We'll pick up a newspaper." Brinson walked back, fiddled with the passenger seat to bring it upright and slid in. "That was really stupid, Dickie," he said as he pulled the door shut. "I hope you haven't fucked us."

Dickie ignored him. "You just navigate," he said, climbing behind the wheel. "And Harlan?"

"Yeah?"

"We still got work to do. Let's say we let bygones be bygones and move on. OK, *partner*?"

Brinson did not miss Dickie leaning hard on the last word.

"You should'a stayed awake for that midnight show, Harlan. It was about a guy back from World War Two who runs moonshine while the cops are tryin' to catch him. Kind'a like us a little, don't you think?"

"I've seen it before. But that movie's got to be ten years old. I liked Robert Mitchum better in 'Cape Fear.'"

"Did you know he wrote and sung the theme song?" Dickie asked

"Thunder Road?'"

"Well, I guess it's actually called 'The Ballad of Thunder Road,' but yeah. That was Robert Mitchum himself singin' it in the movie."

"I think I'd have just called it 'Thunder Road,'" Brinson said. "Catchier title for a song if you ask me."

"Well, good thing he didn't ask you," Dickie shot back. "When are you gonna call Hopwood?"

"After we eat," Brinson replied. "It's going to be a killer in the sun today." He refolded the map. The radio came on loud when Dickie started the engine. Roy Orbison's "Only the Lonely" poured from the dashboard speakers. Brinson punched one of the silver buttons to change the station. The electrified chords of "Bad Moon Rising" tumbled out and Brinson began to sing along. The interior of the Plymouth was steaming and he and Dickie both rolled down their windows to let the wind blow back and through.

Brinson didn't care much for the anti-war "Fortunate Son" but, he decided, he and John Fogerty did agree with on one thing.

They both saw trouble on the way.

♦ ♦ ♦

Surf City

The line at the counter inside Bill's Luncheonette was almost to the door. Mickey had already declined several offers to jump ahead.

"I can wait my turn," she repeated.

When she was in sight of the old NCR cash register a voice called out.

"Chief," it said from one of the booths behind her. "A moment of your time, perhaps."

She turned and saw Mike Gannon waving to her. Despite being alone he had two mugs of coffee and several doughnuts on the Formica table in front of him.

Bill Kuriakos, the owner and proprietor of the tiny business, caught her eye and pointed to the table where Gannon sat. "Hey, Chief Mee-kee. See? He already buy for you," Kuriakos said in a thick, first generation Greek accent. "I tell him you will be here!"

Mickey ducked her shoulders and twisted her body out of the tight queue and toward the upholstered booth.

"Lucky guess," she said. "Cops and doughnuts? Really?"

"Too cliché, remember?" Gannon said with a smile. "Cops and caffiene. That combination has always worked for me. This is a great place, you know. Corner location, pick stucco exterior and striped aluminum awnings – I'd say you couldn't miss it if you tried." Gannon pushed the heavy white mug toward her. "Two sugars and half-and-half if I'm not mistaken?"

Mickey took the cup. "You've obviously been talking to-"

"Doreen," Gannon said, completing the sentence. "We had a lovely supper at the Acme Hotel and then after-dinner drinks at Zorba's Diner. She thinks the world of you. You must know that."

Mickey grimaced. "You took advantage of her sweet nature and pumped her for information. Tell me I'm wrong."

Gannon chuckled. "Nothing of the sort, my dear Chief Cleary. She was most interested in the ins and outs of the newspaper business, especially investigative journalism. One subject just led to another."

"The other subject being-"

"French cruller?" Gannon asked, holding up a frosted pinwheel doughnut. "I have to admit, these are nothing short of addicting. Although they're not your favorite."

Mickey took the doughnut and dunked it in her coffee.

Gannon smiled. "Your favorite doughnuts are the cream-filled ones that come only from the L & M Bakery in Delran, New Jersey, although you don't discriminate between the powdered and the crystal sugar-covered varieties. I've had them myself. They are truly incredible and likely just as if not more addicting than Comrade Bill's."

Mickey pursed her lips. "I think the bakery you're referring to is in Riverside, not Delran. And Bill is Greek, not Russian."

Gannon's smile broadened. "A common misconception and an ethnic error on my part," he said. "But the bakery really is in Delran, a quiet burg quaintly named for the two local rivers, the Delaware and the Rancocas. Don't ever mistake my journalistic flair for a lack of attention to detail. That little bakery sits exactly one block from the dividing line between the two towns, but it's squarely on the Delran side. You can't get near it on a Sunday morning when the Masses let out."

"The other subject being-"

Gannon blew on his mug theatrically. The he reached inside his jacket and pulled out a notebook.

"I had two, or maybe it was three White Russians – a concoction that aspires to greatness but will never achieve cultural significance in the pantheon of American cocktails – so my notes are a little hazy." He thumbed through the small, leather-bound book. "Stop me when I come to something that's patently false."

Mickey took a bite of the sopping cruller and waited.

"Late Spring, 1967. You're the new Police Chief, much to the consternation of the Borough Council but to the apparent delight of Mayor Billy Tunell, a.k.a. the Laundromat King of Long Beach Island." Gannon flipped a page. "Before the summer season even starts, the dead and somewhat mangled body of one Dante D. Ragone, Junior, sole scion of reputed Philadelphia Mafioso Dante D. "Danny Rags" Ragone, Sr., mysteriously appears on a Surf City beach. *Your* Surf City beach, as it were. A boating accident is strongly suspected but as the new Chief, and almost a year removed from a stint as one of the first female beat cops in Philadelphia, you decide you are going to pursue an investigation to rule out, shall we say, malice afterthought and murder most foul, possibly connected to the vagaries and vicissitudes of the *paterfamilias'* organized crime conflicts. How am I doing so far?"

Mickey sipped at her coffee and said nothing.

"Great," Gannon continued. "So over the course of the next thirty six hours, the body of the decedent vanishes, your only Deputy is found dead in his rented lodgings, not one but *two* FBI agents meet their maker in your station house and your father, a decorated ex-Philly cop himself, is grievously wounded, having driven all the way to Long Beach Island from the Great Northeast, presumably on a mission to rescue his only daughter."

Mickey finished the doughnut.

"So far, so good then," Gannon said. He took a long swallow of his coffee. "Now here's where I'm having trouble with the time line. Several hours after these events transpire you ride into town, looking visibly worse for the wear shall we say, on the back of an English motorcycle driven by a young Viet Nam veteran who may or may not now be your paramour, escorted by a veritable phalanx of outlaw bikers. Members of the so-called Sons of Satan, a sinister although alliterative sobriquet I only wish I could take credit for. The New Jersey State Police along with the high-ranking members of the FBI arrive and temporarily lock you up, in your own jail I should add, on suspicion of the murder of the boy and at least one if not both of the federal agents. How am I doing? Am I hitting all the high points?"

"It sounds like a really bad first novel," Mickey replied.

"Agreed," Gannon said. "A terrible one, actually. But that's what's fascinating. It's so unbelievable, so outlandish, so, so *contrived*, it almost has to be true."

Mickey laughed and finished her coffee.

"Warm you up, hon?" a waitress in a starched but stained white uniform and a pink, trifolded cap asked.

"Thanks, Connie," Mickey said.

"And for the gentleman?"

"Fill it to the brim, please," Gannon said.

"You mean the rim?" Connie asked as she raised her elbow.

"Sure," Gannon said. "That, too."

The glass Bunn pot was nearly full and some of the coffee splashed out. Mickey grabbed a paper napkin from the black metal dispenser and blotted tiny puddles of it off the table and the silver Seeburg Wall-O-Matic miniature jukebox to Mickey's left that promised 2 Plays for a Quarter. Gannon flipped another page.

"Where was I? Oh, yes, let's see, an armed armada of outlaw

bikers, locked in your own jail cell. Then, *then,* it's suddenly all over. Just like that. Bodies are removed, suspects are released and everybody goes home to, oh, I don't know, play Parcheesi. Or maybe it was Chutes and Ladders."

"Parcheesi," Mickey said. "At least that part you've got right. It was definitely Parcheesi."

"Don't patronize me, Chief," Gannon said.

"OK, no patronizing, even if we are technically patrons at the moment. So what else have you got in your little brown book, Mr. Gannon? And are you going to eat that other cruller?"

Gannon thumbed another page. Mickey reached for the doughnut.

"Oh, yes," Gannon went on, "So, the body of the dead boy, which you unceremoniously stashed in a liquor store cooler– a nice touch by the way – disappears and then, as if by magic, shows up in South Philly where a funeral service that would shame an Egyptian Pharaoh is held, officiated by none other than His Eminence, the Archbishop of Philadelphia, followed by all-you-can-eat fried calamari and fresh-made cannoli. Tears are shed and mourners faint on cue while old dons and new *capos* come all the way from Cleveland to sip anisette. And, coincidentally and contemporaneously, two prominent Ragone crime family associates conveniently disappear, never to be seen or heard from again."

"Disappear?" Mickey said with a mouthful of cruller. "Now I find that hard to believe, Mr. Gannon. It is 1969. No one can just disappear."

"Don't be coy, Chief," Gannon shot back. "You almost did."

Mickey swallowed and pursed her lips. "You should know by now that coy is not in my playbook," she said.

"OK, point taken. But to this very day, Messrs. A. Louis Petroni, Esquire – Danny Rags' loathsome but long-time *consigliore* – and 'Tommy Shots' Caputo, Danny's Hall of Fame hit man, have not been seen alive or kicking by anyone, anywhere."

"The two gentlemen you mention were involved in a dangerous and highly unpredictable business," Mickey answered. "Who's to say? Maybe they're hiding in Sicily. New wives perhaps, even new families. It's all in that best-selling Mafia book, the one about what good guys they really are. How they're just misunderstood."

"I have read 'The Godfather,' Chief, and I would say it's much more likely that Petroni and Caputo are slumbering with the shad than sunning themselves in Sicily. What I'm saying, Chief, is that there's all this, this *carnage* and then, like a goddamned grade-school blackboard, it's all erased. Wiped clean. Poof. Surf City gets a brand-spanking-new modern police station and you get two cream-of-the-crop deputies slash personal bodyguards. "

The bodyguard comment caught Mickey by surprise. She wasn't sure if Gannon noticed so she let it go.

"How could any of that possibly happen in this day and age, Mr. Gannon, when everything we do is written down and typed up in triplicate?" Mickey asked.

"It *happens*, my dear Chief, when the truth is more dangerous and more damaging than the whitewash or the fantasy. Do you really believe for one minute that some dipshit Commie sympathizer killed JFK all by himself? Fired all those shots in succession with a bolt-action rifle at a moving target nearly three-hundred feet away with pinpoint accuracy?"

"That's what the Warren Commission says happened," Mickey replied. "Do you know something they don't?"

Gannon snapped the notebook shut.

"Who is everybody protecting, Chief? No offense, but it certainly isn't you. You're just the MacGuffin, the Maltese Falcon if you will. So who is it? Ted Williams? Johnny Callison? Neil fucking Armstrong?"

A couple of customers glanced over at the utterance of the obscenity.

"OK, now you're just spitballing," Mickey said. "And you leave Johnny Callison out of this. He won the All-Star Game with that dinger in '64. Only Williams and Musial had done that before. Maybe it's Richie Allen."

"Unlikely. The Phillies don't protect him on the field, much as less off," Gannon answered. "Some guy in the bleachers at Connie Mack threw batteries at him. Batteries, for God's sake. He has to wear a helmet in the field. At *home*." Gannon shook his head in dismay. "A truly towering talent but totally misunderstood and unconscionably underappreciated. He'll be in the Hall someday – you mark my words. And, in case you ever run into him, he prefers to go by Dick Allen – says Richie is a child's name the sportswriters stuck him with."

"Maybe in fifty years he'll be in the Hall," Mickey said. "Maybe not. It's an unjust world and it's not getting any better, at least not that I can tell. And as far as your conspiracy ideas –"

"Chief," Gannon persisted, "This whole country is built on conspiracies and cover-ups. The biggest lies are the true ones. It's the basis of our entire political system and the reason journalism as we know it exists. You think you're ever going to hear what really happened in *My Lai*? You think you're ever going to find out exactly what Nixon and Kissinger are up to in Cambodia? There are people out there saying that this whole moon landing thing was faked – directed by Stanley Kubrick and shot on a soundstage at MGM or some Warner Brothers back lot. All I want is the truth, Chief. Just one time. *This* time. Why is that too much to ask?"

Mickey downed her coffee. She willed herself to remain calm but her head was spinning. Where, she wondered, was Gannon getting his information? There was so much that she knew it wasn't coming from Doreen.

"I do appreciate the coffee and the crullers," Mickey said. "But I'm afraid I can't help you. Nobody's covering anything up. Nobody's protecting anyone. Let me know about the moon landing, though. I'm going to be very disappointed if that didn't happen. I'll never be able to watch Walter Cronkite again." She started to slide out of the booth.

"He told me you'd be a tough nut to crack," Gannon said, shaking his head.

"Who told you?" Mickey asked

"An old friend of yours."

"I have a lot of old friends. On both sides of the river."

"And on both sides of the law, I daresay. This particular one said to remind you that Surf City is just a little drinking town with a big fishing problem."

Mickey put her hand on the back of the booth for support. Doc Guidice. So he was alive, she thought. Gannon put down two crumpled dollars bill for the tip. "Too much?" he asked, looking up at Mickey.

"Yeah. She'll think you're interested in her. Save the other single – it'll get you seven lukewarm beers at The Anchorage over in Somers Point."

"Seven for a dollar?"

"It's their claim to fame. So, this old friend have anything else to say?" Mickey asked.

"Only that simple is always better than complicated, whatever that means. I suspect he's referring to Occam's Razor but he said you'd know." Gannon pushed himself out of the booth. "It'd be simpler if you just told me the truth. I'm going to get it eventually, you know. Better all around if I get it from you."

"I don't think you could handle the truth," Mickey said

Gannon smiled. "I really like that line. Mind if I use it in my story?"

"Sure," Mickey replied. "Just don't say where you got it."

"He says you're a hero, Chief. That's the story I want to write. The story of a hero."

"You like old movies, Mr. Gannon?"

"I happen to love old movies, Chief Cleary. Why do you ask?"

"While you're on the Island check out the matinee at the Colony Theatre over in Brant Beach. It's just the other side of Ship Bottom on the Boulevard. Steve McQueen, Bobby Darrin. It's about what happens to soldiers in a war. You know it?"

"I know it well," Gannon replied. "'Hell is for Heroes. 1962, if I'm not mistaken.'"

"You want to write your story, write it about someone who deserves it," Mickey said, turning to leave. "I'm no hero, Mike. I'm just a beach cop. I would think seriously about the novel, though. I'd read that."

"Female protagonists don't sell in the fiction market," Gannon replied.

"So say the male writers," Mickey answered. "Enjoy your time on LBI – America's Riviera according to our mayor."

She nodded to Bill Kuriakos and walked out.

◆ ◆ ◆

Hammonton Township, NJ
Just Outside the Pine Barrens

Cowboy Barstow dreaded the knock he knew was coming. But he was ready.

His little library had proved its value, the answer coming from an old tome he'd picked up at the Flea Market in Rancocas. Modern fuses and firing solutions reveled in complexity, he thought. The old books were printed when state-of-the-art meant hand built and advanced technology implied only that there were one or two moving parts.

Cowboy knew he was taking an incredible risk, one that could easily backfire in every sense of the term. But it was the idea of a backfire that had sent him searching the dusty pages deep into the night and found him hunched over his battered workbench as dawn filtered in.

What he'd constructed was simple and even an ogre like BoDean, he decided, could manage the simple manual tasks needed to connect and actuate it. He pushed out thoughts of the consequences if it didn't work or, worse, if he'd miscalculated the proportions.

Although his father had been a fire-and-brimstone Baptist preacher, Cowboy did not think of himself as a religious man. But he wafted a silent prayer to whatever deities there were, asking that they grant him this one success. He had known and feared Billy Bowker and so had steered clear of him. But Billy had never asked anything of him and Cowboy had never offered. Now BoDean, Billy's fraternal but nonetheless physically similar twin had suddenly become something of a customer. An unwanted customer who, Cowboy knew, would insist on repeat business as long as the product performed.

Cowboy smelled burnt coffee. He went to the narrow sunlit kitchen and unplugged the percolator which had boiled dry sometime in the night. He'd been reminded repeatedly from a young age that he was born a sinner. He wondered if his act would turn out to be just another soot smudge on his once-alabaster soul or would it finally be one of amends and repentance?

His thoughts lingered on the question until he heard the rustle of tires turning off the gravel road.

Twenty-Six

Surf City

Mickey was surprised to see Rodriguez already at his desk when she walked in. His head was propped up on one balled fist and she couldn't tell if he was awake or asleep.

His head tilted up when she pulled the station door shut.

"Rough night?" Mickey asked.

"You could say that," Rodriguez answered, rubbing at his eyes. "Dip and Charlie got more sleep than I did and they were working."

Mickey went over to the new Farberware double-pot percolator Mayor Billy had bought for them and started to work on a fresh brew.

"So, if I can ask, how did the sleep-over go?"

Rodriguez ran both hands through his wavy dark hair and laughed. "Yeah, well, sleep was not the operative concept. Talking, giggling, screaming, whispering – yup, those we had plenty of let's say. Sleep –" he looked at his watch. "I'd say sleep arrived about an hour ago. You don't need her back right away, do you? 'Cause she's out like a light."

"Not if she's sleep-deprived, I don't," Mickey said. "But do you need to go home and sack out for a few hours?"

Rodriguez stretched and rolled his neck in the way Mickey knew as peculiar to football players and athletes in general.

"If no one takes offense, I'll take a nap on one of the cell bunks before the crime wave hits. It is Friday, you know, Chief."

The radio on his desk was turned to a low but audible volume. Three Dog Night's "One" was playing. Mickey had spent the night alone in her bed. She thought she had finally gotten used to the empty space where Ronnie laid but in the wee hours she had found herself patting the bed next to her to see if Bunny was there. She wondered why she suddenly missed those two bony knees in poking her rib cage.

"I think we'll all be OK with that. What time does Dip come back on?"

"Three by the book. He said if it was quiet he'd be back after lunch. I think he has a girl. Which is good. I was starting to wonder, you know?"

"Dip?" Mickey said as the percolator steamed and hissed.

"Nah, not Dip. He's a Boy Scout. Merit badges, sash and all." Kaylen Fairbrother flashed through her mind as she said it.

"Yeah, well he let it slip that he liked Liberace."

"That's insufficient evidence, I'm afraid," Mickey replied. "Now, if he comes in with sequins on his uniform or puts a candelabra on his desk, then that's a different story."

Rodriguez stood up and smoothed non-existent wrinkles in his uniform blouse.

"Please don't tell me Colombia got up early to iron that for you."

"Damn right she did," Rodriguez answered. "She takes more pride in my appearance than I do to be honest. She would'a killed me if she knew I walked out with a wrinkled blouse."

Mickey listened to the percolator's staccato burps and hummed along with the radio. "Three Dog Night," she said. "Not as strange as Strawberry Alarm Clock I suppose, but still."

"Charlie – who else but Charlie? The guy's a damned encyclopedia, I swear. Anyway, Charlie told me it's an Eskimo saying – means a really cold night. Says when they're out on the ice hunting seals or whales or whatever they eat that they sleep with their sled dogs – you know, for the body heat. So they grade the nights by how many dogs it takes to keep them warm."

"That'll be helpful if I'm ever a contestant on 'Jeapordy,'" Mickey said. "Eskimo Sayings for twenty, Art." The percolator hissed and she waited until it sounded the last drops had perc'ed. "Rich, can I ask you a personal question?"

"Rodriguez laughed. "Guess it depends on how personal."

Mickey poured herself a mug. "Professionally personal, I guess."

"Sure. Ask away."

"Do you ever feel like you and Charlie were hired to be not just my deputies but my, um, bodyguards?"

"Did you say 'bodyguards,' Chief?"

"Yeah, bodyguards." She studied Rodriguez intently. The word had struck home, if only for an instant, but she did not miss it.

"I'm your deputy, Chief Cleary. You do not strike me as someone who needs a bodyguard if any of the scuttlebutt is even halfway true. And while we're on the subject, is it?"

"No, seriously. It can't escape you that you're pretty overqualified for this job. Charlie, too. Why did you take it? Do any of your cop friends report to a woman?"

"Just their wives and girlfriends, ma'am, sometimes both."

"OK, that's funny but I'm asking you a straight-up, and off-the-record question here, Rich. Come on, level with me."

"Look, Chief, this is a great job. My wife is from Puerto Rico and she grew up on a beach. This is a nice safe town that only gets crazy three months out of the year. The rugrats love it here and they go back to the island, P.R. that is, every other month in the winter to see Colombia's parents and they go to a beach there. Charlie can drive to Carolina in a day if he wants to. I see my wife every night and I don't get shot at – so I guess I don't understand the question, if you want me to really level with you."

"OK," Mickey said, adding powdered creamer to her mug, "Just forget I said anything."

"If you think about it," Rodriguez continued, "we're all bodyguards. For each other. That's why they wanted a department roster of four. We're always looking out for you but we know you're always looking out for us. Make sense?"

Mickey poured in the sugar from a glass dispenser she'd "borrowed" from Bill's Luncheonette.

"OK," she said. "So... the non-sleeping part of things went well?"

"They named her Princess Bonnie, so you might have to deal with that. Oh, and she learned 'Be My Little Baby' from the record player and my wife's collection of 45's so you also might be hearing that a lot. And, um, it might be in Spanish."

"The Ronettes? Little young for sappy teen love songs aren't they?" Mickey asked.

"They sing it to their dolls, Chief. *Dios mio.* You got a lot to learn about kids."

Mickey went to her desk and sat down.

"Oh yeah, I put something in your top drawer," Rodriguez said. "A guy dropped it about half an hour before you got here. Said you'd remember him from Tony Mart's – Double D?"

"Doug Doucette," Mickey said reaching for the drawer handle. "Tony's floor manager. Scraggly long hair, tie-dyed t-shirt, right? I thought he'd be at that music festival up in New York I read about. The one with all the mud and the naked hippies doing it in public."

"No, this guy had styled hair and was pretty snappily dressed. Had one of those little alligators on his shirt. Said to tell you he's a record producer now and the tickets are a little gift from him and Tony. There's also a note."

Mickey pulled the envelope out. It was embossed with the Tony Mart's logo,

"Showplace of the World." She reached inside and withdrew the two tickets.

"Tom Jones or Englebert?" Rodriguez asked with a grin.

"Neither. Linda Ronstadt and some guy named Jackson Browne who's I guess opening for her. September the twenty-fourth at – get this – a place called the Troubadour in West Hollywood."

"Florida?"

"Try California," Mickey said. "Yeah. Like I can afford that."

"Oh, yeah. He also said they'd fly you and a friend out – that part was Tony's treat, I guess. I'm your friend, right, Chief? Be good to have a bodyguard in Hollywood."

Mickey thought of the year she'd taken off after the horrific shooting at K & A, fixing cars and growing dope in Northern California. "OK. If Dunn's not back by then you're hired," she said.

"That's another thing I meant to tell you," Rodriguez said. He walked into one of the two open cells and sat on the bunk. "Your little Bunny seemed really happy. But just before they all crashed she said 'Dunn come home.' She know something you don't?"

"Just wishful thinking, I'm afraid," Mickey answered. "Let her believe it for now, I guess. I'm beginning to think that little girl has seen more horrible things than all of us here put together."

"Did you know she never owned a doll?"

"No, but it doesn't surprise me. Did she tell you one of Dunn's buddies let her fire a fifty-caliber machine gun?"

"No, that didn't come up, fortunately. Anyway, the rugrats gave Princess Bonnie one of their dolls and her crown, just so you know she didn't take them. What did the note say?"

Mickey reached back inside and pulled out the folded paper.

"Are we going somewhere after we get back from California?" Rodriguez called over.

"This would be before California it looks like. And this is something at the other Jersey shore – some club north of Asbury Park. Place called, ready? Pandemonium in Wanamassa. Wanamassa? I've never heard of it. But we're supposed to see a band called Child. Says I'll recognize the lead singer right away."

All Mickey could think of was the skinny kid she'd met sweeping the floor at Tony Marts back in '67. Double D had called him "the boss."

"Apparently you looked the other way on a possible Child Labor Law infraction at the club. This guy said you might have changed the direction of American music."

"Yeah, well I guess we'll see about that," Mickey replied. "He was just a nice kid with a broom." She put the tickets, the note and the envelope back in the drawer. It squeaked shut when she pushed on it.

"He said Bob Dylan stole their band. Did you know that?"

"Who's band?"

"The house band. At Tony Mart's. Leon and the Hawks."

"Levon and the Hawks," Mickey corrected. "And how exactly do you steal a band?"

Rodriguez flashed the universal sign for cash, rubbing his thumb across his fingertips.

"Too bad. They were rockers."

"You'll like their new name better."

"Only if you tell me it's not Moby Grape or Thunderclap Newman."

"Nope. They're 'The Band. Just, 'The Band.'"

"Someone just told me that simplest thing is always best. Can't get simpler than 'The Band.'"

"Simple doesn't always mean successful. So Dunn's not coming home today, I take it?"

Mickey frowned. "I just talked to him yesterday and he didn't say anything about it." She picked up a pencil and twirled it in her fingers. "I've got to figure out what to do with Bunny. I don't think she can handle any more tragedy."

"Tragedy?" Rodriguez said, stretching his frame out on the bunk. "What tragedy are we talking about?"

"As soon as I have a few of the missing pieces I'll fill you guys in and maybe we can come up with a plan. What's that saying - the Devil is in the details?"

"The Devil is in a lot of things these days, Chief. I wish it was only the details," Rodriguez said before closing his eyes.

He was right, Mickey thought. The Sons of Satan, The Druids, the Jersey Devil and the late Billy Bowker. All of them intersecting in the Pine Barrens, a place which for several hours had shown her what Hell on earth looked like. Charlie was right as well and that's what worried her – nowadays. It seemed, there was just too much sympathy for the Devil.

♦ ♦ ♦

Portland, Maine

"We need to get going," Declan Winston said.

Yvette looked at her wrists. The indentations from the plastic ties were fading but still visible and her fingers still didn't feel right. She fumbled with two hands to sip the tea Winston had brought her. He held the cup gently to her lips and she began to cry.

"You think Bunny made it?" Yvette asked. Winston set down the cup, took her hands in his and massaged them. 'You hear anything from your friend? *Tu parlez?*"

"No, but Bunny always gets where she's going," Winston answered. "Now it's our turn."

"What about-"

"Someone is coming to collect Private Hopwood and tidy up. I found us a car while you were sleeping. But Harlan and Dickie have almost a whole day start on us."

"Do they know where Bunny is?"

"They might have an idea. I had Dunn's phone number on a note in my pocket. I had torn it in half but there was probably enough there to give them the general vicinity."

"They have your friend's name, though." She felt her hands

begin to warm up under Winston's ministrations.

"No, it was just part of a number. I know where Dunn lives. They don't. Even if they make it to New Jersey they'll have to look for her. Dunn will understand he needs to keep her under wraps. That will let us make up their head start but we need to leave now."

"They hurt you," Yvette said. "They say they cut you with K-Bar, use electric shocks."

"They didn't do any of that – they just wanted me to yell so you would give up where Bunny was or where the key was hidden. Guys in my unit did worse to me for dogging it on maneuvers."

Yvette flexed and extended her long, thin fingers several times. Tentatively she grasped the cup of tea. This time she was able to lift and hold it. She brought it to her lips and took a sip of the cooling brew.

"Where the key they want? Bunny doesn't have it."

Winston lifted up his shirt. A tattooed American Eagle held a writhing serpent in its beak, the snake's tail curling around his navel.

"I was just afraid they were going to take me to get X-rayed next," he said.

◆ ◆ ◆

McGuire AFB
Wrightstown, NJ

Ronnie had tried to sleep but the bone-rattling vibration that earned the aging Globemaster airframe the nickname "Old Shaky" refused to let him. It was just as well, he thought. His musings glided between the carnal and the practical. Mickey had read him the note from Declan Winston. When he felt the C-141 throttle down, indicating the first part of their descent, he began to focus more on the practical. First he head to get home. He hoped the Army would facilitate that but he knew that even if you loved the Army, which he did not, even then it would never love you back, so he wasn't counting on it. A lot of servicemen and women came and went through McGuire, he figured, so maybe he could catch a bus or even call a cab once he was through with the paperwork at Fort Dix.

His thoughts turned to the little girl Mickey called Bunny.

Declan had told him about his plans for the woman he'd met and fallen in love with and her daughter. The irony that they had narrowly avoided the massacre which still held Ronnie in its grip was almost beyond his comprehension. He knew Declan wanted them out of the Viet Nam quickly, before the incoming salvos of repercussions arrived and eyewitnesses conveniently disappeared. Declan did not want them testifying to anything, a sentiment Ronnie understood. The one constant in Army life had always been "payback is hell."

He decided he'd use the rest of the flight to map out a strategy to protect the girl. He didn't know the names Mickey had read to him but had heard the stories: Want your new bride or girlfriend out on the next plane? Here's a little package for you to take with you on your Freedom Bird flight. Deliver it as instructed and your family will be waiting for you. Something had gone south, Ronnie understood that. How far south? He hoped he'd know that by the end of the day. The descent smoothed out the vibrations a bit and Ronnie felt himself finally nodding off. The practical then yielded to the carnal as the big Pratt & Whitney engines droned on but at a lower and, somehow he thought, a more soothing pitch.

◆ ◆ ◆

Ship Bottom, NJ

Mickey stopped at the new Dunkin Donuts on the Boulevard and picked up two cups of coffee and a half-dozen of the jelly doughnuts her dad favored.

When she arrived, his door, she noticed, was open.

"Roll call, Sergeant Cleary," Mickey called. "Literally." She shook the small white cardboard box which she held by the four-square string the pretty young girl behind the counter had tied on.

Hearing nothing, she walked into the small kitchen and sat the box down on the yellow table with its matching set of two hard-worn padded metal chairs.

"Hey, Dad," she called. "Coffee and jelly doughnuts. Going once."

"Out back, Michaela," a voice responded.

Mickey slid past the bedroom door toward the rear of the little house where her dad stood in boxer shorts and a white U-shirt.

"I'm afraid you're out of uniform," Mickey said.

"Ahh, it's OK. I got friends at the top," Patsy answered.

Mickey's shoes crunched softly on the crushed seashells that covered the entirety of the tiny backyard. There was no fence and Mickey watched as a neighbor's square umbrella-style clothesline creaked and rotated in the offshore breeze. Housedresses, aprons and several pairs of enormous panties fluttered with each turn. Mickey held out one of the cardboard cups and pulled off the lid. She thought she heard something in the far corner of the yard, behind some scrub bushes that Ronnie had planted for Patsy to mark the property line.

"You could prob'ly rig a spinnaker with a pair of them undies," Patsy said and reached for the coffee.

Mickey laughed. "I didn't know spinnaker was in your vocabulary."

"My Navy career was pretty short, as you know," Patsy replied. "I never left the Pennsy," he said referring to PNSY, the Philadelphia Naval Shipyard in the old Southwark neighborhood by the docks on the Delaware River. "But I did meet your sainted mother there. So it's famous for two things."

"Birthplace of the U.S. Navy," Mickey answered.

"1797," Patsy said. He sipped at the coffee. "What's she doin' back there? I can't see."

Mickey scanned the tiny sun-bleached property. "What's who doing?"

Just as she said it a small animal came scampering out from behind the bushes and bee-lined toward Patsy. He handed Mickey his cup, bent down and scooped it up. For an instant Mickey thought it was a large rat.

"Say hi to Pixie."

Mickey realized he was holding a small dog. A Chihuahua, she guessed. It had triangular ears, a narrow snout and bulbous eyes. Its tail wagged madly. Patsy leaned his face in and let the tiny dog lick it.

"Wait. When did you-"

"She showed up last night," Patsy said. "Just walked in the door and curled up on the rug. I made her a can of Campbell's condensed soup 'cause she looked skinny. Chicken and Stars."

"I don't think dogs eat soup," Mickey said, still trying to process the information and the situation.

"Licked the bowl clean," Patsy answered. "I didn't have any

dog food."

"No tags?"

"Nope," Patsy replied, stroking the dog's neck. "Naked as a jaybird."

"Where'd you get the name, then?"

"Look at her. Couldn't exactly call her Spike or Mack now could I?" The dog began to shiver and Patsy stroked the tawny fur with one large hand. "I had the TV turned on this morning and that kid's show was on Channel 10 – the one with the Peter Pan lady."

"Pixanne?" Mickey said. She'd heard Rodriguez talk about how much the rugrats loved it.

"Yeah, that's the one." Patsy shifted the tiny dog to his other forearm where it promptly nestled its head in the crook of his elbow and appeared to fall asleep. "Cute little thing, ain't she? Like a pixie, so…"

"Got it," Mickey replied. "I'll pick you up a leash and some other stuff and bring them by later. Did you remember to report a lost dog to the Ship Bottom police?"

"Yeah, I told your friend Davey Johnson. They ain't exactly subtle about checking on me. I assume that came from you."

"I just said if they were in the neighborhood," Mickey answered.

"Well, they're in the neighborhood a lot. I can take care of myself, you know."

"I know you can, Dad," Mickey said. "Don't get too attached, though. Good chance an owner will show up today or tomorrow."

Patsy looked down at the sleeping dog. "Somebody wasn't taking care of her too good," he said. "Your friend Davey said sometimes at the end of the season renters just leave their pets behind to fend for themselves. I'll give her a good home. And don't worry about supplies. We're goin' uptown later."

"I don't think Long Beach Island has any real pet stores," Mickey said.

"We'll go to Woolworths or the Five and Dime. They'll have something. Bring my coffee, would ya?"

Mickey followed him into the house. He laid the still-snoozing dog on the plaid couch the way one, she assumed, would lay a baby in a bassinette. She almost laughed out loud. Her father had never been particularly demonstrative when it came to showing affection toward her or, as much as she could remember, her mother. "It's just not his way," Eileen Cleary used to say. And now, the sight of this burly man cradling a tiny dog like a newborn caught her by surprise. "Well, will miraculous wonders never cease," her mother would have said if she'd lived to see it, Mickey mused.

"Seen that truck around anymore?" Mickey asked.

Patsy took back the coffee from her and they walked the few steps back toward the kitchen and sat down at the table.

"Oh, so now there *is* a truck?" Patsy said, raising his eyebrows.

"If you say there's a truck, then, yes, there's a truck."

"No. I ain't seen it since that last time," Patsy replied.

"I told the local shop to be on the lookout for it," Mickey said. "And both these cups are for you. Just don't give that dog any coffee, OK?"

"BOLO or APB?" Patsy asked.

Mickey shook her head. "Just a head's up is all. What did Davey have to say?"

"Guess their new chief was asking a lot of questions about you."

Mickey leaned in. "Yeah? What kind of questions?"

"Background, mostly. Nibbling around the edges about the Troubles. Sizing up the competition, if you was to ask me."

"There is no competition," Mickey said. "He's got his shop, I have mine."

"Your friend Davey – I told you he has a bad case of the hots for you, right – anyway, your friend says this new chief is on a mission to get this single police force idea for LBI pushed through. Has all these budget numbers and he's in the ear of all the council people on the Island."

"You couldn't get all six councils to agree on lunch," Mickey said. "They'll never agree on this. Billy Tunell won't go along. All it takes is one 'No'."

"Prob'ly right, kid. But watch your back. I'd say if it ever did go through, you'd be his biggest threat. You got the rep with the locals and you're tight with the Feds and he doesn't know anybody."

"Haven't you heard? It's a man's world, Dad. Even James Brown says so. Besides, I thought he was some hotshot motorcycle cop out in L.A. before he showed up here? These councilmen will eat that up."

"Your buddy says that's what he puts out but they're starting to wonder. Doesn't have any shoulder patches or an old helmet or anything. Most guys, if they had that stuff, it would be up on their wall or on their desk the minute they moved in. Sends a message, you know? You were in California. Know any cops back there you could ask?"

"A lot of amateur criminals, Dad," Mickey said. "But no cops. Trust me. No cops." For a second time that morning Mickey recalled her stint on the commune in Humboldt. The mantra for inclusion had been "gas, grass or ass" and to avoid providing the last she'd served as the chief mechanic for the group's rag-tag fleet of VW buses and its incongruous Lincoln Continental. She'd never told anyone there her previous job had been as a Philadelphia Police Officer and she had always pleaded ignorance on matters involving the law. Her commune name, she thought with some regret, had been Moondancer.

"Anyways," Patsy said, "he agrees – the guy is a pipsqueak. Where's your little friend?"

"Bunny? She's crashed out at the Rodriguez's – sleepover with their three girls last night."

"What time is soldier boy supposed to call?"

Mickey reflexively looked at her watch. "Thirteen hundred hours so that's-"

"One o'clock," Patsy said. "Calling here again?"

"Yeah," Mickey said. "Less ears to overhear, we figured."

"I should be back from the store by then. If not, I'll leave the door unlocked. I got police protection now, thanks to you."

Mickey stood up. "See you after lunch," she said.

"We'll be here," Patsy answered, nodding toward the couch. The little dog gave a few muffled woofs and her spindly front legs flexed rhythmically.

"Pixie," Mickey said as she headed for the door. "It fits. But I think Spike would have been pretty good, too." She paused. "Bunny thinks Ronnie is coming home today."

"She's going to be disappointed, that is unless he hitched a ride on one of them F-4 Phantoms."

"Yeah, I know. And I'm running out of things to distract her with. But I still have two bad guys who may or may not be on their way here looking for her."

"I told ya, she could hole up at the Jablonski's. I think old Police Commissioner's get a little protection too. It just ain't so obvious."

They're right on the beach."

"I think I'd rather have her close by. I'm afraid one more separation from someone she trusts would be too much."

"She's tougher than you think, is my bet."

"I think she's pretty tough. She's just seen too much." Mickey pushed open the wooden screen door. It squeaked and groaned as the long coiled spring tethering it to the frame stretched out.

"Ha," said Patsy. "Ain't we all."

Twenty-Seven

U.S. Army Fort Dix
Burlington County, New Jersey

Ronnie got up from the thinly-padded seat on the metal chair and walked around the tiny office. Again. The Army clerk-typist gave him a shrug.
"I'm not some FNG," Ronnie said. "Something should be happening. Can you call somebody? Check on what I'm waiting here for?"
"Hey, pal. You see a phone? Besides, it's above my pay-grade and outside my clearance level, I'm afraid," the man answered in a thick New York accent. "Got smokes though, if it'd help."
Ronnie shook his head. The clerk – his ID pin said his last name was Forscellini - produced a half-full pack of Newport's and tapped one out. "You sure?" he said, pointing the foil at Ronnie.
"Yeah, I'm sure," Ronnie answered. Then, "Where you from?"
Forscellini stopped typing. "The Bronx. Home a' the Yankees. Although they ain't never gonna be the same now that Mantle's retiring."
"He's been the cause of a lot of excitement," Ronnie replied.
"Yeah," Forscellini agreed, "You could definitely say that."
"Got a first name?"
"Who? Me or Mantle?"
"You," Ronnie said and exhaled loudly.
"No, dipshit, I ain't got a first name. It was the Depression. We were too poor for first names."

Ronnie thought for a moment that he had really offended the soldier until he flashed a 'gotcha" grin. "It's Al," Forscellini continued. "Short for Alphonse. Ginzo to the core, I'm afraid." Then he went back to hunting and pecking. The metallic clatter of the keystrokes was the only sound in the room.

Gibson, his M.P. escort, had walked him from the cargo hold of the Globemaster to a Quonset hut not far from the runway at McGuire AFB and then turned and departed without a word. Two hours after that Ronnie had been taken by an Air Force Jeep and driven the two-and-two-tenths miles along a restricted access blacktop road to a sentry-guarded back gate at the Army Base Fort Dix. There an Army jeep with an equally taciturn driver picked him up and drove him to his current location. He had passed rows of howitzers and tanks, most appearing to be there primarily for display. The jeep driver had barely acknowledged him, nodding toward the door Ronnie was to enter was as close as he came to any personal interaction. His thin "orders" envelope had remained unopened. It was if, he thought, they knew he was coming and were dead set on ignoring him for as long as possible. His requests to make even a single phone call to arrange transportation home had been summarily declined without explanation. They wanted him out, he decided, but until he was out they wanted him isolated. The logic defied him no matter how many ways he looked at it.

Ronnie heard a drawer slide open and looked up. Forscellini was reaching deep inside the lower file drawer to his left. "How long since you got laid?" Forscellini asked.

Ronnie could hear him digging for something in the drawer.

"Been away a couple of months," Ronnie answered. "OK. Probably more like four."

"Then you might enjoy this." Forscellini tossed Ronnie a thick, glossy magazine that landed at his feet. Ronnie reached down and picked it up.

"*Penthouse*, huh?" Ronnie said. "*Playboy Magazine* get a new name?"

"This definitely ain't *Playboy*. This is a lot hotter," Forscellini said. "Not even for sale stateside until next month. A mook on his way back from Italy gave it to me. Full bush and beaver shots. Although for myself, I do tend to favor the in-depth interviews and the cutting-edge journalism over the, should we say, prurient photographic content."

Ronnie paged through the magazine. It was tamer than the brutal hard-core stuff passed around in-country but, he thought, it still made *Playboy* look like *Sports Illustrated*.

"They're going to sell this at the newsstand?" Ronnie asked, lingering on a spread-eagle shot of a voluptuous brunette model.

"Right next to *The Sporting News*," Forscellini replied. "The latrine is right outside but, and this is just my personal advice now, you might want to show some restraint and save it for your squeeze."

Ronnie flipped through a few more pages. "A lot of anatomy on display here," he said.

"And I consider myself an advanced student of Anatomy," Forscellini replied. "Especially when pulchritude is accompanied by pudenda."

Ronnie nodded and skimmed some more pages. What was rolling over in his mind was that a grunt Army clerk had the words prurient, pulchritude and pudenda in his vocabulary and had used them all correctly. The photo spread was titillating and Ronnie felt himself starting to respond. But there was something else, he thought. Like a large fly caught in a double-hung window it buzzed just on the edge of earshot, demanding his attention.

It was, without a doubt he decided, the vibe.

◆ ◆ ◆

Surf City

Mickey was driving north on Central Avenue when the cruiser's radio crackled.

"Dispatch to Surf City 1. Copy?"

She plucked the dashboard microphone from its metal hanger.

"Surf City 1. Good morning, Arlene."

"Morning, Chief Cleary," Arlene replied. "Deputy Higgins requests your presence at SCPD ASAP. What's your twenty?"

Mickey squeezed the talk button on the shoulder of the microphone.

"Northbound on Central just leaving Ship Bottom. ETA nine minutes, depending on shoobie density and traffic."

Charlie could have used direct radio contact, she knew, so either something was terribly wrong or he was pulling her chain.

"Copy that, Chief Cleary. Will relay your twenty and your ETA."

Mickey waited, then spoke into the microphone again. "Deputy Higgins give you a Status by chance, Dispatch? You know how much I love the flashers and the siren. Surf City 1, over."

"Affirmative, Surf City 1," Arlene answered with what sounded to Mickey like barely contained bemusement.

"Care to share, Dispatch?"

After thousands of calls over the summer, Mickey knew that formal radio etiquette tended to go by the wayside the closer it got to Labor Day.

"Copy that, Chief. 'Visiting Dignitary' was the message. Proceed Code Five."

Mickey laughed. There was no Code Five. It was their password for find an excuse not to respond. "Tell Deputy Higgins to apprise Mayor Billy of my imminent arrival and that he will be my first order of business."

"Copy that, only it's a different dignitary."

Mickey stopped at a light. A small boy walking with his parents on the street waved at her. She waved back and whooped the siren eliciting a huge smile from the child and terrified looks from the parents.

"Anyone I know, Dispatch?"

"Better not tell you. Ask again later. Dispatch out."

Mickey broke into a grin at Arlene's use of what she knew were two of the Wham-O *Magic 8 Ball* toy's mysterious liquid answers. She crossed South 3rd Street and officially into Surf City's single square mile of sovereign space. She stayed on Central, passing Division Street which marked one of the narrowest points on the entire Island. With a twist of her head she could see the bay and the ocean in one look. A crowd of noisy beachgoers was heading up North 7th Street and she waited for them to cross, waving at the small children who pointed and tugged on their parents' swimsuits. Mickey thought she recognized the Nepp family traipsing wearily, again loaded with a supply of beach equipment worthy of a Silk Road caravan. Another good day for the Farias couple's fledgling rental business, she decided.

She turned right at 8th St and a shower of ersatz raindrops fell from the sweating water tower hitting her windshield with a concussive splattering sound. Mickey flipped on the wipers and pulled into the SCPD station's parking lot which faced out onto Long Beach Boulevard. She noticed there was a police cruiser parked at an angle, effectively taking up both her and one of the deputies' marked and reserved spots.

Mickey slipped into to an empty space, cracked the windows and turned off the engine.

Visiting dignitary, she thought. *Better not tell you.* She shook her head as she exited her cruiser. Now she knew what and who were waiting for her.

The foreign police cruiser was a heavily modified Chevy Camaro SS and looked to be new enough that she checked to see if there was still a sales sticker in the window. Mickey had read about the car in her monthly cover-to cover perusal of *Road & Track* magazine. The cruiser's graphics, she noted, had been started but weren't complete so there were large areas with only thin white outlines against the glossy Fathom Blue paint job. The Ship Bottom borough Seal wasn't filled in but there was one finished spot. Emblazoned across the driver's side door in flowing cursive were the words:

JIM JUSTUS, CHIEF

Mickey bit her lip to suppress a smirk and kept walking toward the station house door. She tried to remember an old saying that Innocentia had taught them in grade school – it was something about imitation, she thought.

Out on the Boulevard the traffic crawled by as renters and day-trippers funneled toward the narrow, dunes-guarded beach accesses. There would be more complaints about having to purchase Mayor Billy's visionary beach badges so close to the end of the summer. She suspected that before day ended, and it was shaping up to be hot, humid and airless, she and her deputies would be coming to the rescue of more than one of the gaggle of high-school girls who were employed to fan out and check all adult beachgoers for valid tags. Over the course of the summer Mickey had threatened more than one irritated and sunburned suburbanite with a hefty fine and possible incarceration for verbally abusing the poor young women. Sam Santaspirito, the borough's attorney, was trying to get the Council to adopt an ordinance making such behavior a formal misdemeanor and doubling the fine for it but Mayor Billy, who at one point had wanted his name and title printed on the badges, was stonewalling him.

The visiting cruiser and the badges occupied Mickey's thoughts as she reached for the door handle. Then she heard the rumble of what her "grease monkey" side knew was a big performance engine. She pulled on the door just as a Plymouth Road Runner drove by heading south. Mickey recognized the color as the custom, slightly darker Vitamin "C" Orange option. According to *Car & Driver*, another of her favorite reads, she knew it had just been released in the fall of 1968 with a no-frills design and a low-end price tag. A muscle car for the masses the article said. This was the first one she had seen on the Island. Ronnie would have classified it as a "suicide machine" if coupled with a young driver and a long, straight stretch of Highway 9 in front of him. The car came standard with a big V8, Mickey remembered, 383 cubic inches and a four-barrel Carter carburetor capable of producing, she thought the specs said, something like 330 horsepower. Her Chevelle could saddle up 360 horses and so, she mused, she could at least catch it if she had to.

The sun was reflecting almost painfully off the car's windshield and passenger-side window so she couldn't gauge the age of the driver. She hoped it wasn't a kid and the steady, well-within-the-speed limit pace plus the lack of any heavy rev's or attempted peel-outs made her think it was probably someone older and, hopefully, someone passing through on their way to somewhere else. She already had, she decided, enough to worry about.

♦ ♦ ♦

"It's not very big, is it?" Dickie Robichaux said.

Harlan Brinson was driving at Dickie's request. Dickie wanted to ogle the tanned young flesh that lined and shimmied on each side of what, from the top of the lighthouse at Barnegat, was obviously main drag for the whole island.

"You talking about this town or your dick?" Brinson shot back without looking over.

"This island. And as for my dick, it's big enough for all this tiny hiney, I do declare," Dickie said. "You happen to know what the age of consent is in New Jersey?"

"Sixteen, if it's like everywhere else," Brinson replied.

"Eighteen in Louisiana," Dickie said. "I like this plum better. Shit, probably don't even need grass on the field to play ball here."

"Dickie, remember - we get what we came for and then we get out. Our LZ is small and our egress routes are limited, unless you're a seafaring man."

"Shit, Harlan, I could navigate that bay we crossed in the dark if'n I had to. Ain't no gators in it, neither. And probably no sharks. I don't like that bridge, though. We could get trapped in traffic on it like skeeters in pine sap. We should think about stashing a little canoe or maybe even a johnboat just in case. I seriously doubt we could find a pirogue anywhere north of the Mason-Dixon."

It occurred to Brinson that Dickey's personality and thought processes had been totally transformed by his years as a tunnel rat in-country. That he now saw the whole world as a closed space and that surviving in it depended on whether he could avoid or kill anyone who stood between him and an exit. The rickety causeway bridge, Brinson realized, was just another version of a tunnel, like the restroom stall had been. He was constantly evaluating his escape options and routes. Dickie wasn't a loose cannon, Brinson concluded. He was more like a flask of unstable nitroglycerin.

"What's our plan?" Dickie asked.

"Let's continue to recon at ground level for now. From what I saw at the top of the lighthouse I figure the whole island is only about thirty klicks north-south and maybe, maybe a klick at best at its widest. Half that where it narrows down. Flat as a dammed pancake except for the sand dunes. We can cover every square inch of it in a day, day and a half. Maybe less if we split up."

"No way we can boost a car here," Dickie said.

Brinson shook his head. "Don't need to. You take the car. We passed a shop a couple of blocks back. I'll rent a bicycle there. Then I'll just buy an ugly Hawaiian shirt, some gook sandals and a pair of wraparound sunglasses and maybe a hat. I'll be fucking invisible. You need to be the same."

"I ain't wearin' no VC thongs, Harlan."

"Fine. Get some cheap white sneakers, then. And some sweat socks and gym shorts. Try and cover up the tattoos – this looks like a working class crowd but it's pretty much all white bread. They'll notice those and remember you. Just act like a gearhead or a fisherman if anyone decides they want to jaw."

"Chuck Taylor Converse All-Stars," Dickie replied. "High-Tops. White. Always wanted me a pair of them. Nine bucks, though."

"Treat yourself," Brinson replied. "We accomplish this one last mission and we'll be lightin' up joints with crisp new twenties by this time next week."

Dickie rolled down the window and stared out as they passed the neat wooden strake and clapboard houses that lined the Boulevard between stands of small retail businesses. "Speakin' of grass," he said, "there ain't none. You notice that?"

"It's a vacation spot, Dickie. Nobody wants to cut their grass on vacation. All the lawns are just sand or stones or crushed up seashells."

"Yeah, buddy. Chez Robichaux is lookin' better all the time," Dickie said.

Brinson slowed down as the traffic thickened. He spied an old car heading north in the opposite lane.

"Check it out. '57 Chevy Bel Air," he said. "My daddy owned that car when I was younger. He traded it in on a Pontiac Catalina one day instead of giving it to me like he promised he would." The two vehicles were stopped almost abreast of each other and Brinson flashed the driver a peace sign. The old man behind the wheel gave him a quizzical look in return. "You get your sneakers, Dickie. I'm getting' me one of those."

Dickie looked over. "What's he's got in his lap?" he asked. "Looks like a damn *coypu*."

"A damn what?"

"*Coypu*. A giant river rat lives down in the bayou. Nutria, some folks call 'em."

"Shit, Dickie," Brinson replied. "It's just a little bitty dog is all."

"Where are we now?" Dickie asked.

"Crossed back over into Ship Bottom a few blocks back," Brinson answered. "Same town we came in through."

Brinson put on his right-turn blinker. It ticked loudly in the warm air of the car. He made the turn onto West 8thth Street and drove another block, intersecting with what the black-on-white sign said was Central Avenue. A square, white cement building with a flat roof and a single front window caught his eye. Painted on the cement and taking up most of the storefront was a huge logo. "Ron-Jon Surf Shop" it said, with the "Ron" and the "Jon" hyphenated and spelled out in vaguely Asian-style letters, like those on the front of every Chinese restaurant menu Brinson had ever seen.

"Let's pull in here," Brinson said.
"Think they got sneakers?" Dickie asked.
"We'll get those at an Army-Navy I saw further back. I don't think surfers generally wear sneakers."
"S'pose you're right," Dickie replied. "Don't know why not, though. You think it'd be easier to stay on the board with a little more traction underfoot."

Brinson pulled into the unmarked asphalt lot next to the little store. The parking area was being enlarged and the air smelled of hot asphalt and diesel fuel. It occurred to him that while Dickie's comment about sneakers and surfboards sounded off-the-wall, it actually made perfect sense. He would, he decided, need to recalibrate his thinking about available options with Private Robichaux. He was in danger of making the classic military mistake. The same one Goliath had made, the same one that cost Custer first his scalp and then his life and the same one Westmoreland made before he was sentenced to a desk job.

They had all underestimated their opponent.

◆ ◆ ◆

Chief Jim Justus was everything Mickey expected. And less.

In the ten minutes she'd been inside the station the only words she'd managed to get in were "good to finally meet you." She found it hard to stay focused, partly because Justus was still wearing his mirrored, aviator sunglasses and she was looking at her own reflection in each lens. With his eyes shielded he reminded her of Clutch Cargo, the animated TV character with a superimposed human mouth that delivered the corny dialogue. Sally Starr, the beloved afternoon kids' TV hostess, had been in town in June and she and Mickey had shared a laugh about Clutch, Spinner and Paddlefoot. There was more to life than Bosco, Our Gal Sal had advised her. His hair was a sandy blonde and slicked with what Mickey figured from the fragrance were generous dollops of Alberto VO5.

Mickey found herself nodding intermittently although she had no idea where in their conversation they actually were. She tried to re-focus her listening and when Justus said "Back in my two-wheel days in California," she took a stab at replying.

"Hey, I worked for a year in California," Mickey interjected, failing to mention it was spent fixing cars and growing marijuana. "We might know some of the same people."

Justus paused, seeming momentarily unsure of how to proceed.

"Oh, I'm sure I'd remember if we'd met," he said with a smile, ducking the implied question and its potential complications.

"I like the new cruiser," Mickey said. "The Council thought I was crazy when I bought mine when I got here in '67. Really sends a message, though, doesn't it?"

"Imitation is the sincerest form of flattery," Charlie Higgins opined from his desk without looking up. "Oscar Wilde said that."

Mickey sucked in her cheeks and clamped them between her molars to keep from laughing.

"And the new uniforms. Same color as the car, aren't they? Fathom Blue by PPG, unless I'm wrong about that," she said.

"Sharp eye," Justus replied and finally removed his sunglasses. "Chief Cleary, you'll find that I like to pick a theme and stay with it. We're on the ocean. The ocean is blue. I think we should reflect that. I'm hoping the public will start to think of the color as Ship Bottom Blue, actually."

"We still like the khaki," Mickey replied. "Same color as the sand. And we spend more time on the sand than we do on the ocean. Actually."

"The Boy Scouts of America share your enthusiasm for the color scheme, so I guess it's hard to argue with it. At least for the moment." He smiled.

"California Highway Patrol mounted units wear khaki, though, don't they," Mickey said. "And those funny tight pants."

Justus hesitated only slightly, but enough for Mickey to notice.

"And NYPD mounted units wear blue," he countered. "I'm on the East Coast now so, as they say, when in Rome. And as for the pants, they're horsemen's jodhpurs, standard for professional riders, equine or mechanical."

Mickey ran a hand through her dark hair. "Well, let's hope uniform color is the only important thing we disagree on," she said as sweetly as possible.

"On the contrary, Chief. I much enjoy being challenged," Justus said. "I think it makes us stronger as a police force."

"And by 'us' you mean?"

"Why, Ship Bottom PD, of course. My little proposal for Long

Beach Island's law enforcement future is just a pipe dream at the moment as I'm sure you're keenly aware."

"I am keenly aware," Mickey replied.

"Then we should definitely talk more," Justus said. He wiggled the temples on his sunglasses. "I'm proposing that all six Chiefs on the Island start meeting formally once a month."

"I can get us a big booth at Tony Mart's," Mickey offered. "Showplace of the World. Take in a show. Let our hair down, as they say now."

"I was thinking of a bit more, how to put it, a bit more formal venue and process. At least to start out with." Justus put his aviators back on. "I've heard a great deal about you, Chief Cleary. I hope we'll have a strong working relationship going forward. We are neighbors, after all, Ship Bottom and Surf City."

"Good fences make for good neighbors," Charlie chimed in.

Justus ignored him.

"We're updating our station house," Justus said. "State of the art stuff, really. Teletypes, transmittable Xerox copies, Motorola electronic beepers. Great stuff. Feel free to stop by when you're in town to visit your father. We're happy to keep an eye on him for you. Just professional courtesy in my book."

"And I do appreciate that courtesy, Chief Justus," Mickey replied. "Dad was decorated police officer as I'm sure you're aware, but he's no spring chicken. He'd be the first to tell you that."

Justus cocked his head. "And it's possible that you may have accrued one or two powerful enemies during your tenure here. All the more reason to-"

Charlie Higgins spoke once again. "Winston Churchill once said, 'It's good if you have enemies. It means you've stood for something.'"

Justus glanced over his shoulder. "Your deputy is a learned man, Chief Cleary. I can see why you keep him close by."

Mickey wondered if the comment was a veiled bodyguard dig at her.

"Indeed he is, Chief Justus," she said. "Smartest guy in the room." The comment sailed over Justus like a loose kite.

"Then I leave you in good hands." Justus squared his narrow shoulders. "I'm glad we had this chance to finally meet. I'm really excited to see what we can accomplish here together. Law enforcement outside a major metropolitan city can get a little blasé, in my experience. It might be time to light a fire under it again." He stepped toward the door. "Call me anytime you need help." He nodded to Charlie. "Deputy."

Mickey moved with him. "I can show myself out," he said and then exited briskly. When the station door swung shut, Mickey looked over at Charlie.

"OK, it was funny but I could have taken him on all by myself you know."

Charlie grinned. "Of course you could have. But how many chances am I going to get to puncture such a pompous windbag? A pompous, *white* windbag to boot?"

"Not many," Mickey conceded. "Not yet, anyway."

"Exactly," Charlie said, spinning a newly sharpened Ticonderoga Number 2 pencil between the thumb and index fingers of each hand. "And the reason I could do it is because you were here to cover me. You were my bodyguard, so to speak."

Mickey sat at her desk. "You've been talking to Rodriguez, I take it."

"Just some harmless office gossip," Charlie said and slapped the pencil down on his blotter. "I need about an hour after noon patrol today, Chief. I'm expecting a call from Darnell. He's refusing the morphine shots so now they've switched him over to the pills. He has to take some to ease the pain, but he said he wasn't going to swallow any last night or this morning so he'd be clear when we spoke. I think he has some more intel on those names in your little girl's letter. I'd like to take the call at home, if that's alright."

"Whatever you need, Deputy," Mickey replied. "And tell Darnell thank you from me. Did Rodriguez get any shuteye?"

"A little. And I will pass your thanks on to Darnell. I do have a bit of a bad feeling about these two gentlemen, though, I must admit. Can't say exactly why. Just a feeling. Like some kind of –"

"Vibration?"

Charlie leaned back in his chair. "Yes. Like a vibration. Something that's all around me yet something I cannot quite see. You understand me?"

"I do," Mickey replied. "And who said that thing about imitating? I thought maybe it was Shakespeare."

"I said it was Oscar Wilde, Chief, but it was actually Charles

Caleb Colton, a minor nineteenth-century writer. Oscar Wilde, a rather flamboyant individual in his own right, borrowed the saying and improved upon it, saying, 'Imitation is the sincerest form of flattery that mediocrity can pay to greatness.' I didn't want to overdo it, you know?"

"Oh, I still think he got the message, don't you?"

"Yes, ma'am. What did your father call him?

"A pipsqueak."

"Truer words, as they say. And if that little Napoleon ever rode a motorcycle in uniform then I am Linc Hayes from *The Mod Squad*."

That made Mickey laugh. "I still think we did pretty good, there, Deputy Higgins."

"I think we did, too, Chief Cleary," Charlie replied. "Tag-teamed his honky ass if you'll excuse my-"

Mickey suddenly felt faint and Charlie's voice sounded very far away. She put her hands on her desk but she still felt like she was falling. Something he said had hit her like an incoming round.

She wasn't in the station anymore. But yet she was. Only it was the old station. A man she couldn't see was saying something. Something about praying to God. Something about – about tag-teaming. Her stomach felt like she was riding the first car on The Thunderbolt roller coaster at Willow Grove Park, hurtling down the big hill.

"Just pray to God."

The pain in her wrists. The voice, taunting her.

"I think they call it tag-teaming."

"Just pray to God."

The worst day of her life.

"Just pray to God."

But there was something else, she knew. Something more.

There was mud on the tires, her father said.

There was mud on the bike. From the Pines, Stellwag said.

It popped inside her head like a party balloon and she heard it clearly.

"Just pray to God his brother isn't there. I think they call it tag-teaming."

The world started to go black.

"Just pray to God."

"His brother isn't there."

His brother *wasn't* there.

Her head hit the desk just as Charlie got to her.

Twenty-Eight

The Pine Barrens

BoDean studied the little device Cowboy had given him. It seemed simple enough. BoDean favored the simple because it worked right more often than the more complicated. He turned it in his hands. The nail keg sat in the corner of his shack, its seams sealed with pine pitch to keep the jelly gas from leaking out. BoDean had thrown some roofing nails and ball bearings into the mix on a whim and then regretted it. But the thought of digging all that shrapnel out of the viscous fuel made him decide to leave it. He hoped this wouldn't make his little gift immediately lethal. That outcome, he considered, would defeat his whole purpose.

He also abandoned any thoughts of using the sharpened badge, lamenting the hours he'd spent carefully preparing it. Instead, he'd placed it on top of the incendiary mix in the nail keg before he'd tapped down and sealed the lid with paraffin wax. The badge would survive, he knew. Cowboy had warned him about leaving "forensic evidence" – clues specific to him, he explained. BoDean didn't intend on leaving clues but he did intend on leaving a message. The badge would do just fine for that he'd decided. It had made it through one fatal inferno. It would make it through another.

The fuse was short, simple and wrapped in a black material that felt like plastic but it was so smooth it was almost slippery. There was a smaller metal box on the crimped onto the end that Cowboy said would create the spark and set the fuse to burning. BoDean questioned whether the fuse itself was too short but Cowboy explained that it would burn very slowly inside this wrapping, allowing BoDean both the time and distance he required. He had intended to use the Zippo lighter he'd borrowed from Billy on the last day he'd seen him alive but Cowboy insisted that the little metal box in his hand would be both more reliable and less visible.

"You don't want be hunched down with a visible flicker or trying to light it in a breeze," Cowboy had said. "Somebody's bound to see you and maybe ask what it is you're doing." BoDean agreed he did not want that.

The metal box in his hand looked like something Cowboy had constructed himself. It had a single black button that cowboy said would send out a radio signal. Remote detonation, Cowboy called it. It also had a funny smell. If it didn't work, BoDean decided, then he and Cowboy would have themselves a reckoning. If it did work, well, he thought, they might just need to have themselves a reckoning at some point anyway.

He set the device on the lid of the nail keg. Outside he heard the loud rumble of unmuffled motorcycle engines. The bastards were tearing up his property again – more of them and riding closer to his shack every time. On BoDean's last reconnoitering sojourn he saw that they'd strung coils of barbed wire around their wooden clubhouse. If they kept coming closer and if the jelly gas worked right again, he figured, the wire would keep them from running off before they fried. The Bowkers had been in the Pine Barrens for generations, he mused. The Droo-ids had been there for maybe a few months. It was, he decided, not even a fair fight.

BoDean walked out into a murky daylight. Darkness came early and quickly in the Pines, thanks to the thickness of the trees and the overhead canopy. It was like the stories his family passed down about the coal country they'd come from. The ground was finally starting to dry out. He kicked thin cakes of tawny mud from his boots. It wouldn't be dark on the Island for a long time.

The sound of the motorcycles grew fainter. BoDean figured they'd come within two hundred yards despite his having marked the property with a hand-lettered sign and several deer skulls. He'd painted the antlers with some fluorescent road-striping paint that Cowboy had lifted for him from shop at the Public Works garage and when the headlights hit them they looked like leering devil-heads.

In the end, BoDean assumed, everybody burned. If he made it as far as the afterlife, he was sure he would too. He looked at the damp underbrush and the moist and mossy deadfall. He didn't mind the rain – it what's kept the whole place from going up in flames around him.

◆ ◆ ◆

Surf City

The radio on Dippolito's desk was playing. The Crazy World of Arthur Brown and their 1968 chart topper, heavy with brass, was just fading out. Mickey could hear Dip talking.

"These guys were at the AC Racetrack couple of weeks ago. Guy that was there said it was nuts. Jefferson Airplane and Creedence Clearwater were there too."

Mickey slowly lifted her head. She was in one of the cells on the bunk. Nothing hurt but she still felt slightly woozy.

"Easy there, Chief," Charlie was saying. "We were afraid for a minute there that we'd lost you."

"Mickey-san OK," she heard Bunny chirp. "She just sleepy. She wake up now. Dunn come home. She be OK."

She pushed herself up on the thin mattress bunk and swung her legs until her feet met the floor. The cobwebs were beginning to clear and she looked around.

"What time is it?" she asked.

"Little after twelve," Dip replied. "You were talking when we laid you down so we figured you were OK. Charlie thought it was probably just exhaustion so we let you rest for a while."

Mickey remembered conversing with Jim Justus and then Charlie after he left. She remembered sitting at her desk. Charlie had been saying something but now she couldn't remember what it was.

"You OK now, Chief Cleary?" Charlie asked. He was standing at the cell door.

"I'm fine," Mickey answered. She looked up at him. "We were talking about something. What was it?"

Charlie's hand was over his sidearm.

"I believe it was about the phone call I need to take in a few minutes," he said. "If you're OK I'll excuse myself for about an hour. Dip came in early and Rodriguez is out on a call. Lost dog, I think."

"Darnell, right?"

"Yes, ma'am," Charlie replied. "I'll let you know what he says when I get back."

The discussion came back to her but she couldn't help feeling there was something else, something missing. Something important.

Charlie patted his piece and turned for the door. Dippolito brought her a cold bottle of Pepsi-Cola.

"Are we out of Tab already?" Mickey asked reaching for it.

"I thought maybe you should have something with sugar in it," Dippolito replied.

"OK, Doctor Dennis," Mickey shot back. She put the clear, tapering bottle to her lips and sucked down a third of it. Bunny came over and sat next to her. She was wearing clothes Mickey didn't recognize. She hoped Colombia hadn't gone out and bought them.

"This is cool," Mickey said pointing to Bunny's white t-shirt with the yellow and black Batman logo. Her shorts were plaid and pleated and Mickey touched the hem.

"Carn-a-bee Street," Bunny said. "Ee- nez say I can keep."

"We'll say OK, but just for now," Mickey replied. It hadn't occurred to her that Bunny would be with her long enough to require several sets of clothes even though, she thought, it really should have.

"I like Ee-nez," Bunny said. "She name me Princess Bon-nee. I wear crown. Tee-air-a."

""Yes, I heard," Mickey answered. "Bunny, why did you say Dunn is coming today."

"He come," Bunny said. "I know."

"How do you know? Did someone tell you?"

Bunny shook her head. "No one tell. I know."

Mickey drew in a breath. She considered putting it to rest right away but decided to let the little girl hold on to her hopes for a few hours more.

"Then we'd better get ready," Mickey said and stood up. She felt fully recovered but the dangling conversation with Charlie still gnawed at her. She took another long swig of the cold Pepsi. "What kind of dog?" she asked Dippolito.

He shrugged. "Didn't say."

"Middle-aged woman. Corner of Sunset and Barnegat?"

"I don't know if it was a woman, but yeah, that's the ten-twenty," Dip replied. "How'd you know?"

"How long's he been gone on that one?"

"Fifteen minutes maybe. Why?"

"If he's not back or if you don't hear from him in another fifteen, I want you to go there and provide back up."

"It's a missing pooch, Chief. I don't think there's really any danger."

"Trust me, Dip," Mickey answered, "He's in the worst kind of danger imaginable. Fifteen minutes, got it?"

Dippolito looked at his watch. "Got it, but I still don't think-"

Mickey cut him off. "I'll take Bunny with me. We've got a couple calls to make." She looked at the child. "Are you hungry?"

"I stay here. I clean guns. Answer phone. Wait for Dunn to come. I know how clean guns. Soldiers teach me."

Dippolito looked at Mickey. "Can she really-"

""I'm absolutely sure she can and no, she isn't going to." Mickey turned back toward Bunny. "You're coming with me, little lady. My papa-san has a new friend I want you to meet."

◆ ◆ ◆

Long Beach Township, NJ

"You ever wish you were back?"

Dickie Robichaux had his shirt off, his eyes closed and was lying on his back on the sand. He had been nearly motionless and silent for the last twenty minutes.

"Never," Brinson answered. "Absolutely never. Do you?"

The exposed low-tide beach was flat, hot and, Brinson thought, surprisingly empty for an August weekend. They were at the southern terminus of the island. Waves with the barest amount of qualifying curl lapped lazily at the shoreline. Behind them stood a multi-story building that a weathered sign identified as Life Saving Station #118.

"You ever get to see *Nha Trang*?" Dickie asked.

"You had to be shot up to go to *Nha Trang*," Brinson replied.

"The Acapulco of Viet Nam they called it. Big field hospital, big provincial hospital. *Nha Trang* never saw a battle or flying bullet. Never got bombed. North of Cam Ranh Bay on the South China Sea. Just across the strait there was an island you could get to in one of the native junks. *Hon Tre.* The native women went topless there all the time. Like it was no big deal. Harlan, I swear I'd rejoin the Army if they'd send me back there."

Brinson was sitting with his arms around his knees looking out at the placid Atlantic.

"If you rejoined the Army, Dickie, they wouldn't send you to *Nha Trang*. They'd send you right back to *Cu Chi*."

Dickie remained quiet a while longer. "You ever go down in a VC tunnel?" he asked.

"Can't say I ever had the pleasure," Brinson said. "I saw enough shit above ground to last me a lifetime."

"Black echo. That's what we called it down there."

"What's it stand for?"

Dickie turned his head slightly. "Doesn't stand for anything. Means a state of mind. It's dark, it's quiet and you're alone. It's what goes on inside your head. And after a while, what goes on inside your head is what takes over."

"Weren't there snakes down there?"

Dickie laughed. "Snakes? Oh, yeah, there were snakes. But I grew up with snakes. Louisiana has more'n fifty kinds scattered around it. Only about seven are poisonous. Canebreaks, copperheads, cottonmouths, pygymy rattlers, two different kinds'a corals and then the big diamondbacks. Anyone of 'em kill you in short order. But the snakes never bothered me, really. And neither did Charlie. He was just me in black pajamas. I knew what he was thinkin', I knew where he was goin' and I knew he really didn't want to be there any more'n I did. There were times, Harlan, when'd we'd just slide by each other in the dark without a word and keep on movin'. We both had to deal with the same shit - ants, spiders with bodies as big as walnuts and scorpions. I hated the scorpions the most. And the booby traps – trip wire grenades and spring-loaded *punji* sticks mostly. You'd pray to God that if you bought it, it was from a grenade 'cause at least it was over in an instant. I ended up in *Nha Trang* when a *punji* went through my leg. Straight through but it only got the meat and the gristle. Missed the artery, the doc said, by less'n a quarter inch. It had me impaled, so I had to use my knife to slit the skin open so the spike would slide out sideways. If I couldn'ta done that, I would'a put one in my temple before the rats had a chance to start in on me. They go for your eyes first. We crawled around down there whenever they ordered us to but Charlie, Harlan, Charlie fuckin' *lived* down there. And the tunnels made 'em sick. Malaria, dysentery, tapeworms long as your arm. They didn't care. That's why they can't never be defeated. They are totally committed. Only American generals are committed like that. American soldiers don't really give a shit. Now, I'm bettin', most Americans probably don't give a shit anymore either. You want to conquer Viet Nam? Put a fucking Hilton Hotel right on the beach in *Nha Trang* and have dink cabaña boys serving ten-dollar mai-tai's. If this war is ever over, I'd go back. But don't anybody ask me to set foot underground again, here or there."

Brinson put his palms flat on the white sand. "You think we should just let it go? Just disappear into the woodwork. Fuck all this shit with Winston, forget about the kid and be content with what we already have?"

"You mean like we should seek an honorable end to this mission?" Dickie propped up on his elbows. "We're fucked whether we do or we don't, Harlan. Hopwood didn't answer, didn't check in. Who knows what kind a shit show it is now up in Portland? Odds are he killed them both after getting what he needed and is on his way to Philadelphia. Yeah, we could stake out the airport and maybe the big train station but how many key lockers in how many places you think there are?"

"Hopwood wouldn't-"

"Sure he would. Lot of bread for one person. Don't bullshit me and tell me you're not doin' the math. I'm doin' it myself."

Brinson noticed that Dickie said this without any discernible trace of malice or anger.

"Or maybe Hopwood's a KIA. Winston could sit on the stuff for as long as he wanted. There's a chance the kid isn't even here, right. Or maybe he went to CID and now they're tracking us. I heard Leavenworth is worse on a good day than Alcatraz was on a bad one. Let's play it out. See if we get lucky."

Now it was Brinson's term to remain silent. The ocean was more than just flat, he thought to himself. It was completely and utterly becalmed. He'd read about sailors stuck in the Doldrums where no breeze blew for days on end and imagined this is what it must have looked like.

Dickie eased himself back down. He appeared totally relaxed, as if he were just another tourist soaking up the sun. "What kind of bike is that, anyway?" he asked.

"A Schwinn Sting-Ray," Brinson answered. "I was hoping for something a little more adult but it was all they had left."

"Banana seat I see. And what do they call those handlebars again?"

"Ape bars."

"And that thing on the back of the seat."

"A sissy bar."

"I knew the last one," Dickie said. "I just wanted to hear you say it. And you think you're gonna be invisible?"

""Believe it or not, Dickie," Brinson said. "On that thing, around here, I will be."

"Has it got one of them dinger bells?"

Brinson brushed sand from his legs. "They were fresh out."

"Too bad," Dickie said and began to mobilize himself into a sitting position. "What's our grid plan?"

Brinson got up and brushed more grains from the clothes he'd bought at the Ron-Jon Surf Shop. Then he reached down, picked up the off- white version of a military jungle hat he'd purchased and stuck it on his head, pulling the brim to obscure his face.

"I'll start pedaling north from here," Brinson directed. "You take the car back to the lighthouse and then work your way south from there. We should be able to meet up in Ship Bottom by seven at the latest. I saw a place at the other end of the bridge looked alright. Emil's, I think it was called. Probably just beer and pizza but we don't need much else."

"What if we spot the kid?"

"Same plan," Brinson replied. "We'll come back when it's dark and grab her. No sense anyone recognizing us from earlier in the day. We just have to be sure of her primary LZ."

Dickie nodded. "I'll loop back and forth on the north end so I'm not visible in one town too much." He stood up and looked at the metal pole and ladder with a crow's nest attached to the top at the Life Saving Station's wooden piling breakwater. "Be nice if they had one of those to climb every klick or so."

"Time to saddle up," Brinson said as he headed off to pull out the bike protruding from the Road Runner's tied down trunk.

"Terrain is mostly blue feature," Dickie said, using military slang for the surrounding water. "We have ourselves a decent chance." He got up and followed Brinson.

"I wish we had a way to break squelch, just in case we get lucky early." Brinson slipped his feet into a pair of new orange flip-flops he'd left by the car.

Dickie Robichaux shrugged. "Stick with the plan, right? Best way to avoid a fugazi."

Harlan Brinson rubbed the sand off his palms."Right. And besides, how hard's it going to be to spot one dink kid?"

Twenty-Nine

Brant Beach
Long Beach Township, NJ

Charlie Higgins was both buoyantly happy and deeply troubled.

Happy that Darnell had, for the first time in months, sounded like the brother, like the man he knew and loved. Troubled by the information that man had imparted.

"They been doping me up good," Darnell had said. "And they been doing it on purpose. " He went on to tell Charlie that his new doctor, a female captain repaying her medical school loans with military service, had been nothing short of appalled at the doses of powerful narcotics he'd been getting and the frequency with which he'd been getting them. She'd told Darnell he could become an addict if he wasn't one already and promised to help him through the process of tapering down his medication which she told him would bring with it the specter of acute withdrawal. "I never touched a street drug in my whole life," Darnell had said with an ache in his voice, "And now I'm gonna be on Methadone like some damn junkie from the corner." Charlie had gotten the name of the woman doctor and intended to contact her but now he was torn, wondering if his plan to transfer his brother to another VA remained a good idea. Still, Charlie was buoyed by Darnell's clear head and the news that his leg prosthesis had arrived and fit him comfortably and that he was going to start therapy to learn how to walk with it.

The good news was tempered mightily, Charlie thought, by the second half of the conversation which concerned one Private Richard Robichaux. He knew Darnell had commanded a specialized unit although his brother was never at liberty to and thus had never before discussed any details of that unit's mission or its location. Darnell, it turns out, had led a platoon of soldiers who specialized in finding the entrances to a vast network of underground tunnels the Viet Cong had dug beneath the jungle to hide and move men and supplies. Then and usually alone, they climbed down into those tunnels to, as Darnell put it, "clear the motherfuckers out." It was dirty, dangerous work often involving lethal hand-to-hand combat and the tunnel rats, as Darnell called them, became "an entirely different breed of soldier. More like rats than men in that you never, ever want to corner one."

In his brother's telling, Robichaux had been a tunnel rat for at least a year when Darnell arrived and as a lieutenant assumed the role of platoon leader. Darnell described Robichaux as a "racist cracker from the swamps" and someone who had chafed immediately at taking orders from a black officer, even though the platoon had several respected black members. Darnell told of a conversation he'd caught just a part of on his way to the latrine. Robichaux was holding court in one of the tents and expounding on how in his way of thinking it "weren't strictly natural" for any black man to tell a white man what to do, even in the military. Darnell had heard the stories about other black officers in-country and so, he told Charlie, he began sleeping with his .45 caliber Colt 1911 pistol under his pillow. The only problem, Darnell said, was that "you can't shoot a damn grenade."

Darnell described to Charlie being choppered to the 12th Evac Hospital in *Cu Chi* where a surgeon he remembered only as Toby gave him the choice of taking his leg off there to stop the ongoing hemorrhage or to leave it on, with the slim hope it could be saved at the much bigger 3rd Field Hospital in Saigon. The surgeon had warned Darnell that if he left the leg, what remained of it anyway, on, that the chances were 60/40 he would bleed to death on the trip even if they went by air. There was a Dust Off helicopter ready and rotating that had one spot left and it would go either to Darnell or a soldier with what Dr. Toby had called a sucking chest wound. He gave Darnell first shot and his brother made his decision.

"So part of me will always belong to *Cu Chi*," Darnell had said.

"In a grave with a thousand other arms and legs." It was the first time Charlie had heard the whole story.

Charlie had taken his Rand-McNally World Atlas with its full color fold-out map of Viet Nam to the office to show Dippolito something. When he got back to the station he wanted to find *Cu Chi* and some place Darnell kept referring to as the Iron Triangle.

The fragging incident, Charlie already knew, had eventually been ascribed to a "preventable but accidental ordnance discharge" and the file on it closed. Darnell said a CID officer out of Saigon had visited him at the 12th Evac in *Cu Chi* but Darnell had been heavily sedated and the officer seemed uninterested in anything other than the simplest explanation.

Charlie asked Darnell if it was Robichaux who had rolled the grenade into his tent. "The guy puts on like he's this dumb swamper but he's not," Darnell had told him. "Every tunnel rat is incredibly brave but if he's not smart, he's dead. I'm sure had had someone else do it." He told Charlie to regard Robichaux as nothing short of a "lethal adversary" in any situation.

Charlie looked at his watch. He wanted to stop at the Surf City 5 & 10 and pick up something for Bunny on his way back. He laughed to himself at the thought of watching Chief Cleary fumbling with any kind of child care. It clearly, Charlie mused, was not her bag.

Lost in these thoughts, he at first didn't notice the group of men gathered around his patrol car which he'd parked on the street. His modest bungalow faced north on West 62nd Avenue, halfway between the Boulevard and Bayview. He had once used his old college stick to heave a lacrosse ball all the way from his front step into the Little Egg Harbor Bay. His house was that close. In the opposite direction, he pegged the distance to the ocean at right around the net-to-net length of four lacrosse fields. The property taxes in the geographically larger Long Beach Township were lower than Surf City's and he liked living in a different place from the one he policed almost every day. His neighbors were only there in the summer and after Labor Day he had the neighborhood almost all to himself.

As he descended the few steps and approached the street his head was down and not until he heard a voice call out did he look up.

"Hey, black boy," it said.

For an instant he was certain he'd imagined it.

♦ ♦ ♦

County Road 545
New Hanover Township, NJ

Ronnie Dunn was out of uniform in more ways than one. Following the interminable processing that freed him once again from his military service, a considerably more talkative grunt had chauffeured him in a new jeep from Fort Dix's back gate to a secondary cyclone fence line topped with Dannert wire. The gate had a simple Yale padlock and the whole thing seemed designed to impress rather than to actually impede. Once outside the fence, the young corporal whose name Ronnie remembered was Mike Flood, mostly because the kid said it so often and ran it together like it was one word – Mikeflood – had helped him with his duffel and wished him luck before executing a perfect K-turn and peeling out in a hail of dust and road dirt.

That had been an hour ago. The rare street sign told Ronnie he was on Texas Avenue and he had not seen a vehicle pass in either direction since he began walking. He had been instructed at Fort Benning to travel in his olive drab ACU, something not really designed for a long trek on baking asphalt. He had his blouse tied around his head and his pant legs rolled up. The heat from the macadam was coming straight up through his boots. The ditches on either side of the road looked even less inviting.

Ronnie knew the general local geography and wayfinding had always been his special gift. His green GI undershirt was soaked and his dog tags clacked with each step. The kid said there was a phone booth just outside of Browns Mills, but that was still a fair distance ahead. "There's a hospital there does these open heart operations," Mikeflood had told him. "Guess it's a pretty big deal." Ronnie thought of Dale Gibson the MP and his brother's characterization of the doctors who did those operations. Ronnie faintly recalled hearing about the place, an old TB hospital that was turning to heart care since tuberculosis was going to be completely eradicated in the United States by the end of the Sixties.

The small amount of folding money and pocket change Ronnie had carried with him from Fort Benning had disappeared between the last two Quonset huts without explanation or apology. He was literally penniless and if not for his military ID card and his tags, it occurred to him, he would qualify as a vagrant. Mikeflood said Browns Mills was about 8 klicks from where he was dropped off. Ronnie knew his walking pace was barely over two miles an hour. He was not even halfway there, he realized. And at the rate he was sweating, hydration was going to be an issue sooner than later. He pondered the irony of surviving Asian jungle warfare only to succumb to the American military bureaucracy.

Small shimmering pools appeared on the road stretched in front of him, the superheated air creating mirages of cool liquid. Ronnie dropped his duffel, checked his watch and decided he'd take a ten minute rest which he would repeat at one hour intervals. There were no trees and thus no real shade. The sun was nearly vertical overhead and even the telephone poles cast a tiny shadow. He thought it statistically unlikely that a vehicle going in his direction would not eventually appear. The only question was, would it stop?

◆ ◆ ◆

Brant Beach

In the second instant Charlie knew that he had not imagined it. There were three of them he quickly assessed, one at each front seat door and one with his hands on the hood. He didn't see a gun but the cruiser obscured the kid on the far side and so he couldn't be sure.

"Yeah, you. Jigaboo," the voice continued. It was the kid at the hood. He straightened up and crossed his arms on his chest.

Charlie patted for his nightstick but the ring on his belt that held it was empty. He had left it by his desk, he remembered, in his haste to be on time for Darnell's call. His hand moved toward his gun.

"You're thinkin' where's that white chick and that spick just when you need 'em, ain't that right, you fuckin' jungle bunny?"

Charlie raised his left arm to distract their attention and with his right hand unsnapped his holster.

"Sticks and stones, fellas," Charlie said in as non-threatening a tone as he could muster. "Now, I come from North Carolina and, believe me, you cannot call me a name that I have not already heard many, many times before." He turned slightly to obscure his hip on his gun side. "So why don't you fine northern gentleman reconsider your confrontational tone before things get seriously out of hand."

"Things are already seriously out of hand." It was the kid on the far side of the patrol car speaking. "We're here to straighten that out." It was a Philadelphia accent, Charlie thought. Close if not identical to the one he'd heard at the scuffle on the beach. He pressed his palm against the stock of his Smith & Wesson M917 and spread his fingers.

"And just how you plan to do that?" Charlie asked. If they weren't armed with anything serious he'd take a few lumps, he knew, but he'd do more damage than they could handle. He glanced down the street for their wheels. The only car he didn't know was a distressed, rust-brown Ford Fairlane with dented Pennsylvania plates. Charlie made a quick mental note of the tag number. They hadn't come with a getaway driver, which he figured improved his situation immensely.

The kid on the far side of his car raised a baseball bat.

"Let me guess," Charlie said. He began to ease his gun from the holster. "Looks like an Adirondack. Probably a 28 or maybe a 31 which means you swung it playing PAL or Little League ball. Dribblers to the first baseman, most likely. If you hit it at all, that is."

"Fuck you, eggplant," the kid answered.

Charlie felt the long barrel and then the muzzle of the .45 caliber slip free of the leather.

"Ah, eggplant. That tells me you're of Italian descent. Are your buddies both dumb-ass Wops, too? Or did you bring along a Polack and maybe a bog-trottin' Mick so you wouldn't lose your nerve."

The kid smacked the bat against his open palm. "You just keep talkin', Sambo," he growled, his face notably redder now.

Charlie smiled. "Never wait for a pitch to hit, son," he said. "Didn't they teach you that? Always *look* for a pitch to hit."

The three started to move toward him. Charlie brought his right arm straight up and brandished his sidearm. "Don't be stupid now," he said as he leveled it at the one closest to him. "'Course, I'm bettin' stupid's all you brought with you today outside a'that little-dick bat."

"You black bastard," the one with the bat yelled. Charlie swiveled slightly, took a slow breath and fired.

♦ ♦ ♦

Surf City

"You papa-san's little dog like me boo-coo," Bunny said. "Boo-coo lots."

The shock of what she heard next froze Mickey where she sat. Arlene's voice was shaking and she was speaking so loud into her microphone at Dispatch that all her S's were coming through blurred with static.

"Shots fired. Shots fired."

That's all Mickey heard at first although she knew there was more. They were sitting in the Chevelle letting the air conditioner run when the long shrill beep that signaled an emergency cut the humid air.

"All units respond. West sixty-second and Bayview. All units respond."

West 62nd and Bayview registered next. It was an address she knew.

"Shots fired. All Units respond Code 1. This is a 10-48, repeat, this is a 10-48."

The information hit Mickey all at once. The address was Charlie's house in Brant Beach and Code 10-48 meant Emergency Officer Assistance. Coupled with the never-welcome "shots fired" she assumed the worst, hit the flashers and then the siren.

"Cool!' Bunny said as Mickey shifted into gear. She immediately shifted the Chevelle back into Park. She had almost forgotten Bunny was there.

"I think that little dog misses you already," she said as calmly as she could. "Would you like to go play with him some more?"

Bunny's face lit up. "Peek-see. I go play with Peek-see. Peek-see lick my face. Peek-see like me boo-coo."

Mickey reached over and unbuckled the child's seat belt. "Tell my papa-san I had to go in a big hurry for work. I'll be back as soon as I can. Go! *Didi mau!*"

Bunny opened the door and jumped out.

"CLOSE THE DOOR," Mickey yelled over the siren. Patsy was standing in the doorway, the little dog in his arms. Bunny slammed the cruiser door shut with both hands and ran toward him. As Mickey backed up and then pulled out she saw Bunny disappear through the doorway. Patsy held a hand to his head in the sign for "Call" and Mickey returned an extended thumb as she threaded her way to the Boulevard. She could hear the sirens from other responding units and then saw their blue strobes and cherry-tops heading south. In the rush of adrenaline, sights and sounds, she made scant note of the orange car turning west toward the bay.

♦ ♦ ♦

Brant Beach

The bat exploded with a thunderous crack simultaneously with the first shot. The kid dropped it and put both hands to his face which, Charlie noticed, was bleeding profusely. The other two froze at the sound and he used the split-second pause to put a round at each of their feet, sending chunks of asphalt and gravel spraying into the air. Fright-induced profanities flew and Charlie used his improvised version of a flash-bang to advance on his cruiser. The kid with the bat was on the ground and out of the fray for the moment Charlie figured, which left only two slightly dazed and confused punks to deal with. Charlie holstered his gun and charged right at them. Extending his arms, he hooked the nearer one with his left, dragged him across the car's freshly Simonized hood and used him like a battering ram to take down the other one who was still standing. It was only the wail of police sirens approaching that kept him from pounding the two heads within his reach into bloody pulps on the pavement in anger. He glanced over at the third kid who was moaning and still holding his bloody head. The bat had been above the kid's head when he fired so Charlie was sure he hadn't fatally wounded him and most likely hadn't even hit him. Whether a sharp chunk of the Adirondack was stuck in his skull was another matter.

"Now don't either of you two dipshits move a muscle," Charlie barked. "You done messed with the wrong eggplant. *Boys.*" He almost spat the last word at them.

The roar of engines and the squeal of tires announced the arrival of reinforcements. Charlie heard car doors opening and a chorus of "fuck"-heavy commands being shouted. Two of the Long Beach officers were standing over him.

"Charlie, you OK?" one asked.

"Yeah," Charlie replied. "Yeah, I'm good." He released his grip on the boys on the ground and pushed himself to his knees, panting. "How's that one?"

A Beach Haven patrolman Charlie knew only as Jimmy G. was tending to the bat-holder.

"Got some shrapnel, looks like," he said without a trace of sympathy. "And a pretty good scalp wound. I ain't a doctor but I'm guessing he'll live." The he laughed.

Charlie got to his feet and brushed dirt from his uniform. There were large sweat stains beneath each arm.

"So who are these morons and what's their beef," one of the Long Beach guys asked. His nameplate said Belz. Charlie thought his first name was Mike.

"Just that," Charlie replied. "Morons. Beyond that, my guess is they're either drinking buddies or coworkers of the guys whose heads we busted on the beach. Same accent, I think. That's their car down the street. The piece of shit with Pennsy plates."

"Classy wheels," Belz replied. "Hardly worth the impound cost."

Charlie straightened his uniform and watched as Belz's partner and another of the Beach Haven officers cuffed the boys on the ground and pulled them roughly to their feet.

"Cancel the bus," Jimmy G. yelled over. "No ambulance ride for this *putz*. We'll wrap his head in a towel. The ER can wait until after he's booked." He reached behind the still moaning boy and cuffed him.

Belz came over and stood next to Charlie. "You gotta know how much I hate to do this to you but-"

"I'll follow you back and give you a complete and detailed statement. I discharged my weapon so I'll have a stack of papers to fill out at our shop, too. Might as well get started."

"You're sure you're OK, right?" Belz asked.

"The very last game of my senior season I got into a fight with the whole Princeton lacrosse team. Score ended up in a tie but the fight went our way. And they were some tough white boys, I will tell you that much. We drank with them later that night. So I suppose I didn't have to use my weapon but I just didn't have all day to spend whupping their asses, you know?"

Belz patted him on the back. "Ahh, don't worry. You didn't

shoot 'em, pardner, you just shot *at* 'em. Big difference."

Charlie turned around at the approach of a sound he knew well – Chief Cleary's big-ass Chevelle engine. He watched as she screeched to a halt and the driver's door flew open. He eyed her as she her quickly assessed the threat situation and then started walking toward him. When she got close she smiled.

"Who fired the shots?" she asked.

"Just me, Chief, I'm afraid," Charlie answered. "But I couldn't hit the broad side of a barn from the looks of it. I missed all three of them. Badly."

The Chief chuckled. "Less paperwork that way though, Deputy," she said.

"That is true, ma'am," Charlie responded. Jimmy G. approached holding something in front of him. Charlie saw that it was the barrel of the baseball bat. It had survived almost completely intact. The tapered end above the handle was a jagged array of ash wood spikes and splinters-in-the-making.

"Souvenir," Jim G. said, handing it to Charlie.

Belz whistled. "Whoa. Nice shootin' there, Tex," he said. "That handle can't be more than an inch in diameter. Damn, son, you are one deadeye dick."

"Little League Adirondack, just like I thought," Charlie said, turning the barrel to read the wood-burned labels in the middle and at the end. "And check this out, Chief Cleary. It's the Mickey Mantle model. From what you tell me, your Deputy Fairbrother would be proud."

"Yes he certainly would," the Chief replied. "We'll have to put it up on the wall at the shop."

Charlie lowered the bat fragment to his side. "I'll give my statement to our Beach Haven brethren on my way back but then you and I need to have ourselves a serious sit-down conversation. Where's Bunny?"

"She's at Patsy's. Why?"

Charlie looked around. "Best keep a short leash on that young'un 'til we get some things sorted out. I'll explain later." He saw the look that crossed the Chief's face and furrowed her brow.

"Don't worry," he said. "We got plenty of wagons to circle."

Thirty

County Route 545
Outside Browns Mills, NJ

Ronnie was due for another ten-minute rest when he heard the engine. He unwrapped his uniform blouse from around his head and cocked an ear. It was definitely coming from behind him and so, to his great relief and minor astonishment, that meant it was heading in the same direction he was.

He unfolded the blouse, shook it out and then slipped it back on. He'd already doffed his undershirt and so he started buttoning up the blouse. He had it about halfway when he heard the car's engine throttle down behind him. At least the driver was slowing up, he reasoned. Ronnie dragged his duffel and stood on the narrow dirt and gravel shoulder with his thumb out.

The sun reflecting off the windshield made it hard to see what kind of car it was that was approaching. As it drew closer and, Ronnie noticed, slowed even more he recognized it – a late model Pontiac, probably a Tempest. And it was a convertible to boot. It was apple red and gleamed like it had just been Turtle Waxed. The unique grill, with its ship-like center prow and the dual side-by-side headlights came closer. On the driver's side of the grill there was a GTO badge.

A snippet of music flashed through his mind's ear.

Wa-waaah, Wa-wa-wa-wa-waaaahhhh

He thought it was Ronnie and the Daytonas. The coincidence did not escape him as the car came to a rolling stop abreast of him.

"You lost soldier?" the driver asked above the rattle and roar. The car shook slightly even at idle RPM's.

Definitely a V-8, Ronnie decided, which meant something like three hundred plus horses if it had the four-barrel carburetor. Ronnie remembered reading a feature on the car in one of Mickey's collection of hot rod magazines. It really was shaped like a Coke bottle when seen from the side, he thought.

"Sir. No sir," Ronnie replied out of reflex. The driver was not wearing a uniform.

"You're not AWOL, are you?"

Ronnie laughed. "Sir. Definitely not, sir. My ETS became official about three hours ago."

"Well then hop in," the driver said. "Just throw your duffel in the back seat. Bet you're tired of humping it."

"I am but it's pretty dirty, sir" Ronnie replied slinging the duffel strap. "You sure you don't want me to put it in the trunk?"

"Nah. Just throw it in," the driver said nodding to the rear of the vehicle.

Ronnie lifted the duffel bag and dropped it in the bench back seat. The car's upholstery was also red, he noticed He opened the passenger side door, rolled down his pant legs, brushed off the seat of his fatigues and slid in. He pulled the door shut and when he turned, the driver already had his hand extended.

"Cole," the man said with a big smile. "Cole Prejean."

◆ ◆ ◆

Somewhere in the Pine Barrens

Mike Gannon was now completely and irretrievably lost and he knew it. His watch said one o'clock but it was if he'd entered a whole different time zone somehow. What sunlight filtered down was weak and smoky and it seemed more like early evening than it did mid-afternoon.

He'd repeatedly nodded his head in understanding when the bartender at the Piccadilly Tavern – he thought that was the name on the sign, anyway – had given him directions. Gannon was a city kid, used to *turn right, turn left* or *keep going straight* kinds of instructions and realized that's what he should have asked for. But some odd form of male insecurity had made him embarrassed to admit he couldn't navigate his way out of a paper bag. The directions might as well have been given in Egyptian hieroglyphics. The compass headings and driving distances the man had recited, and which Gannon had tried to scribble down, became useless once the canopy of tall pines thickened and he couldn't even tell where exactly the sun was.

The he heard the rumble of an engine. No, not just one engine he realized, but several. The leaves rustled as the sound grew louder and small animals skittered by his feet running from the intrusion. A large deer – he thought it was deer anyway – flashed by about twenty yards from him, its white-tailed rump bouncing with every stride.

Gannon got out of his car. He hoped it was some locals who, if they couldn't lead him to his destination, could at least point him in a proper direction. The soles of his scuffed and deeply creased Florsheims sunk in the mossy soil which at one point almost pulled his feet clean out of them. Within a few more steps the thin, faintly elastic Gold-Toe socks were soggy and covered with tiny fragments of twigs and leaves. As he slowly advanced he held on to slippery tree branches and the occasional knurled and knobby trunk for balance.

A motorcycle with a single rider passed by on the backwoods excuse-for-a-road he had turned off a just few minutes before. Gannon realize his shouts would never be heard above the bike engines and so he continued to plod onward. He had, he guessed, about fifty more yards to cover. The riders seemed to be coming single-file. Most wore sleeveless leather vests and had arms that were heavily tattooed. He had a bad angle to see exactly what was on the back of all their vests but he guessed it was supposed to be the head of a hooded monk or perhaps the Grim Reaper. It also looked like there was white lettering arcing above and below the figure but he couldn't make out what it spelled. Gannon had wanted to interview the leader of the Sons of Satan. A little local digging indicated that people on the Island thought they were a rough bunch but that they generally kept to themselves. Not quite The Wild Bunch, he surmised. They hadn't yet taken over any small towns. He was sure they held the key to the missing parts of Mickey Cleary's story. He wasn't completely sure that the riders on the trail were the gang he was looking for.

Gannon continued to press forward through the underbrush.

He was just about to raise his arm to draw attention when he stopped. A motorcycle with a sidecar came into view. It was moving slower than the pack and was apparently having trouble getting traction on the wet forest floor. It skidded back and forth and its driver was rapidly shifting gears and gunning the engine to adjust. But what caught Gannon's attention and caused him to rethink hailing the group was not the rider but the sidecar's passenger. Gannon had expected to see what he often referred to in his puff pieces as a Motorcycle Mama. Instead, the bullet-shaped sidecar held what looked to Gannon like a middle-aged man in a soiled white dress shirt. His head and torso bobbed in an exaggerated manner with each bump and turn. It took Gannon a second to realize that the passenger couldn't brace himself because his hands appeared to be tied or otherwise restrained behind his back. His eyes were wide and even with the gray duct tape across his mouth Gannon could read the look on his face.

Pure, unmitigated terror.

Gannon had brought his ancient Brownie Starflash camera along with several rolls of Kodak 127 Ektachrome film but they were locked in the car's trunk. Even if he could get to it, he figured, the big silver reflector bowl on the camera's top would give him away. He pressed as close as he could to a big pine and willed himself invisible. It sounded like three or four more motorcycles passed by before the rumble began to fade. If he followed the freshly made bike tracks backwards, he reasoned, he should be able to find his way to the main road and civilization.

When the engine noise seemed far enough away he began picking his way back to the car, composing his new story in his head. He already had the new lede:

"Behold the forest primeval. Or, more accurately perhaps, the forest of prime evil."

With the words buzzing in his head he didn't see the man in the leather vest standing by his now-muddy Dodge Dart until he spoke.

"Observe anything interesting?" he asked.

◆ ◆ ◆

Brant Beach

Dip and Rodriguez had pulled up minutes after Mickey arrived. Charlie was getting into his cruiser, still holding the Adirondack.

"Nice you guys could make it," she chided.

"You missed all the excitement."

"We were both at Sunset and Barnegat, Chief," Dippolito said.

"Yeah," Rodriguez interjected. "Why didn't you ever tell me about that *chica*?"

Mickey started to laugh.

"I take it Charlie's OK?" Dippolito asked.

"Three idiot punks against Charlie?" Mickey said and exhaled sharply. "Shit, that's not even close to a fair fight in my book."

"Who fired the—"

Mickey cut Rodriguez off. "Charlie did, but they were just warning shots. We'll debrief when we get back to the shop."

"What's he got in his hand?" Dip asked.

"He got a broken-bat single. I'll explain later." She scraped the ground with her toe. "Dip, help the Long Beach guys look for the other piece of that bat, would you? Rodriguez, you go back and hold the fort. Charlie's going to be a while. I have to make a stop in Ship Bottom and then I'll meet you there."

"Copy that, Chief. And the rugrats want to know if Princess Bonnie can come for supper tonight," Rodriguez added. "Colombia said it's fine. We're having tacos. I bet her royal highness has never had a taco."

"We'll see about supper. Call Mayor Billy. See if he'll be in his office this afternoon or if he and Loretta will be canoodling."

"Canoodling? Is that some fancy kind of canoeing?"

"Well…it may involve a man in a boat."

Rodriguez scratched his head. "You lost me, Chief. Maybe you can explain that later, too."

"Ask Charlie next time you're out for a beer. The man knows everything, like you said."

Rodriguez reset his patrol hat, tapped the bill in salute and headed back to his cruiser. Dippolito came up holding the other end of the bat.

"Not much left, Chief. Just the knob really," Dip said.

"Should be a number stamped on the bottom?" Mickey said.

Dippolito turned it up. "Three-one. Thirty-one."

"Charlie guessed it was a 28. He'll be disappointed he was wrong."

"It was still a hell of a shot, especially since he did it on the dead draw," Dippolito opined.

"Well, nobody's dead or seriously wounded, so that's what's important." She tapped her campaign hat against her uniform pants. "What was Rich doing when you got to Sunset?"

"He was backing out of the front door like the place was on fire."

"And the dog? What kind was it, did he say? It wasn't a Chihuahua by chance, was it?"

"Springer spaniel the lady said. A male."

"Wait, you talked to her?" Mickey said.

"Yeah, of course. She seemed real nice. I think we kind of surprised her, though."

"Surprised her? Dip, she called us, remember."

"Well, then Rich must'a got there a lot sooner than she expected. She was wearing a slinky kind of bathrobe and, Chief, I swear I tried not to look but I'm not sure she had her underwear or a bathing suit on underneath it."

Mickey burst out laughing.

"OK, Dip, sometime in the next twenty-four hours I want you to talk to Rodriguez and Charlie. Preferably at a bar and after at least two beers. Got it?"

"Copy that, Chief. What should I do now?"

Mickey looked at the quiet street. There were no lookey-loos in sight. All at the beach, she decided. "Drive around the loop a couple of times to remind people we're out and about and keeping an eye. Call the State Police. See if they can connect our friends from the beach to these guys – make sure you tell them to deal directly with the Long Beach boys so we don't step on any toes. Oh, and check the houses across the street. Make sure one of Charlie's rounds didn't end up in someone's parlor. Meet us at the shop when you're done."

"Copy, Chief," he said and walked away.

Davey Johnson from the Ship Bottom PD sauntered toward her. She hadn't seen his patrol car roll up. "Wow," he said, "A real Gunfight at the B.B. Corral."

"That's pretty clever," Mickey said. "Hey, thanks for looking out for my dad, Davey."

"My pleasure, Chief. I tell Justus it's only part of our routine patrol grid but we check more often than that. He spends more time counting our hours than anything else."

"No phantom truck?" she asked

"Not the one he eyeballed. Not just yet, anyway."

Mickey tugged on his uniform sleeve. "Ship Bottom Blue?" she said with a smirk.

"Ship Bottom Blues is more like it," Davey replied, shaking his head. "He's a little tyrant. Starts every friggin' sentence with 'back in California.'"

"I met him today," Mickey said. "He is definitely a trip."

"A rather short trip," Davey replied with a wink. "I think that might be the whole problem." Mickey remembered Charlie's comment about Napoleon.

"Could be. Where is he anyway?" Mickey asked. "I figured he'd beat the Long Beach boys here."

"At Zeke's place out in Manahawkin getting the custom paint job he ordered finished. I bet he's shitting a brick right about now."

"Zeke still running a low-end chop shop?"

"Don't ask, don't tell," Davey answered.

"Speaking of asking, you still engaged?"

"Nah, that kind of fell apart. I don't think the Sheehan's envisioned their daughter making do on a beach cop's income. You still-"

"Yes, I'm still," Mickey replied with a nod. "One of these days you're going to hear me singing 'Hey, la, my boyfriend's back, but not just yet it seems.'"

"That was The Angels, unless I'm wrong. Few years back, though."

"1963," Mickey said. "I remember because I was brand new and the North Philly girls were singing it out the windows of their row homes. Sometimes, if I was on my second or third walk-by they'd change it to "hey, la, my beat cop's back."

"Cute. Little different down here, I suppose."

"Ususally. But not today," Mickey said and placed her hat squarely on her head. "Definitely not today. This situation had FUBAR written all over it but luckily things stayed north." She turned to leave and then stopped. "I'm heading to Patsy's right now so you can check this one off your list. And if I hear of a nice single girl, I'll let you know."

"And if you get a Dear Jane letter you be sure to let *me* know," Davey replied.

Mickey gave him a little wave and headed for the Chevelle.

◆ ◆ ◆

The Pine Barrens

Gannon's mouth had gone to pill-bottle cotton.

The man in front of him was lean and lanky and seemed, he thought, relatively unperturbed by Gannon's presence. He worked up a scintilla of saliva, waited until it coated his tongue and then spoke.

"You a Son of Satan?"

Gannon noticed that the man had a set of military dog tags dangling from his neck. When he smiled, Gannon thought it looked like he'd just come from an expensive orthodontist appointment.

"Well, it's not exactly how I describe myself when I call my mother. But that's the name of my motorcycle club, yeah." He leaned a hip against the Dart's from fender. "Didn't know they ever made this in a convertible, tell the truth. Not sure *why* they did to be honest."

"They didn't make a lot of them, I don't think," Gannon replied. "Do you guys worship Satan, by chance?"

"Worship Satan?" the man chuckled. "I don't think half our members could *spell* Satan without looking at their patch. You have any idea how close you just came?" he asked.

"I'm beginning to suspect," Gannon said with a rasp.

"Who were they?"

"Call themselves the Druids. And they don't call their mothers very often, I suspect."

Gannon felt his body posture relax. "That guy in the sidecar?"

The man ignored the question.

"I'm Stellwag," he said. "Steven Stellwag. You could say I'm in charge of our little band of brothers."

Gannon began walking toward the Dart.

"Can you guide me out of here?" he asked.

Again the question was ignored.

"You the reporter from Philly who's been sniffing around our club's good friend Chief Cleary?"

"I am a newspaper journalist, I am from Philadelphia and, yes, I did come down the shore to talk to Mickey Cleary about some events that may or may not have occurred in 1967."

"It was the Summer of Love, man," Stellwag said with a grin.

"I didn't come to write about love, unfortunately," Gannon replied. "*You* wouldn't be interested in talking to me about those events, would you?"

"Not about Chief Cleary, I wouldn't."

"How about other things?"

"I might," Stellwag said, "But only if you find those other things more interesting than old news from '67 that, as you say, may or may not have happened."

Gannon was almost to the car's rear fender.

"I always put the best story on the front page," he said. "You know of a better story?"

"You just saw what you just saw. What do you think?"

"I think I wish I hadn't seen it. But now that I have." Gannon reached for his notebook.

"Now that you have is a problem. A problem for them and a problem for you." Stellwag's brow furrowed.

"I have to tell somebody," Gannon complained. "I have to report it. I mean, they're going to kill that man, aren't they?"

"Maybe," Stellwag said. "But you don't know that for sure, do you? Maybe they just want to talk to him, see what he knows. Maybe they just want to frighten him into not talking about what he knows. Maybe some college kids hired them to scare the living shit out of one of their pledges. Maybe they're initiating a Prospect."

"Would a Prospect be wearing a white dress shirt?"

"There's a thousand stories in the Naked City and probably twice that many out here in the Pine Barrens."

"What am I supposed to do, then?"

"Wait 'til your sources tell you somebody's disappeared or 'til a body shows up." Stellwag swatted a bug on his inked and muscled forearm then flicked it off. "You've got a hell of a story then. If you're brave enough or maybe foolish enough, you've got an eyewitness account to go with it."

"I think I'd go with 'sources who wish to remain anonymous' for obvious reasons," Gannon said and sidled around to the driver's side. "So, can you show me the way out of here. I can just follow the motorcycle tracks if you'd rather not."

To Gannon's surprise, Stellwag took two steps and opened the Dart's passenger side door. "If you want to talk about those other things, there's no time like the present. Best to put a little time between that parade and your egress. Might run into a few stragglers protecting the rear if you go back that way." He slipped into the front seat, pulling his knees up so they would fit.

Gannon got in, fumbled for his keys and then pulled his door shut.

"Steven Stellwag. It's got a good ring to it. Alliterative, and the ST combination is especially strong."

Stellwag pulled a pair of rectangular blue-tinted sunglasses from his vest pocket. Gannon recognized them as the style favored by military aviators. "My real first name is Claude," he said with a smile. "But if you ever call me that or print that?" He slipped the sunglasses on. "*I'll* kill you."

Gannon turned the key in the ignition. He put the Dart in Reverse and slowly backed up, wondering exactly what he'd gotten himself into.

Thirty-One

Brant Beach

Dickie let the Road Runner idle just off the main drag on a side street named, according to the sign, East Paulding Avenue. He turned around in a shallow driveway and pointed the car west, inching forward until he had a view of the action halfway down the road across from him.

The screaming sirens and speeding cop cars at had commandeered his attention. He abandoned the hot, boring and so far fruitless box-grid search in Barnegat in favor of chasing down something potentially more exciting. If Harlan asked, and Dickie knew he would, Dickie's rationale would be that a commotion attracted a crowd and that a crowd allowed for the efficient recon of a larger number of civilians in one place. Unfortunately, as far as he could tell, whatever the commotion was had attracted more cops than crowds. He wasn't even certain he could see anyone who wasn't wearing a uniform.

Shocking Blue's "Venus" was pouring out of the radio. He turned up the volume doubting that a loud radio would draw any more attention than a cluster of police cruisers in any of these towns. *She's got it,* he hummed to himself. *She's got it.* The song faded out in a wail of plaintive electric twangs and a pulsing bass line. A motor-mouthed DJ came on and Dickie was anticipating another loud and fast summer song. When he heard the whiny and slow-starting strains of Zager and Evans' inexplicably popular "In the Year 2525," he pounded one of the silver station-selector buttons. To his dismay the Youngbloods' sappy "Get Together" began bleeding from the speakers.

"Yeah," Dickie said. "That's right. Everybody get the fuck together right now," and punched another button. A pounding back beat and an immediately identifiable baritone told him that Elvis had not left the building. "Caught in a trap," he thought as the song blared out. He turned the volume up louder and recalled his conversation on the beach with Harlan. "Can't walk out," he sang to himself.

When Dickie looked up the police cars were dispersing. He turned down the radio and shifted into Drive, keeping his foot planted firmly on the brake pedal. Three cars, all from different island towns judging by their markings, stopped at the corner across from him. Two turned to his right and headed north, the third turned to his left and sped south. Dickey flipped on his right-turn signal and slowly released the brake. He had just shifted his foot to the gas pedal when a family carting a large, pink and black striped umbrella and two oversized rafts and dragging several plaid beach blankets crossed in front of him. He pounded the brake. The Road Runner's nose, he figured, was less than a foot from the two giggling little girls who were looking at him through the windshield. Just about the dink kid's age he figured, but they were both tanned and blond and classically American. All they needed, he decided, was a little dog tugging on a swimsuit and they could be a Coppertone billboard. One of them waved. Dickie waved back and tapped the horn.

After they passed he spied another cruiser across the intersection waiting to turn north. Deciding it would be better to be behind it than ahead of it, he waited until it turned and then he pulled out. He kept a safe trailing distance behind the cop car which, he noticed, was a nice-looking Chevelle SS from Surf City and bore the Police Department's phone number across its trunk:

HY4-8121

He thought he remembered Harlan saying something about the word Hyacinth and a phone number in Winston's pocket. Maybe, Dickie decided, he would reverse his grid and cruise Surf City first, now that he was pointed north. The Army had taught him the expression "go south" to describe a deteriorating situation. Maybe there was some greater cosmic benefit to be derived, he wondered, in going north. Maybe he'd have more success if he stayed on this heading. He'd lost focus on the road and so didn't notice the cruiser's brake lights and left turn signal. The Plymouth screeched to a stop inches from the Chevelle's bumper. The cruiser turned left, its driver glancing only momentarily back at him. It took him a second to register that the driver was not only a cop, it was a female cop. And not bad looking from what he could tell. At his court martial, Dickie recalled, one of the jury of officers had been a woman and another had been black. Women cops and Negro officers, he thought, passing judgment on him. It was if his rightful place in the world didn't even exist anymore.

Dickie made a left at the next corner and slowly doubled back. Now he really wanted to see more of this girl cop – see what she had from the neck down, anyway. The idea of a pretty woman with a gun slung on her hip titillated him. Stuck in a line of cars held up by an old woman trying and repeatedly failing to parallel park, he watched as the Chevelle stopped in front of a small wooden bungalow. The girl got out and let herself in the front door of the little home. It didn't look like an official call, Dickie thought. She hadn't even knocked. Boyfriend, he wondered? It occurred to him that even cops had nooners. Anyway, what little he saw he liked.

Horns were starting to honk and tempers were starting to flare in the cars ahead of him. Dickie actually hoped it took a while longer so he could watch the woman exit and get a look at her from the front. He was assuming her particular model came standard with high beams.

More cars stacked up behind him. He saw a tanned teenager in baggy trunks and a blue t-shirt that said "WaterBrother" on the front jump out of an idling Mustang. The kid swapped places with the old lady and expertly slipped her aging Lincoln Continental into a parking place in three quick moves. Dickie was impressed, since the baby-blue sedan looked to be about the length of an aircraft carrier. A cheer went up from both passers-by who'd stopped to watch the spectacle and the line of stuck drivers. Horns now blared in celebration as traffic began crawling forward again. The old lady, Dickie figured she had to be at least eighty, turned, smiled and gave everyone her thin and bony middle finger.

He tapped the accelerator, keeping one eye on the bungalow. If it was a nooner, then he'd have to roll by later if he wanted a second chance to check her out. The knot of cars slowly loosened and he resumed his reconnaissance run. No harm in checking out Ship Bottom twice, he thought.

On the Road Runner's radio Jackie DeShannon was encouraging him to "Put a Little Love in Your Heart." Dickie changed the station.

♦ ♦ ♦

Mickey was surprised to find Patsy asleep on the couch.
"Dad," said, rousing him." Where's Bunny?"
"Watching TV," he said groggily. "Sally Starr should be comin' on now I thought. Kid said she never heard of Popeye and Olive Oyl. I figured it'd be, you know, educational."
Mickey looked at the old black-and white set. The sound was turned all the way down. Mickey reached over and turned it back up.
"*And now we return to...The Secret Storm*" an announcer cooed. A commercial for Shake & Bake Seasoning had just finished.
"Bunny?" Mickey called. There was no reply. "*Bunny,*" she said in a louder and stricter tone. Again, no answer. "Dad, where is she?" Mickey struggled to keep an even voice. Patsy sat up.
"She was right there." He pointed to the TV. "Drinkin' a Hawaiian Punch I got her. Happy as a clam. Hey, where's Pixie?"
"Forget the damn dog, Dad," Mickey barked. "Where the hell is Bunny?"
Patsy rubbed his head. "Maybe she took her for a little walk. I bought a leash when we went downtown."
"Fuck, Dad," Mickey said. "How could you let her-" She was halfway out the front door when she heard Patsy's screen slam around back. Mickey bolted through the living room and past the kitchen.
"Peek-see hot," Bunny said. "She need drink. I give her my red punch."
The little dog was panting madly. Patsy went to the sink. He filled and then came over with a cereal bowl of cold water. Pixie ignored it. "I sure hope she don't have the heat prostations," he said.
"Who? Bunny?" Mickey asked.
"No," Patsy said. "Pixie. She don't look so good. I better get the fan." He grabbed the brown metal Sears box fan from the window, plugged it in and turned it on. It rattled and hummed

and then pushed out a stream of slowly cooling air. The dog lay down, its tongue lolling worrisomely to one side. Patsy unhooked the leash from the tiny cloth collar and pushed the bowl of water toward it.

"Bunny, where did you go?"

"We take walk," Bunny answered. "Talk to people. They like pet Peek-see."

"How far did you go?"

Bunny traced a square with her finger. "We stay on path whole time."

Mickey assumed she was referring to the sidewalk which meant they might have only gone around the block. "No street?" she asked.

Bunny shook her head slowly. "No street," she said." Where my punch? "

"I'll get you a fresh one," Mickey said.

"Fruit juicy Hawaiian punch," Bunny sing-songed.

"There we are," said Patsy. The little dog was coming around and lapped daintily at the full bowl. "She's okay, just worn out. You have to ask me before you take her outside, Bunny. Got it?"

"You sleep," Bunny said. "Peek-see scratch at door. I take for walk after she pee. We have fun."

Mickey pulled the big can from the refrigerator. It had two triangular holes punched in its top. Mickey grabbed Bunny's glass, poured out the warm remnants and refilled it. She held it to her chest.

"You heard the man. Ask next time, got it?"

"Five by five," Bunny answered and reached out her hand. Mickey gave her the bright red concoction which she guessed probably contained a pound of pure sugar.

"That stuff has vitamins, right?" Patsy asked. "That's why I bought it."

All Mickey could do was laugh. "Sure, Dad. Lots of vitamins. I'm sure it builds strong bodies twelve ways."

"I think that's Wonder Bread, kid," Patsy replied.

Bunny smacked her lips after downing the entire glass. "I stay here. Play with Peek-see. Drink more punch. I wait for Dunn here. You bring. Tomorrow we find Mama."

"You're coming with me," Mickey said. "Pixie's had enough excitement for one day." She looked at Patsy. "And so have I."

"Yeah," Patsy said, "What was all the fuss going south? I heard somethin' about shots on the scanner."

"I'll fill you in later," Mickey answered. "Stupidly isn't strictly illegal but sometimes, Dad, sometimes it's damn near lethal." Mickey glanced down. Pixie was now up on all four legs and lapping at the water with more enthusiasm. "In the car, young lady," she instructed Bunny. "Tell Patsy thank you and Pixie you'll see her later."

"You tell," Bunny said. "Patsy you papa-san." She went over to pet the dog.

"Thanks, pap-san," Mickey said and winked. "We'll be back later."

"OK, Michaela," Patsy said. Pixie trotted over to him and he scooped the dog up. "But what did she mean 'wait here for Dunn'?"

Mickey put a finger to her lips and led Bunny out to the car.

♦ ♦ ♦

Lebanon State Forest
N.J. State Highway 72

To Ronnie, Cole Prejean seemed like a man on a mission.

Ronnie's dead-reckoning told him they were at the southern border of the Pine Barrens, the Lebanon State Forest on official maps, named for the old Lebanon Glass works. He figured they would be emerging from the dusky *demimonde* fairly soon.

"Ever been way back in there?" Prejean had asked.

"Time or two" Ronnie had replied.

"Not too inviting, is it?"

"That's exactly how they like it." Ronnie's last comment had lulled the conversation for a while.

As the flickering, almost strobe-like sunlight flashed over them Ronnie pondered his vehicular savior. Prejean said he'd done ten years in uniform and had been out for just as long. His haircut and his apparent fitness level made Ronnie wonder. He said now he did some "consulting" work for the armed services and was finishing up a stint as a civilian contractor at Fort Dix.

"Strictly white collar stuff, though," he'd said. Teletypes, mimeo machines, Xerox copiers. And these new things called computers. Finding a way to connect them all instead of shipping or hand-carrying documents all over the globe. Inside of five years the side that's getting information seamlessly and accurately from one command to another is the side that's going to win. It's always been that way – grunts fight the battles but eggheads win the wars. Alan Turing, Albert Einstein and Robert Oppenheimer, just to name a few."

"What do we do with all the guns and missiles, then?" Ronnie had asked half-seriously.

'Good question," Prejean had answered. "Battles are fought and wars are waged mostly for political theater and career advancement. Other than taking out Hitler and Hirohito, ever known a war to really change anything it set out to change?"

Ronnie admitted he did not have a good answer to that one. Prejean said he had family on Long Beach Island and was treating himself to, as he phrased it, "the Holy Grail of East Coast vacations, right? A week at the Shore."

Ronnie looked up at the thinning canopy. He pondered the statistical likelihood that the only car he saw would not only be going in his direction but would be going all the way to Long Beach Island. It was theoretically possible but still it seemed that everything about his departure and arrival, including the unexplainable and interminable delays, felt less like a series of random occurrences than it did a sequence of pre-planned maneuvers.

"Not much of a talker, are you?" Prejean said with a smile.

Ronnie apologized. "Trying to get used to the idea of being a civilian again, I guess." He noticed that Prejean did not ask him the usual set of questions – how long he'd been in, where he was deployed, what action he'd seen. The man seemed content to know that he wasn't AWOL and that had a girlfriend in Surf City he was going home to fornicate with.

"My girlfriend's dad lives in Ship Bottom," Ronnie offered. Prejean had said his destination was his brother's place there, not far from the causeway terminus. "If you want to drop me off I can get to Surf City without any problem."

"Wouldn't think of it," Prejean replied. "Any man that served his country like you have qualifies for a door-to-door ride in my book. Tell me about your girl."

Ronnie told him a little about Mickey. He intentionally left out the part about her being the Chief.

"I think it's great that women are being recognized for their abilities and not just for their proportions," Prejean said. "When I got out there were no women officers in my command chain. I imagine that's changed. Your girl must be a cut above to be where she's at. Chief of Police. I bet that caused more than one pair of testicles to retract."

Ronnie remained silent.

The Tempest roared out of the forest and onto a brightly lit stretch of straightway. Prejean gunned the engine. Ronnie grabbed the window frame as they approached and then took a mild curve at high speed. After negotiating it Ronnie yelled "*Ole'*" and gave him a thumbs up. Prejean had told him the car's rich color was a factory paint job called Matador Red.

"Damn straight *ole'*. Fuckin' A, ole'," Prejean said and let the car coast for a while.

Ronnie waited until the engine noise dropped and then looked over at Prejean.

"I appreciate the lift," he said. "But if it's OK with you, can we just cut the shit right now?"

Prejean didn't react. He just let the car continue to glide and pulled it onto the highway's narrow shoulder. When the Tempest finally came to a stop he reached for the glove box.

Thirty-Two

The Pine Barrens

The dark interior of the Sons of Satan clubhouse had the baked-in aroma of body odor and stale beer. Gannon sat on a long davenport. One leg was missing and had been replaced by a cinderblock. It had three mismatched, torn and stained cushions. He tried not to think about what the stains were from.

"All of the guys in the Club served in-country," Stellwag was telling him. He sat in a leather La-Z-Boy recliner that seemed to be not only in good shape but of a recent vintage. Rank has its privilege, Gannon thought to himself. "All saw action and all were honorably discharged. Most have at least one decoration for valor."

Gannon had his notebook out and was scribbling furiously.

"So why are they – and you for that matter – holed up in a modern-day no-man's land?"

"Casualties of war," Stellwag said. He pulled a pack of Lucky Strikes from his vest. "Smoke?" he asked, holding the pack out to Gannon.

"Maybe later," Gannon replied.

Stellwag tapped out a cigarette, held it in his lips and withdrew an Army-green Zippo lighter. "Beer?" he asked, lighting the cigarette. "We got plenty."

"Again, maybe later," Gannon replied.

"Let me get you one anyway," Stellwag said. "It'll help put the boys at ease to see you with it. Drinking it is strictly up to you." He rose from the recliner and crossed to a large refrigerator. "Schaefer

OK?" he asked. "Some of the boys are partial to Ballantine Ale so we got that, too."

"Sure. Schaefer's fine. Although I doubt I'll be having more than one," Gannon replied, mimicking the television jingle.

"You're a funny guy for a reporter," Stellwag said, returning to his recliner with two bottles. He handed one to Gannon. "But you're funny in a very sly way."

"And you're a smart guy, Mr. Stellwag. Do I call you Mister?"

Stellwag smiled. "To these guys I'm still an LT. So if you want to be formal just call me lieutenant and even though you're a civilian I grant you permission to address me as LT."

"Got it," Gannon said and continued to write. "El-Tee. So, we were talking about your brothers-in arms. My question is why aren't they working regular jobs, buying houses, having kids and backyard barbecues in the leafy suburbs? That's what the guys home from World War II did. That's how we got Levittown – both of them."

Stellwag tapped a long ash onto the wood floor.

"Some tried and failed. Some didn't bother trying. After you've crawled around in the jungle picking leeches off your skin, after you've seen guys impaled by *punji* sticks, after you've seen the inhuman things that a committed enemy is capable of doing – stocking produce at the A & P or peddling lawnmowers and chainsaws to guys in Ban-Lon at Sears just is not an option. What our countrymen don't understand is that there was simply no way for us to come home and not bring the war back with us."

"Why not just stay in the military then? It's a solid career, good pension."

Stellwag laughed and tapped out another Lucky.

"Because it's still the military. Even if you love the Army, Mr. Gannon, it won't ever love you back. None of these guys wanted to be officers. Hell, most of them never even wanted to be sergeants. This club is modeled on the military but without all the regimental bullshit. We don't have a flag but we do have a patch. And we will fight to protect that patch."

Gannon paused his scribbling. "Who's your enemy now, lieutenant? Um, did I do that right?"

Stellwag nodded. "State Police narcs, the ATF, IRS, New Jersey Forest Fire Service, the dipshits who want to level the Pines and build an airport for jets."

"The Druids?" Gannon interjected.

Stellwag smiled. "I was wondering when you were going to get to them. Before we start down that road I want to tell you something you should write down." He lit the second Lucky Strike. "We're not hiding out here. We're dealing. Dealing with what we've seen. Dealing with what we've done. What, and this is what you need to print, what we were asked to do and what we were ordered to do. For our country. For people like you, so you can say what you want and write what you want and fuck who you want."

"I'm not sure I-"

Stellwag leaned forward.

"Some of these guys wake up screaming at night. Sometimes I find one of them out in the brush yelling there's VC inside the wire. They divide the world now into just two things, friendlies and unfriendlies. It's that simple. This humble abode is their refuge and these guys are their comrades. It's all they know anymore. The devil in military indoctrination is that it's extremely, not to mention permanently effective."

"Is that where Sons of Satan comes from?"

"Maybe, but mostly it just sounds threatening and evil. Would you be sitting here if we were 'The Smokin' Aces'?'"

"And are you threatening and or evil?"

"We don't hurt anyone that hasn't tried to hurt us first. And as for evil? Lucifer was a fallen angel, an outlaw if you will. No, we're not evil – we just don't take any shit. You want evil? Now let's talk about the Druids."

"They're outlaws like you and your men. Why talk to me about them? Why-"

"Why not just take all the weapons and ordnance we've accrued and drive them out, right?"

"Succinctly put and... yes."

"We could do that tonight if we wanted. Be a little bit of a skirmish but the outcome would not be in doubt. They have more manpower but we have superior firepower, tactics and training. Wouldn't even be a fair fight."

Gannon stopped writing. "Are you planning on using me as a weapon, Lieutenant Stellwag?"

Stellwag grinned and took a swallow of beer.

"The pen, Mr. Gannon, is mightier than the carbine. Do you

know who's ultimately going to decide the war?"

"I'm assuming Kissinger and Nixon, that is if Kissinger ever bothers to tell Nixon what he's doing."

Stellwag shook his head. "Not even close." He drained the bottle of Schaefer and picked at the label. "You are."

Gannon put down his notebook and reached for his own beer bottle. "Don't want it to get warm," he said. "Care to tell me how I am going to decide the Viet Nam War?"

"Not you personally, maybe. But your compatriots in journalism. I shuttled around plenty of correspondents. Plucked a few out of bad situations. Talked to them all. They'll bring this bullshit war to an end before Nixon or Ho Chi Minh ever will. Hearts and minds works both ways."

"And the Druids?"

"You saw that little caravan today. Used to be one or two locals did the dirty work for the Mafia. Now you've got not just wiseguys but drug dealers, loan sharks, gamblers, all saddled with people who are, let's say, inconveniently alive. The Druids have identified a market and they are actively exploiting it." Stellwag leaned back. The recliner creaked.

"You're talking about a modern Murder Incorporated. Do you know the movie?" Gannon asked.

"No, but I know the concept. The Pine Barrens is a great place to disappear, as they say, whether you want to or not."

"The guy in the sidecar."

Stellwag nodded. "Not the first one to pass by. You must have sources – see who's missing and start from there."

"You strike me as someone who's had some education."

"I went in after my second year of college," Stellwag replied.

"Drafted, I assume?"

"Nope. Enlisted," Stellwag said.

"What were you studying?"

Stellwag put down his empty beer. "To be a journalist, what else?"

◆ ◆ ◆

N.J. Route 72 East
Near Woodland Township

"When did you figure it out?" Prejean asked.

"I haven't figured it out," Ronnie replied. "But I've been suspicious since I stepped on the bird at Lawson and I was the only passenger. The MP escort, all the delays. Zero answers or explanations – even for the Army it was a bit much."

Prejean popped open the glovebox. Ronnie half expected to see a revolver or a knife. Instead he saw a tightly rolled manila envelope.

"Pull it out and take a peek," Prejean said. "We'll stop in some place called Mud City before continuing on to this island of yours. Fifty klicks or so."

"Thirty five," Ronnie corrected. "Manahawkin is more developed. If we stop there we can get something to eat and I can make a phone call. If you can spare a dime, that is."

"Your money's in a bag in the trunk, by the way. Expenses are on me for right now. You read that report and we'll debrief in – where did you say again?"

"Manahawkin," Ronnie replied. "We'll pass a big marquee for the Drive-In Theater. I'm surprised your brother didn't mention it."

"Fuck you, soldier," Prejean said pleasantly. "Read the report."

Ronnie bent back the thin metal clasp and extracted the papers and the two photographs that came with them. Both were induction photos. Crisp uniforms, smiling, shaven faces and Old Glory hanging perfectly in the artificially-added background. Ronnie flipped each picture over. Harlan Luvern Brinson. Richard Jean-Baptiste Robichaux.

"Impressive handles for a couple of grunts," Ronnie said. "I didn't think you were allowed to name a guy Luvern."

"Brinson made it to Sergeant as you'll see. If he hadn't been an almost intentional fuck-up he was smart enough he could've gone to West Point if he wanted. IQ off the charts. He's the brains behind the whole enterprise. And Luvern is a very common name throughout the Midwest. Nobody bats an eye." Prejean had one hand on the top of the black steering wheel.

"Jean-Baptiste?" Ronnie asked. "His folks have a thing for John the Baptist?"

"Jean-Baptiste LeMoyne de Bienville," Prejean replied. "Founded the great city of New Orleans in 1718. Old Dickie, and he goes only by Dickie – during Basic he nearly beat a guy to death with a metal cafeteria tray for calling him Richie – Dickie has deep Cajun roots. Deep like all the way to the bottom of the bayou. The 'x' at the end usually means a previous generation was functionally illiterate – which, down in swamp country, should never, ever be mistaken for stupidity."

"How'd he get hooked up with Brinson?" Ronnie asked hoping he could skip large parts of the thick file.

"Their courts-martial were back to back in the same building. They met in a hallway while their lawyers were taking a piss."

Ronnie put the file on his lap.

"Is Declan Winston-"

"Dead? No. He's very much alive. A little worse for the wear maybe, but alive. He was a gunner on your PBR."

"He was. I picked off a VC sniper hiding in a palm tree when we were on patrol on some Mekong backwater. Declan was convinced the guy had him lined up in his scope. So –"

"Life debt?" Prejean chuckled.

"Something like that," Ronnie said. "He said I have ESP or something."

"Do you?" Prejean asked.

"I get a feeling once in a while," Ronnie answered. "I can't tell what's going to happen. But sometimes I just know that things are about to go south. What about Yvette, the Vietnamese girl's mom."

"It's a small world, after all," Prejean said. He moved his hand to the bottom of the wheel. "She and the little girl were survivors of the unfortunate civilian engagement at *Mi son*. They were visiting Grandma's village or gathering firewood – something that kept them out of harm's way. But they were witnesses to the aftermath of the shit that went down. Anyway, she's OK, too. They didn't really hurt her. I still don't know how that little girl, one, got away and two, got herself all the way to your island with just a name and a town on an envelope"

"That's why Declan wanted them out ASAP," Ronnie said. "They were witnesses."

"And that's why he hooked up with the Dynamic Duo you see in front of you."

"Brinson is Batman and Dickie is Robin, I take it?"

"Close," Prejean said. "Harlan never gets his hands dirty."
"Robichaux?"
"Not exactly a Boy Wonder but someone to be reckoned with. He was a tunnel rat and a damned good one by all accounts. Couple of Purple Hearts, a Silver Star. Filleted open his own leg to get free of a *punji* stick that had him impaled when he was underground all alone. No telling how many tunnels he cleared all by himself. Half of the *Cu-chi* complex it sounds like. Dickie could have been a true war hero."

"Until?" Ronnie asked.

"Until he fragged his LT," Prejean said. "Black fella, but I don't think that had anything to do with it. Dickie was into heroin dealing, but so were a lot of guys, commissioned officers included. They were just getting this smuggling thing started but it was pretty simple. Stuffing the bricks into hollow places in jeeps and APC's heading stateside. About two-thirds of their shit was confiscated. Dickie knew the suppliers but outside of that he didn't have a solid distribution outlet. He thought his LT was going to rat him out and so the guy got fragged. I went and interviewed the LT at the Evac hospital in *Cu chi*. I couldn't find enough to pin it on Dickie but our friends at JAG still figured out a way to drum him out a month later."

"The LT, he survived a fragging?" Ronnie said, surprised.

"Lost a leg," Prejean answered. "Had a chance to maybe save it by evac'ing to Saigon but he gave up a spot on a Dust Off chopper to a guy with a chest full of shrapnel from a mortar round. He's in a VA in Nebraska at the moment. I was on my way to interview him again when I got wind that these two were on the move and diverted to Fort Benning."

"No good deed goes unpunished," Ronnie said. "But where does our buddy Luvern fit in?"

"Harlan, like I said, he was pretty smart, he had a lot of contacts on the Admin side and at I Corps which meant access to all the military clerks and the local friendlies doing the immigration paperwork. They cooked up this scheme to ship the heroin home with guys in exchange for greasing their war brides' paperwork. Anybody check your duffel when you shipped home?"

Ronnie shook his head. He thought of the weapons and explosives he'd carried next to him half-way around the world.

"What are the chances?" Prejean said. "Think about it. Either lawyer doesn't have to take a tinkle and none of this shit ever happens. Other shit, yes. But not this shit. Like I said, it's a small, small world."

"Are they on the Island," Ronnie asked.

"I think we have to assume so," Prejean replied. "From Winston's info and the TOD of a guy we think Dickie stabbed in a bathroom at an interstate rest stop, they could have made it here by last night or maybe this morning. How much chance do we have a spotting them, do you think?"

"LBI is a pretty small world, too. You probably couldn't avoid running across someone even if you tried."

"That's good for us, then," Prejean said.

"Works both ways," Ronnie said. "I think we need to skip Manahawkin. You got enough gas in this beast?"

Prejean glanced at the instrument panel and nodded.

Ronnie looked hard at the pictures again. No long rifle shot was going to stop Dickie Robichaux, he thought. This was going to end only one way – up close and personal.

♦ ♦ ♦

Surf City

Mickey's chair was uncomfortable. She shifted her hips several times but it failed to make things any better. Mickey fretted about leaving Bunny at the station with Dippolito but she didn't want to be out driving around with her in public either. Finally she stood up and approached the Mayor's receptionist who also served as the sole clerk at City Hall. She had been a late summer hire and Billy Tunell had carped frequently to Mickey about the amount of time it was taking her to learn his many quirks and idiosyncrasies.

"He does know I'm here, right, Margaret?" Mickey asked her.

"Oh yes, dear. I'm sure of it. I'll buzz him again if his door doesn't open in the next minute. But I was going to tell you I think you might know my son. Douglas? "

"Douglas. No, I don't think I –"

"Maybe you know him as 'Double D.' Edmund and I never liked or approved of that childish nickname, by the way. He used to work at Mr. Marotta's establishment but now he's some kind of producer. Music, I think he said. Flits here and there, all over the country. Hardly ever home long enough for a good meal. Edmund told him he needs to get a real job. Music producer. I mean, where's the future in that? Anyway, I'm sure he mentioned your name."

"Yes," Mickey said. "I believe I might have met him once at Tony Mart's."

"He is still single, dear. Edmund says he just needs to meet a nice local girl and that will -"

"Well don't keep us waiting."

The voice was Billy Tunell's. Mickey had not heard his office door swing open.

"Come right in, my dear, dear Chief Cleary. Right this way. Margaret – would you bring us three Dr. Pepper's please? And call that contractor again and tell him I want an answer on the storm culvert problem by five o'clock or he'll be hearing from Sam Santaspirito. And he knows what that means. Tell him the two entities no one wants to hear from are the Spanish Inquisition and Sam the Holy Ghost."

He ushered Mickey in and closed the door. There were two small glasses on his desk, each containing a dark liquid. A large man with a big smile and an impressive mustache sat in the chair across from Mayor Billy's desk. She recognized him immediately.

"Chief Cleary," the man said. "Pardon my not getting up. My hip. You understand."

"Hello, Tony." Mickey said. "How are things at The Showplace of the World?"

"Where Friends Meet," the man known up and down the shore as Tony Mart said.

"Thanks for the tickets, by the way. And the offer of the trip," Mickey said.

"I'll be dishonored and eternally shamed if you don't accept them," Tony replied.

"I have to report any gifts to His Honor, you know."

"Report them in triplicate if you like, dear girl. My little nightclub – actually it's not just a nightclub it's an institution – lies outside your jurisdiction so a rare kindness does me no good and does you no harm. And as for influence, that I already have in abundance. And may I humbly admit I don't need or want any more."

Mickey sat down and pointed to the glasses.

"Your homemade anisette, I assume," she asked.

"Ah, you remembered from your very first visit. I would offer you some but I know you'll decline as you are obviously on duty. How is Ronald Dunn. Not home yet, I hear."

Mickey noticed how much bigger and more comfortable the chairs in Billy Tunell's office were. "No, not yet," she said. "Soon we hope. He was supposed to call with any new information earlier today but I haven't heard from him. Either that or I missed his call."

"Yes, you've been busy. I heard about the excitement to your south," Tony said.

"Is there anything you don't hear about?" Mickey asked.

Tony Mart ran a finger along his mustache. "In a word my dear – no. Is there anything I can do to assist?"

"You have a cure for stupidity and ignorance?"

"A sorrow and a pity that I do not. Once the miscreants are returned to their homes across the river, you can be assured that a stiff reprimand awaits them," Tony said with a pleasant smile.

Mickey knew what that meant. "Are you in our fair borough on business or pleasure?" she asked

"My business is always a pleasure, so I can say both without fear of contradiction."

"We're having trouble with our big storm drains," Billy Tunell interjected. "Debris, rodents, mosquitoes – they're apparently teeming with every variety of vermin and pestilence except poisonous snakes and scorpions from what it sounds like. Tony has friends in the construction business. We were just discussing a remedy."

"Are you talking about those big silver pipes that come out from under the road on the beach and on the bay side?" Mickey queried.

"The very same," Tunell answered. "Technically they're called culverts and they're supposed to keep us afloat in the event of a heavy rain or a big sea surge."

"They look like the openings to tunnels," Mickey said.

"I suppose in a way they are but I wouldn't suggest spelunking in one any time soon," Tunell said with a little theatrical shiver.

"Spe-what?" Mickey asked.

"Spelunking," Tunnel answered with mock disbelief. "Strictly speaking, the exploration of underground caves. Which is what they might as well be. The guiding principle being – don't climb into one."

"Not on my list," said Mickey.

"I also hear that you've become rather, shall we say, maternal in the last few days," Tony said with a bigger smile.

Mickey wondered – was there anything the guy didn't know about that went on anywhere on the Island?

"You could say that," she offered. "Like a lost dog – she literally followed me home."

"Much like your father's new friend," Tony added. "I do have an especially soft spot in my heart for children and dogs, you know. Until your situation is, shall we say, more well understood I'm prepared to offer you some trifling assistance."

Mickey sat up in her chair. "What kind of assistance?"

Tony, in response, sat back. Tunell, she noticed, remained quieter than she was used to and sipped nervously at his anisette.

"I must be getting back to The Showplace," Tony said and rose easily from his chair. So much for the bad hip, Mickey thought. "Grant Smith and the Power are finishing up their engagement and I expect another sell-out. But I have brought along someone who will elaborate." Tony nodded at Tunell. "Your Honor, a pleasure as always. Chief, Gunther's Bus is playing next week. They're a great band that deserves more commercial success than they've enjoyed. I'll leave passes for you and Ronald. Hopefully he'll be home by then to use his."

Mickey stood up. Tony turned and left through a side door Mickey had never really noticed existed. What she did notice was that he left the door open. Through it she heard words exchanged in low tones and shuffling footsteps. She looked over at Tunell. He downed the last of his anisette. When she looked back, a man was standing in the little doorway. He was hunched and drawn and rail-thin. It took her a minute to recognize him. When she did, she had to sit down.

"Doc?" she said. "Doc, is it you?"

"Hey kid," the thin man said. "Bet you didn't think you'd be seeing me again, did you?"

♦ ♦ ♦

Bunny had Charlie's radio turned all the way up and was doing something that vaguely looked like dancing.

"Wah-too-see," she said, phonating each syllable slowly. "Ee-nez teach me."

The Archies chart-topping and, to Dippolito's ear, incredibly annoying hit "Sugar, Sugar" was playing. Bunny only knew two of the lyrics but she belted them out whenever they arose.

"Sugar, sugar," she shouted. This was followed quickly by "Candy giiirrrlll." Again and again and again. Dippolito was going to lose his mind, he thought.

"Hey Bunny," he said. "It's hot in here, isn't it? Want to go outside for a minute?"

Thirty-Three

Philadelphia International Airport
Tinicum Township, Pennsylvania

Yvette Tran looked on nervously. Their little contingent was huddled in the Eastern Airlines terminal and the airport was crowded with vacationers and businessmen escaping the sweltering City of Brotherly Love. The outside temperature was pushing ninety and the humidity was close to the same. During the short time they'd been outdoors on the softening asphalt tarmac and until they'd entered the cool of the terminal, Yvette thought she was going to choke on the fumes wafting from the nearby oil refineries and tank farms.

The two CID officers were in plainclothes to attract as little attention as possible. When they had pulled her and Declan over on the big road outside of Boston she at first didn't realize who they were and what they represented. She thought they were in league with their former captors and that she and Declan would be kidnapped and, this time, surely killed whether they divulged any information or not.

When the first officer flashed his shiny U.S. Army wallet through the car window Yvette had begun to cry and couldn't stop herself for several minutes. She had already given up hope that they could rescue Bunny in time. When she saw the Army man's wallet and the great eagle on it she knew then they were going to have help. She knew then there was a chance she would hold little Good-Night in her arms again.

Yvette had never been on airplane until they left on the big jet from Saigon. Now she had been on two, counting the small one the Army had provided to get them all to this place called Philadelphia where Declan had hidden what it seemed everyone was after.

The CID man motioned her closer.

"Might as well see what all the fuss is about," he said to her. They were standing in a narrow hallway just off of a very big hallway where people pushed strollers and dragged bulging suitcases along the polished floor. Announcements she didn't understand echoed from loudspeakers she couldn't see. If not for the cool air, she thought, she would swoon.

They were next to a long wall of dirty and dented boxes Declan called luggage lockers. Some of the lockers along the bottom were large enough to fit a suitcase. But most, she noticed, were smaller and arranged along the top rows. Many had small keys sticking out from round locks. Some did not, though.

She watched as Declan withdrew a key from his pocket.

"Want to do the honors?" Declan asked the CID man with the very short hair and the birthmark on his cheek.

"No thanks," the birthmark man said. "I know where it came from. It's all yours."

"Hey, I washed it real good," she heard Declan say.

The CID man laughed. "I don't care if you fuckin' sterilized it, man. I'm not touching it."

The other CID man had a square, brown leather suitcase whose top opened like a mouth. He set it on the ground at Declan's feet. He had longer hair and a mustache that did not make him look older, Yvette thought.

"It better be in there," the birthmark CID man said.

Yvette watched as *they* watched Declan slip the key into the little round lock.

"Why'd you pick 417?" the one with the mustache asked.

"Bunny's birthday," Declan said. "17 April. Not like I was going to forget."

"Good thing. I see you filed the number off the key. Gutsy move there, cowboy."

Declan laughed. "I knew who I was dealing with." He turned the key and the locker door swung open with a loud groan.

Yvette closed her eyes.

The birthmark CID man breathed out loudly.
"Well, son of a *bitch*," was all she heard him say.

♦ ♦ ♦

Ship Bottom, NJ

Dickie Robichaux was on his third loop and he was tired of the endless repetition of salt water taffy shops, fudge shops and ice cream joints that started just south of the lighthouse and never stopped. He'd gotten a burger and a vanilla shake at a place called Bill's in Surf City. The old guy at the grill asked him how he wanted it.

"Burnt to a crisp," Dickie had answered and the old boy came through.

"Medium rare – that make you sick. You want eat meat – you got to cook it first."

Bill was Dickie's kind of guy.

Dickie had cruised by the little house in Ship Bottom several times looking for the lady cop. Had told Bill about her while he was sucking out the last of the shake with a collapsing paper straw.

"That Cheef Mee-kee," he'd said. "Mee-Kee Clear-ee." Dickie couldn't place the accent. A Russky, maybe. He looked the part. Bill said she was a regular customer. He concurred with Dickie's assessment of her physical attributes. "I tell Cheef Mee-Kee she should run to be Miss Magic Long Beach Island." He told Dickie it was a beauty pageant like the Miss America put on by the lifeguards after Labor Day when all the tourists went home. Dickie tried to imagine what she looked like in a bikini.

On his way back to the Road Runner he had spied a phone booth on the diagonal corner. He crossed the street and thumbed through the thin, swing-up phone book thoughtfully provided by the New Jersey Bell Telephone Company. He didn't find any listings for a Cleary in Surf City but he did find one in Ship Bottom with an address that matched up with his sighting. The first initial was 'P' and not 'M' but Dickie figured Mickey could easily be a nickname. Had to be her, he decided. That's why she didn't bother to knock – it was her house.

Dickie jumped in the Plymouth and fired it up. He'd cruise Surf City one more time and then hit Ship Bottom. He prayed that

Harlan would be early. He was tired of this recon. Tunnel clearing had been an all or nothing proposition. He couldn't stand this in-between shit much longer. He'd had eyes on what seemed like a thousand kids with straight black hair the length of the dink girl's. A bunch of them had turned out to be boys. Not one of them had been Asian.

He looked at the shoebox on the passenger seat. Nobody had Converse High-Tops in his size so he'd settled for a pair of Bata Bullets he'd found in an Army-Navy store run by an old guy named Enrico who went by Ricky. What Dickie found most interesting about Ricky, other that he had never served in either the Army or the Navy, was that his heavily waxed handlebar mustache was a mixture of hair originating from his upper lip and long, thick hairs growing right out of his nostrils. Dickie Robichaux had seen some shit in his time but, he had to admit, he had never seen that.

Traffic was barely crawling as lines of people trudging wearily home from a hot day on the beach clogged the crosswalks. Dickie saw he was stopped just shy of the Surf City Police building. He watched the crosswalk intently, eyeballing the nearly continuous line of tourists. When he glanced over at the cop shop he saw the back of a child with straight black hair to the shoulders being shepherded inside by a patrolman wearing the same khaki uniform the chick had worn. He looked like a Boy Scout leader, Dickie thought.

Dickie hadn't seen enough to tell even whether the kid was male or female. Could have been either, he decided. As he inched forward in the heat it occurred to him that chances were good that a lost or runaway kid would end up at a police station. He put on his blinker, intending to circle the station again. Harlan was supposed to be the big brain, the mastermind, Dickie thought with some dismay. He should have thought of that earlier, before Dickie had spent all day sucking car exhaust fumes and sweating like a pig in the Road Runner. He was beginning to think Sergeant Brinson was maybe more expendable than he realized. If Winston had somehow escaped that moron Hopwood, Dickie reasoned, even if Winston had copped the heroin for himself, a lucrative deal could still be arranged but only if Dickie had the kid. He would have to think hard, he decided, about whether to even tell Harlan about what he'd just seen. He had the car and he had the gun, Dickie mused. Harlan had a bike with a banana seat. He suddenly liked his odds a whole lot better.

Dickie made two more recons of the station. As he passed, a cruiser with Surf City markings pulled into its small parking lot and an impressively built black police officer got out and went inside. Dickie looked at his watch and decided he'd head for Ship Bottom to meet Dickie. The snail-like traffic would give him plenty of time to think.

◆ ◆ ◆

The Pine Barrens

BoDean Bowker looked up at the only wall clock he owned. Its face was an old and rusted ripsaw blade and the hour numbers were painted on. Loose Nuts had given it to him a few years back. He put the bone necklace on and placed the larger device Cowboy had given him in a brown paper bag. He'd crimped the smaller device onto the fuse and slipped the fuse into the hole he'd drilled at the base of the nail keg, then carried the keg to the bed of the pick-up and covered it with an old tarp. He liked the idea of not being directly connected to the keg. Cowboy said the weak radio signal would travel fifty yards but no more. If it didn't work, Cowboy said, just try moving closer and push the button again until it did. Once he got the electrics of it figured out, BoDean decided, he wouldn't need Cowboy anymore.

BoDean knew he needed to gas up the truck and he wanted to stop by the Pic-a-Lilly for a shot and a beer before he set off on his mission. He wanted to look at his brother Billy's picture above the taps. Then he'd head for the island. If he was running early he'd just drive around Mud City. He'd cross the bridge only after it got dark.

Tomorrow he'd wake up knowing more peace than he had known in two years, he realized. Tomorrow he'd wake up and decide who needed to pay next for what they'd done to his brother.

He touched his fingers to the well-worn wrist bones hanging on his chest. The he picked up the paper bag and walked out the door.

◆ ◆ ◆

Surf City

Doc Guidice looked even smaller sitting in the big chair.

"You look good, kid."

"I really did think you were-"

"Dead?" Guidice rattled out a laugh. "I'm a lot tougher than I look, you know," he said. His eyes still had the little twinkle Mickey remembered from their first meeting on the beach.

"Well, you know. Petroni and Caputo so..." she said.

"Ahh, Artie and Shots. Won't see them no more." Guidice winked. "That's from that book. 'The Godfather.' I must'a read to Danny five maybe six times now."

"You read it to him?" Mickey asked, her voice registering her surprise.

Guidice shifted in his chair. "Danny Rags isn't doing so good, Chief. Neither am I as you can see. I got the emphysema, ironically from bein' around too many heavy smokers. Who knew that could happen, huh?" He coughed as if to accentuate the statement. "Danny's got the diabetes and it's just eating him alive. Can't see, can't even make pee anymore. On the kidney dialysis machine twice a week. I don't think it's gonna be long, frankly."

"Did he send you here?" Mickey asked. Billy Tunell had left them alone in his office and the silence hung in the air.

"He did," Guidice finally replied. "He knows you were just trying to do right by Little Rags. Trying to find out what really happened to his boy so's his family would know. And you did. Danny never forgot that once he got past the grief. He's given a fortune to those nuns of yours. And you probably headed off a full blown street war in the process. He's afraid that when he goes the young Turks will go to war anyway since his only son is dead. Says he should'a banged Maria more often so he'd'a had three boys like Vito Corleone. He really loves that book, I gotta tell you. Say it's like that Puzo guy stole his life story."

"OK, but why did he send you here?"

"He say he owes you one and he wants the debt paid before he goes."

"How is he going to do that?"

"Said he hears things. Said word gets around."

"What things? What word?" Mickey leaned in closer so she could hear the answer.

"You know that animal in the Pines? Billy Bowker. The one we used to pay to take out the garbage? The one your *amichetto* sent to his own personal *inferno*?"

Mickey didn't answer.

"I know you can't say, being a cop and all. Well, his cursed mother had a litter of two and that animal has a brother. A fraternal but not an identical twin brother."

Mickey's head began to swim. Spoken phrases and voices announced themselves.

Pray to God.

Pray to God his brother isn't there.

Tag-teaming.

The phrase Charlie had said that she couldn't remember after she blacked out.

No such things as ghosts.

She really had seen him.

Funny kind of mud. On the tires.

Patsy.

"Hey kid, you OK. You don't look so good. Let me get some water."

Guidice's voice was faint but getting louder. Mickey looked down at her hands. They were welded to the arms of the chair. Her legs felt as if they weren't even there.

"Here you go, nice and slow."

He was holding a glass to her lips. She swallowed a little and the rest ran down her chin.

"Easy now," he said. "Here, you take it."

Mickey felt him pry her fingers loose, wrap them around the cool glass and guide it to her lips. She was able to drink from it now and her head began to clear. She finished the water and set the glass in her lap.

"He's going to try and hurt Patsy, isn't he?"

"That's what Danny says." Guidice had seated himself again. "He wants to help."

"By doing what?"

"What do you think?" Guidice said. A crinkly smile crossed his lined and sun-weathered face.

"I think I can't have any knowledge of what you're telling me," Mickey said.

"Why? You think that cheapskate Billy would spring for a bug in here? Ha. You know better than that, kid. That lousy bog-Irish bastard has the first dime he ever stole." Another combination of a laugh and a phlegmatic cough followed.

"You're putting me in an impossible position here, Doc. You do realize that."

"I'm not doing anything of the sort, kid" he said. "Wheels are turning. What's gonna happen is gonna happen. You got nothing to do with it. Nothing at all. But when it happens, Danny wants to you to know it squares things with him. *Capisce?*"

"What do you mean 'wheels are turning'?" Mickey asked.

Jackie Mariani - the son, not the old man - and Rico Marcelli are on their way to the Pines right now. They're Danny's best. Lots of made bones between the two of them guys. When it's done you'll find a box of Salt Water Taffy on your desk. From James, not Frailinger's. And every piece will be *anisette*. Then you'll know you can quit worrying. Hey, it's better than a fish."

"Doc, really, I don't know-"

"Yeah, that's right. You don't know. Anybody asks, and they won't, you weren't aware that the *maiale sporco*, the filthy pig, even had a brother. Danny says there isn't anything that connects you or Patsy to any of it. Even Marcelli and Mariani don't know what the hit's about. Just business. It's a gift, kid. A gift from a dying man. Just accept it. It's the simplest answer. What are you gonna do, put Patsy under constant surveillance or police protection? You think his little yappy dog is gonna scare anybody off? This is what needs to happen. Anything else is *pazzo*."

Mickey felt flushed. "No, what you're telling me is crazy, Why don't we just arrest him?"

"For what?" Guidice said. "For being a dead guy's brother? Listen to me for once, would you? Don't make this complicated." He pushed himself up from the chair. "I gotta get back. Danny likes to hear good news right away." He winked again.

"Don't tell me. From the book?"

"Did I say six times? Probably more like nine or ten now that I think about it."

Mickey stood up. Guidice reached out his hands for hers. She gave them to him.

"We all got Penance to do so we're clean when we go," Guidice said softly. "Danny's doing his and I'm doing mine. But sometimes there aren't enough Our Fathers, Hail Mary's and Glory Be's so you gotta get creative. Danny wants you to know he appreciates what you did and so does the family. I'll tell him you look good and that you and he are square. Say hi to Patsy. Never figured that old Harp for a dog guy."

"Is Billy driving you back?" Mickey asked.

Guidice shook his head. "Danny's *consigliore* brought me over in his shiny new Corvette. Tommy Santucci. Nice kid. Right outta Penn Law. Top of his class. He almost gave me a heart attack drivin' on the Schuylkill Expressway. Kid, I miss the old days. You look out for yourself, OK?"

"OK, Doc," Mickey said. "Tell Danny-"

Guidice interrupted her. "Danny who?" he said.

Mickey began to speak but then stopped herself.

"That's my girl," Guidice said as he shuffled out. "Simple, right? And don't forget to invite me to the wedding. Soon, OK? Before I croak."

Mickey watched him go and waited. She heard an outside door open and a big engine crank into life. Then she turned to leave.

When she arrived back at the station Bunny was coloring in her book in one of the cells and humming to herself. Dippolito and Rodriguez were at their desks. They looked at her expectantly when she entered and went to her desk. She had radioed Dave Johnson and asked him to park outside Patsy's house until she could get there. She hoped there weren't any more major problems to deal with. Her plate, she decided, was more than full.

"Where's Charlie?" she asked, pulling out her chair and seating herself.

Dippolito and Rodriguez looked at each other.

"He's out back," Rodriguez finally offered. "He got a phone call. Then he went out back and hasn't come in. I'm guessing it was some bad news." He made the Sign of the Cross twice in rapid succession, pulled a tarnished crucifix on a silver chain from his blouse and kissed it.

"Dip, how's Bunny doing?" Mickey said.

"She's fine Chief. Been coloring in that book most of the time."

"Did she eat anything?"

"Nope," Dippolito replied. "Said she wanted to wait for Dunn. Ronnie, I guess I should say." Mickey breathed in sharply.

"Charlie say anything?"

"Nothing, Chief," Rodriguez answered. "Just got up and walked out without saying a word. He didn't look too good. No offense meant, but if a black guy can look pale, then he did."

Mickey processed the scant information. She stood back up and walked through the silent station to the back door. She glanced over at Bunny who, engrossed by her big box of Crayolas, did not look up. Mickey walked to the door, slowly pushed open the aluminum screen and stepped out onto the shallow concrete apron. Charlie was standing very still, his gaze turned outward toward the bay and apparently very far away. He did not register her arrival. To her great surprise he held a burning cigarette between his fingers and several crushed butts littered the ground at his feet. She had no idea he even smoked.

"Deputy," Mickey said. "Everything OK?"

The big man turned around. Tears stained his smooth cheeks and his eyes were red.

"Charlie?" Mickey said. "What is it? Is it your mother?"

"I got a call, Chief." He said in a halting voice. "Darnell is dead."

Thirty-Four

The Pine Barrens

Lieutenant Stellwag had assigned Everett "Haystacks" Calhoun to guide Gannon back along a different road than the Druids had used. Calhoun was not quite as big as the eponymous professional wrestler but, Gannon thought, his bulk and his girth were truly impressive. The patch on his vest identified him as the club's sergeant-at-arms.

Calhoun was literally squeezed into the Dart's modest back seat, being unable to fit in the passenger one. Gannon thought for sure he'd be following Calhoun's bike but, he was advised, the big Harley-Davidson would make too much noise. Calhoun would be walking back from wherever he disembarked the Dodge.

"You know that girl police chief in Surf City?" Calhoun shouted, a bit louder than was necessary but Gannon wasn't going to tell him that.

"Yes I do," replied Gannon.

"Tell her I'm still mad at her."

"I'll do that," said Gannon. "Should I tell her why you're still mad at her or will she know?"

"She should know but she might'a forgot, I suppose."

Gannon tried to cock his ear while still keeping the Dart on the rutted dirt road.

"And if she forgot?"

Calhoun shifted his weight and the Dart's tires slipped a little. The Torsion-Aire front suspension was being sorely tested.

"First time we run into her she said she knew I wasn't the leader."

Gannon put both hands on the wheel. The uneven distribution of weight toward the rear was digging the tires into the soft sandy soil. Gannon tried easing off the accelerator.

"No, man" Calhoun said. "Give it more gas, not less. You gotta keep your speed or we'll bog down." Gannon complied and the Dart responded. "Anyway, I told her I was the club's leader. She said she knew right away I wasn't because, she said, the fat one is never the leader. Tell her that kind'a hurt my feelings."

"How long ago was this?" Gannon asked.

"Two years. Maybe a little longer. If the LT ever decides to retire, I'm gonna run to be the next president of the club. Tell her I'll come visit her when I get my president's patch sewed on. Hey, hold up right here." Gannon squeezed the brakes and the Dart came to a slippery halt. "Turn it off." Gannon twisted the key and the engine quit.

Calhoun tapped him on the shoulder and pointed to the right. A large, newer model pick-up was coming up a smaller trail. Gannon sat quietly as it passed thirty yards in front of them and continued on down the road. The cab window was rolled down but driver did not even glance in their direction.

"Friend of yours?" Gannon asked.

"I thought maybe it was the Bowker fella. Kind'a looked like him but that ain't his truck. Let me tell you, that motherfucker is seriously *de*-ranged. His land butts right up against the Druids'. Whas' that song on the radio they're always playin'? Something 'bout seein' trouble on the way?"

"Bad Moon Rising," Gannon said. "Creedence Clearwater Revival, if I'm not mistaken."

"If you say so," Calhoun replied. "OK, we can keep going now. Try and stay in those truck tracks if you can. Be easier on your tranny and that little six-cylinder go-kart engine you got under the hood." Calhoun let out a belly laugh that Gannon felt through the back of his seat. He wanted to tell the big man that the Dart's engine was actually the larger V-8 and not the Slant Six, but decided to let it go. Gannon started the motor and used the 'three-on-the-tree" lever to shift the manual transmission into low gear.

"Hey. You gonna write anything about me?" Calhoun asked.

"I will if you want me to," Gannon answered. "Where are you

from? Let's start with that."

"The great state of West Virginia," Calhoun replied. "A ways from Wheeling. Always thought I'd be diggin' coal in the mine or maybe in the shine business with my kin, married to some toothless hill woman and livin' in the holler."

Gannon hoped he could reproduce that nugget of literary gold verbatim when he got to his typewriter.

"But the Army had other plans. So here I am today, ridin' in the back a'this kiddie car convertible with you. Go figure that one."

"Did you see combat?" Gannon asked.

"I did more'n see it, fella. Trust me, I did plenty more'n see it."

"Were you wounded?"

Calhoun pulled up his vest, exposing a continental shelf of pale fleshy midriff. It was riddled with thick, criss-crossing scars.

"Guy on my near flank stepped on a Bouncing Betty. That's a mine," Calhoun said rubbing the still-pink scar tissue with his fingers. "Killed him straightaway but the shrapnel got me. MFW they call it. Multiple Fragment Wounds. I thought I was headed for a toe-tag. Ended up having eighteen separate surgeries. Had a bag for almost a year."

"A bag?" Gannon asked.

"C'lostomy bag. Can you imagine shittin' out your side for a whole year? But I had to 'til they did number eighteen and hooked me back up. Happiest day of my life."

Gannon slowed as they came to an intersecting road. This one appeared it might even have some gravel on it.

"I'll get out right here and hump it back," Calhoun said without registering any annoyance or hesitancy about having to make the trek. "Get the door, would'ya?"

Gannon got out, pulled the driver's seat forward and offered Calhoun an arm.

"Best if I do it myself," he said and pushed up and out with an almost athletic grace. Before Gannon knew it the huge man was standing next to him.

"Calhoun is spelled the 'ou' way. Don't you be puttin' two 'o's in it now."

"You'll find I'm a stickler for accuracy," Gannon replied. He wondered if he should offer to shake the big man's hand.

"And don't forget to tell that girl Chief what I said." Calhoun began to walk off.

"I won't," Gannon said. "And thank the lieutenant for his hospitality and his help."

Calhoun continued walking as if he hadn't heard a word.

♦ ♦ ♦

Surf City

Mickey moved a step closer. Shock registered on her face.

"Charlie," she said. "I, I'm so sorry. Fuck, Charlie. What happened?"

Charlie wiped the tears from his cheeks and squared his shoulders. Mickey knew he was struggling for control. She didn't know if he would or could say anymore than he already had.

"Who called you? Mickey asked.

"Lady doctor from the VA. A new one. Darnell really liked her. Trusted her. Said he was getting so much narcotics he might be addicted already. Said she was going to draw down the doses and help get him off that shit. He even got his new leg. He was happy, Chief. And he was *clear*."

"What did she say? What did she think?"

Charlie tossed the cigarette on the ground. She watched him take a deep breath.

"She said she wasn't in a place where she could talk a lot. Her voice got real low, like trying to whisper almost. She said they found him dead in his bed. Nurse said she checked on him at midnight and just thought he was sleeping. Didn't check again until almost seven this morning. Said the nurse called her in a panic saying Darnell had CTB."

"What the hell is CTB?"

"Ceased To Breathe."

Mickey momentarily ceased to breathe after he said it.

"So what did she think happened?"

Charlie's jaw quivered slightly as he tried to give her an answer.

"She said she thinks maybe somebody dosed him during the night. He still had an IV for the antibiotics. They could have snuck it in there without even waking him up, she said."

"Dosed him with what?" Mickey asked.

"Morphine, probably. She said it goes missing from the medication carts all the time and never gets accounted for. Chief, they put him down like some damn dog." Charlie uttered the last sentence with a quaver in his voice.

Silence took over until Mickey broke it.

"Who would do that, Charlie?"

Charlie Higgins clenched and unclenched his large fists. "I think it might go back to the heroin smuggling and the guys who fragged him," he said. "The CID man who talked to him at the hospital in *Cu chi*, that was right after they amputated his leg off, was going to come and interview him again Darnell said. Soon as he finished up the assignment he was on. Couple of days he hoped."

"Do you need some time off?" Mickey asked him.

"I will, Chief. But first we got our own business to take care of. Remember I said we needed to have a conversation?"

Mickey nodded.

"Well we need to have it right damn now."

◆ ◆ ◆

Ocean County Rte. 72
New Jersey Mainland

The big marquee at the Manahawkin Drive-In was undergoing a switch when they drove by, Prejean pushing the GTO past seventy miles an hour and weaving around the increasing eastbound traffic, Ronnie thought, like a movie stunt driver.

Two kids had been finishing up changing the sign, one clambering down a shaky-looking extension ladder and the other holding it at the bottom, his neck craned all the way back.

STARTS TO-NITE!
$5 A CARLOAD   NO PASSES
STEVE MC QUEEN   JACQ BISSET
BULLITT
HELD OVER! MIDNITE ONLY
SATAN'S SADISTS

Ronnie had leafed through the file and grown more impatient with each passing mile.

"Move motherfucker!" he yelled at an elderly man driving what his father always referred to as an "Ol' 55" regardless of the model year. The sedan, Ronnie thought it was a Studebaker, was doing no more than thirty. The driver shook his bony fist out the window as they passed it.

"Any pinch-points ahead of us?" Prejean asked.

"The causeway bridge in Somers Point," Ronnie replied. "Luck of the draw. We might cruise right across or it could be a parking lot all the way into Ship Bottom."

Prejean looked at Ronnie's feet. Ronnie had taken off his boots and tossed them in the back seat next to his duffel.

"You don't look like Abebe Bikila,so," Prejean said. The car slowed as he slipped his foot off the accelerator, reached down and removed both his sneakers without untying them. He handed them to Ronnie. "What size are do you wear?" Prejean asked.

"Ten and a half," Ronnie said taking the sneakers and untying the laces. "But why-"

"Elevens," Prejean said nodding to the pair of new-looking low-top black Converse All-Stars. "If we get stuck on that bridge, you hump it in on foot and I'll come find you and your girl."

Ronnie pulled on the shoes and tied the white laces. They were a little loose and Ronnie knew that would mean blisters if he had to run in them. "Who is B.B. Alpha-Kilo?" he asked.

"Bikila," Prejean corrected. "He won the 1960 Olympic Marathon in Rome. That fucker ran all twenty-six miles of it barefoot."

Ronnie looked down at the road rushing under the wheels and the asphalt baking in the August sun. He decided he'd prefer the blisters.

Prejean continued dipping in an out, crossing the center line and eliciting a brass section of panicked horns from oncoming drivers.

"Remind me never to play 'chicken' with you," Ronnie said.

"Son, every one of my assignments is about playing 'chicken,'" Prejean replied. Ronnie let the comment sit. A stretch of empty road opened up in front of them. Prejean hit the gas. Consecutive road signs blurred by.

     Entering Stafford Township
     Gateway To The Jersey Shore!

and then

      NJ Hwy 9
      3 Mi Ahead

"Do we take 9 South?" Prejean asked.
Ronnie shook his head. "Those two lanes will take you almost anywhere but not to Long Beach Island. Just stay on this road and we'll run right into the bridge. Literally."
Prejean gave him a thumbs up and continued to accelerate. Ronnie thought he'd read that the Tempest GTO possessed a limited-slip differential. He would have to remember to ask Mickey. He was positive she would know.

◆ ◆ ◆

Surf City

Mickey left Charlie with his thoughts and his pain and walked back inside the still-quiet station.
"Bad news?" Dippolito asked.
Mickey held up her index finger. "I think Charlie would prefer to tell you himself. He's composing himself and he'll come back in when he's ready."
Rodriguez began to get up from his chair. Mickey waved him off. "He would want to come to us. Let's give him that."
Mickey walked over to the cell where Bunny colored, still humming softly.
"I'm going to go get us something to eat," she said and sat down on the rumpled bunk. "Burgers and fries sound good?"
Bunny continued coloring, stopping only to stick a Burnt Umber crayon in the built-in sharpener on the flip-top Crayola box.
"Bunny?"
"We wait for Dunn. Then we have fries and burger. Shakes, too. We wait."
She still had not looked up.
"Bunny," Mickey said as gently as she could. "Bunny, listen to me. Dunn didn't call today. I'm sure it was because the Army is keeping him busy. But I don't think he's coming home today. I wish he were because I really miss him and I want to see him very badly. I don't want you to be sad or disappointed."
"Dunn come. You see." She withdrew a blunted Cerulean Blue crayon and twisted it in the sharpener. "You see. We wait."
Mickey let out a long exhale. "Bunny," she said in a slightly

sterner tone. The screen on the back door groaned and Charlie came in. Bunny reacted but pretended not to notice and went back to humming, slipping in "sugar, sugar" and "candy girl" almost in whispers.

Mickey got up. She walked out of the cell, over to her desk and sat down. Dippolito's desk radio had been playing and he switched it off. Charlie walked to his desk and stood by it. He'd pulled himself together, Mickey thought.

"Outside of my actual family," Charlie said in a steady voice, "Everyone here is like my family. Everyone here is just as close, just as important to me. I have received word that my baby brother Darnell has passed away unexpectedly this morning at the Veterans' hospital in Omaha. The COD is being listed as a cardiac arrest and probable heart attack but an autopsy will be performed along with some blood tests to further determine just what happened. I've spoken to his doctor – a nice young woman named Jessica – and she assures me she will follow up on her end and keep me informed."

"Deputy Higgins," Mickey said, "I know we all agree that if you need time to-"

"I'm sure I will, Chief," Charlie said. "But the autopsy and the tests, I'm told, will take several days to complete and then they will release his body. I will call my mother and my brothers and sisters tomorrow and tell them the unfortunate news. I may need to take some time next week to arrange for Darnell's final trip home and see about his funeral arrangements and burial back in North Carolina. Until then, I will continue to work as usual. It's especially important that we all look after one another. Chief Cleary will explain more about that in a minute but-"

Charlie paused and looked down at his side. Bunny had slipped out of the cell and was tugging on his belt.

"You brother die," she said without a trace of emotion. "Mama-san say people who die watch us. Keep safe. They watch all time from sky. All dead people from our village watch me and Mama from sky all time. Even babies. You brother watch you from sky now. Keep Charlie-san safe." She nodded her head once in affirmation and walked back into the cell without another word.

Charlie wore a look of astonishment. Then a smile slowly crept to his lips.

"Out of the mouth of babes, as it says in *Psalms* Chapter Eight

Verse Two, thou hast ordained strength. I couldn't have said it any better. Chief Cleary, would you like to brief us on the situation at hand and our planned response?"

"Everybody have a seat," Mickey said. "This is going to take a minute. Dip, put your radio in the cell with Bunny and turn it up – I don't want her hearing this right now."

♦ ♦ ♦

Our Lady of Mount Carmel Church
Hammonton, NJ

The priest introduced himself as Father Angelo. Cowboy wasn't sure how to address him so he went with the always reliable "Your Honor." This elicited a deep laugh and an affectionate pat on the back from the portly cleric.

"I don't believe I've seen you before," Fr. Angelo said. "What brings you to us today?"

"I, I need forgiveness, Your Honor," Cowboy stammered.

The priest chuckled. "My son," he said. "We *all* need forgiveness. We all *seek* forgiveness. May I ask, are you a Roman Catholic by chance?"

"No, Your Honor, I, I'm not," Cowboy replied. "Is that a, a sin?"

"I would consider it more of an oversight than a sin," the priest said gently. "Do you have a particular denomination, then?"

"I got a twenty and two fives, I think," Cowboy said.

"No," Fr. Angelo said. "I mean do you, ah, do you attend a particular church or belong to a certain congregation, perhaps? Lutheran maybe? Baptist or Methodist?"

In Cowboy's hand was his cowboy hat. He rubbed it against the leg of his dungarees as if were brushing something off.

"No, no, Your Honor," he said. "But I seen the cross and then the church and it just seemed like this would be a good place to, you know, apply for forgiveness."

"Forgiveness is not something you apply for," Fr. Angelo advised. "It's something that man asks for and God grants. Does that make sense?"

"Sure, sure it does," Cowboy replied. "So is there a special office or department I need to go to?"

"Well," Fr. Angelo said, "We do have a confessional, which is like an office. My office is right next door and there's a connecting window. It's very private and what's said inside it never leaves it. Does that sound like what you're looking for?"

"Yes, yes it does," Cowboy said. "Is there a fee, you know, like a deposit or a cover charge?"

"There is not," the priest said. "God just asks that you enter with a full heart and a clear mind."

"Is it near here or do I have to drive?" Cowboy asked.

"Fortunately it's just a few steps away, right inside the church," Fr. Angelo said and extended his arm. "May I show you the way?"

"Sure, sure," Cowboy said. "Let me just go turn off the engine."

"Of course, take your time, my son" the priest told him.

Cowboy walked slowly toward the vehicle he'd parked just off the road. He had a couple things on his list. Forgiveness was just one of them. Everything was going according to his plan with one exception.

He opened the door, twisted the key and shut off the engine. He dropped the key in his front pocket. He'd have to get used to driving BoDean's truck for a while. Cowboy's had tinted windows due to his eye surgeries and BoDean's did not. But he knew wouldn't be getting his back anytime soon.

Thirty-Five

Bonnet Island
Manahawkin Bay

"I think this is it," Prejean said. "Make me and Chuck Taylor proud, soldier."

A line of cars stretched to the horizon on the wooden bridge. Ronnie had been a track star at Holy Spirit High School, outstanding at the mile. Only an equally stellar career as a wide receiver in football had kept him from setting records in cross-country as well. That was sometime back but to stave off the boredom of his detention at Fort Benning he'd run part of the perimeter fence every day without fail. He wasn't as fast but he'd had no trouble keeping a decent pace and figured that each run covered roughly ten miles out and back. In the middle of Manahawkin Bay he calculated he was less than 2 miles from the causeway's terminus in Ship Bottom and only another half mile to either he and Mickey's place or the Surf City PD.

"Got any water?" Ronnie asked.

Prejean popped open the matching red center console and withdrew a clear bottle with a screw top.

"Plain water in a plastic bottle?" Ronnie asked holding it up.

"Stupid idea, I know," said Prejean. "But it's all I got."

Ronnie unscrewed the top and chugged the lukewarm liquid. Then he grabbed the file folder, opened the door and stepped out. He nodded to Prejean and set off at a fast trot next to the line of idling cars. Bonnet Island was dead ahead, halfway between the

GTO and Ship Bottom and he could see its western shoreline and smell the tang of the bay as he ran.

Some of the non-moving cars beeped at him or gave him the peace sign. It seemed that each one he passed had a different song on the radio. He zipped by a Sunshine Yellow Plymouth Barracuda convertible pumping out "Twenty Five Miles from Home" by Edwin Starr and quickened his pace. When a white Ford Fairlane Torino blasted Sly and the Family Stone's "Hot Fun in the Summertime," he felt like it was just for him. He switched the folder from one hand to the other as he crossed the mid-point of Cedar Bonnet Island. The road started to arc downward before him toward Long Beach Island. Home was literally in his sights and his legs felt like they were turbocharged. Sweat poured from his forehead but he felt stronger with every yard he covered. He thought of Mickey, her dark hair and her bright smile and ran even harder.

As the bay side of LBI grew larger it seemed like the music grew louder. When he crossed the foot of the bridge and stepped on the Island for the first time in months he heard Sam and Dave belting out "Hold On, I'm Comin'" from a metallic lime green Mercury Cougar. He was certain it had been cued up just for him.

Hold on, he thought. *I'm comin'*

♦ ♦ ♦

Surf City

"We even know what these guys look like?" Rodriguez asked. "Or what vehicles they're driving? Plate number maybe?"

"We have a partial but unconfirmed description on the truck that my da-, that retired officer Cleary in Ship Bottom believes was conducting surveillance on him. Officer Cleary thought it was a Chevrolet pick-up, sixty one or sixty two, fair amount of rust and it may have a light brown mud stuck to the tires and the undercarriage. Davey Johnson from SBDP is on site there now. The driver of that truck, we assume, is the twin brother, fraternal not identical but close enough, of someone both Ronnie Dunn and I engaged in the past. That brother is deceased. This one is not."

"Not yet," Charlie said in a low tone. Mickey let it pass without comment.

"I'll type up a description," she continued, "but for right now just go with a white male, mid-thirties, weighing well over two hundred pounds with short sandy or light brown, tightly curled hair." Mickey felt the hairs on *her* neck stand up as she described Billy Bowker from memory. "Likely lives back deep in the Pines so dress might be noticeable for that. Short and sweet, look for a male Piney who's built like a bear."

"What about the other two? The ex-Army guys?" asked Dippolito.

"Bunny has eyeballed them both up close," Mickey said. "I'll talk to her when we're done and see what she can give us. I'd like to keep her out of this as much as possible but that may prove difficult. For now, I'm guessing that they will stand out from the locals and the shoobies. Maybe a little rougher-looking. When I spoke to Ronnie yesterday he said they'd probably have arm and chest tattoos – maybe of a military or patriotic nature but not necessarily. He said 'Born to Kill" was a popular one."

Rodriguez spoke up. "Lot more civilians with tattoos out there these days, Chief. Even on the women. We start hauling in everybody with a tat? You're gonna need a bigger jail."

"They'll probably avoid being seen together, either," Dippolito said. "If they were smart, they'd split up. It's a small island. Two men hanging out together would draw attention around here."

Rodriguez shot Mickey a glance.

"Dip has a point," she said. "We're dealing with three potential suspects and probably two vehicles. If our ex-military friends came all the way from Maine, they probably did it in one vehicle. I'm guessing something fairly unobtrusive, a car that would blend in as opposed to one that would stand out."

"Stand out like, what, like a souped up Chevelle SS?" Rodriguez said.

Mickey threw her pencil at him. "Yeah, like a Chevelle SS. Nobody likes a smart-ass, Deputy."

Charlie cleared his throat. "My late brother indicated that one of the ex-military guys is an expert at hand-to-hand combat with lethal expertise. Darnell said to avoid, as he put it, 'cornering' him. He did not know nor did he have any intel about the other one, but rats of a pack are like birds of a feather in my experience."

"One's the brains, one's the brawn, maybe," Mickey said. "We think they're responsible for at least one death we know of out-of-state. We ideally want all three of them alive and kicking, especially the military guys. They may be involved in something much bigger and I'm sure the government will want to talk to them." She nodded to Charlie. "But do not underestimate the capacity for violence from any one of them. It's more important that all of us are alive and kicking this time tomorrow.""

"Are they armed and do we know with what?" Rodriguez asked.

"The military duo for sure. The victim in Connecticut was stabbed. They're still looking for the knife. I'd count on at least one gun if not two. Perp probably ditched the murder weapon but you can get a knife or gun around here about as easily as you can get saltwater taffy. As for the hillbilly, they all have shotguns so look for an empty rack on the truck I guess."

"What about Bunny?" Charlie asked.

Mickey looked over at the cell. Bunny continued to color. Her head and shoulders swayed slightly with the music.

"Still working on that one," Mickey replied. "I'll send out for some dinner for us. SBDP has the description of our friend from the Pines and his truck. Whatever I can get from Bunny I'll type up as well. I've given SBPD everything I have but in the next hour we need to have all six departments up to speed and on the lookout. We may not be one shop, but that doesn't mean we can't work that way."

The radio crackled.

"Surf City this is Dispatch," Arlene said. "Be advised, Ship Bottom 1 is in pursuit of a white male in military fatigues. White male in military fatigues. Do you copy?"

Mickey flipped down the black toggle switch on her unit and depressed the button on her microphone. "Dispatch, this is Surf City. Copy that. Surf City 2 and 3 are rolling. What's the ten-twenty?

"Shore and East Bay. Repeat Shore and East Bay, Copy?"

"Shore and East Bay. Copy," Mickey answered. She looked up. "That's just on this side of the bridge. I really hope we just got lucky."

Rodriguez and Charlie flew out the door.

"Dip," Mickey said. "Stay with Bunny. I'm going to check on my dad real quick and then I'll swing back. She can't be alone. Eyes on her all the time. All the time. If you have to pee, hold it 'til

I get back. Got it?"

"Copy, Chief," he said.

When Mickey looked over again Bunny was standing with her hands gripping the cell bars. Her eyes were wide.

♦ ♦ ♦

Ship Bottom

Patsy watched the cruiser that had been parked across from his little house flip on its cherry tops and pull away in hurry.

"Wonder what all the excitement is," he said to the small dog in his arms. "It's getting' dark, little girl. Let's go for a walk and see if we can find out what's goin' on."

The dog's tail wagged happily. Patsy put her down and grabbed the new leash from the table near the door. He hooked it on the collar and patted his pants for his house keys. "Must'a left them in the bedroom," he said. "Ah, we won't be that long." The dog was pawing and scratching at the wooden door. Patsy pushed it open and it walked outside.

♦ ♦ ♦

BoDean watched the old man leave. He was taking a chance, he knew, but when he'd hit one those random and inexplicable gaps in traffic, he'd kept going and crossed over the bridge without even having to slow down.

The street fronting the long block looked deserted. BoDean felt ridiculous wearing the clothes he'd bought, a loud print shirt and ill-fitting shorts. The hat was the worst, he thought, but it had the widest brim he could find and obscured his face almost completely when tilted down. Only his dirty socks and his low-top boots felt familiar.

He waited to see if the police cruiser was looping back. When it didn't, he got out of Cowboy's truck and walked slowly to the rear of it. He dropped the tailgate and hooked an arm around the nail keg. With his other hand he draped an old shop rag over it. He checked the street for any new arrivals then walked purposefully to the side of the house. A couple of nighttime scouting trips had told him where the single bedroom was and he set the keg outside the flimsy wood wall below the open window. The fuse and the smaller metal box he obscured with some fragments of seashells that had been used in place of grass to border the property. He pulled off the rag. The small keg was almost the same shade of wood as the house. BoDean thought it was almost invisible.

He checked for any nosy neighbors and pedestrians once again. Then he walked away from the house in a different direction, crossed the street and returned to the truck. BoDean climbed back in. He pulled the ridiculous hat down low.

And he waited.

Thirty-Six

Holgate
Long Beach Township

Dickie was stretched out on the rapidly cooling sand in front of the Life Saving Station. "Boy, once it gets dark here it gets dark fast, don't it?" he said.

Brinson was pacing the beach above the pilings with a piece of driftwood in his hand. "Not fast enough," he replied. "I hate waiting."

"You know what you're going to do yet?"

Brinson stopped pacing. "A fire is always good," he said. "Brings the cops and the fire trucks. Snarls everybody up for a couple of hours at least. All it'll take is a gas-soaked rag in the nearest car's tank and –" With his free hand he reached into his pocket, withdrew a silver Ronson lighter clicked a flame into life. It glowed brightly in the fading daylight. "An instant Dante's *Inferno*. And a fire at a cop's house? Shit, you can bet your ass every unit and warm volunteer body on this island will come running. The streets won't be clear for hours. Now this all hinges on the kid being at the cop shop, you realize that."

"She's there. The more I think about it the more I'm sure of it. Sure it was her I saw."

"You being sure of it doesn't make it true, Dickie."

"I have instincts, Harlan. Good instincts. And I have learned to trust them. They're why I crawled out of every single one of them tunnels in *Cu Chi* alive and Charlie didn't. She's there."

"We need her alive, Dickie." Brinson said.
"She will be," Dickie answered. "Even if nobody else is."

◆ ◆ ◆

Ship Bottom

Ronnie looked at the blue-uniformed officer in disbelief.

"On the ground, dirtbag," the policeman shouted. Although it was almost dark, the officer still wore mirrored aviator sunglasses and Ronnie figured him for no taller than five foot eight. His voice was high and tinny and for a moment Ronnie thought he was going to laugh. But Ronnie looked at the Colt 0.45 caliber service revolver in his hand and decided this was not currently a laughing matter.

"Sir. I'm a U.S. serviceman on his way ho-" Ronnie tried to say.

"We know exactly who you are," the cop said. "Face in the dirt, asshole. And I mean now."

Ronnie dropped to his knees. He held his arms out, holding tight in one hand the folder which was quivering in the bay breeze. He was afraid the two photographs would blow away so he slid the folder toward him as he hit the deck and covered it with his chest. He heard sirens and saw flashing lights bouncing crazily off car windows and chrome bumpers. He flexed his neck and said, "Sir. Please. I think you're making-"

A gunshot followed. Ronnie flinched but quickly realized he wasn't hit.

"Next one's in your ear, motherfucker," the high voice yelled. "Do..Not..Move. I repeat. Do..Not..Move or I will shoot you."

Tires screeched, car doors slammed and Ronnie heard the sound of leather soles slapping asphalt pavement.

"Alright. Pat him down for a piece and then cuff him boys," the high voice said. "He's going downtown."

Ronnie found it almost surreal. The cop sounded like he was spouting lines from old black and white movie, he thought, or maybe he'd been watching too much "Dragnet." The running footsteps got closer and then stopped. Ronnie raised his palms from the pavement.

"Oh, holy shit," a familiar sounding voice said. "Oh for Christ's sake. I do not believe I am seeing this shit. Dunn? Ronnie Dunn. Is that you?"

"Afraid so, Davey," Dunn replied, the words muffled by the macadam. He slowly started to get up.

'What's going on here?" the high voice demanded. "You *know* this man, Officer Johnson?"

"Chief Justus, I'm sorry to do this but I must respectfully inform you that you just fired a shot at Chief Cleary's boyfriend, Ronald Dunn. I'm telling you this because I am sure she'll want you to explain that to her when she arrives on scene."

Ronnie was up on his knees, still clutching Prejean's folder. A siren whooped and Ronnie turned his head. But he didn't need to see the car.

He knew the sound of the engine.

♦ ♦ ♦

BoDean kept the truck window up which mad it hotter inside the cab. He didn't want it idling, think it would draw more attention. He wanted the truck to appear parked for the evening. He'd never been in a vehicle with tinted windows before and decided if he ever traded the old Chevy in it's something he would order. It escaped him how the glass could possibly let him see out but not let anyone could see in. He felt like he was in a deer blind.

The old man was on his way back with the little dog. BoDean had to laugh at the sight, the big burly ex-cop walking a sissy little dog on a leash. Thing looked more like a varmint than a pet, he thought. He watched the man approach the dwelling in the truck's rear-view mirror. The little dog was tugging on the leash and didn't want to go inside. BoDean watched with growing alarm as the dog yipped and tried to pull the old man around to the side of the house where BoDean had set the nail keg. It was almost dark but still much earlier than he wanted to set it off. The dog would be collateral damage but BoDean saw that as an unanticipated bonus. He hated little yippy dogs.

BoDean judged his distance from the house at about forty yards. He reached into the paper bag and withdrew the metal box with the black button. Fifty yards, Cowboy had said, no more than fifty yards. With his left hand he touched the bone necklace. He watched as the dog strained at the leash. It was only ten feet from the keg. BoDean's breaths became shorter and quicker.

He could hear the old man now.

"What is it, girl, What is it? A rabbit? What is it?"

BoDean moved his thumb over the black plastic button. The funny smell from the little box was stronger inside the closed environs of the cab. BoDean watched as the old man leaned down and picked up the little dog, cradling it like baby with one meaty forearm. The dog continued to yap and the old man continued to talk to it, but they were heading toward the house's front door now. BoDean moved his thumb off the button. Then he rolled down the window to let in some fresh air and put the metal box down on the seat. He'd waited more than two years. He could wait a little longer.

◆ ◆ ◆

Route 72 East, Stafford Township
New Jersey Mainland

Mike Gannon turned off the Dart's engine. Whatever was going on up ahead had snarled traffic badly and he hadn't moved in twenty minutes. It seemed like poor planning, he thought, to have a series of popular beach towns on an island with only one way on and off. Surely there were plans for another, or maybe even two other bridges in the future. The sun was behind the trees to the west and the air was cooling rapidly, but it was still a beautiful summer evening and Gannon decided he'd leave the top down.

It occurred to him that he'd come for what he hoped would be one great story, had found another and now might not be able to write either one. He had debated making the call from the lone phone booth he'd encountered after escaping the Pine Barrens. But he couldn't get the look on the man in the motorcycle sidecar's face out of his mind. Stellwag had said they would probably spend a day "working him over," polite parlance, Gannon assumed, for torture before they offed him. He'd almost run out of dimes trying to explain to the State Police the exact nature of the crime he was trying to report. He had later seen two State Trooper vehicles heading in the opposite direction and could only hope they were responding to his tip.

Whenever he got back to Surf City he would have to come up with something else to report otherwise the days would be docked from his vacation allotment. Not that long ago, he rued, dreams of a Pulitzer danced in his head. He thought maybe he could still make something out of Stellwag's story – the disaffected Vietnam vets, shunned by the country they risked their lives to defend, banding together in the backwoods. Maybe an LT Robin Hood and his not-so-Merry Men angle. It reminded him of an old movie with Robert Mitchum but he couldn't recall the title. Something with "lightning" he thought. He kept going over the gilded copy Haystacks had given him, finally repeating the words "toothless hill woman" over and over to try and keep it fresh in his mind.

If he wrote about the Druids, he knew, they would quickly figure out who had ratted on them. He did not want to spend the rest of his life looking over his shoulder or having someone start his car for him every time. He desperately wanted to use "The Forest Prime Evil" lede somewhere – he doubted he would ever come up with a catchier phrase even if he was still tapping out copy at the age of a hundred.

Gannon turned on the radio and looked at his watch. He decided he'd listen for exactly fifteen minutes and then he would turn it off so it didn't drain the Dart's AC Delco battery too much. He tuned the radio to WDAS at the far right end of the dial, knowing they would not be playing "Sugar, Sugar" or "In the Year 2525." Georgie Woods, "the guy with the goods," was spinning nothing but smooth R & B and soul hits.

Gannon doubted that much could have happened since he'd been off the island and decided he'd wait until morning to share an inconvenient truth with Chief Mickey Cleary.

She was already yesterday's news.

Thirty-Seven

Ship Bottom

Dickie pulled over at the corner of East 6th and Long Beach Boulevard to let Brinson off.

"This is the widest part of the island," Dickie said. "You got the address, right?"

"I got it, don't worry," Brinson replied

"Twenty-one hundred hours. That still the plan?" Dickie was looking at his watch. Brinson checked his and nodded. "I have to admit," said Dickie, "I made fun of that bike but it'll work perfect for this mission. You will be, like you said, invisible."

"I won't be able to pop smoke so don't screw up the ORP."

"5th and Shore," Dickie replied. "It's a dead end corner and not well lit, so if you need cover 'til I get there just hang in the shadows. I'll have the kid. After that it's one right turn and we're off the island and on our way to Philly to get rich. "

"And Dickie," Harlan said. "If you're not there to pick me up-"

"Yeah, I got it," Dickie replied. "I'll be there. But you got two minutes from the time I pull up to be in the car. Otherwise, pardner, I am already gone."

"Copy," Brinson said. "Tonight we head out for the Promised Land, *Mister* Robichaux."

"I'd feel better if we had a chance to case it first." Dickie replied.

"You worry too much, Dickie," Brinson said. He unbuckled his lap belt.

"Yeah, well, that's OK. The shit I worry about don't happen," Dickie answered.

Brinson got out, went straight to the trunk and pulled out the Sting-Ray. An overhead street light flashed in the chrome handlebars. Dickie watched the lid of the trunk come down, saw Brinson mount the bicycle and then push off heading west. Dickie figured anyplace else on earth and Brinson would stand out like a hard dick. But not here. Because this wasn't, as far as Dickie could tell, quite like anyplace else he'd ever been.

◆ ◆ ◆

Mickey had a hard time processing what she was seeing.

A man in what did appear to be military fatigues was in the process of getting up from what she assumed was the prone position common to arrestees. He was bathed in a sea of car headlights and police cruiser spotlights and looked like a rock star up onstage at Tony Mart's. He had short-cropped hair and a muscular build and was holding something in one hand.

Jim Justus was standing about ten feet away, his long-barrel Colt clutched in his right hand but hanging next to his side. He appeared to be mumbling something at her. Mickey edged closer.

"Chief Cleary," she thought she heard the Ship Bottom Chief say. "I, I didn't know. I couldn't have known. I just got the description and assumed this was our susp-"

Her attention had shifted to Justus and so it startled her when the man in the fatigues spoke, apparently to her.

"Well it's about damn time you got here, Cleary," he said.

For a second she thought she was going to faint.

"Pardon my French," Ronnie said as he settled himself in the Chevelle's front bucket seat across from her. "But who the fuck is that?"

Mickey pulled her door shut.

"That," she said and then stopped. In one move she grabbed Ronnie's collar and pulled him toward her. She put her mouth on his and kissed him as hard and as deep as long as she could. Only when she sensed both of them needed to breathe did she lean back. She heard car horns bleating in appreciation.

Ronnie smiled. "River deep," he said.

"Mountain high, motherfucker," Mickey replied. "Pardon my

French"

Ronnie's smile grew even bigger. "OK, he said, "But, seriously. Who is that guy? He fired a live round at me, you know."

"Well at least he missed, didn't he?" Mickey replied as she slipped the key into the ignition and turned it. The Chevelle purred. "And I like the new 'do." She pointed to his military haircut. His hair had been long and sun-streaked the last time she'd seen him

"You think he missed on purpose?" Ronnie asked.

"Only a fifty-fifty chance, I'd say. He's the new COP in Ship Bottom.

"I know how you spell 'cop,'" Ronnie deadpanned.

"Chief of Police, Private Einstein. Jim Justus."

"Justice, like in Miscarriage of Justice?"

"No," Mickey answered. "Like 'Just Us,' which is what I'm hoping for as soon as we possibly can. But right now, soldier boy, we got shit to do."

"Speaking of," Ronnie said, "Today was some strange shit," Ronnie said. "Sorry, some strange stuff."

Mickey laughed. Before he'd left he was working on dropping his barracks-level use of profanities to a manageable level. She was just as bad as he was, she thought. Mickey shifted the Chevelle into Reverse and began backing up, trying to extricate herself from the tangle of vehicles and rubberneckers. It was going to take more than a simple K-turn she decided.

"Strange stuff. Like?" Mickey said. She had really enjoyed that kiss and was hoping she'd have to stop long enough to do it again.

"Like they cut my hair at oh-dark-thirty before I shipped out. Like they could have just given me a bus ticket and my civilian clothes. Instead I got an MP and an entire cargo plane all to myself. Like those civilian clothes and my small amount of money and pocket change went missing. Like I've been back in New Jersey since this morning but they kept delaying me, like they were waiting for something."

"Waiting for what?"

"Waiting for the guy that picked me up and drove me here to arrive. Not one car passed me in either direction on seventy-two until he showed up. These two dipshits, Brinson and Robichaux, are on everybody's radar, not just yours it seems."

"Yeah," Mickey said, "Well I hate to tell you but they're only two-thirds of our problem."

Traffic slowed in front of them. Mickey debated hitting the siren and the flashers and decided against it for the moment.

"Two-thirds?" Ronnie said. "I don't understand, Mick."

She squeezed the brake pedal down as a line of red taillights brightened and glowed in the darkness.

"Turns out there *are* such things as ghosts," she said. The Chevelle came to a stop and she leaned over and kissed Ronnie even harder. It reminded her of a date at a Drive-In movie or a roadside Passion Pit.

"Missed you too," Ronnie said when she broke it off. She was almost panting, she realized.

"When we put all this *stuff* to bed, that's the first place we're heading. Hope you had your Wheaties, 'cause I'm counting on some serious *nhuc duc*, soldier boy. As in boo-coo *nhuc duc*."

Ronnie looked over at her with surprise on his face. "Don't tell me. Your little friend Bunny taught you that."

"Yup, And the hand signal, too, which I obviously can't do right now. So who's this guy that picked you up and where is he?"

"Guy named Cole Prejean. French name, I guess. When you look at it, it looks like you'd say Pre-Gene but you don't."

Mickey flashed on the she'd met Doc Guidice and he'd given her a pronunciation lesson. "Like Judah Jay," she remembered him saying. Ronnie kept talking.

"Anyway, this guy is Army CID he says. Said he grew up in Louisiana and knows guys like Robichaux well. Called himself and Robichaux coonasses, whatever that is. And there's something about the 'x' at the end being important."

"CID. That's, what – Criminal-"

"Criminal Investigative Division," Ronnie said. "The Army's version of the FBI."

Mickey recalled Charlie mentioning something about a CID officer interviewing Darnell.

"He give you those?" She pointed to the sneakers on his feet.

"He did, actually. Combat boots are not designed for flat-track sprints. I prefer Puma's but I have newfound respect for Chuck Taylor. You still haven't told me about the other one-third of our problem."

"What's in the packet?" she asked.

"A lot of bad news about our two friends but –" He reached inside the folder. "A picture of each of them – old pictures taken at induction but something to go on anyway."

Mickey glanced over at them. She breathed out heavily.

"I was afraid I was going to have to ask Bunny to describe them. Now I don't have to. You know, she kept saying you would come home today."

"Really? How would she know that?"

"You're the one with ESP. You tell me. Did your friend Pre-Gene say anything about-"

"They're both OK. They'll bring them here as soon as they've secured the merchandise at the Philly Airport."

"The mer-"

"The heroin," Ronnie continued. "Like three-quarters of a million bucks worth of it. Just sitting in a luggage locker. No wonder they're willing to go to such great lengths to get it. Now, what's this you were saying about another third?"

Mickey realized she was avoiding telling him. Once she did, she thought, then, then it would be real. And she did not want it to be real. And if she kept quiet and accepted Danny Rags' dying gift to her, maybe it would never become real. She took a deep breath.

"Our friend Billy Bowker has a brother," she said. "A twin brother if you can believe that. Like one backwoods psychopath wasn't enough" She watched Ronnie take in the information. "We think he means to hurt Patsy."

"Is he on LBI now?"

"Maybe," Mickey said, choosing her next words carefully. "But it's also possible he's been unavoidably delayed. Perhaps permanently delayed."

"Who told you all this?"

"Doc Guidice," Mickey said. "I talked to him this afternoon."

"Juice is still alive?" Ronnie said, using the old doctor's youthful street nickname. He rubbed at his forehead. "That's hard to believe."

"He's a tough old bird Too tough to whack, it seems."

Mickey accelerated gently as the road before her cleared. "We'll swing by Patsy's place and make sure he's OK. The Ship Bottom boys are supposed to be keeping an eye on him for me. As close as they can manage to continuous surveillance. Fair warning, he's got a dog now."

"Didn't see that coming," Ronnie said.

"Neither did he. Lost or abandoned, probably. It just trotted in and plopped itself down like it owned the place, he said."

"Let me guess," Ronnie said. "Big dog, right? A Collie like Lassie is my bet."

Mickey laughed. "OK, she said, "Let's go with that assumption for now." She flipped on the blinker as they approached the intersection with Patsy's street.

"So why would Bowker's brother be unavoidable delayed?" Ronnie asked.

"What is it you soldier boys say? That information is on a 'Need To Know' basis only?"

She saw Ronnie running the possibilities through his head.

"Anyway," she continued. "Dad saw his truck. Old Chevy, no later than a '62, caked with mud. From some dirt road deep in the Pines, probably. We don't have a plate but that's enough to go on. Never doubt an old cop. I should have known. We should be able to make it. Billy Bowker wasn't exactly a criminal mastermind, so."

"Maybe this one got all the brains," Ronnie said. "DMV run his name?"

"It's a Friday in August. Dip had a call in but they never called back." Mickey made the left turn and shut off her headlights. "You check your side," she said, "I'll check mine." Out of habit, she checked both. She saw a few pick-ups but none that matched the description or looked particularly out of place. She passed one with tinted windows, a new automotive trend that Mickey hated. "They really need to outlaw those," she said, pointing out the truck parked on Ronnie side. "Scares the crap out of me when I pull a car over that has them."

"Everybody's got something to hide, I guess," Ronnie said as they pulled up across from Patsy's little house.

"Yes they do," Mickey said. She mused that if she accepted Ragone's gift then she would forever have something to hide along with everyone else. She shifted the cruiser into Park and killed the engine. Ronnie started to get out.

She pulled him back by his fatigue blouse, leaned across and kissed him again, hard and deep and long.

The police car had approached with its headlights off and BoDean so didn't notice it until it slid past the truck. It was *her* car, he realized with a jolt. He looked at the device and its beckoning black button. It was a golden opportunity, he thought, to settle all his scores in a true blaze of glory. The old cop, the Chief and, like a cherry on the top, the yappy little dog. BoDean reached over and picked it up, cradling it in his palm.

He rattled the wrist-bones hanging from his neck. He could hear his brother's voice. Somewhere during the nosy Bank Examiner's long ordeal in the Pines Billy had taken a break. He and BoDean had used the pause to fortify themselves with a half Mason jar of Billy's White Lightning, he recalled. Billy thought torture of and murder as skills too often practiced by what he called *ama-choors*. He felt they needed to be passed on and so he often shared advice despite the blood, the anguished screams and the pleas for the mercy of a quicker death. "Always remember, brother," Billy had told him as that long night had dragged on, "There is suffering. And then there is *pro-longed* suffering. *Pro*-fessionals *pro*-duce *pro*-longed suffering."

Billy watched her get out of the car. A man with short hair and wearing some kind of military clothes got out from the other side. He didn't recognize the man or the uniform but now it was dark and the two quickly disappeared through the house's front door. BoDean thought he wanted to a professional. He resisted temptation and put the metal box back on the passenger seat.

A few minutes later she and the man emerged, got back in the police car and drove off. BoDean checked his watch. He rolled down the window just far enough for him to be assured that the blackout windows hadn't fooled him into thinking it was darker than it really was. It wasn't. He started to roll the window back up when he saw something that caught his eye in the truck's rearview mirror. It took a minute for him to see clearly but it looked like it was an adult man pedaling slowly on a kids' kind of bicycle. He noticed that the man looked like he'd shopped at the same place BoDean had for the garish clothes BoDean currently had on.

The man on the kiddie bike was moving too deliberately BoDean thought, weaving from one side of the street to the other. He was checking out the parked vehicles, BoDean realized. As he watched, the bike slowed and came to a stop at the car parked behind him. Then the man straddled the bike and moved forward awkwardly using only his feet, like a duck waddling across a paved road. Bo Dean tilted his head so he could see the man better as he approached the truck's rear fender and stopped again. BoDean thought he meant to siphon gas, given that the truck's tank would have the largest capacity and that the price of a gallon had just passed north of thirty-six cents. But BoDean didn't see a hose or a gas can. He did notice the man had something in his hand, though. BoDean though it might be a rag.

♦ ♦ ♦

Higgins and Rodriguez had already checked in and Mickey and Ronnie were heading north on Barnegat Avenue trying to avoid the crawl on Long Beach Boulevard.

Charlie had said they were helping SBPD, Charlie referred to them as the Bottom Boys, clear out the cars so causeway bridge traffic could get moving again. He also passed on a message from Davey Johnson saying, in Charlie's words, that Napoleon was keeping him at Waterloo and he'd be back to stake-out Patsy's place as soon as he could.

"I'm going to have to apologize for not believing her," Mickey said to Ronnie. "She just kept saying "Dunn come home. Dunn come home' It was weird. Either a very lucky guess or maybe there really is the power of positive thinking."

"Bunny Vincent Peale," Ronnie quipped. "You know, plus the *nhuc duc.*"

"Hey," Mickey chided, "She said you guys, the soldiers, taught her that."

"I'm sure we did," Ronnie agreed.

"I'm going to let you tell her the good news about Coo-pral Winston and, what's her mama-san's name?"

"Mama-san?" Ronnie said. "First boo-coo and now mama-san?"

"What can I say," Mickey replied. "I'm a quick learner."

"Her mama's name is Yvette, if I'm not mistaken. A nod to the French Colonials who made exactly the same mistake we're making now."

"Pretty name," Mickey said. "You know, I haven't heard back from Dip yet." She grabbed the microphone and toggled a switch. "Surf City 1 to Base. Dip, do you copy? Over."

Static filled the car's interior.

"That's weird," Mickey said and tried again. "I told him to leave the shop. Surf City 1 to Base.," she repeated. "Dippolito, pick up. Dippolito, do you read? Over."

They were only three blocks from the station.

"That's my next car," Ronnie said. He pointed to an orange Plymouth Road Runner parked at a slight angle on the side of the street ahead of them. One tire was up on the curb and it looked like the trunk was popped. Mickey thought she had seen the car twice, once in Ship Bottom and then again in Surf City. She remembered it because it had come up very close behind her in Surf City when she slowed to make a left turn. She had made a quick note of the front license plate – the boring New Jersey beige with black lettering. The car Ronnie was pointing at had a Pennsylvania rear plate. But it was the same car. Mickey was certain of it. She let up on the pedal as they came even with it and then looked in Ronnie's rear view mirror as they passed, slowing the Chevelle until she could see the front bumper. Just below it a silver rectangle framed a New Jersey plate.

"What do you think?" Ronnie asked.

"I think... something's... wrong," Mickey said and punched the gas.

Thirty-Eight

Surf City

  Jeffrey Silverman's first car was not his first choice.
  But in the darkness of this dusty beach road it was a previously unrecognized and unappreciated gift from God, he thought. Thanks to the genius of the automotive interior designers at the Chevrolet Motor Company, he was about to consummate actual carnal relations with, if not quite the bleach blonde *shiksa* of his dreams, then the brunette girl who'd sat next to him in A.P. Trigonometry class all year at Cherry Hill East High School, Berry Feldstein. His fevered and ultimately fruitless pursuit of the perfect and thus unattainable Heidi Abramowitz had spanned all of the previous two years and then some. In contrast, his courtship and now his imminent ravishing of Bouncing Berry, a name she'd given herself, had covered only the last two days. Her family, she said, was spending a week at the Shore. She had come up to him at Skee-Ball game in the back of a sweltering boardwalk arcade and asked if she could play. Some polite chit-chat had ensued, including Berry's sharing the fascinating tidbit that Skee-Ball had been invented and patented in 1908 by a guy in nearby Vineland, New Jersey. When it came Berry's turn to roll, she'd reached down and picked up not one but two of the nine Masonite spheres in the rack and looked Jeffrey right in the eye.
  "I just love the way balls feel in my hand," she'd said.
  Jeffrey had almost suffered a seizure.
  After that, they had retired behind the arcade and just below

the boards for some heavy petting. Tonight's assignation had to wait, Berry had told him, until her parents were sure to be inebriated enough that they wouldn't notice what time and in what state of dress she came home.

The 1960 Brookwood station wagon was, in Jeffery's own estimation, a real beater but it was built like a tank. Jeffrey had nicknamed it the Green Dragon in a less than successful bid to improve his coefficient of cool. Its factory Cascade Green PPG Duracryl paint job had cascaded into something barely identifiable as color and patches of rust grew like lichens around every edge. Jeffrey didn't care. The Brookwood wagon's second and third row bench seats folded down flat creating a screwing surface he calculated was considerably larger than his bed at home. He'd padded the hard seatbacks with one old quilt from the attic and three beach blankets plus a throw pillow he'd snuck from the davenport in the house they rented every summer from the Matlick's.

Jeffery had his pants off and his boxers down.

"Let me get on top," Berry said. He assumed this was so she could do the bouncing.

Jeffery had looked up ways to keep from having it all over too soon. A visit to the local pharmacy had revealed a "desensitizing lubricant" jelly called Detane which promised, according to the ad featuring an attractive couple on their way to the boudoir, "greater marriage compatibility." Jeffery had somehow found the nerve to ask the old druggist what he thought.

"Depends," he said. "You want to go for a long time and not feel it or you want to feel it and maybe pop off a little quicker." He explained that the slippery substance actually contained a powerful local anesthetic and that Jeffery's erect penis would "stay hard as a rock but feel as dead as a doornail."

Jeffery had thanked him for his candor and put the box back on the shelf, purchasing only a new package of Trojan rubbers and the smallest bottle of Aqua Velva he could find.

Berry was starting to moan. He watched her deftly doff her panties and drop them by his ear. She leaned down and stuck her warm tongue inside his mouth as she climbed aboard the good ship Silverman and shimmied up the mainmast.

Bouncing Berry was making good on her Skee-Ball brag when someone began knocking on the curved glass window that wrapped around the Brookwood's rear fender. Jeffrey assumed it was a policeman until Berry screamed and slipped off him, cowering by the hump of the passenger wheel well.

When the knocking ceased the drop-down tailgate banged open. Someone who was definitely not a policeman was yelling for them both to get out. He tried to say something but nothing came out. He thought of the set of keys he'd left hanging in the ignition and tried to imagine why anyone would want to steal a ten-year old Chevy beater. A station wagon at that. Jeffrey felt himself being pulled roughly by one ankle. Berry was crying and the not-a-policeman was shouting "shut the fuck up" at her repeatedly as he slid helplessly toward the back bumper. His feet dropped downward but his legs were hamstrung by his half-mast boxers and he tumbled awkwardly into the street. He saw the shouting man pull Berry out and toss her to the curb as if she were a rag doll. Jeffrey was desperately trying to get his underwear pulled up when he saw in rapid sequence the face of the terrified little girl and then the gun in the man's hand.

♦ ♦ ♦

When Mickey pulled and saw Dippolito's cruiser still parked where it was when she left she felt momentarily relieved. The front door of the station was closed and, Mickey assumed, locked. She parked the Chevelle and she and Ronnie got out.

"Wait at the front door for me," she said. "I want to go around back."

As she walked around the building she could see that the back door was open a good six inches. She unholstered her gun and slipped it out. When she got to the door she yelled through the screen.

"Hey, Dip you in there? Dippolito. Everything OK in there? Bunny? Bunny. Are you inside?"

A little chill ran through her and a wave of nausea arrived. Mickey swallowed hard and pulled open the screen door with her free hand, then extended the hand holding the gun in front of her. She kicked the inner door open all the way.

"Dip? Bunny?" she called. All the lights were on. Her eyes went first to the two cells. Empty. Then to Dippolito's desk. Papers were strewn all over it and his chair was six feet out of place. She didn't see any blood.

"Dip? Bunny? This not funny, OK. Dip, where are you?"

She heard the door creak behind her and wheeled around, pointing her revolver at the sound. Then she heard a rasping almost gurgling sound inside the otherwise silent station.

Ronnie pushed in through the back door.

"Christ, I almost shot you," Mickey said. "I said wait out front."

"Yeah, right," he said. The he cocked an ear. "Over there," he said pointing to Dippolito's paper-strewn desk.

Mickey took two steps and saw the new Flagg Brothers duty boots Dip had been so proud of sticking out from under the desk. His feet were still in them.

"Aw, fuck," Mickey yelled. "Fuck. Dunn, give me a hand here. It's Dip."

He was alive, Mickey could see, but she figured barely at best. She crouched down and cradled his head. His face was blue and mottled and his neck looked like it was five sizes bigger. His breathing sounded like wet sandpaper and bubbles foamed at his lips.

Ronnie crouched next to her.

"Somebody fractured his larynx," Ronnie said. "Do you have a knife and a tube or a plastic straw?"

"Let's just call the ambulance," Mickey replied.

"He'll be dead in about two minutes if we wait for them. We have to make a hole in his windpipe."

"Here?"

"Sharp knife. Straw. Even a Bic pen will do. Pull out the point and the ink barrel."

Some forgotten image of Dip whittling on a balsa wood stick popped into Mickey's head. She rifled through Dippolito's desk drawer and found his Boy Scout Jamboree folding knife. She handed it to Ronnie who began pulling out the various blades until he found the one he wanted.

"Won't he bleed out all over?" Mickey asked.

"The tissues are so swollen they'll choke off any significant bleeding. Here, help me tilt his head back. Did you find a tube? Anything round and stiff will do." Mickey turned away as Ronnie drew the blade across Dippolito's neck. She grabbed a thick Magic Marker. "Will this work?" she asked.

As Ronnie predicted the neck wound oozed only a precious few drops of blood. The rasping respirations were getting worse.

"We'll make it work," Ronnie said. He grabbed the marker, pulled off the cap and twisted the collar that held the pointed nib until it popped out. Then he used the knife to saw of the rounded bottom. ""Pray for luck, he said. "This is the worst part. Call the ambulance."

As Mickey stood up she saw Ronnie stick a finger in the fresh neck wound. It looked like he was feeling for something. Then he took the truncated marker tube and jammed it in the new hole in Dippolito's neck. A few seconds later as she was dialing the Fire Station she heard a pop and then a wet, blowing sound. Blood, phlegm and what looked like tissue extruded from the marker barrel.

"Shit, I think it's still plugged," Ronnie said and then shocked Mickey by leaning down, putting his mouth around the marker tube and sucking hard on it.

She gave the briefest report possible, saying only "This is Cleary. Medical emergency. Police Station. Now," and hung up the phone. It seemed like sirens could be heard the second the receiver slapped the cradle.

Ronnie brought his head up and spit out a disgusting liquid mess on to the floor.

Mickey could hear the difference right away. Air was moving in and out of the marker tube. Dip's neck was still swollen but his face was getting pinker by the second. Ronnie wiped his mouth on the green sleeve of his fatigues.

"I was wrong," he said. "*That* was the worst part." He rubbed his lips with his hand.

"Should we put a pillow under his head?" Mickey asked.

"No," Ronnie answered. "We have to keep his neck bent back a little – helps keep the windpipe from kinking."

The sounds of first sirens, then engines, then slamming door and raised voices grew nearer."

"He looks better," Ronnie said.

He looks grotesque, Mickey thought to herself. "Is he going to live?" she asked.

"Depends on how low his oxygen got and for how long. "He could live and never wake up."

"I should have left Charlie or Rich with Bunny," Mickey said.

"This is my fault. I should have looked out for him and known better."

"This had to Robichaux," Ronnie said. "Unless you would have left Charlie *and* Rich here, this would be one of them."

"Shit, I forgot the door," Mickey said. She sprinted to the front of the station, pulled the locks and swung it open just as the ambulance crew arrived. "It's Dip," she said as they shouldered past her. She moved to hold the door for the rolling stretcher.

Mickey wasn't sure how much time had passed but it seemed like the stretcher with Dip on it was clanging by her before she knew it.

"We're taking him to AC," one the medics said on his way out the door.

"How'd you know how to do that?" Mickey asked.

""I'll tell you later. This guy's got Bunny and he's moving. He has to be heading off the island."

"Let's go, Mickey said.

"You go. Start looking – take his picture with you and give out the description to anyone you can."

"Where are you going?"

"Me and Chuck Taylor will sprint home. Is my bike gassed up?"

"If that's how you left it, it is. Will it start after four months?"

"That bike would start after four years," Ronnie said. "I'll grab it and I'll get going."

Mickey paused. "You take the Boulevard – you can weave in and out on that thing. I'll go to Barnegat Avenue. Hopefully that mess at the bridge is still acting as a roadblock."

"Call the Cavalry," Ronnie said. "Everybody needs to saddle up, ASAP."

"Copy that," Mickey replied."Somebody needs to watch my dad's place. I'll work on that."

Mickey moved closer and then remembered the mess on the floor and how it got there. "Yeah, I'll kiss you again after you've brushed your teeth a couple hundred times. Promise. But right now we can't let anything happen to Bunny. Not after all she's been through."

"We'll find her," Ronnie said. "We will find her.

◆ ◆ ◆

Ship Bottom

BoDean looked around and climbed back into Cowboy's truck. The rag the guy had tried stuffing into his fuel tank was still clenched in his fist and he tossed it on the floor in front of the passenger side seat. The air in the cab grew thick with the scent of gasoline.

He'd tucked the asshole's limp body in the bed of the truck and covered it with the tarp. He'd dump it or burn it once he was back in the Barrens, he figured. He'd walked the bike down a block further away and leaned it against a tree. It was a rental, he'd noticed, so someone would either steal it or return it. Less work for him either way, BoDean calculated. He was worried the rag might be what Cowboy had called that f'rensic evidence. He should have thrown it in the back with the body, he now thought. As he leaned over to retrieve it he saw the light in the old cop's bedroom window go off and, as if in response, a switch inside him turned on. The waiting was finally over. He tapped his brother's bones for luck, rolled down the window just far enough to peer out and picked up the metal box.

Pro-fessionals pro-duce pro-longed suffering he said to himself as if reciting a prayer or an incantation. He felt the black button under his thumb, the same one he'd sliced on the sharpened badge days earlier. BoDean closed his eyes and conjured up Billy's face, his toothless smile and his cackling laugh. He pushed hard on the button.

All the lights were out but the little dog scratched again at the front door. Patsy took her outside and waited. After Pixie had finished piddling, Patsy picked her up and was about to go back inside when he heard a sound like a sudden breeze and saw a bright glow reflected in the window pane. He thought a street light had popped or maybe even a transformer had blown high up on one of the poles.

He turned around, looked down the quiet street and was amazed and perplexed at what he beheld. Maybe thirty or perhaps forty yards away was a truck with its windows all glowing as bright as an arc light. Only to Patsy it looked like the illumination must be coming from inside the truck. He was transfixed by the sight. Pixie yapped but Patsy remained motionless, fascinated and horrified at what was unfolding in what seemed like slow-motion. A tongue of flame shot out of the driver's side window and then withdrew, almost as if it had been sucked back in. He heard a muffled scream, one unlike any he'd ever heard before and then saw a hand, just a palm really, slapping frantically at the dark window glass on the driver's side. He covered the little dog protectively with his other arm and began to back up. There was noise like a faraway explosion and then more flames escaped the window. The screams were endless and something other than human. And then they stopped.

Patsy could now see that a fire was raging inside the truck's passenger compartment. He quickly put the dog inside and went to see if he could help. When he got to about twenty yards away he could feel the heat. Then he saw flames lick out from the undercarriage and knew what would happen next.

Patsy's legs moved like they hadn't moved in twenty years. He bolted through the front door, grabbed the little dog off the couch, kept going to the back door and then out to the furthest part of the sea-shelled back yard.

The next explosion he heard was louder. It shook the ground and rattled the window panes. Glowing debris shot up and then fell slowly from the sky like the tail end of a fireworks barrage. The little dog shivered and shook in Patsy's arms. He patted her head and rubbed her neck, as much for his own comfort as hers.

For an instant BoDean thought it hadn't worked. In the space of a heartbeat he saw a little flash emanate from the box in his hand and then it was if the very air around him was catching fire. He tried to open the door but his hands felt like soft rubber. He batted at the windows, unable to see, the pain becoming unbearable. He screamed but the sound seemed like it came from somewhere else, belonged to someone else. Every breath he took seared his lungs. He reached for his face and found only a molten mass of flesh. He heard crackling and popping and, in the instant before he died, he realized it was his own body being consumed by flame. ♦ ♦ ♦

Surf City

Mickey's frustration was mounting. She didn't know what kind of car she was looking for. She knew they wouldn't be on foot. She was willing herself to remain collected, to think like a cop and not like a daughter or – a temporary mother.

She was headed south on Barnegat Avenue, now just a few blocks from Ship Bottom when she saw it. A flash that lit the sky. A second later she heard the boom and felt the pavement shake. She toggled the radio and listened for chatter. It didn't take long.

"Dispatch to all Fire and Ambulance units. Possible explosion. West 5th Street Ship Bottom. Repeat. Possible explosion. West 5th Ship Bottom. All available units respond Code 1. Repeat. All available units respond Code 1. Possible fatality. Repeat possible fatality." Mickey recognized the throaty voice of Sherry, the night Dispatch operator. She also recognized the 10-20. West 5th was the street Patsy lived on.

Rich Rodriguez was pissed.

He didn't have time for this shit right now. He hit the lights and whooped the siren. The skinny kid wearing only his underwear was waving frantically. As he drew closer he could see someone else. It looked like a girl of about the same age curled on the sidewalk in a fetal position. Rodriguez rolled up and jumped out.

Charlie Higgins had just crossed the border into Surf City when he heard the explosion. He wheeled the cruiser around and headed to where he saw the light in the sky. The Dispatch channel on the radio crackled and Charlie listened. He knew who lived on West 5th Street. He whispered a silent prayer that he would not arrive there to find the unspeakable. He hit the roof lights and sped south. He began to repeat the simple plea, "Please, Jesus," over and over as he drove.

Dickie Robichaux looked at his watch. Twenty-one-forty hours. Harlan was ten minutes behind schedule but that had worked out even better. He watched the glow in the sky, felt the shudder of air suddenly super-heated and waited for the sirens. When the first one wailed, followed quickly by a chorus of others, he figured he'd wait another five minutes and then start moving. After he'd tied up the kid and taped her mouth, he popped up the second row bench and laid her on the floor behind the front seat. She would be invisible to anyone they passed. She'd finally quit wiggling and the muffled whining had mostly trailed off. He knew exactly where every cop on Long Beach Island was headed. He was going to go in the opposite direction. He was still debating whether or not he would stop to pick up Harlan.

Thirty-Nine

Ship Bottom

Davey Johnson got there first.
He parked his cruiser and ran down the street. What had once been a pick-up truck was engulfed in flames, the heat intense. Anything not metallic had been burned away and the skeleton frame glowed eerily. A Chevrolet emblem lay on the ground, hurled by the blast. Smoke was still rising from it.
Davey hustled by and went right to Patsy's house. He was sure Patsy did not own a truck. He pounded on the door and then pushed his way inside, calling out. The place was empty. He cleared each room as he'd been taught and then moved to the back door. He walked out and saw Patsy and his little dog huddled near some bushes in the back yard. He ran to them, his boots slipping on the uneven shells.
"Sergeant Cleary, are you OK?" he yelled as he drew closer.
"I'm OK, Davey. I'm OK. We're OK. He stroked the dogs head. We're OK."
"You house looks OK," Davey said. "I think it's safe to go back in now. I'll go with you."
"We're OK, Davey. We're OK," Patsy repeated. Davey thought he might be in mild shock.
"Good, Officer Cleary. That's good. Let's get you and your little girlfriend back inside, shall we." Patsy took a step and Davey put a hand on his shoulder. "That's the way," he said. "Easy does it."
"Did you call Michaela," Patsy asked.

"Not yet," Dave replied. "I came here first to make sure you were OK. I'll radio her in just a minute. I want to check your house and then I'll get her on the radio, OK."

"Yeah, OK," Patsy said. "You want a beer when we get to the house? I got lots."

Davey Johnson laughed. "Maybe later," he said. "Definitely later I'll take you up on it."

'Yeah, OK," Patsy said.

Davey led him in through the back door and took him to the couch. "You two sit right here. I'll get you some water and then I'm going to check around outside."

"Davey," Patsy said.

"Yes, Sergeant Cleary?"

"I'll take that beer now, if you don't mind."

His bartending chore completed, Davey walked the outside of the house, shining his flashlight up and down looking for any drifting embers which could wreak havoc on a wooden dwelling. As he was inspecting the final outside wall, he spied a barrel sitting below the bedroom window. He shined his light and saw a black cable snaking from the bottom of the barrel. He crouched down and was met with the odor of diesel fuel. Davey pocketed his flashlight, picked up the heavy barrel and began lugging it to the far corner of the yard. He could still feel the heat from the burning truck on his back.

♦ ♦ ♦

Surf City

Traffic was a mess which, Mickey decided both helped and hindered her search. If she was stuck then so were Robichaux and Bunny. "Don't corner him," Darnell had warned Charlie. He's a rat, Mickey thought. Better to trap him. Then her radio crackled.

"Dispatch to Surf City One. Do you copy, over?"

"Surf City One, copy. Whatc'ha have for me, Sherry. Over."

"Surf City One, Ship Bottom Three is on scene at site of the explosion and fire. He reports that involved vehicle is a truck with at least one occupant who is deceased. He reports that Sergeant Cleary and his pet are fine and his dwelling is secure. He will stay

on scene unless you need him. Over?"
"Copy that. Surf City One sends thanks. Copy?"
"Copy. Dispatch out."
Mickey heaved a sigh of relief and felt for a moment like she might cry. She bit down on her cheek and steadied her hands on the wheel. The radio squawked again.
"Surf City Two to Surf City One. What's your twenty, Chief?"
"Approaching Division southbound on Barnegat. Copy?"
"Copy. Stay there as I am en route to you from Shore and North 3rd with two juveniles who say they can ID suspect and vehicle. ETA two minutes."
Mickey's heart rate jumped.
"Copy that. Go Code 1."
She heard the siren and guessed thirty seconds was more like it. She pulled the cruiser over and hit the roof lights. She checked her rear view mirror and saw a familiar motorcycle and rider approaching.
Ronnie pulled up alongside the driver side window.
"Nothing?" Mickey asked.
Ronnie shook his head. "Be nice if he had one of those ESSO Tigers or an Atlantic Red Ball on his antenna. What's going on in Ship Bottom? "
"Truck exploded on my dad's street. He's OK. Davey's there."
"How's the dog?"
"The dog's fine, too. I'll tell Dad you asked." Mickey saw Rodriguez at the intersection. "Rich says he's got two juvies who can ID Robichaux's vehicle."
"I think the fire is a diversionary tactic," Ronnie said. "If they're still working together, that is."
"How would that-"
"Everybody knows where Patsy lives which means everybody would respond."
Rodriguez rolled up in his cruiser and killed his flashers.
"Traffic is a mess and there's only one way off," Mickey countered. "What good is a diversion?"
"Gives them a chance to hole up, maybe wait it out or even find another way off the Island."
"What other way?" Mickey asked.
"The Bay," Ronnie said. "I'd go either all the way north to the light or all the way south to Holgate by the old Life Saving Station.

A guy from the swamps would be right at home crossing it."

Rodriguez walked over and stood across from Ronnie. He nodded to Mickey."Chief," he said. "Might want to come over to my unit to talk to them. The boy isn't exactly dressed for the occasion. Any word on Dip?"

"They were taking him to Atlantic City. If I hear anything, you'll know," Mickey said.

Rodriguez looked over at Ronnie. "Heard Tom Thumb took a shot at you. Good thing it wasn't Charlie."

Ronnie gave him a puzzled look.

"Charlie our deputy, not Charlie the Viet Cong," Mickey clarified.

"Got it," Ronnie replied.

"Dunn thinks the fire is a diversion," Mickey said. "You buy that?"

"Military guys would use military tactics," Rodriguez answered. "Makes a certain amount of sense. The entrance to the bridge is still all locked up. They're not getting out that way. So do you want to talk to these two young lovers?"

"Did they see Bunny?"

"She was with the guy when he came up on them. Said she looked scared but otherwise OK."

"I don't need to talk to them," Mickey said, drumming her fingers on the car door's interior. "What's he driving?"

Rodriguez pulled out his notepad. "1960 Chevy Brookwood station wagon. Light green, lot of rust, banged up whitewalls. It belongs to the kid. He calls it the Green Dragon. They were about to do the deed when the guy shows gun, pulls them out from the back seat and takes off with the car and Bunny."

"Two doors or four?" Mickey asked.

"He didn't say and I didn't ask, why?"

"They made a lot fewer of the four-door. Either way, we should be able to find that beast," Mickey said. "Put it out on the radio but caution Do Not Approach. I don't want to put Bunny in any more danger than she already is. Treat it like a hostage situation, which is really what it is now. Charlie's brother said not to corner this guy."

"Copy that, Chief. What do I do with the lovebirds?"

"Take them home. I think they both may have some 'splainin to do. I'm going to get blocks set up at Harvey Cedars and Brant

Beach. We'll either push these jokers to the ends of the island or trap them in the middle. Have you seen Charlie?"

"Not for a while," Rodriguez said. "Let me get on this and then I'll join the search. See you later, Dunn. Better luck next time."

"*Adios, amigo,*" Ronnie replied.

"Where to now?" Mickey asked.

"Let's track north," Ronnie said. "I got a feeling on this one."

"It started, I see," Mickey said nodding at the bike.

"It's a Royal-Enfield," Ronnie shot back. "Of course it started. Built like a tank-"

"Goes like a bullet," Mickey said, completing the company's advertising slogan. "Yeah, yeah. I know."

Ronnie kicked the engine into life and roared off. Mickey killed the roof lights and made an illegal U-turn. She hoped Dunn's feeling was right because now she had a feeling of her own.

Forty

Ship Bottom

Charlie Higgins listened intently and then hooked a left. If things were alright at Chief Cleary's father's place then he was going where he was needed. But first he needed to prepare. When he crossed the line into Surf City he found a small parking lot next to Rider's Market, a mom-and-pop grocery store he liked to frequent. They always stocked a supply Goldenberg's Peanut Chews, a vice Charlie believed bordered on addiction but for which he was unapologetic. He often bought the whole box.

Charlie pulled in and turned off the engine. He got out and went to the trunk and opened it. The large nylon bag had not been disturbed in months. A lapse on his part, he realized, not cleaning the contents. He hoped it would not mean the difference if it came right down to it.

He unzipped the bag and rummaged for a minute. The first thing he withdrew was the newly available 0.44 AutoMag he'd purchased on his last trip home. He'd altered his holster so it would fit the bigger gun and he exchanged the 0.45 Colt revolver for the semi-automatic pistol and tucked extra clips in his pocket. He put his service weapon in the bag. Then he pulled out the scoped Remington 270 rifle and an extra box of Winchester cartridges. He shouldered the rifle by its sling, grabbed the cartridges and slammed the trunk closed. Then he walked back along the driver's side. His radio was crackling.

"Surf City 1 to Surf City 2. Charlie do you copy? Over."

Charlie reached in grabbed his microphone.
"Surf City 2, copy, Chief."
"Where are you?"
"Just stepping out over the line into our fair borough."
"You got the vehicle description?"
"'60 Brookwood wagon. Chevy. That's some heavy metal thunder, Chief. Where do you want me?" Charlie assumed they were dispensing with radio chatter formalities.

"Why don't you post up in Barnegat, near the light and we'll see if we can push these guys toward you. Barnegat PD is starting a sweep south with both their units. On the chance they slip through I need you up there to be a backstop."

"Copy that, Chief Cleary."

"And Charlie, this is a Do Not Approach, Do Not Engage hostage situation. He or they have Bunny."

"It's Robichaux, correct?"

"That is affirmative. He is the driver. Unknown as to whether his partner is with him or in the wind. But we know he has Bunny."

"Copy, Chief. Instructions understood. Surf City 2 out."

Charlie laid the bolt action rifle barrel down on the passenger side. If it needed to be done, he thought, he wanted to be the one to do it. For Darnell and now for Dip as well. He pulled the door shut and fired up the engine.

Mickey saw the Enfield in her side mirror and pulled over. Ronnie came up, stopped and reached into a bag hanging on the bike's handlebars. He let the engine run.

"Here," he said and handed her a large Army-green walkie-talkie.

"Where did you-"

"My duffel bag of tricks," Ronnie said. "Where else? If I spot them I need a way to let you know and vice-versa."

Mickey noticed it was already turned on. She hit the squelch button and static came from Ronnie's unit. "I feel like a commando," Mickey said.

"And this is a rescue mission, not an attack," Ronnie replied. "So be Chief Cleary and not Sergeant York. Wait for backup. If we can separate them from Bunny, ballgame's over."

"If," Mickey said. "OK, let's – what do you guys always say - Saddle up?"

Ronnie laughed, gunned the bike and took off. A song floated in Mickey's head. If Bunny had ESP then she was sending it out to her. "Hold on. We're comin'."

Dickie liked his plan more and more as he drove north. The visual recon they'd done from the top of the lighthouse had ended up being the key. Dickie remembered several things – there were boats tied up on the bay side. Small boats with outboards. Pull starts, so no ignition key required. There were also large storm drains that ran from the bay side to the beach side underneath the roads. He figured the corrugated pipe diameter was at least five feet. He'd have to crouch or belly crawl, pushing or pulling the kid with him, but he could manage it. He'd managed much worse, he thought. Dickie looked at the gun on the seat next to him. He could just leave the little dink in the car and try to disappear or he could go for broke. He couldn't get to Harlan if he wanted to and now, he decided, he didn't want to. Without Harlan slowing him down, getting in the way or maybe double-crossing him, going for broke grew steadily more attractive.

Dickie looked back over the seat. The kid stared at him and tried to speak but the tape muffled it to almost nothing. She was still alive, he thought. That was all he needed to know.

If he stayed to the beach side, he calculated, and ditched the car there, then he could hump it through the pipe and steal a boat on the bay. They would find the care but they would be looking for them on the wrong side of the island. It would delay them long enough, he figured, for him to get to the mainland.

The kid was banging the back of his seat with her pointy knees.

Dickey shifted the wagon back into gear. He disliked the three-speed column shift but the engine felt like it was probably a V-8. And it was heavy, even for a wagon. Dickie thought maybe close to two tons. It was a battering ram on wheels and that, he decided, provided him with a tactical advantage.

As he pulled out slowly a guy on a bare-bones motorcycle cruised past him. It wasn't an AMF or one of the Harley-Davidson's that he favored, just two wheels, a seat and a loud-ass motor. Sometimes simpler was better, Dickie thought.

Forty-One

Harvey Cedars

Billy Tunell had told Mickey that Harvey Cedars' odd name came from a time when the north end of the Island was covered with white cedar trees. How Harvey entered the geographic nomenclature was a matter of some debate, but apparently it did not refer to an actual person or family named Harvey. Billy also shared that the area which was now Surf City, around the same time that the cedar trees were in charge, was known as the Great Swamp. As this did not jive with the mayor's vision of and marketing strategy for America's Riviera, she was forbidden to pass on her newfound knowledge under penalty of dismissal.

Mickey scanned in a wide arc as she drove up one side street and then down another. She occasionally caught glimpses of other cruisers doing the same. Radio chatter went back and forth noting locations and declaring them clear.

Then the walkie-talkie buzzed. Mickey picked it up and held it to the side of her face.

"I got him," Ronnie said. The rushing air, he had to be moving she thought, was distorting his words and she couldn't make out the location. She did notice that he'd said "him" and not "them."

"Dunn. Say again. Where is he?"

Again, wind-whipped words and garbled phrases were all she heard.

"Dunn," she yelled into the unit. "Pull over and transmit so I can hear you."

Two static bursts told her he understood.
Mickey's pulse quickened and her breathing increased.
Her walkie-talkie popped again.
"I passed him pointed north. He was still south of the turn for High Bar Island. 25th, maybe."
"Just him? Just Robichaux?"
"Afirmitave," Ronnie answered.
"Any sign of Bunny?"
"I did not see her on my fly-by. But I know she's in that car."
"OK," Mickey said, " Stay with them but do not engage. Cavalry's coming."
She turned on the roof lights and hit the siren.

◆ ◆ ◆

Loveladies

Dickie saw the lights before he heard the sirens. Time to rock and roll, he decided. Judging from the sound he didn't think he could make the lighthouse ahead of them but he might make it to the pipe which jutted from the dunes. It didn't matter – improvising was always what he did best.

He stepped on the gas and turned up the AM radio. Stabbing with a finger at the silver buttons, he passed on The Fifth Dimension, The Cowsills and the Isley Brothers until finally a song he liked finally poured out of the one crappy speaker. Creedence Clearwater's "Green River" made the dashboard thump and Dickie began to sing along. He'd been disappointed to learn that the band's brand of "swamp rock" had originated in the hippie haven of San Francisco and not in Baton Rouge or Metarie. If his life had been different, he thought, he'd have traveled all the way up to New York to watch them play in a farm field. The sirens were getting louder. Dickie looked for the next right turn.

A turn he knew would take him east and straight toward the vast, dark ocean.

◆ ◆ ◆

Barnegat Light State Park
Barnegat Light, NJ

Charlie parked at the far end of the lighthouse's gravel parking lot and shut off the engine. He heard sirens and saw the glimmer of roof lights and cherry tops speeding in his direction. He grabbed the Remington by the stock and pulled it toward him

He didn't understand why the Barnegat Light was not a more popular tourist attraction. The Park Service had been more than accommodating, not closing it to the public until ten p.m. in July and August when the days were the longest. The only thing they hadn't done, Charlie thought, was to hire a full-time lighthouse keeper.

Some high-power spotlights had been installed over the winter and they bathed the structure in white light from three angles. It was beautiful, stately and almost majestic in its way, Charlie thought, with its white bottom half and its tapering, brick-red upper half.

He opened the cruiser door and stepped into the humid night. The wind was coming in gently from the ocean and the dune grass swayed with occasional gusts. Maybe the answer, Charlie mused with a smile, maybe the answer truly was blowing in that wind.

He slung the rifle over his shoulder and walked toward the base of the lighthouse. It was deserted, again, on a beautiful evening when there should have been a line of people waiting to catch a last birds-eye view of the fleeting summer.

Charlie glanced at the historical plaque that had been erected and kept walking.

Once he reached the rock jetty, he trod carefully. He looked at the water. The air and the sea temperatures were equilibrating and he saw no coamers, only a small and gently breaking surf. He picked his way long the huge flat, black stones for about thirty yards. The rocks were dry, he noticed, which was unusual. Usually breakers kept them wet and slick. He looked up at the lighthouse. The light and the huge Fresnel lens had been removed long ago. Maybe someday someone would rekindle the lamp, refocus the light with a new lens. He'd climbed each of the two hundred and seventeen steps and looked down from the height of a sixteen-story office building, taking in the island from stem to stern and from port to starboard. Charlie had wanted Darnell to see it. He'd wanted him to mount those metal steps on his one God-given leg and his other man-made one. He wanted Darnell to feel the cool air and watch the lamps wink on as darkness fell, making the Island look like the lights on a ship ready to cast off and sail away.

Charlie knew he would tell Darnell these things when he brought him home. But first he had business to attend to. He hoped Bunny was right. He hoped Darnell looked down on him and protected him now for he knew, in his heart, he had not done enough to protect Darnell.

Deep down between the jetty's rocks he heard scurrying movement.

Rats, he knew.

Mickey caught sight of the wagon just as it turned. It was a dead end, she realized. Just the beach and the ocean in that direction. Ronnie came toward her from the opposite direction, skidded through a U-turn and then rode up next to her.

He pointed. Mickey nodded. Then he took off, trailing the wagon by fifty feet, leading Mickey by the same.

Then the big Brookwood accelerated headlong toward the dark Atlantic. East 9th Street was a long straightaway, reaching toward the ocean further than any other cross street. He would have to slow down, Mickey knew. There were no side roads and no turnarounds ahead of him.

Suddenly she knew what his intentions were.

She picked up the walkie-talkie. "He's going to take the sand," she yelled into it.

She watched as Ronnie throttled back, letting her catch up. They would bracket him, she decided. She pointed at Ronnie and then at the big wagon's passenger side. Ronnie nodded.

The Brookwood's twin cat's-eye taillights glowed in the deepening gloom but did not brighten. He had not touched the brakes, Mickey knew. As they approached the end of the street the dunes rose up. The Brookwood accelerated. She thought of the kid's name for it. They were chasing a Green Dragon and Dickie Robichaux was no Jackie Paper. Ronnie's bike crossed in front of her and flanked the car on its right side. Mickey knew she would have to gun the Chevelle to get it across the soft sand. If she just could keep it moving the beach at low tide would be hard and flat. The Chevelle was not built to be a dune buggy and Mickey wasn't sure how it would perform once it left the paved road. She hoped Robichaux was not going to drive into the ocean in some weird, suicidal gesture that would take Bunny with him. If he turned right on the beach he'd have the whole length of the island to run. If he turned left, the possibilities were extremely limited and shrinking by the yard.

The Brookwood hit the narrow path between the dunes at full speed, scraping the wood pilings sunk deep in the ground, the wagon was so wide. But it barely slowed. A spray of white sand hit Mickey's windshield. Out her side window she saw Ronnie take the dune's humped berm at high speed, the bike launching into the air then up and over. She could not see the results of the landing.

She felt the Chevelle's door bump the round pilings which were like sawed off telephone poles wrapped in rope. The cruiser began to bog down. She knew she had enough power but she didn't know if she could get enough traction. She downshifted and then poured on the gas. The Chevelle bucked. Sand flew all around her as the rear tires spun, desperately seeking for purchase. Suddenly it seemed like a catapult had grabbed and propelled her forward with a bone-jarring thud. There was sand on the rear-view mirror but she could see it was Rodriguez in his cruiser, pushing her forward. Suddenly the Chevelle took off, speeding toward the dark waves. Mickey pulled hard on the wheel and the tires skittered on the sand. She braked and tried to steer for the water's edge. With each yard she picked up both traction and speed. She saw Ronnie, hauling his bike toward the ocean, its tires sinking back in the sand with each heave.

The Brookwood was now at least three hundred yards away. She knew Rodriguez's maneuver had gotten her on the beach but if he'd gotten himself dug in, then he was closing off the access path like a cork in a bottle.

Mickey could see a line of cruisers moving north on Long Beach Boulevard, to her left and parallel with her direction of pursuit.

"There's nowhere to go, asshole," she yelled realizing only she could hear it.

The big wagon had found hard, wet sand and it took off like an animal sprung from a cage.

Mickey headed for the tire tracks and felt the Chevelle respond.

Ronnie, she saw, was back up on his bike and gaining on her.

"Where the fuck are you guy going?" she yelled at the windshield.

Ronnie was taking a wider track, the Enfield motorcycle zipping through the lapping surf and kicking up a rooster tail of foamy spray. In her rear view she saw Rodriguez, the headlights of his cruiser steadily closing on her. She figured he must have gotten the same push from behind he'd given her.

Oily smoke belched out of the Brookwood's tailpipe like ink from a fleeing squid. That could only mean, Mickey knew, that he was flooring it. It raced toward the lighthouse and the end of the beach.

"He's gonna wreck it on the rocks," Mickey shouted to the empty car. She assumed he had now decided to go out in a blaze of glory without letting Bunny go.

Then the pair of twin taillights brightened. The wagon fishtailed wildly on the beach and came to a sliding stop. As Mickey continued to approach she saw the driver's door fly open.

Charlie watched with an almost detached fascination as the sound and the fury grew ever closer. The pursuit, he saw, had crossed over from the road onto the beach and Charlie felt a little disappointment that he had missed the chance to experience that. He reasoned that in every act of our lives we had assigned parts. He knew what his was and he knew the spotlight would eventually find him. Then he brought the rifle down and chambered another Winchester 0.27 cartridge.

The salt water spinning back like a fountain from the front tire was stinging Ronnie's eyes and he had to keep wiping them clear. The Enfield wobbled a little each time he let go of the handle bars. He was gaining on Mickey and the station wagon that he thought looked more like an Armored Personnel Carrier with windows. A small but nonetheless rogue wave slapped at the bike broadside, forcing Ronnie to kill the throttle and dismount. Ronnie needed the motorcycle to be true to its model name, Interceptor, but he was afraid the salty ocean water was going to foul the bike's 736 cc engine and put him out of commission. He dragged the bike sideways up the mildly sloping shore, hopped on and tried to get it started again. The Chevy APC and Mickey's cruiser grew further away as he jumped on the starter.

Mickey slowed and felt the cruiser hydroplaned beneath her. She had no idea if the Chevelle would even stop on the brine-soaked sand. Ahead she saw Robichaux for the first time in the flesh as he got out of the car. He was squat and stock and even in the poor illumination of her approaching headlights, he looked physically formidable. Mickey tapped the floor-button and her high beams came up. She thought maybe she could blind him as she got closer but he did not even pause to look back. The cruiser was still slipping underneath her and she took her foot off of the accelerator and tapped the brakes as if she were driving on black ice.

The over-powered Chevelle engine throttled down but then the car went into a slide, the back end sliding wildly and forcing Mickey into a "doughnut" in the sand. She pulled the steering wheel in the direction of the slide like they'd taught her in pursuit training, downshifting and braking at the same time. The cruiser slowed and straightened out but she was still three hundred feet from the Brookwood. She could see Robichaux pulling something, no, she realized, pulling *someone* from the wagon's backseat door. And that someone was Bunny.

He had her in one arm as if she were a small mannequin or a large doll. He then hoisted her over his shoulder and started trotting toward the road and away from the waves. His free left hand was down by his side and, Mickey could see, in it he held a gun.

She had more control now but less speed and questionable braking ability. She had to slow down or risk running into the Brookwood. "Some heavy metal thunder," Charlie had said – the Chevelle, she was sure, would sustain the brunt of the damage from any collision occurring at speed. She could not risk running into it.

There was so much happening so fast Mickey found it hard to maintain focus. She saw no sign of Dunn. There was a large culvert peeking out from under the road with a tangled pile of what looked like dried reeds and driftwood cluttered below its dark maw. The kind, she assumed, Mayor Billy had been talking about in his office. Robichaux's path seemed to be arcing toward it. As she closed the distance on the Brookwood a terrifying thought arrived unbidden. The mayor had said the big pipes were, and Mickey remembered his exact words, "teeming with every variety of vermin and pestilence. That wouldn't stop Robichaux, Mickey concluded. Ronnie had called him a tunnel rat and this would be just another tunnel. He would be right at home with the pestilence. And she knew he would not hesitate to drag Bunny into it with him.

Dickie was ten feet from the big pipe's mouth. He did not see a grate. The kid was squirming and trying to kick even with her tape-bound ankles. Dickie's right arm was wrapped around her like a C-clamp. The pipe's diameter was plenty large and Dickie figured pulling or pushing her along wouldn't be a problem. He doubted there were poisonous snakes and there were definitely no scorpions so about the only thing he might have to deal with would be rats. And rats had never been a problem before.

When they got within five feet Dickie felt suddenly and violently ill. He stopped, peering into culvert which now took on the appearance of what he imagined was the mouth of Hell.

He'd always experienced a feeling of dread and sometimes impending doom before he'd dropped feet first into a tunnel's spider hole in *Cu Chi* or anywhere else in the Iron Triangle. But once he was surrounded by the dark, the cool earth and the loamy aroma, his adrenaline levels surged and the sensations quickly passed.

But this wasn't *Cu Chi* or *Cholon*. It struck Dickie the way a preacher back in Terrebonne Parish had described the way God struck Paul on his way to Damascus. Dickie blinked and the entire outside world went silent. Black Echo. He looked into the pipe and beheld a living vision of writhing snakes, hissing scorpions and chattering rats.

And in that instant Richard Jean-Baptiste Robichaux knew one thing.

He was not crawling inside it.

Forty-Two

Barnegat Lighthouse
Barnegat Light, Ocean County, NJ

Philip Bartholomew Stanley didn't mind the late hours. "Phil the Thrill" to his small group of friends and fellow Park Service employees was tasked with securing the lighthouse promptly at ten every night during July and August and the five and a half hours of overtime each and every weeknight plus the fourteen hour weekend shifts swelled his checking account nicely. He was planning on using the extra money for a mid-December trip to Nashville, Tennessee to see Janis Joplin perform. He also wanted to see Kris Kristofferson and Skeeter Davis, if only to hear the latter sing her hit ballad, "The End of the World."

Phil the Thrill had his head down and was fumbling with the ring of keys on his belt. His summer uniform shorts let the mild ocean breeze tickle the hair on his legs.

He heard the man before saw him

"Get down on the ground, asshole," the man shouted. He had a funny accent that Phil the Thrill could not immediately place. Like folks he'd encountered from the Pine Barrens but maybe, maybe just a bit thicker.

"Get the fuck down now," the man yelled, this time even louder.

He was sturdily built, the Thrill could see, and he had what looked a child slung over his shoulder. He wondered if the child were perhaps ill. He was about to offer the full assistance of the

New Jersey State Park Service when the man raised his arm. In what seemed like one continuous, liquid sequence, the Thrill saw the flash, heard the loud firecracker pop and watched the stones and gravel at his feet explode upward in a shower of sharp and stinging shrapnel.

It was time, and he thought this without actually thinking it, to get the fuck down.

Mickey let the Chevelle roll to stop and jumped out.

She could hear the Enfield coming up the beach behind her. She'd seen Robichaux pause with Bunny at the opening of the big storm culvert and then start running toward the lighthouse.

She patted her holster and took off running after them

As she ran, she saw a flash and heard the sharp pop of a gunshot. A man near the base of the lighthouse went down in a hail of stones and dust. How many more casualties would there be, she wondered, before this was all over?

Even though Robichaux was carrying Bunny she was not gaining on him. She wondered if he had ever carried his wounded comrades the same way, the way Ronnie had described to her. She watched as he and Bunny entered the attached building at the base of the lighthouse. She always thought it resembled a small two-story house with a single central door and a peaked roof. The previously open front door slammed shut and a few seconds of banging meant, she surmised, that Robichaux was trying to barricade it from the inside. She heard the metallic clang of the spiral steps being ascended.

Ronnie pulled up next to her but he left the Enfield's engine idling.

"I think he's decided to lock himself inside the light," Mickey said.

Ronnie used both index fingers to wipe his eyes. Mickey noticed he had a thin crust of dried salt clinging to his forehead and cheeks.

"That's a dead end plan," Ronnie said. "After all this, why would he do that?"

"He has Bunny and he has a gun," she replied, "His only chance is to use her to bargain his way out."

"Every dog has his day," Ronnie replied. "And it is August."

"You go cover the bay side. I'm going to see if I can't get inside."

Ronnie looked at her. "You did your job, Mick. Rescue mission remember? Not an assault. Bunny is the safest she's been since he took her. Without her alive and kicking he's got nothing to negotiate with. He's a dead man. One thing from what I read in Prejean's report is that this guy is not stupid. You said it yourself right away. It's a hostage situation. Just treat it that way. Technically, it's now a kidnapping anyway. You could call the FBI if you wanted to, right? I mean, Dickie's not going anywhere unless he packed wings."

Mickey took several deep breaths, a technique Charlie had taught her to help step back from the brink. Ronnie was right, she thought. Bunny was in very little danger now. The threat was real, but it now was contained. Now there was time.

More police cruisers began arriving, crowding for space inside the lighthouse's small parking lot. The sounds of sirens sailed on the sea breeze and then faded out. Engines idled and then stopped. The white base of Barnegat Light was alive with kaleidoscope colors. It reminded Mickey of a show on the main stage at Tony Marts. She could still hear the steady but fading bang on the circular stairs as Robichaux moved upwards with little Bunny.

"I'll call Evan Driscoll," Mickey said.

"I'm sure he gave you his personal number several times," Ronnie said with an arched eyebrow.

"*Several* times," Mickey affirmed. "I have his card in my wallet."

"I'm sure you do," Ronnie said and gave her a Cheshire cat grin.

Rodriguez's cruiser pulled up behind them.

"I'll have Rich call him," Mickey said. "Just so he doesn't get the wrong idea."

As Mickey watched, a red Mercury Cougar with a blue flashing light attached to its windshield pulled into the lighthouse parking lot.

"Who's that, I wonder?" Mickey asked.

"That's my ride," Ronnie said. "Prejean, the CID officer. The bigger fight may turn out to be who has jurisdiction here. You, the Barnegat boys, the Army or the FBI when they show up?"

"Depends on what suit is trump, I guess," Mickey replied, recalling that it was her father who'd taught her how to play Pinochle.

Rodriguez approached them. "That... was by a mile the coolest thing I have ever done," he said with a wide grin.

Ronnie mounted the bike. "Meet you up there. Better bring your bullhorn."

Dickie was tiring and he knew it. But the kid had stopped squirming, at least. He'd lost count of the steps. It seemed like there were more than the first time he'd climbed it with Harlan. And that seemed like a month ago.

The walls were narrowing more quickly now. Dickie looked up and thought he could see the platform at the top.

He kept humping upward even though his legs were burning. Finally he mounted the last pie-shaped step and felt the cool night air blowing in. The kid wasn't moving at all now. If she was dead, Dickie figured, then he was too. He slid her off his shoulder and sat her against the inside wall. He wasn't convinced they wouldn't take a shot at him the minute he peeked his head out. It looked like she was breathing, at least. Dickie pulled the tape off her mouth and her eyes opened.

She looked right at him.

"They kill you," she said.

"I know," said Dickie. "But they won't kill you. And neither will I, so just listen to me, do what I say and we'll both get out of here alive."

"They kill you anyway," the kid said matter-of-factly. "I always hear soldiers say – they kill anything that moves."

The boulders were hard but they were smooth and flat and Charlie was not uncomfortable. He thought he saw something at the top of the lighthouse and brought up the rifle, keeping the scope an inch from his eye. He saw shadows and guessed that it was Robichaux inside the lighthouse's glass enclosed lens room. And that he probably had Bunny with him. Charlie knew he would have to come out on the parking lot side to make his demands. He studied the observation platform through the Leupold M8 4x scope. Unless he was carrying Bunny on his shoulders, Charlie calculated he had the perfect angle.

Forty-Three

Barnegat Light State Park

Mickey motored the Chevelle off the beach and into the crowded parking lot. Yellow wooden saw-horses had been set up and a crowd of onlookers was forming behind them already, she could see. The phrase summer stock theater occurred to her and she flashed on the memory of seeing "Man of LaMancha" with Howard Keel at the Camden County Music Fair. All she wanted now was Bunny safe and sound. She did not think that it was an impossible dream.

She parked the Chevelle and hoped out. Ronnie came over with his new friend.

"Cole," he said. "Say hello to Chief Cleary. Chief, Cole Prejean, Army CID."

Prejean extended his hand and Mickey shook it.

"What do you think?" she said. "Want to throw Rock, Paper Scissors to see who's in charge of this-?"

"SNAFU?" Prefean replied.

"I was thinking FUBAR. Or, what's the other one you guys like – shit show?" Mickey said.

"You, your department and, really, all the Island departments have done strong work here tonight. My compliments. I understand you've chosen to involve the FBI, given the new kidnapping scenario and the current hostage situation."

"I had Deputy Rodriguez contact them and request assistance. They'll be on scene within the hour. They're sending a team of agents and a hostage negotiator. They wanted to send their snipers but we said no to that one."

"Be aware, they'll send them anyway," Prejean said with a chuckle. "In an unmarked van. The Feds, they do love their unmarked vans. I have informed command at Fort Dix and at CID HQ. That would give us air support if we need it."

"Air support?" Mickey said. "What, like those planes they sent to shoot King Kong off the Empire State Building? Wouldn't that qualify as overkill?"

"In the Army," Prejean shot back, "There is no such thing as overkill."

"I've got a psychopath and a terrified little girl up there, Mr. Prejean. What I don't need down here is a FUBAR or a shit show starring a bunch of John Wayne wannabes."

"Well put, Chief Cleary. Rest assured I and thus the U.S. Army are in total agreement. Robichaux is our creation and we'd like to have him alive and talking. We believe he is involved in something much larger than his partnership with Harlan Brinson who, we now believe, is deceased."

Mickey looked at him.

"We believe he was immolated in that truck fire near your father's house earlier this evening. There was another fatality involved in that fire as well, the owner of the truck we think. We're trying to get that corpse ID'd as soon as we can. It's odd. That body had gold fillings on it but they appear to be from someone else's mouth. It's a pretty tangled web at the moment but we're working on it. I've also asked Dix command to post a couple MP's at your father's until we figure all this out. He'll be well protected until we're sure a credible threat no longer exists."

"I appreciate that," Mickey said. "I really do. Is there anything my department can do to help you?"

"I'd like to speak with your Deputy Higgins, if I could. It involves his brother, Darnell."

You mean his *late* brother Darnell?"

Mickey saw the shock on Prejean's face but he instantly composed himself.

"Darnell is dead? When did this occur, did he say?"

"Last night at the VA he was in. Charlie said his doctor thinks he got dosed with morphine or something."

"I'll look into as soon as this situation is resolved. Is he here?"

"His cruiser is over there," Mickey said. "But I haven't seen Charlie. I'll connect you as soon as I do. I know he'll want to talk to you."

Prejean nodded. "I'm sorry to hear about Lieutenant Higgins but all the more reason I need Dickie alive. Time for the rat to start ratting."

"Well put," Mickey said.

Prejean turned and headed for the Cougar.

"CID guys all like that?" Mickey asked Ronnie.

"No," Ronnie said. "Most are way, way worse."

A murmur arose from the assembled officers and the growing crowd of spectators. Mickey heard the sound of something loud approaching from afar but couldn't decide what it was. As more and more necks craned upward, Mickey began walking unhurriedly toward the base of the lighthouse.

"Where are you headed," Ronnie asked. Prejean, she noticed, was motioning him over.

"Just need to check on something," she said and kept moving.

Dickie was wearing Bunny like a flak jacket. Her legs were locked around his waist and her arms were around his neck, fingers interlaced. Her head was right next to his, cheek to cheek. For the moment, he figured, he was bulletproof.

As he stepped from the lens room out onto the observation deck the beauty of the scene struck him. He looked out, not down and saw the ocean curling around the island's tip. The lights looked like a string of jewels stretching south. He saw headlights lining the connecting bridge and, further to the west, the darkened site of the future Chez Robichaux. He felt calm, he realized. He felt at peace. He had a sense of purpose and he had a plan.

When he finally allowed himself to look down he was amazed and pleased that the multitudes assembled below were all there for him. He was a rock star gazing out on an appreciative audience. Things got a little brighter and he realized that powerful car spotlights, probably from police cruisers, were being trained on him one by one. He now remembered one of the Park Service guys telling him and Harlan that the lighthouse was one-hundred-and-seventy-one feet tall and they would climb two-hundred-and-seventeen steps to reach the little room that once housed the light and the lens.

Dickie thought he heard someone on the shaky metal steps but in the next instant he heard a familiar sound – a chopper or maybe choppers. It made Dickie smile because to him that sound had always meant rescue, redemption and R & R. It or maybe they were Hueys, he knew, by the pitch of the engine and the whump-whump of the rotors. It had always been the sound of friendlies, the sound of salvation. The stiffening ocean breeze gave way to something else. He saw a single helicopter approach and recognized the outline of a sniper seated at the cargo door. The sound grew loud and the rotor wash started to blow back his hair.

He held the child closer, tighter. He felt her hand at the back of his head and an instant later realized he was wrong. It was not her hand. It was too cold to be that.

It was the barrel of a gun.

"Show's over, Dickie," he heard a woman's voice say over the rising din. "Step back and put her down. You put her down right now or I promise you I will blow your fucking brains all over both of us."

Charlie knew all about windage but the disturbed air kicked up by the helicopter's blades confused him. He had the shot lined up and he knew he would not miss but now he had to wait, hoping the chopper would shortly move off and restore the opportunity that he felt he was entitled to.

A memory, sudden and unbidden, came to him. He and Darnell were hunting in the Carolina pines years ago. Darnell had a deer in his sight and was ready to shoot. Charlie had tapped him on the shoulder and gently pushed the rifle's barrel to the side. He'd seen it was a fawn and said softly to Darnell, "Not yours to take, little brother. Not today."

When Charlie looked back through the scope Dickie Robichaux was standing at the railing at the top of the lighthouse, his face turned away. He did not have Bunny. Charlie slid his finger from the trigger. He felt his brother's presence. Then he glanced up, searching for something familiar in the coal-dark sky and among the diamond stars.

Mickey had one arm curled tightly around Bunny who was shaking almost uncontrollably now. She held her other arm straight out, the Colt's long barrel still trained on Robichaux's head.

"Put your arms up so they don't shoot you," Mickey said.

He tilted his head, arms remaining by his side.

"Come on, Dickie, don't fuck around now. It's over. Show them your hands."

He turned his face just far enough to look at her. And spoke.

"Charlie never got me," he said. And then he smiled.

"What did you say?" Mickey asked, squeezing Bunny tighter to her.

"Charlie," he repeated. "He never got me."

Mickey tried to speak but found she could only stand with her mouth open and her eyes wide as Dickie Robichaux gracefully vaulted the waist-high railing, spread his arms like a high-diver and disappeared from sight.

SEPTEMBER 1969

Forty-Four

Long Beach Township

Mickey set the glass down in front of Gannon.

"A White Russian," he said, his delight apparent. "You remembered."

"Bartender looked at me funny," Mickey replied. "But when I told him it was for my friend he said, 'I sure hope she enjoys it.' Bottoms up, sweetheart."

Mickey reseated herself on the metal folding chair and squeaked its cracked rubber leg caps closer to the long table. Bunny was drawing on the white paper tablecloth with her new box of Crayolas.

"When do they announce the winner?" Gannon asked.

"Pretty soon, I think. You going to use this in your story?"

"Not unless Bert Parks shows up in a thong. Too cliché, my dear chief. You know *me* better than that. I'll mention it to the editor of the Society pages, though."

A loudspeaker shrieked with feedback.

"Folks," the emcee said, his one hand around the thin chrome stand that sprouted an oversized microphone. "In just a little while we'll be announcing the winner of this year's Miss Magic Long Beach Island Pageant. I know you're all excited but our panel of impartial judges faces an especially difficult decision this year, as

I'm sure you all agree."

Appreciative applause broke out from the assembled and mildly inebriated crowd. The contestants, dressed in evening gowns and seated demurely on a stage comprised of abutted cafeteria tables, all gave identical parade waves and smiled broadly.

"And while you're at it," the emcee continued, "How about a big hand for the Long Beach Township Beach Patrol who have sponsored the Miss Magic pageant since it began way back in 1958." He wore a mint-green crushed velvet tuxedo jacket along with a pink ruffled shirt and a monstrous butterfly bow tie.

Applause, whoops and hollers rang out and echoed in the acoustically unsophisticated hall. The island's remaining lifeguards had started the party early.

When the clamor died down, Gannon leaned over toward Mickey.

"I'm sorry you're not the hero," he said and sipped the milky cocktail. "I assume that's still OK?"

"I never wanted to be. You know me better than that. I will settle, though, for being the heroine of that crappy first novel when you get around to writing it."

"Deal," Gannon said and tipped his glass. "You know, maybe this drink will catch on. It just needs to, oh, I don't know, it just needs to abide for a while I think."

"Not sure what that means," Mickey said, "But let's go with it for now."

"Bunny's OK with being the heroine?" Gannon asked.

"I think so. Yvette and Declan are around here somewhere. You can ask them again if you'd like."

"Feeling any separation anxiety?" Gannon asked.

Mickey gave him a funny look.

"Oh come now, my dear Chief. You're going to tell me you did not become attached to her? It was obvious she became very attached to you."

"I did. But I'm not her mother."

"I know," Gannon said. "But without you she-"

Ronnie came up with his arm around Declan Winston. They had started their party early, too.

"Tell them the story," Ronnie said. "But tell it the way you told me."

Mickey saw Gannon reach for his notebook.

Ronnie and Winston sat down. Winston downed the remains of his beer.

"OK," he said. "So we're standing at the luggage lockers in the Philly airport. I ask one of the CID guys if he wants to open it. He says no, since he already knows I had to poop it out. So I open the locker and there's... nothin', *bupkis*, completely empty. I didn't know if the two of them were gonna shit or go blind. They both start reaching for their sidearms. So I reach up in the top of the empty locker and pull down *another* key. I had stuck it there with bubble gum. So now we need to hump it to the Greyhound Bus Station to open another locker. That's where the bricks were. I have to tell you, once I handed them over it crossed my mind that if they weren't really from CID that Yvette and I were going to get capped PDQ. Fortunately they were legit and so here we are."

Ronnie laughed out loud. "You have to realize what tightasses these CID guys are. I'm sure that when that locker opened and it was empty they both had visions of being posted to Greenland." He stood up. "Winston and I are going to get another beer. Anybody need anything?"

"I take a Tab," Bunny said without looking up. "What Mickey-san drink."

The two men left for the bar and Yvette came over and sat next to Mickey.

"I want to tell you again," she said. "I thank you very much, *merci beaucoup* for taking care of Bonne-Nuit. I worry about her every minute until I see her face, touch her hand. *Merci, merci beaucoup*, Mickey Cleary. We come back visit you *tres souvent*, very much off-ten. Maybe next time they not drink so much, *n'est ce pas?*"

"That'd be great. I'll even take time off." Mickey swallowed hard and fought back tears. She knew they were leaving in the morning to start their new lives in Declan's home state of Virginia.

"Where are, eh, *rugrats?*" Yvette asked her.

Mickey laughed. "Rich, their dad, had to work tonight. Colombia, their mom, she said she was afraid it would make them all too sad."

"Sad to leave," Yvette said, "Make happy to come back."

"Very happy," Mickey said and wiped at her eyes. Yvette leaned over and kissed her on the cheek. "Bunny always love you," she said. "I tell her you mama-san number two." Mickey grabbed one of the folded paper napkins and blotted her face.

"Yvette," Winston called. "Come meet Mickey's papa-san." Yvette touched Mickey on the shoulder and glided away.

Gannon took the opportunity to move closer.

"Funny. I have it in my notes somewhere that Cleary's don't cry," he said. "Do I need to print a retraction?"

Mickey took another napkin and tried to stem the continuing flow of tears.

"You print one word about this," she said in a thick nasal voice, "And they'll be looking for *you* in the Pine Barrens. I still have friends, you know." She used the napkin to blow her nose. Then she took an ice cube from Gannon's glass and touched it to her cheeks.

"You ever get an explanation?" Gannon asked. "I mean one that actually makes sense?"

Mickey gave a long exhale.

"The little barrel that Davey found. It was basically a gasoline bomb, I guess."

"Yes. A flame *fougasse*, it's called. Very old. Very nasty."

"Yeah, well anyway. They had to send the Bomb Squad all the way from Philly PD. The FBI ended up with it. And you know what else was in it? A badge I lost a couple years ago. Another little touch for your novel."

"So how did BoDean Bowker manage to fricassee himself in a truck that wasn't his?"

"My, um, friend at the FBI says the fuse on the foo gas, or whatever you called it, was nothing but coaxial cable with parts that probably came from an old Erector Set stuck on the end. Harmless. Useless. Certainly not a remote detonator of any kind. So either something Bowker had in the truck blew up or the cab was filled with volatile fumes and just ignited. Like being trapped in a cloud of pure fire."

"A gruesome end, as they say. Who owned the truck?"

"Some Public Works guy over in Hammonton. He said BoDean just asked to borrow it. Had no idea what he was up to."

"I'd hate to be the insurance adjuster on that claim," Gannon said and took another swallow of the White Russian. "And the body in the back of the truck? That was Robiscek's -"

"Robichaux," Mickey corrected.

"Yes, Robichaux, thank you. That was Robichaux's partner in crime?"

"The Army has dental records on everybody that's ever enlisted and they say absolutely, positively it was him. Far as I know, nobody has a particularly good answer for that one yet."

"Two birds with-"

"One fire. Talk about, what was that word you used over doughnuts at Bill's? Contrived?"

"As I said, truth is stranger than fiction, Chief. Or, in the *lingua vulgaris*, you just can't make this stuff up."

"I'll drink to that," Mickey said and picked up her now lukewarm beer.

Yvette and Winston came over and gathered up Bunny and her crayons.

"We have an early day tomorrow and a long drive," Winston said. "Thanks again for everything. It'll never be enough but-"

"It's already enough," Mickey said. "Come here, you," she said to Bunny. "Give me a hug."

Bunny wrapped her skinny arms around her. "I come back see you. We have boo-coo fun. You promise."

"I promise," said Mickey.

"You go home now," Bunny commanded. "You and Dunn need do *nhuc-duc*. So you make baby."

"Bunny!" Yvette scolded.

"It's OK," Mickey said. "I know all about it. I'd tell you, but it's a long story."

Applause rang out as they turned away. Mickey had missed the big announcement.

"Who won?"

"Betty Sprague," Gannon answered. "Pretty girl. Definitely belongs on the Society pages. And thanks again for inviting me to this. I honestly had no idea."

A petite brunette with upswept hair was receiving the tiara-like crown and a large state fair-type white ribbon.

Mickey smiled. She still had Princess Bonnie's sparkly tiara on her bedside table.

◆ ◆ ◆

Mickey was soaked in sweat. She tumbled off Ronnie and reached for the glass on the bedside table.

"Now that's what I call *nhuc-duc*, soldier boy," she said. "Some damn fine *nhuc-duc*. Not to mention boo-coo. Do they give out medals for that?"

"They give one for Distinguished Service," Ronnie said between panting breaths.

Mickey took a drink. "Now I understand what they mean when they say battle hardened."

Ronnie did not have enough air left to laugh. "You've been around that reporter too long," he said and then reached for his own glass.

A tiny votive candle flickered, bathing them in an ochre glow. "Tonight was a really good night," Ronnie said. "And that, that was a little bit of heaven."

Mickey lay on her back and nestled close to him. She reached to set her glass back down. It bumped something on the table. She looked over and saw the little tiara shimmering in the votive's light.

"Yeah," she said. "A good night. A *Bonne Nuit.*"

Mama Cass was on the radio singing "Dream a Little Dream of Me."

Mickey leaned over and blew the candle out.

Forty-Five

Elon, North Carolina

Charlie Higgins looked up and down the block but saw no one. He checked his watch. The afternoon was hot and Charlie was beginning to sweat, having opted for an outside table in the sun at the little restaurant on Williamson Avenue. Nicely dressed students from the nearby eponymous University strolled by, textbooks in hand or shouldering backpacks. When he glanced again Cole Prejean was seating himself across from him.
"Hello, Charlie," Prejean said.
"What have you got?" Charlie asked him.
"Cold comfort, I'm afraid," Prejean replied and produced a thick manila folder. "But comfort nonetheless. Unlike many of his comrades, Lieutenant Darnell Higgins' ultimate sacrifice shall not be vain. And if you commune with him any spiritual way, I want you to give him a message. Something I know he will understand and he will appreciate."
"And what would that be?" Charlie asked.
Prejean smiled. "Payback is hell."

ACKNOWLEDGEMENTS

Once again, the feat of bringing the story rattling around in an author's head to the printed page requires the talents, efforts, assistance and patience of many people. I hope I haven't missed any of them. The author wishes to thank Joe Marquart and Bob Rocca, my first writing mentors and all those who encouraged my writing career; my cabal of critical readers, notably Dr. Kate Galluzzi, Mrs. Nancy (Miss Donahue) Croce and Bruce Forshay, USN (Ret.) for their input, suggestions and encouragement; Terry Persun for his Fast & Furious formatting; Graphic artist Jim Zach at ZGraphix for another memorable cover concept; Kellie Jo Heimer at Control Print Creative; Steve Schukei for his help on automotive details; Ryan Martz & Doug McCarthy at Fire & Pine who graciously provided the map of LBI for a story that hinges on both fire & pines; Laura Hope-Gill, MFA, my writing mentor and Master's Program Director at Lenoir-Rhyne University; a grateful nod to Doreen Cramer at The SandPaper and to Margaret (Pooch) Bucholz for their help on getting the little LBI details right; and to my friend and mentor, betterselling, OK fine, *best*selling author Bob Dugoni who always likes to see his name in a book.

Also, I want to thank those old friends, mentors and colleagues who allowed their names to grace characters in this story: in no particular order, William P. Tunell, MD, the greatest mayor Surf City never had; James C. Guidice, DO, who is still imparting priceless pulmonary wisdom to yet another generation of physicians; Tom Morley, DO; Jack Mariani, DO and Rick Marcelli, DO, orthopedic surgeons who've fixed more bones than they've made; Mike Flood, DO; Thomas F. Santucci, Jr., DO; Dale Gibson, CCP & Mike Belz, CCP, my long-time perfusionists, colleagues and co-conspirators; George Joo, NJSP (Ret.); medical school colleagues and now caring, accomplished physicians Phil (still The Thrill) Stanley, DO, Mary Beth Harman, DO, Mark Nepp, DO and Michael Ganon, DO; Linda Johnson, wife of my good friend Dave Johnson, DO, who was taken from all of us too soon; and high school classmates Louis A. Petroni, Esq. and Daniel J. Ragone, Jr., MD.

Both Mrs. Loretta Lamarro and Sister Innocentia really did teach me at St. Peter's Parochial School in Riverside, NJ. I'm glad they can live on in these pages.

ABOUT THE AUTHOR

DANIEL J. WATERS is a native of Southern New Jersey. He graduated from Bishop Eustace Preparatory School, St. Joseph's College in Philadelphia and the University of Medicine and Dentistry of New Jersey and has been publishing stories and essays since 1981; his work has appeared in the *Journal of The American Medical Association, The New Physician, The Examined Life* (University of Iowa) , *Intima: A Journal of Narrative Medicine* (Columbia University) and in *Typishly: An Online Literary Journal.* He practiced open-heart surgery for thirty years and is the author of "A Heart Surgeon's Little Instruction Book" and "A Surgeon's Little Instruction Book", collections of surgical wisdom, advice and aphorisms as well as the novels ***Surf City Confidential*** and ***Threshold.*** He holds a Graduate Certificate in Narrative Healthcare and a Master of Arts in Writing from The Center for Graduate Studies/The Thomas Wolfe Center for Narrative at Lenoir-Rhyne University in Asheville, NC. He currently serves on the adjunct faculty of Des Moines University where he teaches Narrative Medicine and Medical Humanities. He and his wife Pamela have three grown children and live in Clear Lake, Iowa.

Visit our website at www.bandagemanpress.com

Contact the author: drdan@bandagemanpress.com

CRITICAL PRAISE FOR "SURF CITY CONFIDENTIAL"

"A gripping debut. Waters creates a cauldron of colorful characters simmering in an intricate plot. The revelations come in a wild, tense finish. One of the best books I'll read this year."
—Robert Dugoni, #1 NY Times, Wall Street Journal & Amazon Bestselling Author

AMAZON READERS AGREE: 100% FIVE STARS

"Set in a small coastal town in the late sixties, this is a fast paced story that kept me turning pages into the night. This book is a very impressive first novel, comparable in pacing and character development to the work of Ken Follett or John Sandford."

"A real page-turner set in a milieu that will be familiar to many readers - the Jersey Shore. The book delivers on its promise and then more! Perfect summer (or any other season) reading."

"Enjoyed this so much! Having grown up in that era I was amazed at the detail. Remembered things I hadn't thought about in years. Love the dialogue and surprise ending...."

"Difficult book to put down! Many twists and turns to keep your interest to the end! One really great read."

"SURF CITY CONFIDENTIAL" and **"THRESHOLD"** are available in Paperback and Kindle e-Book formats on Amazon.com and at select local booksellers and libraries

Made in the USA
Middletown, DE
09 March 2024